Facing the L

# Facing the Light

## ADÈLE GERAS

ORION

First published in Great Britain in 2003 by Orion,
an imprint of the Orion Publishing Group Ltd.

A CIP catalogue record for this book
is available from the British Library.

ISBN 0 75285 154 3 (hardback) 0 75285 155 1 (trade paperback)

Typeset in Perpetua by
Deltatype Ltd, Birkenhead, Merseyside

Printed in Great Britain by Clays Ltd, St Ives plc

The Orion Publishing Group Ltd
Orion House
5 Upper Saint Martin's Lane
London, WC2H 9EA

For
The Magnificent Seven:

Jane Gregory and Jane Wood
Laura Cecil and Laura Watson
Linda Newbery and Linda Sargent
and Broo Doherty

Thanks to friends who encouraged me during the writing
of this book: Jon Appleton, Eileen Armstrong, Jane Barlow,
Annie Dalton, Anna Dalton-Knott, Anne Fine, David Fickling,
Mary Hooper, Dan Jones, Alison Leonard, Helena Pielichaty,
Celia Rees, Rosie Rushton, Ann Turnbull, Jean Ure,
Frances Wilson, Jacqueline Wilson.

As always, I'm grateful to my family: Norm, Jenny and,
especially, Sophie for her excellent advice throughout.
This book would never have been written without her
belief and enthusiasm.

What you don't know can't hurt you but she does know and she must forget what she knows. It is secret secret secret. She must pretend she doesn't know and never did or it will hurt her. The house . . . that's where the secret lives and all she wants is not to know somewhere far away.

She is standing at the window. There's not even a breath of wind to move the white curtains and the grass outside lies dry and flat under the last of the sun. Summertime, and early evening, and she isn't in bed yet. She's nearly eight and it's too soon for sleeping. Everyone is doing something somewhere else and no one is looking. The shadows of trees are black on the lawn and the late roses are edged with gold. There's a piece of silvery water glittering through the weeping willow leaves. That's the lake. Swans swim on the lake and she could go down to the water to see the white birds. No one would know and what you don't know can't hurt you.

She has to go, to flee, across the carpet woven with flowers and twisted trees, and then the door opens and she's in the corridor and it's dark there always, even when the sun is shining outside, and a thick stillness takes up all the space and spreads down the staircase and she moves from step to step on tiptoe so as not to disturb it. Paintings on the walls stare at her as she passes. Still lifes and landscapes spill strange colours and their own light into the silence and the portraits scream after her and she can't hear them. The marble floor in the hall is like a chequerboard of black and white and she makes sure to jump the black squares because if you don't something bad is sure to happen and maybe she just touched one black square on her way to the garden but that wouldn't count, would it?

Then she's on the grass and the air is soft, and she runs as fast as she can down the steps of the terrace and over the lawn and past all the flowers and between high hedges clipped into cones and balls and spirals until she reaches the wild garden where the plants brush her skirt, and she's running and running to where the swans always are and they've gone. They have floated over to the far bank. She can see them. It's not too far away so she starts walking.

Something catches her eye. It's in the reeds and it's like a dark stain in the water and when she gets a little nearer it looks like a sheet or a cloth and there are waterplants and grey-green willow branches with skinny-finger leaves hiding some of it. If only she can get nearer to where the water meets the bank she can reach in and pull it and see what it is. The water is cool on her hand and there's something that looks like a foot poking out from under the material. Could it be someone swimming? No one swims without moving.

Suddenly there's cold all around her and what she doesn't know won't hurt her but she knows this is wrong. This is bad. She should run and fetch someone but she can't stop her hand from reaching out to the dark cloth that lies on the surface of the lake. She pulls at it and something heavy comes towards her and the time is stretched so long that the moment goes on for ever and ever and there's a face with glassy open eyes and pale greenish skin, and hair all loose and sliding like a terrible spreading growing billowing weed that drifts across the silvery water and moves in and out of the open mouth and she feels herself starting to scream but no sound comes out and she turns and runs back to the house. Someone must come. Someone must help, and she runs to call them to bring them and she's screaming and no one can hear her. Wet drowned fingers rise up from the lake and stretch out over the grass and up into the house to touch her and she will always feel them, even when she's very old, and she knows the fingers and she knows every fold of the sodden cloth and the unseeing eyes streaming with silver water and the hair undone. Now she knows them all and she can't ever ever stop knowing them.

# Wednesday,
# August 21st,
## 2002

I'm allergic to my mother, Rilla thought. She leaned back in the bath, closed her eyes, and let the vanilla-scented foam and the hot water cover her. It happened every single time. The snake had come back. She could feel it, uncurling from where it lived, so deep in her head that for most of the time she forgot it was there. A white snake, that was how she imagined it, twisting and uncoiling and somehow winding itself around the separate parts of her brain to give her the only headaches she ever had. Tension headaches was what the doctor said when once Rilla had mentioned the problem, but of course she hadn't told him what caused the pain. She knew exactly. It was Leonora, her mother, and not just her. I'm allergic to the whole package, she told herself; Willow Court, Gwen, the entire set-up. Every time I have to visit the place, it's the same: the white snake tightens the scaly loops of his body around bits of my head, and I can feel my heart beating strangely too. She smiled. Usually, after only a few hours in her mother's presence Rilla recovered sufficiently to function in a more or less normal manner, but there was no getting away from it: the prospect of visiting Leonora filled her with something approaching dread.

What was she afraid of? She looked around her bathroom, her haven, her lair. It was the room she loved best in the whole world. Her small house (*How clever of you, darling, to find such a sweet little place. And in Chelsea!* Leonora had said at the time) was, depending on your point of view, either sadly in need of total redecoration or the height of bohemian chic. Rilla herself thought that she and her house went well together. We're past our best, she often thought, but we've still got what it takes, oh yes. At least she had managed actually to buy a house of her own, which was more than could be said for Gwen, her elder sister, who had never lived anywhere but at Willow Court, under Leonora's gaze. Rilla couldn't for the life of her understand how her sister survived. She seemed happy enough, but you could never really tell with Gwen. Maybe she'd been dying to get away for years and not said a word. The martyrdom involved would have been typical, but in all probability Gwen had grown used to her own captivity. If anyone had asked her why she and her husband chose to spend their days in the depths of Wiltshire, she'd doubtless have murmured something about what a privilege it was to be entrusted with the care of the paintings of their grandfather, Ethan Walsh (the Walsh Collection was what she called it) and so boringly on and on. She wouldn't mention that her constant attendance on Leonora and her lifelong devotion to the house and property made it the most natural thing in the world for her to inherit Willow Court when Leonora died. Well, Gwen was welcome to it. Rilla would have regarded having to stay there forever as some kind of prison sentence, but was aware that most people didn't share her taste.

For most people, she thought, read my sister and my mother. Why should I care what they think? I'm forty-eight years old and my bathroom is my business and no one else's. She looked at the candles on the long shelf beside the mirror. There were half a dozen of them, and she lit them every time she bathed, night or morning. The small, plain candlesticks that held them were made of opaque glass: blue and pink, and a pearly white that Rilla liked best of all. No one else saw the point, and how could she ever explain the lift in her heart when she stared at the moving flames, or how the shapes of the coloured wax growing into weird encrustations on the candlesticks pleased her, and how their faint fragrance spoke to her of peace and beauty and every sort of soothing? And the plants. There was a jungle of them above the basin and on the windowsill, and the greens (with almost every leaf a different shade, some blueish, some tinged with yellow, or brown, some striped, others streaked or blotched or spotted) made a garden for her, and one, moreover, that needed little attention because she let it run riot deliberately, revelling in the fronds and tendrils that spilled over the sides of their pots and trailed down past the tiles, touching the side of the bath.

Gwen had been the first to see the bathroom after it was redone, and she hadn't needed to say a word. It's me, Rilla thought. There must be something wrong with me if I can remember it all so clearly from years and years ago. How she'd stared at the bath and basin in silence, then turned and said, 'Are you sure it's not just a little too much?'

Rilla had been madly in love with Jon then, just about to marry him, and everything she did was exuberant, happy, full of passion. Jon Frederick was a pop star, and while he was never, even at the height of his fame, quite at the very top, they'd been one of London's bright young couples in those days. She'd just been in a movie, *Night Creatures*, which was a silly sort of thing but at least it had paid well, and urged on by Jon she'd commissioned the artist Curtis Manstrum to paint the bath and basin. He was famous for his fountains and had perfected a technique of covering basins with highly coloured decorations which could withstand years of water falling on them. He'd done such a splendid job on Rilla's bathroom that a magazine came and photographed it and for a while it was the talk of London – the talk, anyway, of those people in London who made a habit of talking about such things.

'What's the matter with it?' Rilla had answered Gwen, and for the first time she saw everything through her sister's eyes: blue and green and pink in Matisse-inspired swirls that made you feel dizzy just to look at them, covering every inch of porcelain, dazzling the eye with their singing brightness.

'Well . . .' Gwen hestitated. She doesn't know the right words, Rilla thought. She's the granddaughter of a famous artist and she still hasn't a clue. She has all those paintings all around her every day and she can't bloody think of a single intelligent thing to say. In the end, and only because she'd been asked directly, Gwen murmured, 'The colours are rather strong, aren't they? And all those patterns look a bit fussy to me. Over the top. Don't look so crestfallen, Rilla! You did ask. And it's not me who is going to be bathing here, is it?'

'No, right,' Rilla said. 'I saw what you had done in your ensuite bathroom. Peachy pink as far as the eye can see; peach basin, peach bath and peach His and Hers towels folded neatly on the heated towel rail.'

'There's no need to be nasty,' said Gwen.

Rilla had bitten back the 'Fuck you, too,' which came into her head and quickly led the way out so that her sister's delicate tastes should no longer be affronted. To this day she could remember how Gwen's words had made her feel in the wrong, exposed as someone altogether too noisy who called attention to herself. Disapproved of.

So why did she keep visiting? Why did she not distance herself from the whole damn thing? Love, as usual, was the answer. Twined in among all the other feelings that filled her whenever she thought of her family, entangled in everything, bound in so strongly that to try to cut it out would destroy her utterly, was the love she felt for her mother and her sister. She couldn't help it. All that nonsense about blood being thicker than water was, it appeared, no more than the truth. It was as though Leonora and Gwen were parts of herself, parts that she found difficult and irritating most of the time, but still pieces of the fabric. Also, there were things she remembered from her childhood which still shone, after everything, and you didn't throw such memories away in a hurry. You kept hold of them as a kind of talisman to guard against the others, the things you couldn't bear to think about.

Rilla sat up and squeezed a spongeful of water on to her shoulder. They love me too, she thought, even though they disapprove of me, Gwen and Mother. Even if I'm not quite the sort of person they'd mix with if I wasn't their blood relative, they, too, probably need me in their lives. She wondered whether or not Gwen still recalled an earlier bathroom incident from when they were little. Rilla hadn't forgotten. She'd taken her felt-tipped pens one day and drawn all over the white walls. It wasn't an accident. She could remember thinking: the walls will be prettier with fishes all over them, and she'd gone and taken the felt-tips out of the nursery and brought them into the bathroom and spread them out on the side, by the sink, and then she'd set about making lovely fish outlines and colouring them in carefully with her best shades of turquoise, purple and orange. They looked beautiful. How happy Mummy would be when she saw them swimming there, across the wall! Rilla was only seven and she couldn't reach very high up even if she stood on the chair, but there were lots and lots of fishes and she'd added some seaweed too, otherwise it wouldn't be the proper sea. When she'd finished she called Gwen to come and have a look. Gwen went white all over. The colour left her face, then came back again, all red and blushing, as though she were ashamed.

'She'll be angry, Rilla. You've spoiled the whole wall.'

'No, I haven't,' Rilla laughed. 'I've made it pretty. Look at the fishes! Don't you like it?'

'It's horrible and I'm going to tell Mummy. You're going to be in *such* trouble. Wait and see.'

Rilla got out of the bath and found one of the enormous soft towels that covered her from head to toe. She smiled. I *was* in trouble too, she thought. No supper that night, and then no visit to the circus, and watching out of the window as Gwen went off with Mother in the car to see the clowns and the elephants. How I wept and sobbed and begged, but Mother was quite unmoved. *You have to learn, Rilla dear,* she'd said. *Before you go galumphing into things and being naughty because you haven't thought properly.* Even after all this time, the injustice rankled. So often, things she'd done to please Leonora were somehow misunderstood. Rilla wondered sometimes whether her highly-decorated bathroom was a way, after all these years, of getting her own back at everyone who thought her childish fishes and seaweed did nothing but spoil a nice clean wall.

'Galumphing' was the word which really hurt, the one that got under the skin and stayed there for more than forty years. Galumphing, which came trailing implications of bigness and weight and excessive clumsiness. Rilla made her way into the bedroom. Ivan was awake, humming tunelessly as he looked at the paper. She had to get ready. She wanted to be at Willow Court as early as possible and definitely before dinner.

Sitting in front of her dressing-table, Rilla peered into the triple mirror and saw far too many reflected images of her lover, lying already fully dressed on the bed behind her. She couldn't decide which was more depressing – looking at him, or contemplating the wreck that she'd suddenly turned into. Back in the bathroom, it was easy to pretend that she was still the creamy-skinned, gorgeous creature in the photograph that mocked her from behind the massed bottles of perfume. More fool me, she thought, keeping a movie still from more than twenty years ago. I must be a masochist. That hair, rippling over a pillow trimmed with lace, and those perfect shoulders in the satin nightie . . . no wonder the monster, or whatever it was in *Night Creatures*, was tempted. The rings she was wearing in the photograph were still around somewhere, ornate silver set with moonstones and opals. She'd been allowed to keep them, for a wonder. Vaguely, Rilla thought about whether it would be worth turning the flat upside down to find them. Probably not. Half the photograph was white roses, spilling off the bed and almost out of the frame, like an avalanche. David, the director, had spent such ages piling them up, arranging the fur rug over her feet, and making sure she was leaning back against the bedlinen at just the right angle. I should take it away, she thought. It's ridiculous to keep it there as a reminder. Maybe I could cover it up completely with a scarf or something.

She stared at herself and sighed. She smiled. That was a mistake. Could all these wrinkles and dark circles and general sagginess of neck and chin have sprung up overnight? I'm only forty-eight, she thought. Sod's Law, that was what it was. There was Gwen, two years older and all milk and roses with never more than a spot of powder and a dab of lipstick on special occasions. No bloody justice in the world. She could hear her mother's voice saying, as she always did, *Fairness has nothing to do with it, Cyrilla darling. Your sister is one person and you are another and you are both precious to me.* Leonora was the only person in the whole world allowed to use the really too silly name she'd saddled her younger daughter with at birth. Her sister only had to contend with Gwendolen. It wasn't brilliant, but at least people had heard of it. When Rilla first went to school, everyone asked, is Cyrilla a family name? But they could barely suppress their laughter whenever it was spoken, so she very quickly shortened it, and short was how it had mostly stayed.

Of course, if her father had lived, he might have tried hard to suggest something more sensible, but Rilla was willing to bet that her mother would have carried the day as she usually did. Peter Simmonds, Rilla's father, had died in a car accident six months before she was born. Rilla knew it was quite irrational, but she'd always felt faintly guilty, as though she herself were to blame for the crash, which, according to Leonora, had been the indirect result of telling Peter she was pregnant again. The subject wasn't one Rilla had discussed with Leonora, but both she and Gwen grew up with stories about the relationship that had existed between their parents. By all accounts, this love was like something out of a fairytale: transcendent, immutable and deeper by far than the rather ordinary passions experienced by other people. Certainly it took Leonora some years to recover from her husband's death. Rilla thought she recalled the house being quiet, and her mother in black weeping at the breakfast table, but didn't know whether the silence and sadness in her head were truly memories or only stories that had been told to her later by Leonora and which she was imagining. Photographs of her father, a tall, rather military-looking man with reddish hair and an unsmiling gaze, were there in albums which were hardly ever looked at these days.

'What for do you look so sour, beloved Rilla?' came Ivan's lazy tones, husky partly from last night's cigarettes but mostly from well-rehearsed affectation.

'Nothing,' said Rilla, 'only it's going to take a hell of a lot of slap to reconstruct something resembling my face.' She kept her voice light, so that Ivan shouldn't know her true feelings. She had no intention of trying to explain the fear in her heart at the prospect of the days ahead.

'You are beautiful, my darling,' said Ivan. 'You have a twilight beauty.'

'And you are full of shit,' said Rilla, applying rather more foundation than Monsieur (or possibly Madame) Lancôme would have recommended to her cheeks and forehead, and making sure to blend in thoroughly around the neck and chin line.

That was one thing you could say about working (or in Rilla's case most often *not* working) in the movies and the theatre. It did teach you all about the possibilities, the magic, the transforming power of make-up. Everyone was busy constructing selves that they thought might appeal to others. Ivan, for instance, had a really rather remarkable resemblance to a vampire and played it for all it was worth. He was foreign, he was tall and skinny, he had lots of teeth and very pale skin and eyes he himself described as 'hypnotic'. He went in for Hammer Horror décor in his flat, which Rilla tried to avoid as much as she possibly could by managing to contrive that they always ended up here. She smiled again at her own reflection in the mirror. Her house was not exactly Ideal Home, but even if it was as flamboyant as Ivan's, it was also cosy and there was nothing remotely Gothic about it.

'You are happy now,' he said. 'You are remembering last night.'

'Don't flatter yourself, sweetie,' Rilla said sharply, and instantly regretted it. He wasn't the best lover in the world, but he was better than nothing. 'I'm sorry, Ivan. It's just that I'm a bundle of nerves about going back to my mother's house. I can't help it.'

'You smile,' Ivan continued, 'while I am weeping. What will I do without you? How will I bear it? How will I live?'

'Oh, do grow up, darling, honestly! It's only a few days. There's no need to be melodramatic about it.'

'You do not love me. You could not speak so if you had love in your heart.'

She couldn't deny it. She didn't love him, of course she didn't, but it was quite sharp of him to have spotted it. Rilla thought she put on a reasonable show of affection and certainly she was always whole-hearted about the sex, but her heart, well, that was foreign territory, and had been out of bounds for years. It was sometimes hard to square the way she was now with how she'd been in the days of Hugh Kenworthy, her first love. Months would go by and Hugh would simply never enter her mind, but when she *did* turn her thoughts to that time (sixteen years old, feeling everything so passionately that it seemed as though her skin were missing) she experienced something like a flood washing through her, a mixture of that old desire that made it hard for her to catch her breath, and vestiges of the rage she felt towards Leonora for what she had done. Rilla pulled her thoughts round to the present.

'It's nothing to do with love,' she explained patiently. 'I've told you all about it. Mother's seventy-fifth birthday party is strictly a family affair, otherwise of course I'd take you. You know that.'

Rilla outlined her mouth with a colour called Sepia Rose, and added lipgloss, believing that one couldn't glitter and shine too much. She had no time at all for matte and beige and the whole less-is-more philosophy. Cream cakes, red wine and Prawn Bhutans with extra naans were what she craved. She hadn't been quite truthful about the family affair. Partners, husbands, boyfriends, girlfriends were all invited, but Rilla never for a moment considered taking Ivan. She knew exactly how her mother would react to him. She'd be oh so polite, and smile the smile that made the Mona Lisa look positively open by comparison and say something like, *Welcome to Willow Court, Mr Posnikov*, but her greenish eyes would take in the slightly grubby fingernails, and her nostrils would dilate almost imperceptibly and her eyes would strip away all the pretences and discover who knew what awful truths about poor old Ivan. What would be made entirely clear to him, without so much as a word being spoken, was the feeling that he was not, to coin another of Leonora's phrases, *one of us*.

'Do get up, Ivan, please,' said Rilla. 'I have to decide what to take. I really want to get to Willow Court as soon as I can.'

She began to throw garments from the wardrobe on to the bed. Why was almost everything she owned either silky or satiny or feathered or beaded or somehow like a costume from a show? Whenever she visited Willow Court, she felt the need to find a disguise, a costume which wouldn't instantly make Leonora wrinkle her mouth. Why couldn't she manage neat skirts and crisp blouses? She would probably spill something on them if she did wear them.

'I choose for you!' Ivan declared. 'I know what you need. I am dress designer, no?'

'Okay,' said Rilla. 'Imagine you're dressing me for a three-act play set in a country house. French windows, drinks on the terrace. You know the sort of thing.'

She moved to the chair by the window and sighed. 'You can't possibly do any worse than I did.'

With surprising care, Ivan picked up one garment at a time and laid most of them aside with the merest hint of a despairing sigh. Finally he said, 'I think this will be enough, no?'

Rilla looked through what he'd chosen and saw that yes, indeed, the green chiffon might do nicely for a summer party, that the claret-coloured gypsy skirt could conceivably pass muster with the white linen blouse, that the black trousers and several silk jersey T-shirts might not be too hideous for morning strolls in the garden. Ivan added a couple of rather fine scarves ('Georgina von Etzdorf . . .' he breathed reverently as he laid them gently on the pillow) and then turned to choose a necklace from the ones looped over a corner of her dressing-table mirror.

'This, I think,' he said, picking out a long string of obviously fake pearls. 'Never before have I seen this – pearls which are not round!' He made the sound that was the nearest thing to a laugh he allowed himself.

'Yes, I love those,' Rilla said. 'They're from America. Square pearls! They'll do.'

She closed her eyes, and let Ivan rummage around in her earring box. What did it matter, really, when it came down to it? However she was dressed, the whole visit was going to be excruciating. The one thing she tried every minute of her life not to think about, to thrust into the darkest, most secret corners of her heart was known to everyone who was coming. What if they spoke of it? How would she bear that? Rilla closed her eyes and drew a deep breath to steady her thoughts. Willow Court. So many ghosts, so much pain, and her mother, Leonora Simmonds, monarch of all she surveyed, especially the paintings. Oh, my God, Rilla thought. What did we do to deserve those paintings in our family?

Rilla let the sound of Billie Holiday's voice fill the car: blue and velvety and freighted with pain. Sweet, but with an edge of darkness all around it, like a border. From time to time she joined in with the lyrics, filling the spaces in her head with the sound of her own voice. She knew that the landscape was streaming past the window, but she didn't even glance at it. She'd seen it far too many times before, on her way back to Willow Court. Gwen'll be walking round from room to room, she thought, checking that everyone has the right towels. She'll have made sure the paintings are newly dusted. And I'll be in the Blue Room, where Mother always puts me because it faces the back. No view of the lake. Rilla shivered in spite of the heat. She hadn't been down there for years but in her worst dreams she still saw the water shimmering with a sort of fluorescence. No, think of Gwen. That's safe. Tidy and organized Gwen, who wore well-cut trousers in proper material that cost a small fortune but nevertheless just looked like common-or-garden trousers. Her shirts, too, were the very best, and Rilla knew for a fact that each one cost an arm and a leg, but whatever was the point when the colours were so self-effacing? Apologetic pink, wishy-washy blue, and minimalism's favourite shade, cream, which did nothing for Gwen, did she but know it.

It wasn't that her sister wasn't attractive. She was. She had the figure of a young girl, and not a chubby young girl either. Her dark hair had greyed to the kind of elegant salt-and-pepper others paid a fortune for in salons, and her skin was like ivory. Rilla longed to put her in burgundy and peacock and old gold, but Gwen wouldn't hear of it. Perhaps all her poor brother-in-law had been looking for when he'd pursued other women during the early years of their marriage was a bit of colour. Rilla felt a pang of shame even thinking such a disloyal thought, but that didn't stop it being at least a possibility. James Rivera, who'd probably started life as Jaime, was wasted on her sister. He was handsome and dashing and just Spanish enough to have an exotic surname, but educated in this country, so not foreign enough to scare the horses. 'What if . . .' was a stupid game to play at the best of times, but Rilla had sometimes wondered rather idly what would have happened if Hugh Kenworthy hadn't been occupying her every thought, asleep and awake, in those days. Would James's eye have fallen on her? Would she have wanted it to?

She hardly ever thought about this any more, but in the old days one of the main items of family gossip, whenever two or three of them got together away from Willow Court was, does Gwen know? Almost from the day her sister married, Rilla could tell James was unfaithful to her. He was always 'up in London', or 'away for the night', and there was the occasion, which Rilla had never spoken of to anyone, when she'd seen him and – what was her name? Milly? Molly? Something like that – one of the young girls employed to help with the children in any case, looking flushed and dishevelled, coming out of the gazebo holding hands with James. And he'd seen her seeing them. Milly, or Molly, didn't last long after that. Gwen *must* know, Rilla thought. She can't not know. How typical of her to say nothing. Rocking the boat was not her thing. Her stoicism appeared to have paid off. Nowadays, James seemed to be as good as gold, though he was rather too fond of alcohol, and Rilla had often noticed her sister's worried frown and pursed lips as her husband helped himself to yet another drink. Order, that's what Gwen was interested in. Order and the Walsh Collection. Thank Heavens Leonora had at least one of her daughters to carry on after she'd gone. Being stuck in that enormous pile surrounded by more spooky pictures than you can shake a stick at was Rilla's idea of Hell.

And then she was there, at Willow Court. The wrought-iron gates were standing open. The leaves of the scarlet oaks leading up to the house were still green. Rilla's mouth suddenly felt dry. She slowed the car right down. She knew that Leonora and Gwen would have been looking out for her and would be waiting for her on the front steps and sure enough, there they were, like figures in a tableau. She could see them from quite a long way away: Leonora upright and self-possessed, standing one step above Gwen. Rilla stopped the car and got out as elegantly as she could, conscious of her mother's eyes on her. She ran up the steps to kiss her sister.

'Darling,' she said, and threw her arms around Gwen, suddenly filled with affection. Perhaps she ought to make more effort to see Gwen on her own. Maybe she should invite her up to London to stay? 'How super to see you! I'm early, aren't I? Hardly any traffic at all, amazingly enough.'

She went up to the next level to embrace her mother.

'Rilla!' Leonora was smiling, but she stood quite still as her younger daughter kissed her. Powder smelling like icing-sugar, Rilla thought, and soft skin, and somewhere in her core something that doesn't want to bend, to relax. Something frozen.

'Mother, you look wonderful. As usual.' And it was true. Leonora's skin was hardly wrinkled at all, and her green eyes undimmed, it seemed. As for the bone structure, well, as Ivan was forever telling her, there was no better basis for beauty than good bones. Rilla knew that any bones she had were rather too well-covered, and she waited for her mother to make some sort of allusion to any weight she might have put on since the last time, but no, on this occasion Leonora said only, 'You look lovely, too, Rilla darling. It's been such a long time since I've seen you. I've missed you, so I'm very pleased you've come down a little early.' Leonora paused, and scrutinised her daughter more carefully. 'And you do look a little tired, too. Never mind. You can have a nice long rest now that you're here.'

Rilla only just stopped herself from saying, Fat chance! Leonora *did* love her, she realized with the familiar pang of guilt she felt whenever she had to remind herself of this fact. She just found it hard to communicate her affection in a normal way, that was all. Rilla mumbled something about getting her bags out of the boot and taking them upstairs.

'You're in the Blue Room, darling,' said Leonora. 'I know you feel comfortable in there. Gwen will help you settle down, and then you've got plenty of time to change for dinner. I shall be dealing with letters in the conservatory, but do come down when you're ready. I'm longing to have a chat, if you're not too tired after such a long drive.' She smiled at Rilla, then turned and went inside, walking as she always did – slowly, and as though people were looking at her. Which, Rilla reflected, they very often were.

She walked to the back of the car with Gwen. Together they took out the luggage and went into the house carrying one bag each. Tangles of television cable snaked over the black and white tiles of the hall.

'They're here already, then, are they? The TV people?' Rilla said as she followed Gwen upstairs.

'Sean Everard, he's the director, he's coming tomorrow,' said Gwen, turning her head to talk over her shoulder, 'but the rest of the crew's here. They're doing what they call "establishing shots". They're very good, really. We hardly know they're around most of the time. They're staying down at the Fox and Goose, and they have all their meals there too.'

She almost bumped into a man squatting on the landing with a camera over his shoulder.

'Oh, gosh, Ken!' Gwen said. 'I didn't notice you there. And I'm very sorry, but I thought it was understood that this part of the landing is out of bounds. I discussed it all with Sean and I'm sure I mentioned it to you.'

Ken said, 'Sorry, sorry. I was looking for Mrs Simmonds's bedroom. There's a picture in there of some swans, I believe . . .'

'Oh!' Gwen relaxed a little. It was obvious to Rilla that if Leonora had said he could be up here, that was different. 'That's fine, then. Only it's along the other corridor. You turned right instead of left at the top of the staircase. It's easily done.'

'Right!' said Ken and wandered away. Rilla noticed that they were outside the old nursery.

'The dolls' house is still in there, isn't it?' she asked.

'Oh, yes. But Mother's absolutely adamant that they mustn't film that.' She strode along the corridor to the Blue Room with Rilla close behind her. Nothing in it had changed since the last time she'd visited, but Gwen had put buff-coloured roses in a vase on the table by the window.

'Lovely Buff Beauty, Gwennie, thank you so much.'

Gwen blushed at the childish nickname. 'You like the ones that go on flowering all through the summer, I know . . .' she murmured and put down the bag she was carrying. She turned to go, started saying something like, 'I'll see you later,' but Rilla interrupted her.

'I'm going to have a look at it. At the dolls' house. Come with me, Gwen, go on. Surely there's time? You don't have anything to do exactly now this minute, do you?'

Gwen hesitated, then said, 'Oh, all right, then. But only for a moment.'

'Good.' Rilla stepped out of the Blue Room and looked along the corridor. 'I'll make sure no one catches us.'

'Stop teasing, Rilla.' Gwen laughed and sounded all at once much younger. '*We're* allowed in the nursery. It's just the TV people Mother wants to keep out.'

'Can't imagine why . . . has she said? The dolls' house was Ethan Walsh's crowning achievement if you ask me.'

'She likes to keep it to herself for some reason,' Gwen said. 'She's always adored it, and of course it brings back memories for her. I can't stay long, I'm afraid. James will be back from the wine merchant very soon and you're supposed to be unpacking.'

Rilla had always loved the nursery. In the old days, it had been Nanny Mouse's domain, but for the last few years the old lady had been living in a cottage down at the end of the drive by the gates, looked after by a nurse-companion. She would have been sad to see it all quiet and echoey, stripped of toys, its bookshelves empty. It was not the room it used to be; the room Rilla had for years considered the centre of her world. Gwen's grandson, Douggie, Efe and Fiona's son, could have slept there whenever they visited, but Fiona liked to keep him near her still. He was only two and a half. Perhaps when he was older, he'd bring the room to life again.

Gwen opened the door and there was the dolls' house in its usual place against the wall. Rilla smiled. Mother was not a sentimental person, but when it came to this, which she often referred to as *almost my only link with my mother*, she behaved in ways which could only be described as somewhat eccentric. Okay, Gwen was right, and it had been made for Leonora by her father, and her mother had decorated every room. Perhaps she didn't want everyone in the world peering and poking at it, but still, not allowing the film crew to see it was taking matters a bit far. Also, only older children were actually allowed to play with it. Leonora would never permit toddlers to smear their grubby fingers over the wallpaper, or mistreat the tiny pieces of furniture. Everyone in the family knew that it was still very much Leonora's own possession, and if they thought there was anything at all strange about a woman of over seventy being attached to what was, after all, a child's toy, they never said so.

Making the house had been a labour of love, that was clear. Rilla found it hard to imagine her artistic grandfather, who'd been a bit of a Tartar by all accounts, getting down to child level, as it were, to create this most beautiful residence. Grandmother Maude, who was hardly mentioned in anything written about Ethan Walsh, had decorated it throughout, with exactly the same care that she had lavished on Willow Court. She had also made three little dolls to live in it – exact copies of herself and her husband and daughter. They were tiny rag-dolls, but so carefully stitched together that every feature was not only clearly visible, but recognizable too. Ethan was the biggest of the dolls, with a dark moustache and heavy eyebrows over piercing blue eyes. Maude had nut-brown hair drawn into a bun at the nape of her neck, and wore a blouse with a high collar made of lace. The Leonora doll was in a dress cut from the same lilac fabric she wore in one of the portraits, the famous one which showed her sitting on the edge of a bed. The dress was trimmed with the lace Maude had used to make a collar on the figure of the mother. Each doll had a smile embroidered on to its face in pink silk. When she was a little girl, Rilla often said that you could see they were a happy family.

'She used to let us look at them at Christmas time,' Gwen said. 'Do you remember?'

Rilla nodded. 'That's right. Didn't we have some miniature holly or something that we decorated some of the rooms with?'

'Wreaths,' said Gwen. 'They're in a box in the attic, I think. With all the other Christmas stuff.'

'She didn't let us play with them at all, though, did she?' Rilla could remember Leonora saying, *I can't let you have them for your games, darlings. They're so fragile, don't you see? But you like the new family I've bought for the house, don't you?* 'She gave us our dolls as a sort of distraction, I suppose, but we did love them, didn't we?'

'Of course we did,' said Gwen. 'I can't remember it bothering us at all that we couldn't play with the ones Grandmother Maude made. I don't even know where Mother keeps them these days.'

Because hardly anyone came into the nursery, there was a quality of chill in the silence that filled the whole room. Rilla thought that the dustsheet covering the house looked a little like a shroud. God, she thought, I'm letting my imagination run away with me.

Gwen nodded in the direction of the dustsheet and smiled at her sister. 'Go on then,' she said. 'Let's have a look at it.'

Rilla stared at the tall, rather narrow shape of the house under its white draperies. The roof was at the level of her waist. She reached for a corner of the sheet and lifted it, raised it up and folded it over, so that the dolls' house was revealed.

'I used to call it Paradise Mansions,' she said. 'Do you remember?'

'That really annoyed me,' Gwen laughed. 'I played with it first when you were no more than a baby. I called it Delacourt House. And the family were the Delacourt family. That was their proper name.'

Rilla said nothing, but she could still see herself, kneeling down in front of the dining-room, picking up the mother doll and pulling off her shawl and throwing it on the floor, and making her lie down on one of the upstairs beds. How furious Gwen used to get! She knew that even now Gwen was feeling a shadow of the outrage she felt then, at the violation of *her* things, *her* dolls.

'You used to want to murder me when I changed things round that you'd already decided on, didn't you?'

'Oh, nonsense,' said Gwen. 'We were only children, weren't we? Children are all little savages.' Her voice was light, casual, but Rilla knew she was right. Gwen came and knelt beside her on the floor. Rilla knew that however much her sister pretended that all this dolls' house nonsense was ancient history, it wasn't really. Bits and pieces of the past lay just under the skin, like buried splinters.

Rilla crouched down to look at everything more carefully. There were three floors, with the rooms arranged on either side of a long staircase. Kitchen and dining-room on the ground floor, drawing-room and study on the second floor, and two bedrooms and a bathroom on the third floor. In the attic space under the roof, Ethan had squashed in a tiny room for the maid. He'd made all the furniture, with beds for everyone and chests-of-drawers to stand beside them. Downstairs, the sideboards and the tables and chairs were intricate masterpieces of carpentry. Every wall was covered with some of the paper that Maude Walsh had chosen originally to hang in Willow Court. It was faded now, but you could still see the patterns: William Morris's Willow, of course, and some by Walter Crane of a pomegranate tree with white birds in it. The sloping roof was a masterpiece of painstaking craftsmanship, and this, surprisingly was Maude's own work. She had painted sheets and sheets of thick paper with an intricate pattern of rooftiles in water-colours and these had been skilfully glued to the plain wood. Leonora had often told them the story of how the new roof had been a birthday surprise from her mother, just before her eighth birthday, just before Maude's tragic death. Over the years, the greys and browns and pale saffrons had faded so that now it looked just like the real thing: weathered and rough; the authentic slatey-yellow of proper tiles.

Rilla suddenly thought what a sensation it would cause among art critics if they could see it. It must be worth a small fortune. How come her own stepdaughter Beth never spoke about it these days? Why didn't Gwen's children, particularly Efe (who was very mercenary, it seemed to Rilla, always fascinated by the price of things) realize what a treasure was stashed away up here?

The dolls were all present and correct. Queen Margarita (whom

Gwen called Mrs Delacourt) and her husband, and the two children, Lucinda and Lucas (Dora and Dominic for Gwen) and the maid, who was called Philpott by both of them. They were all peg-dolls with painted faces and unmoving bodies, but what life they'd breathed into them! Rilla had known what they thought and felt and wanted to do. She tidied their house, and arranged meals for them on their little table, but Gwen always said she did everything wrong, and once she pushed Rilla out of the way so roughly that she'd bumped her head on the runners of the rocking-horse and cried for hours. *Serve you right.* Rilla could remember to this day what Gwen had shouted at her then. *You shouldn't have moved them. I put them where they're supposed to be, and you moved them. You mustn't, that's all.*

'We did have fun with them, didn't we?' she said to Gwen.

'Yes, of course we did.' Gwen stood up again. 'Even though I seem to remember I always thought you got things wrong constantly. I suppose I wanted it all to myself. Didn't want to share it. Aren't children horrible a lot of the time?'

'Not me! I was totally loveable!'

'That's what you think!' Gwen was laughing. 'I know I've just denied wanting to murder you, but what *is* true is that you could be a real pest. But I suppose I was a bit bossy, wasn't I?'

'A confession! Wonders never cease, Gwen.'

Rilla stood up and lifted the sheet to cover everything again. The outline of the roof was sharp against the dark paper of the wall, and under the white avalanche she'd just created the dolls lay quietly. For a split second, Rilla found herself wondering what they thought of the whiteness blocking their windows. She laughed out loud, wondering whether this could be the onset of the menopause. *You're losing it, Mum!* was something Beth sometimes said to her, affectionately.

'Come down when you've unpacked,' Gwen said, 'and I'll go and see to the drinks. It's going to be such fun, Rilla, isn't it? This party?'

'It'll be great,' Rilla answered, and felt that she was telling no more than the truth.

'And where,' said Leonora, turning to Gwen, 'are you putting Chloë and her young man? What's his name? Philip something. Smart, that's it. Doesn't he do something rather fascinating for a living?' She took a sip of wine from her glass and applied herself to buttering a Bath Oliver and arranging dainty crumbs of Stilton on it.

'He's a picture restorer. He works at the V & A, I think, though of course, he's very young and junior. Chloë says he's longing to see the Willow Court paintings.'

The last of the evening sunshine found its way into the dining-room, glancing off the yellow velvet curtains and falling on to the window seat where Gus, one of Leonora's two cats, lay curled up like a furry marmalade-coloured cushion. His brother, Bertie, was fond of soft duvets and only came downstairs when hunger called him to the kitchen.

'In my old room,' said Gwen. 'Chloë's always liked it.'

Rilla concentrated on peeling an apple. It had only been her and Gwen and Leonora at dinner, after all. There was no sign of James anywhere. As though she were reading Rilla's mind, Leonora said, 'James, I take it, is still in town?'

Gwen nodded. 'Yes, he phoned me just before dinner. He's chatting with wine merchants and so forth, and seeing about the marquee, I think. Liaising, he calls it. In any case, he said he'd pick up a sandwich or something on his way home.'

Rilla laughed. 'James would never chat to anyone if he could possibly *liaise*, would he?'

Gwen smiled, rather half-heartedly it seemed to Rilla. A dreadful thought suddenly occurred to her. Is it possible that Gwen thinks James might have slept with me, all those years ago? Could she honestly believe I'd sink as low as screwing my own brother-in-law? Surely not! Rilla dismissed this thought and helped herself to another cup of coffee. James might actually be liaising on this occasion, but on the other hand he might not. She glanced at Gwen. In all the years since their marriage, she and James must have worked out a way of coming to terms with his past infidelities. Nowadays, she was a little tense when he came home late and somewhat the worse for wear, but she had put her foot down about driving right from the very beginning, so at least that was not a worry.

'That's how my father died,' Rilla remembered her shrieking at James during one blazing row she'd witnessed between the two of them. Gwen had been pale with fury and her voice sounded quite unlike her normal measured tones. 'I'm damned if you're going the same way.'

Why did Gwen put up with it at all? She must love him, Rilla supposed. She wondered briefly whether she could stand life with James and knew she couldn't. She wouldn't have been able to overlook the women, right at the start of the marriage. As far as she was concerned, it would take only one tiny slip, one kiss even, and she'd be off. Or send him, the man, whoever he was, packing. Fidelity wasn't surely too much to ask for. Or was it? Did people nowadays even care? She had no idea, and on her present form, she wasn't likely to find out. Who the hell found true love at her age?

She bit into her apple and turned her attention to what Leonora was saying. Something about her work. Rilla sighed inwardly, opened her mouth and prepared to make two cameos on afternoon soap operas sound like star parts for the Royal Shakespeare Company. Talking yourself up, it was called, and she'd grown rather good at it over the years. She tried not to sound defensive. There was nothing wrong with a mother showing some interest in what her daughter was doing. Grow up, Rilla, she said to herself, and launched into an account of the last commercial she'd been in.

In some cupboards, wire hangers made a sound like wind-chimes when you hung your clothes up, but not at Willow Court. Leonora didn't believe in wire hangers. You might just as well take your best dresses and shred them at the shoulders, she used to say, with typical exaggeration. Still, Rilla had to admit that padded hangers covered in material that felt satiny to the touch were both pleasurable and oddly comforting. At least my garments will be in good shape, she thought. Even if I'm not.

She'd been here for some hours and everything was all right. She had managed to look out of the window, earlier on, and there was the kitchen garden in the afternoon sunshine, looking restful and pretty and not a bit threatening. She had to be careful of some places, of course, even in the house. If she wasn't on her guard all the time, he'd appear in front of her eyes and the pain of that was too much to bear.

If there was one thing in the whole world you never forgot, not ever, it was a dead child, and Mark was always with her, contained in her flesh and in every atom of her body, gathered more closely into her than he'd been in the months before his birth. There was no way that he could not be, but it was only here, at Willow Court, that she sometimes heard his voice, and even actually *saw* him, behind the curtain in the drawing-room where he loved to hide, or sitting on the bench in the Quiet Garden with a cat on his lap. This, she thought sleepily, is a haunted house. I should be used to it by now, but I dread it. I dread the sight of him, the impossibility of it actually *being* him. And of course she couldn't sleep in her old room.

Rilla wondered who *would* be sleeping there. She'd ask Gwen. Dinner had been quiet and peaceful tonight, but from tomorrow everything was going to be different. Gwen's younger son, Alex, was getting a lift down with Beth. Efe, her eldest, would arrive in the afternoon with his family and Sean Everard, the TV director, was expected before dinner. There would hardly be time to turn round, and no time at all for heart-to-hearts of any kind. Not too much time for Leonora to interrogate her even further about work (*How long is it since you've been in a film, darling?*) or the current state of her love life or ask her in a roundabout way what she intended to do about her weight. (*Efe goes to the gym every day, you know. Even when he's busy.*)

Well, bully for Efe, Rilla thought, and reached into her enormous carpetbag to find her secret supply of chocolate bars. It was going to be a long time till breakfast. She peeled the wrapping off a Crunchie and lay down on the bed, biting into the gorgeously yellow honeycomb filling, feeling the sweetness fill her, feeling her mood lift. Dinner had gone much better than she'd feared. Nothing contentious, nothing difficult had come up at all. Maybe it wouldn't be so bad, this time here with the rest of the family. Leonora would be as nice as she possibly could be and make the effort to show some affection, and I must as well. Maybe everything would be fine, or better than fine. Maybe.

Thursday,
August 22nd,
2002

Beth Frederick found her breath catching in her throat at the thought of seeing Efe again. *Efe*. Pronounced 'Eefe'. She was the one who'd named him, when they were both two years old, and she couldn't manage to say 'Ethan'. He was Gwen's eldest child. They had practically grown up together. In those days, Rilla and Dad used to spend most of their time at Willow Court, even though they lived in London. That had changed suddenly, after what happened to Mark. Thinking of her little half-brother, even after all this time, was painful, and so Beth concentrated on Efe. She didn't want to cloud with any ghastly memories from the past the happiness she was feeling at seeing him again.

It was nearly time to go. She looked around her flat and thought of the layers of tissue paper between every garment in her suitcase and how impossible she found it not to line up the shirts in her drawer and the sheets in her linen cupboard. It was probably a good thing that she lived by herself. She would have hated to share the space with anyone. Anyone except Efe.

She knew that certain members of the family felt sorry for her. *Twenty-eight and still living alone*. Leonora thought that and said it too, sometimes. Beth didn't mind. She was happy in her work, and couldn't imagine anything worse than marrying the wrong person as so many of her friends seemed to have done.

Yesterday, before leaving work, she'd printed out Efe's latest e-mail, and for once it was interesting and intriguing as well as ending in the best possible way of all, with an affectionate sentence before his name. She knew the whole thing by heart, and wouldn't be separated from it. It was folded up and hidden away in her handbag, in a silky little pocket in the lining that she hardly ever used.

*Hey, Beth! What a fantastic few days coming up, eh? But I do have something of utmost urgency to put to you. Can't say anything now, but we'll talk more at Willow Court. The whole matter is rather important and may have quite serious repercussions. Look forward to seeing you there, kiddo. Love and kisses, Efe.*

It was the longest message she'd ever had from him, the Efe equivalent of a thesis. And *love and kisses* was unprecedented. She wished she could imagine it meant something romantic, but admitted to herself that it probably didn't. *Kiddo* was a bit depressing, with its definite older-brother overtones, but you couldn't have everything. And what did he mean by 'repercussions'? What on earth did he have up his sleeve? She was curious to know, of course, but mainly she wanted to see his face again.

All through their childhood Efe had led, and Beth followed him slavishly. She loved him better than anyone else in the whole world. *Even though they're only step-cousins, and not related by blood in any way, Beth and Efe are devoted to one another*, Leonora told everyone, and that was the family wisdom. He confided in her still. Whenever he had a problem, she was the one he came to, in spite of being married now and head of his little family.

Usually, Beth kept her feelings for him locked away inside herself, and tried to ignore them. Efe was filed away in her heart. She was vaguely ashamed at how childish she was about everything to do with him. Anyone who knew that she printed out and kept every single e-mail he sent her would realize how very immature she was. It wasn't as though they actually said anything interesting. Five words was normal: *Hi, Beth! How's kicks? Efe* was the kind of thing he usually wrote, unless the message was an arrangement like *Don't forget Friday supper chez nous. Ciao.* His indiscriminate scattering of foreign phrases was the sort of thing that led his sister to call him 'a prize wanker', but Beth found it endearing. There was also the rare note which ended *love, Efe*, and these she treasured more than the others, which was seriously pathetic.

Beth felt her heart gripped by a physical pain. The day that Efe told her he was marrying Fiona McVie was the first time she'd admitted it to herself. Stupidly, she had never quite realized before that she loved Efe in an altogether uncousinly way. At first she felt guilt, as though the emotion might have been in some way incestuous, but it wasn't. She was unrelated to him. She was allowed to love him. And he loved her, didn't he? For one wild moment, she'd nearly said it. Nearly blurted out the words that would have spoiled everything: *Don't marry Fiona. Look at me. Look at how much I love you. Look at how well we get on.*

'Getting on' was not what love was about, though, was it? Beth knew that. Efe didn't fancy her and that was that. Fiona was so pretty, like a blonde doll, with long legs and even longer eyelashes and a voice like silver bells, beautiful, but slightly irritating too. Metallic. Rather too high-pitched. There was nothing about her that one could dislike, except perhaps her complete and utter adoration of Efe and the way she always did exactly what she thought he'd like, almost obliterating her own desires and opinions. Still, Beth felt a sour emotion not far removed from hatred whenever she saw her. Even thinking about Fiona with Efe was enough to fill her with anguish. In her wallet, she kept a copy of one of the photographs that Alex, Efe's brother, had taken at the wedding. It comforted her and tortured her in equal measure and she hardly ever took it out, but she knew it was there, herself and Efe together at the wedding reception.

Efe looked glorious. He was almost too good-looking; tall, dark, with long-lashed eyes that changed colour from green to grey to almost blue, depending on what he wore. In this photograph, he could have been advertising Ralph Lauren, and she looked ridiculous. All that frilly nonsense she'd had to wear as a bridesmaid had nearly killed her, quite apart from what she was feeling about Fiona. Her hair had been pulled away from her forehead and tied back. She was standing against a wall, and Efe was looking down at her with something like love in his eyes. That was what she liked to think, anyway. Whenever she took the photo out and examined it carefully, though, she could see the truth. He was looking normal – affectionate and friendly, but no more. All the love was in *her* eyes, turned to look up at him. Love, and something like desperation. There were times when she felt like tearing up the photo, but something always stopped her, a vain hope that the next time she looked, magically, Efe's expression would be different – filled with passion, seeing *her* as the person he wanted to spend the rest of his life with.

Sometimes she chided herself for her ridiculous fantasies. There was no reason on earth why Efe should make those come true and leave Fiona for her. He liked beautiful women and Beth knew that no one could call her that.

She was slim, and her dark hair fell almost to her shoulders in a well-cut bob. She wore little make-up, and what she did wear was very expensive. *But you're a good-looking girl. You don't make enough of yourself. I could show you.* Rilla said that all the time and would have liked nothing better than to manage her stepdaughter's 'look' as she called it. Poor old Rilla! Beth realized how frustrating it must be for her that she had a daughter whose style was understated and elegant. No one would have guessed she was the offspring of a rock star. Beth was neither shy nor self-effacing, but she hated clothes that called attention to themselves. *You're like a funeral mute*, Gwen's daughter Chloë often told her, in despair at her eternal plain colours, and it was probably true. Her clothes were safe. She simply put them on and forgot about them, and that left her free to devote her energies to more important things.

Beth was personal assistant to Jack Eldridge, the senior partner in a firm of architects where dark trouser suits and silver earrings were something like a uniform. Eight years ago, when she'd started working there, Jack had been impressed by the fact that she was related to the Walsh family of Willow Court.

'It's a most magnificent house, isn't it?' he said. 'You're very lucky to have partly grown up there.'

Beth agreed. She loved every inch of Willow Court. It had been built in the early days of the nineteenth century, in imitation of a classical style. The E-shaped building was surrounded by gardens. There were terraces of flowerbeds in front of the house, edged with low-growing lavender bushes, and full of blooms all year round, it seemed. Winter pansies grew before the tulips appeared in the spring, and later, drifts of Busy Lizzies in white and pale pink blossomed in their turn and, of course, roses in profusion. You could walk down the steps between them and make a soft crunching noise on the tiny gravelstones. The formal garden (white wrought-iron gazebo and hedges clipped into neat shapes) gave way to a smooth lawn, which fell in a curve of green to the wild garden, where poppies and cornflowers flourished alongside wild flowers whose names Beth didn't know. The tall grasses planted down there, set with occasional decorative boulders, made an organized jungle that was always busy with butterflies and dragonflies and the hum of bees when the sun shone. And beyond the wilderness, there was the lake. This was where the willows that gave the house its name wept their leaves into the water, and where the swans congregated. Beyond the lake, shadowy trees sloped up the hill to the village church, whose spire was just visible above a rolling ocean of a green that was nearly black in the evening and when the clouds were thick in the sky.

Beth liked the back of the house best of all, though. There, the kitchen garden had rows of vegetables laid out 'like in Peter Rabbit'. She'd said that when she was not much more than a baby, and the name had stuck. It was now known as the Peter Rabbit garden. You had to walk through it to reach the Quiet Garden, which had an enormous magnolia tree in the middle of the lawn with a bench built round it that you could sit on for picnics. No bright flowers grew here. According to family legend, this was by order of Ethan Walsh's wife, Maude, who couldn't abide the startling yellow of daffodils, or the vulgar scarlet of certain roses. The border was filled with delphiniums, lupins, phlox, foxgloves and hollyhocks in muted shades of pink and blue and mauve. Rhododendrons, azaleas and camellias were white. The roses twined around the trunk of every tree were peach, buff, cream and palest pink, and on the far wall fruit trees grew in fan shapes against the rosy bricks. Espaliered, Rilla told her. They're espaliered fruit trees, she'd said, and little Beth rolled the word round in her mouth and fell in love with the music of it on her tongue.

Adult Beth smiled to remember this. She really ought to go and pick up Alex. Efe's younger brother had no car and she always gave him lifts when she could. He would, she knew, be waiting for her outside his flat with his rucksack and assorted carrier bags on the ground beside him, looking like a student. His wavy dark hair would be flopping over his forehead, and he'd have flung his clothes on anyhow with no thought about how he appeared to other people. Efe called his style shambolic, but Beth found it rather touching. Before she left, though, there was still the ritual to perform. She sat down with her hands folded on her lap, feeling a little foolish, as always when she gave in to this ridiculous superstition. The Russians, according to Rilla, always sat down for a few minutes before making a journey. It was considered lucky. Beth didn't know if it really *was* a Russian tradition or if her mother had lifted it from some production of *The Cherry Orchard* she'd been in thousands of years ago. It didn't really matter, because Beth wouldn't have considered going anywhere for a few days without first sitting with her knees together and her hands folded, in the hard chair at the kitchen table. An armchair didn't count, for reasons which had never been explained.

Beth smiled, as she often did when she thought of Rilla. She's batty, she said to herself, but fun, which is more than most people can say for their parents. And we get on, which is also a bonus. She often wondered whether it had something to do with the fact that Rilla wasn't her real mother, but someone her father had married before she knew about things like wicked stepmothers. Maybe that was why she had no trouble at all loving her. Chloë claimed to hate her mother, and Beth remonstrated feebly with her from time to time. It was difficult to see how anyone could hate Gwen, who was a mild, gentle sort of person, but Chloë, who was spiky and aggressive and rather boringly rude these days, seemed to have a positive talent for disliking people. Beth realized that she'd been lucky, ending up with Rilla out of all her father's girlfriends. She was warm and affectionate and funny and forever flinging together unexpected ingredients and exotic spices and making wonderful smells – and a dreadful mess – in the kitchen. Also, she was self-absorbed, which Beth never minded, because it meant that she herself had been allowed to do more or less what she'd wanted to all her life. But from quite an early age, Beth realized that Rilla needed looking after, and organising. She was untidy, not only in her cupboards and drawers but also in her head. She'd gone down to Willow Court yesterday, and Beth imagined what her packing must have been like, imagined her stuffing garments haphazardly into some bag that had seen better days. She smiled as she stood up and went to fetch her suitcase. Then she locked the flat and made her way down to the street.

As she drove to Alex's flat, she reflected on family secrets. No one knew about her feelings for Efe. They had given up, most of them, worrying about her being so firmly unattached. I bet they've decided

I'm a virgin, she thought. Well, let them! Beth never spoke about her sex life. They, Leonora and Gwen and even darling Rilla, thought she was on the shelf. Beth smiled to think of their reaction if they knew. Just because you were suffering from unrequited love didn't mean you had to do without sex. It was just that you never committed. Never got involved. Wouldn't let yourself. She was exactly like many of the men she knew.

These days in Efe's company would be a test. She couldn't wait. Quite apart from curiosity about his news, she was longing to see him, to talk to him, to be near him, to smell his smell when they kissed 'hello' and at the same time she dreaded it. It would be an ordeal. Fiona would be with him, and so would Douggie, and every time she looked at them she'd feel like the little mermaid in the story, as though she were walking on knives.

'You drive, Alex, go on,' said Beth. 'You know you're longing to.'

'Sure you don't mind?' Alex grinned at her. They'd piled his belongings on to the back seat with Beth taking great care to see that everything was tidily stacked.

'No, go on. I'm exhausted. I'll probably be rotten company. I might even fall asleep.'

'I'm used to that,' said Alex. 'You being rotten company. Go to sleep and see if I care. I'd rather listen to whatever crappy stuff you've got in the tapedeck.'

Beth slapped him with a newspaper that he'd somehow managed, in spite of her best efforts, to keep about his person. She pulled it out of a pocket and batted him over the head with it. Then she turned round and tucked it into one of the carrier bags on the back seat.

'You're not touching that till we get there,' she said. 'I don't trust you not to drive and read at the same time. And don't think I'm ignoring your dig at my music. It's the Buena Vista Social Club. Take it or leave it.'

'No, that's okay. Quite civilised for you. Branching out, are you?'

'Shut up and drive, Alex. I'm going to sleep.'

'Right,' Alex said, and pressed some buttons. The music filled the car, and he saw Beth relaxing into her seat and closing her eyes.

There were very few people in the world Alex felt comfortable with and Beth was one of them. He was two years younger than she was, and he'd always known how much she liked looking after him. By rights, she should be married with lots of children of her own, but as she wasn't, Alex enjoyed watching her mother everyone who came into her orbit. She tried as hard as she could to organize Rilla; she took an interest in his love life and all his attempts to be evasive counted for nothing. She had a gift for making him speak, and he confessed things to her that he wouldn't have dreamed of telling anyone else, not even Efe. Worries he had, like, why didn't he feel what he was supposed to feel for all the various women he'd had short and unsatisfactory relationships with? Beth had patience and never minded listening to him mumbling and muttering. She also, very comfortingly, did it while feeding him delicious meals because she believed he never ate properly.

Alex was on the staff of a good newspaper and photographed beautiful women much of the time. He got sent around all over the place to take shots of this starlet and that pop singer and the other society person for one or another page, and sometimes he even got lucky and pulled somebody, but one-night stands were what they always turned out to be. Love never seemed even to be a possibility.

It wasn't just he who made confessions, though. Alex was willing to bet he was the only person who knew that Beth was in love with someone. She'd made him swear not to tell a soul, and he never had. She'd told him about it at Efe's wedding, and fair enough, she'd had a bit to drink, but no one could have called her pissed. She knew what she was saying. It wasn't a very long conversation, but he remembered it well.

*I'm broken-hearted, Alex. Have I told you?*

*No, but you can, Beth. You know you can tell me anything.*

*I do know that. Yes, I do. But I can't speak about this. It's secret.*

*Even from me?*

*From everyone. It's secret and it's hopeless and I'm going to grow up and forget all about him.*

Alex had wanted to ask every sort of question. Who is this person and why can't he love you and are you quite sure he doesn't, but in the end, as usual, he'd said nothing. Later he decided that Beth's secret love was probably married. Nothing more secret and terrible than that. Nothing out of the ordinary at all. Married and not going to leave his wife. One day, he thought, I'll ask her about it again.

He changed gear, and turned his mind to Willow Court. It'd be great to see Efe again. They didn't meet nearly enough in London. This morning there had been a brief text message on his mobile that mentioned needing to discuss something. Urgently. That was typical of Efe. Everything for him was urgent. Top priority, etc. etc. Alex had always idolized his elder brother. There was only a two-year difference in their ages, but when they were kids, he'd followed Efe around and Efe put up with it because a brother who didn't say much and never told tales was quite useful. Alex remembered a game of Cowboys when he'd been tied to one of the willow trees down by the lake for hours and hours after having been captured by Efe's cattle rustlers, which was basically just Efe and Beth. They'd threatened to come back and shoot him and then they'd gone up to the house for tea and totally forgotten him in some other excitement. According to Beth, it wasn't till bathtime that Gwen suddenly noticed he wasn't there and Efe was sent to untie him. Efe's version was that they'd been prevented by the adults from getting back to the lake again, but Alex never even listened to his brother's excuses. He'd just rubbed his wrists where they'd been bound and trudged up through the wild garden to the house.

It never occurred to him to complain about it to anyone and probably it wasn't hours and hours that he'd been tied up for anyway. His love for Efe was so great and unquestioning that, in those days anyway, he'd have put up with anything just to be allowed to be a part of the bigger boy's world. He'd been about six years old when that happened, but he'd always had a hazy idea of the passage of time and that hadn't changed at all.

Another thing that hadn't changed was his inability to speak. Ridiculous to find yourself tongue-tied at his age, but words often struck him as being like a lot of little black insects, flying around in the air when people spoke them; wriggling about in lines of print and causing nothing but trouble and misunderstanding. It was Leonora who'd told him about the things that could never be called back, *the sped arrow, the spoken word*, and all his life Alex had watched words humming through the air and doing damage. He saw how his mother flinched when Chloë was being particularly nasty to her; he noticed how Leonora never managed to speak properly to Rilla, as though her love had somehow got bottled up on the journey between her heart and her mouth; he knew his father thought it was a joke, calling his mother silly, or a fool, or some such, but it wasn't really. It was meant. Words were always meant in some way, and Alex wasn't going to risk saying too many in case they hurt someone when he spoke them.

He was looking forward to seeing his grandmother. Efe always said he was Leonora's favourite, but Alex sometimes wondered whether that was quite true. There was something, some special relationship between her and Efe, which you couldn't quite put your finger on, but yes, she did love him too, in a different way. She was not the same person with Alex that she was with other people. With him, ever since he was a tiny baby, she'd been girlish. She'd played games for hours at a time. She'd played puppets and put on silly voices when they were alone. She'd read to him every night, and Alex never discovered whether this worried his mother or not. She never said. Even now that everyone was grown-up, he was the one Leonora wanted sitting next to her, and when he was at Willow Court he was generally the person chosen to find things for her, or carry them about for her as she moved around the house.

'Don't worry, dear,' she'd say to Mum. 'I've got my Alex here now.'

She occasionally called him that. 'My Alex.' He smiled. The others would bring her expensive presents for her birthday and she'd like his best of all, an album of photos of every single thing – corners of the house, animals, flowers in the garden, individual portraits, groups – the whole of Willow Court life between leather covers. On her actual birthday, the album would be empty, but as soon as she opened it, he'd tell her about his surprise. A history of the whole celebration in pictures. She'd love it. She loved anything that showed Willow Court and the paintings in a good light.

Ethan Walsh's paintings. They all talked about them a lot, and spent ages setting up visits for this or that art expert to come and look at them. Every summer, people came trooping past them dutifully but

Alex wondered whether anyone apart from him and Leonora actually looked at them. That was another bond between them. They understood what was going on in the pictures. They realized that there was more, much more, to them than just paint on canvas, or pastels on thick paper, or watercolours.

For one thing, they were uncharacteristically modern. Most of them had been painted in the early years of the twentieth century, and you could see the influences on them of Impressionism and Surrealism, but there were tricks of perspective there that were very much more modern than that. Some of them, also, harked back to the work of the Pre-Raphaelites. They had that sense of drama, of things being arranged for effect. And then there was the matter of light. Certain of the paintings (the portrait of Leonora herself as a girl, for instance) seemed actually to shed light outside the frame. Night scenes showing imaginary landscapes (mountains, seashores, forests) had moonlight spilling out of them, skimming surfaces, touching the edges of things, making shadows that contained more than you first thought. Walsh hid things in the pictures. Did anyone else realize this? Did they see the eyes in the reeds behind the swans? The clawing fingers at the ends of tree branches? A suspicion of darker things underneath the smooth surface of the world he was depicting? And did anyone notice that the colours were always strangely luminous? There were unexpected combinations in the still lifes that couldn't possibly be exactly true. The painting of a blue teapot, for example, was one of Alex's favourites. The real thing was still used by Mary, the housekeeper at Willow Court, and his mother, and there was just no comparison. The blue paint sang and vibrated and flooded your heart with something like joy. The real thing was okay. Nothing to write home about. Just a teapot. That was Ethan Walsh's real gift, Alex thought. He made things more than they were in life. Better. Brighter and filled with light. And that's what I want as well. That's what my photos do, or what I want them to do. Be like life, but more than that. Have the same luminescence about them that the Walsh Collection has.

'Wake up, Beth,' he said. 'We're here.'

He looked down at her. She opened her eyes and smiled at him.

'I'd like to take a photo of you looking like that,' he found himself saying.

'You're mad, you are!' Beth answered. 'I must look ghastly, all crumpled and sleepy. You should have woken me earlier, Alex. I could have driven for a bit.'

'No, that's okay. I love your car.' He smiled at Beth. 'And what's more, you can't be a backseat driver if you're sound asleep, can you?'

Beth stood in the corridor. She could hear Fiona and Douggie giggling in their room. They must have just got here too, she thought. She listened for a while, but couldn't hear Efe's voice. I should go and say hello at least, she thought, and sighed. She'd already unpacked and arranged everything in the drawers. She was in her old room, the one she always had when she came to Willow Court, with windows overlooking the drive and the wide sweep of lawn at the front of the house. She'd looked out of them as soon as she arrived and saw that the marquee for the party was already being put up. Men were swarming all over the lawn carrying slender steel tubes and hammering together a silver skeleton to hold up the vast greenish folds of the tent, still lying on the grass. Leonora was in the room next door on one side and Chloë on the other. I can't face them, she thought. Not Fiona and Douggie, not just yet, but they'll know where Efe is. She stood listening to Douggie's childish words, gathering herself as though for a battle or some kind of confrontation, and then knocked lightly on the door.

'It's me, Fiona,' she said. 'Hello.'

'Oh, Beth, how lovely! Douggie and I were just having a little game of Lego before lunch. Come and play with us.'

Fiona was perfectly dressed in designer jeans and a white blouse that practically had the words *please do not mistake me for an ordinary white shirt. I am more expensive than anything you've owned in your whole life* printed all over it. She was tall and her hair always looked as though she'd that moment stepped out of the salon. How did she do it? Beth's gaze was drawn, as it always was when she was with Fiona, to her wedding ring. A mist of rage clouded her eyes for a moment and she blinked. It isn't Fiona's fault, part of her said. She doesn't know how I feel about her husband. It's nothing to do with her. It's his fault, he's the one who should know what I feel. Not her. She made an effort to smile.

'I can't really,' she said, and crouched down to kiss the little boy, who looked so much like his father. 'I've got to go and find my mother and say hello to Chloë. Is she here yet?'

'Oh, yes, we're all here now, I think. It's going to be a wonderful party, don't you think? And I'm dying to meet the television director, aren't you? Efe says he's really, really famous.'

'Where is Efe, by the way?'

'He's gone out with James. To the village, I think. You know what he's like when he gets here . . .'

Beth nodded. She did know. He liked to walk around everywhere to make sure that all was as he remembered it, that nothing had changed. She knew how he felt, because she, too, liked everything to be as it always was.

'I'll see you later, Fiona,' she said, edging towards the door. 'I'll just go and say hi to Chloë.'

'Right,' said Fiona. 'Super to see you.'

Beth hadn't really meant to go and find Chloë. That was just the first thing she'd thought of to say to Fiona, but now that she was safely out of there, she might as well just say hello. She walked back to Chloë's room and knocked at the door.

'Come!' said her voice, an unmistakable mixture of the brash and the girlish. Beth stepped into a room that was already so Chloë-esque that she had to laugh.

'Chloë, honestly! This room's a tip!'

'Fuck off if you're going to be like my mum, Beth!' Chloë said, but she was grinning. She didn't stir from her place on the bed, which didn't look like a Willow Court bed at all, but more the sort of thing you'd find in a cheap doss-house. The duvet had vanished under piles of grubby underwear and crumpled bits of paper, and it looked as though Chloë had turned her make-up bag upside down on the pillow. Lipsticks with their tops missing, eyeliners sticky with age, powder-puffs that were so revoltingly grubby you wondered whether they were capable of putting more than dirt on any cheek or nose, lay about all over the place. And her clothes were scattered on the floor, together with the clumpy-looking shoes she always wore. Her lips were outlined with a colour as near to black as it was possible to get. Her white skin and fair hair cut into spikes were supposed, Beth knew, to make her look dangerous, but only succeeded in making her look vulnerable. She was wearing a floral dress, with a rugby shirt over the top.

'I'm an art student,' Chloë said, lighting a cigarette. 'This is what art students do, didn't you know? This isn't a mess. It's an installation, so there.'

'Leonora will have a fit if she catches you smoking. You know what she's like about that.'

'I don't care, if you want to know. I'll spray some of my perfume about. Or I could lean out of the window. I'm using this tin as an ashtray. She ought to be grateful I'm not stubbing my fags out in her waste-paper basket or something.'

The tin she mentioned contained, Beth noticed, a little hillock of stubs that had built up, like an arrangement of small yellow rocks. Chloë continued.

'I've considered making an artwork out of this tin. Stub City, I'd call it. Have you seen Efe and Fiona? They're about somewhere. Oh God, it's going to be gruesome, this party. Days and days of Fiona. I can't bear it, Beth. She's the sort of person who doesn't sweat. Know what I mean? And she comes round to my flat and looks as though she's trodden in something nasty.'

'Knowing your flat, she probably has. Your floor has so many sticky things on it that most people don't make it across the room.'

'What rubbish! A bit of lemonade that I spilled once and didn't clear up properly. You're like an elephant, you are. Never forget anything. Or forgive.'

Beth went over to the open window and leaned out. Behind her, she could hear Chloë, still chattering away.

'Fiona's got a cheek! She comes round to my flat and she's, like, picking at her food and saying nothing, until at last she can't bear it any longer and murmurs something like, *Why don't you get a cleaner? Can you believe it, Beth?*'

'What did you say?'

'Well, nothing actually. I didn't want a massive row to break out, but I was thinking of all sorts of stuff I could have said, like, because

I'm not a spoiled brat like you. Because I wouldn't allow anyone else into my space, and most of all because I don't want to be the kind of tosser who says *oh, my cleaner is an absolute godsend* at dinner parties. Also, because I can't afford it, and anyway why don't you fuck off out of my life, which is how *I* like it and not all plastic and magaziney like yours with my plastic and magaziney brother!'

Just in time, Beth stopped herself objecting to the remarks about Efe. 'Never mind, Chloë. I'm sure one day you'll get the chance to tell Fiona exactly how you feel about her.'

'Better not, if I want to remain on speaking terms with Efe.'

Beth looked down into the garden at the front of the house, and there he was, as though Chloë talking about him had made him materialize. She waved, but he was too far away. He was walking with James, coming nearer and nearer. Even at this distance, Beth thought, you can tell how elegant he is. She swallowed hard and began talking to Chloë to stop her mind from turning to thoughts of Efe's long legs. She said, 'What present have you got for Leonora?'

Chloë leapt off the bed.

'I'll show you. It's brilliant! I'm so pleased with myself.'

She rummaged around in one of the suitcases that was lying on the floor, its contents spilling out of it. 'Here,' she said. 'Look at that. Isn't it lovely? Though I say so myself. I found it tossed into a skip, looking like nothing on earth. Horrible pink glossy paint all over it.'

Beth looked at the little chest of drawers. It was about eighteen inches high and must have been a toy of some kind, long ago. Every trace of pink had gone and it was re-painted in a shade somewhere between blue and green. Chloë had distressed the paint so that it looked as though the wood was beautifully weathered. There were seven drawers in all, four little ones at the top and three longer ones below those.

'I've put something in each drawer – there's one for each decade of Leonora's life – Look!'

Beth looked. There were dried flowers, a locket, a wedding ring in a lace hankie, a miniature flower-pot, little pictures of Bertie and Gus, the cats, done in needlepoint; something beautiful and tiny in every single drawer. It was exquisite.

'It's amazing, Chloë. You're brilliant and she'll be thrilled to bits.'

Beth smiled. 'I must go and find Rilla,' she said. 'And where, by the way, is Philip?'

'Gone to the village for something or other. He'll be back later.'

She almost ran down the stairs to the hall. Efe was walking about outside. She would see him very soon. She was going to ignore Fiona and just concentrate on Efe. Days and days of being with him. A triangle-shaped wedge of sunshine lay across the bottom step, flooding it with light.

It seemed to be true, what they all said. The elderly – Leonora refused to think of herself as 'old' – needed less and less sleep as time went on. Nowadays, she often found herself wide awake as soon as it was light, which meant that she needed an afternoon nap almost every day. She didn't know exactly what time it was, but she'd been asleep for a while. Lunch had been rather tiring, with Douggie needing attention and Efe's wife . . . Fiona . . . making a fuss about everything. It was time to get up. Mr Everard . . . Sean . . . would be here soon, and she'd promised to talk to him. And before that, she had to go and visit Nanny Mouse.

The sky outside her window looked like four o'clock. Leonora pushed away the sheet that covered her, put her feet to the floor and felt around for her slippers. Slowly she stood up. Every time she lay down, she checked herself as she got up, moved her arms above her head, did a sort of bend of the knees, just to make sure her limbs hadn't seized up while she wasn't paying attention. She smiled, satisfied that everything was in working order for yet another evening. It had been a very busy day already. Gwen – darling, reliable, kind Gwen – had been rushing about for weeks, organising everything.

The party would, she told herself, be wonderful. An occasion for rejoicing. And like a reflex, she felt the pain that was always there, somewhere inside her, whenever she was really happy. It was a mixture of regret that Peter couldn't be with her, sharing the pleasure and the ache she could still feel when she remembered him. She'd often heard others say that one of the worst things about losing someone you loved was the way they faded from your mind; the way memories of their physical presence disappeared in the end. In her case, it was exactly the opposite. She could still summon up Peter's smile, the touch of his hands, his mouth on hers. She sighed. Also, somewhere in a place she couldn't exactly reach with her mind, there was something like a shadow. Why was that? A kind of sick dread? True, when the girls were together, there were quite often fireworks, always had been. From their earliest childhood, they had been at odds, in spite of her best efforts, but surely at the ages of fifty and forty-eight they were old enough to keep their feelings under control? She knew that they loved one another, but there was always some kind of competition going on between them. They were both, she knew, seeking her love and approval, and she tried, she really and truly *did* try, just as she had ever since they'd been tiny, to be even-handed and fair in her dealings with them. She recognized, though, if she were honest with herself, that Rilla just sometimes rubbed her up the wrong way, irritated her in ways that Gwen never did. How hard it was to be a mother! How difficult to admit, particularly when your children were adults, that they were only people, after all, and naturally you got on better with some than with others. Which, of course, made no difference whatsoever to the love you felt. Nothing could alter that, but how much easier everything would be if love were enough. It wasn't. She knew that very well. Better than anyone. Still, everything had gone well last night, which was a blessing.

And, of course, it wasn't just Gwen and Rilla on their own, as it had been in the old days. The grandchildren were all here too, with their – what was the modern phrase? – partners. How silly that sounded! What was wrong with 'sweetheart'? She hadn't had a chance to talk to Efe properly yet. He'd gone off with James to walk around the garden and she'd only managed to greet him briefly. Leonora knew that what she felt for her eldest grandchild was out of the ordinary. Love, certainly, but something else too. A particular kinship, because they were alike in so many ways and because Efe reminded her of his namesake, her father. She knew more about him than anyone, though sometimes she wished she didn't. She pressed her lips together and decided this was not the moment to think about all that. She pushed it to the very back of her mind and opened a drawer in her dressing-table.

Without thinking about why she was doing so, she took out from under a neatly folded pile of scarves a square purse made from some kind of thick cotton. The letters roughly and clumsily embroidered there (*MUMMY*) made her eyes fill with tears. Rilla had stitched the purse at school, and though she was never the best needlewoman in the world, she'd loved her enough then to make this present for her. Leonora kept her precious dolls in it. No one else knew where they were hidden. She opened the purse now and took out the little doll that looked as she herself had once looked: pretty, very young, in a lovely dress. Oh, how I wish I could be her again, Leonora thought. Not an old woman with too many sorrows.

She felt her head swimming, and hastily replaced the dolls. Calm down, Leonora, she said to herself. She closed her eyes, breathed deeply, and felt a little better. Sometimes, she imagined her head divided into compartments, rather like her jewellery box, each lined with scarlet velvet and tightly shut for most of the time. That's how it must stay, she thought. I will close that drawer and go back to thinking about the days ahead. She would, she knew, have her work cut out trying to foresee and head off any trouble arising between members of her family. She was still capable, surely, of seeing that everyone behaved themselves. That couldn't really be troubling her, could it? So what was it?

She sat at her dressing-table and picked up the silver-backed brushes that had belonged to her mother. Poor Maude, Leonora thought. What would she think of the fact that she was now known to most people simply as the wife of Ethan Walsh? A shadow, there one second and gone the next, crossed the glass in front of her eyes and she turned to see what it could have been, her heart beating rather too fast in her chest. Nothing. A trick of the light. Possibly even the reflected image of the painting that hung on the wall above her bed. That must have been it, the white of the swans on the water, seeming to move. Not really moving at all.

Leonora soothed herself by looking at the photograph that stood on her dressing-table. Alex had taken it a couple of years ago. She smiled to think of her younger grandson and how, from the very first time he'd held a camera when he was no more than six years old, he'd almost never put it down. Whatever the occasion, there he'd be, snapping away quietly instead of talking to people. She would never have admitted to having a favourite grandchild, but there was, she felt, a special bond between her and the rather quiet little boy who had always seemed to enjoy her company and never required anything from her that she couldn't give. Even as an adult, he was still her darling, and she didn't think anyone quite appreciated how talented he was.

He has a gift, Leonora thought, for seizing the right moment, and quite often for showing more about people in the shot than they realized. There they were, she and Gwen and Rilla, fixed forever as they were that day, sitting on the bench under the magnolia tree in the Quiet Garden. I look good in that blouse, she thought, with Mummy's pearls around my neck. Gwen had Gus on her lap, and the blue of her cardigan was flattering. Rilla looked happy in this picture, which made a change. She wasn't often seen to smile in photographs and Leonora knew that was because Rilla felt it made her look too fat. She had on a long, gold-coloured dress, quite unsuitable for the country, and Leonora felt a momentary irritation, mixed with the concern that she always felt for her younger daughter. It wasn't as though she was a stranger to Willow Court. She knew that it wasn't a long-dress sort of place. Also, she was wearing altogether too many necklaces, which was typical of her. Leonora stared at Gwen looking down at the cat on her lap, and at Rilla looking at Gwen. Not me, she thought. I'm looking straight at the camera. Meeting its eye. The magnolia tree was lovely, studded with its pink and white tulip-like flowers. We seem happy enough, Leonora thought. She sighed, and turned her attentions to her face in the mirror.

It was quite passable for nearly seventy-five, she thought, but that white hair. Where had it come from? When she wasn't confronted by her own image in the glass, and on good days when her legs and arms obeyed her, it was easy for her to think of herself as Leonora Simmonds the beauty, the young mother whose two little daughters were her pride and joy. Her treasures. Concentrate on the good things. Don't give houseroom to shadows. Keep problems in their place. That was always her style. It was what made her *a force to be reckoned with*. She smiled. Sean had called her that. She'd liked his words and summoned them up now to help sustain her till she saw him. A force to be reckoned with. She made her way slowly to the bathroom. It was getting late. She wouldn't be able to stay with Nanny Mouse for very long.

Nanny Mouse was so old that everyone had lost count. She'd been Leonora's nanny then Gwen's and Rilla's, and she'd always been called that. Anyone who met her asked, of course, how she had acquired her name and had to be told, rather boringly, that Leonora had called her that when she was tiny and unable to say Miss Mussington. Mouse she had become, and Mouse she remained, and the name suited her well. Even in her young days there was something rodent-like about her small hands and neat waist, and the way her teeth protruded ever so slightly. She'd worn her hair in a bun at the nape of her neck for nearly a century, and her clothes were as fixed as the seasons – black skirt, woolly cardigan, and a high-necked white blouse in the winter; navy blue cotton dress (long-sleeved, however hot the weather) in the summer. Nanny never removed her cameo brooch, which was pinned to the front of whatever she wore. The children used to giggle and say she probably pinned it to her nightie.

She lived in Lodge Cottage, the pale, square little house at the bottom of the drive beside the main gate. Leonora had decided ten years ago that she was too old to live alone and for all that time, Miss Lardner had been Nanny Mouse's companion, looking after her day and night with the utmost devotion. Which was pretty good considering Miss L was no spring chicken herself, as James often said. She must be sixty-five at least, Leonora thought. Miss Lardner was a quiet, rather enigmatic person, who kept herself to herself. She was tall and well-built and no one ever called her by her given name, which was Doreen. She talked to Nanny, cooked for her, and made sure she didn't slip in the bath. And was well paid. For her part, Nanny, who had looked after everyone for more years than most people survived on this earth, resented the waning of her powers and spent many happy hours grumbling at poor Miss Lardner who seemed to take it all with equanimity. *I'm quite used to it*, she always said. *She's an old lady after all. I don't mind.*

Miss Lardner was waiting when Leonora arrived.

'She's in a good mood today, Mrs Simmonds,' she said, opening the door. Leonora's first name did not cross Miss Lardner's lips, and after all these years it would somehow have been awkward to mention it. The front room of the cottage was golden with sunshine, and she smiled. There was Nanny Mouse, asleep in the chair by the unlit fire. The table under the window had just been polished and a vase stood ready.

'I knew you'd bring flowers,' said Miss Lardner. 'If you give them to me, I'll put them in the vase and bring them in with the tea.'

'Thank you,' said Leonora, handing over the roses Gwen had picked earlier that morning. Nanny loved roses best of all, or she used to, and Leonora went to a great deal of trouble to find the best of the late-flowering varieties to bring whenever she visited, even though she wondered how much of anything the old lady actually took in. Sometimes she seemed to be, in Efe's words, on the ball. The phrase had made Leonora laugh the first time he'd said it. Nanny Mouse and balls of any kind inhabited quite different worlds. Most of the time, however, she was totally out of it, another of Efe's expressions. Now the old lady sat quite upright in the chair with her eyes closed, but otherwise looked much the same as she always did.

'Nanny Mouse has been freeze-dried, like a string bean,' Alex said once, and it was true. She seemed *fixed*, and that was something to be grateful for, but Leonora knew that somewhere, in some way, the old lady's body was ageing, growing weaker, and that fairly soon she would no longer be with them.

'I'm not sleeping, Maude dear,' Nanny Mouse said quietly into the golden afternoon. 'You can come and sit down and tell me things.'

'You startled me, Nanny!' Leonora said, kissing the cheek that smelled the way it always did, of lavender talcum powder. 'And I'm not Maude. I'm Leonora.' She sat down in the chair on the other side of the fireplace and began to talk. Nanny Mouse liked to keep up with what was going on at Willow Court. She was particularly interested in the filming.

'The television people. Are they coming to see me?'

'Of course, Nanny. You'll be in the film. You're the only person in the family apart from me who actually knew Ethan Walsh.'

Nanny Mouse nodded. 'I did. He was good to me. In his way, you understand. He wasn't much of a one for women. Poor Maude!'

The old woman fell silent then. She was holding a handkerchief, twisting a corner of it with her fingers. Silence began to grow in the room, seeping into the shadowy corners the sunlight couldn't reach. Leonora spoke to disperse it, to distract Nanny. The whole family knew that she found it painful to talk of a time when she was very young, whether because it made her feel older, or for some other reason never given.

'The children are here, Nanny. I'll bring little Douggie to see you. You remember him, don't you? Efe's son? My great-grandson. Of course you do. He's such a lovely little boy.'

'But he mustn't wander,' Nanny said, looking up and leaning forward and plucking at Leonora's knee. 'Terrible when they wander. Were you here when he wandered away?'

'Douggie's never wandered away,' Leonora said, and she could feel her heart beating in her throat. Nanny wasn't talking about Douggie. Change the subject. She said, 'You should see the food up at the house, Nanny. We've got pounds and pounds of strawberries. Enough for an army. I'll send some down to you tomorrow if you like.'

'Strawberries,' Nanny Mouse repeated. 'Oh, yes, I do like them! We had them for the wedding, didn't we?'

'My wedding, yes,' Leonoara said, trying to keep up.

'He was dead by then, of course, or maybe he died just after that.'

'Daddy? Yes, he died just before my wedding. I used to think how awful it was that I couldn't be properly happy on my wedding day, because my father had just died.'

'And good riddance!' Nanny Mouse said firmly. Miss Lardner came into the room just then and showed off the vase of late roses.

'Look at these, Nanny!' she said. 'Mrs Simmonds has brought us some lovely roses.' Nanny Mouse stared at the pink and cream-coloured flowers and the dark green leaves, not seeing them.

'No one knows anything,' she said to Leonora, her hands like mouse-paws trembling in her lap. 'No one hears what I say any more, and I say good riddance. I'm glad he's dead.'

She leaned back in her chair, tired from the emotion she'd expended. There were tears in her eyes. Leonora sighed. She knew that Ethan Walsh was a subject best avoided. Poor old Nanny is irrational when it comes to Daddy, Leonora thought. A little soft in the head, I expect. Well, she is frightfully old. It was time to change the subject again.

'Alex is going to come and see you, Nanny. Everyone's here for my birthday.'

'Is it Leonora's birthday come round again? Will she have a magician?' Nanny Mouse's eyes sparkled. Leonora looked at her and shivered. Please God don't let me become like this, she thought. How ghastly to have a kind of wilderness in your head, and be forever wandering around in it, not sure at all of where anything was or when things happened. How unbearable to be so lost! She closed her eyes. I pray it never happens to me. I couldn't bear it. I couldn't bear to be lost in my own head.

Sean Everard found that he was smiling to himself almost all the time these days without even knowing it. People kept telling him so. His PA, Jacy (whose lack of a letter 'k' had long ago ceased to annoy him) said he looked as though he'd lost a penny and found a pound. Purely in career terms the whole thing was a feather in his cap. When he'd gone to pitch the programme, he'd told himself not to hope. Who was going to finance an hour-long documentary on the life and art of Ethan Walsh? Okay, he was well-known and his reputation was riding high these days, but still, there wasn't much crowd appeal in an English painter who lived all his life in one place and didn't do anything more sensational than make amazing images. Sean couldn't believe his luck when the Powers That Be had okayed the project and when Leonora Simmonds, the artist's daughter, had agreed to see him. He admitted it. He was as excited as any kid.

He'd done his research and discovered that she was a formidable woman. It was easier for her, he supposed, than for many others, to be forceful and charismatic because of the money that had come down to her from her great-grandparents. She'd never had to work, and even being widowed at a ridiculously early age had not stopped her doing everything she intended to do. Her husband had probably been insured, which can only have added to her security if not to her happiness. They must have been very much in love, Sean thought, or surely a woman as attractive as Leonora would have married again? What she had done after her husband's death was to throw herself into all sorts of charitable work, as well as managing the estate and looking after the pictures. Then, later on, she'd served on committees of all kinds. Now, Leonora was on the board of three small museums, and a governor of several schools. Not a woman, Sean thought, to sit at home and sigh and gaze out of the window, like the Lady of Shalott.

And now he was going down there for her seventy-fifth birthday party. It had been *her* idea to include the festivities honouring her in the programme about her father. She might be delicate-looking and old-fashioned and so on, but she was a shrewd cookie when it came to public relations.

'I'm an asset, aren't I?' she'd said to him, and she was flirting. There wasn't any question about it. Did seventy-five-year-olds still fancy people? Leonora wasn't the kind of woman you could ask about that outright, but whatever. She liked him and that was great, and better than great, because here he was now, bowling along the M4 to Wiltshire with the top down and the scents of summer flying past his nose. Okay, maybe there was an admixture of petrol fumes on the one hand and manure on the other, but Sean refused to smell those. Flowers. Grass. Blue sky and cottonwool puffs of cloud, which didn't have a proper smell, of course, but the air wafted various fragrances into his nose and he was someone who always accentuated the positive.

Ethan Walsh, Willow Court, those pictures. Sean had been obsessed with them for more than thirty years. As an eighteen-year-old, in 1970, he'd been taken to the house by an aunt with a greedy interest in other people's gardens. The avenue of what he'd been told were scarlet oaks leading up to the front door was like nothing he'd ever seen before, and very impressive but, as for the rest of the garden, well, Sean had nothing against flowers and bushes and greenery, but houses were more his thing, and so he'd made his way inside. Hadn't asked anyone, but just strolled up the steps to a sort of terrace and the French windows had been open and he'd gone in and found himself in an empty room. All the usual things that are always in rooms must have been there, chairs, tables, sofas and so forth, but Sean didn't see them. On the wall above the fireplace were three paintings, hung in such a way that the eye moved from one to the other harmoniously; hung so that the colours of one led on seamlessly to the colours of the one above it, and then on to the one beside it. He gazed and stared and his mouth may have fallen open. It was the first time he'd seen real paintings. The blue! You could put out your hand and touch it and it would have been cool and shining under your hand. That was magic. One picture was a still life of apricots in a white china bowl on a table. Soft-bloomed apricots, pink-gold against the crockery and the blue and white checked cloth laid over the table just visible in one corner and Sean looked at it and felt that if he could only sit there, in the painting, right next to that fruit, everything troublesome and difficult would fall away and he would be perfectly, ridiculously happy. Those apricots would be all he ever needed. Next to the still life was a landscape, and Sean recognized it as the view up the drive to the house, but painted in autumn to show off the disconcerting scarlet of the trees, and a small, grey, rectangular building in the far distance.

He and his aunt had driven up this same avenue less than an hour ago, but this picture made the place look . . . what? Mysterious and full of secrets, with every window like a closed eye, and the trees with leaves the colour of blood leaning towards the house. Sean shivered as he stared at the thousand colours on the canvas that seemed to have been used to produce the stormy sky at the very edge of the painting. The third picture was best of all, and showed a young girl of about six, sitting on a bed. She was dressed in lilac, or lavender, some pale, purplish colour, and the light was probably coming through a window, and the landscape of linen behind her, the sheets and pillowcases, looked like a mountain range: white peaks and dark valleys of cloth all the way up to the top of the canvas. A brass plate under this picture announced *Leonora Walsh 1934*. He had no idea then, but this was the woman he now thought of as his Leonora.

He arrived at Willow Court at exactly the right time and there it was, the vista that had made him catch his breath all those years ago – a long line of trees crowned with leaves which held, deep within their greenness, the promise of scarlet. It was strange, and beautiful and somehow appropriate. Fitting.

Leonora herself had been standing at the front door when Sean drove up and he felt himself specially privileged. He looked round at the beautiful room he'd been given and checked to make sure his tie was straight. Then he picked up his portable tape-recorder and made his way to the conservatory.

'Come in, Sean, come in,' Leonora said, indicating that he should sit in the chair next to her. 'You can put that machine down on this table. Is that all right?'

'Perfect! Are you sure you've not been interviewed before?'

Leonora smiled. 'I am treating this as a conversation between friends. I hope you won't be too busy with your equipment to have a biscuit with your tea? Mary's made them specially. She's our housekeeper. Oh, how silly I am, you met her last time, didn't you?'

'I did,' Sean said, 'and I am always ready for a biscuit. This is such a beautiful room.'

It wasn't a formal conservatory, but more like a sitting-room with glass walls, and wonderfully quiet, with only the faint snoring of Gus coming from the depths of the sofa where his beautiful, long-haired ginger coat made a pleasing contrast to the green, white and pink cabbage-rose pattern of the upholstery. Sean knew that Gus had a brother, Bertie, who preferred the bedrooms to the public rooms of the house. The cats were really Albert and Augustus, Sean had been told, but no one in the family ever called them that.

The plants here were massed against the glass and some of them had grown and spread right up to the high ceiling, pressing against the panes there as though trying to escape. All the cushions had tapestry covers (Gwen's work, he'd been told) and the table was covered with seed catalogues, books, and Leonora's correspondence.

'Shall we start then?' Sean asked.

'Yes, I'm ready.' Leonora folded her hands in her lap.

'Let's begin with your early childhood. Tell me about that.'

'My mother died when I was eight.' Leonora put her cup down on its saucer and gave a small nervous cough. 'My father was always busy. Painting, I suppose. I was mainly brought up by Nanny Mouse. She was very young in those days, but they promoted her when I was born, to look after me. I think my mother was rather delicate. You'll meet Nanny Mouse. She's still alive, though very frail now, of course. She's over ninety. She lives in the little cottage at the bottom of the drive. You must have passed it as you drove up here.'

'Has the estate been in the Walsh family for many generations?'

'Oh, no, dear!' Leonora laughed in a way usually described in novels, Sean thought, as 'silvery'. 'My grandfather bought the land after making a fortune in some boring bit of industry – I've never been quite sure what – bits needed for various engines, I think. Frightfully important without being at all *visible*, if you know what I mean. And in fact when Daddy – Ethan Walsh, I'd better call him, hadn't I? – told *his* father that he wanted to go to London and study to be an artist, there was the most enormous row. Well, in those days young men were expected to follow in their fathers' footsteps and so forth, not go off to be bohemians and fritter their time away on what were called "daubs," very often. It must be quite hard for you young people to understand.'

'No,' Sean smiled at her. 'I think quite a lot of parents even today might consider art a rather uncertain career path.' God, he thought to himself, how bloody pompous I sound! I must watch that. 'May I turn to the subject of your mother?'

'She was very quiet. Unassuming. He was the . . . what's the modern word? The charismatic one. She never seemed to be there, that's what I remember. Whenever I asked Nanny Mouse where she was, I was told she was resting or writing letters. Something like that. I'm rather vague about her death, because I was really quite ill around that time. I remember that. But everything changed completely after she'd gone. Daddy was terribly affected by her death. It was ghastly. He was most dreadfully, dreadfully wounded. I can't recall him as particularly affectionate to her while she was alive, but of course children don't see everything, do they?'

'Where did he meet her?'

'In London, at art school. She was quite a gifted watercolourist, I believe, when he met her, but of course once she was married, she had no more time for all that.'

'So she gave up her art to be with him?'

'Yes. Nanny Mouse told me once that they quite scandalized everyone by eloping to Paris and marrying there. Maude Cotteridge was a penniless orphan and my grandfather wouldn't have been best pleased at the match. The gossip was . . .' Leonora bent forward and lowered her voice '. . . that they lived together before they were married. Their affair was the talk of artistic London, apparently.

You'd have thought she'd be miserable here in the country, wouldn't you, after being used to London up till her marriage, but she loved the garden. She added all sorts of things; the gazebo and the Quiet Garden at the back are hers entirely. The border there. Have you seen it? Well, you'll see it when you film it, won't you? It's as beautiful as any painting. And the espaliered fruit trees on the wall, they were her idea. In those days, when Ethan and Maude were first married, Willow Court had four gardeners. We have to manage with two these days, but of course I have very green fingers, so the garden has been a kind of hobby for me. A bit of luck for the estate, wouldn't you say?'

There she was again, flirting with him. He smiled at her.

'That's great,' he said. 'We've made a good start, but we'd better stop for now. I must go and change for dinner.'

'I've rather enjoyed it. Tomorrow I'll take you up to my father's studio.'

'Yes, I'm greatly looking forward to seeing that. And I'm most grateful to you for being so helpful to me. To this film. I hope it lives up to all your expectations.'

Leonora looked up at him. 'I'm sure it'll all be wonderful,' she said. 'If you don't mind, I'm going to sit here for a while. Drinks on the terrace at six o'clock.'

'Lovely. I'll see you later,' said Sean, and left the room, shutting the door quietly behind him.

Leonora closed her eyes. For a moment, she had the impression that she wasn't alone in the conservatory. Perhaps Gwen had come in to see where she was. She breathed in, and her nostrils were filled with a fragrance she recognized, lily of the valley. Who used it? Where did she know it from? Maybe James had brought it back for Gwen from one of his trips abroad. Or perhaps it was Rilla, or even Chloë, but why was it so familiar? She opened her eyes to see which of the women now at Willow Court had crept in here while she was sitting with her eyes closed, but she was quite alone. The fragrance hung in the air, and there was no one at all. Only Gus, snoring slightly and dreaming cat dreams. I imagined it, Leonora thought. It's in my head. She shivered slightly and shut her eyes again. I'll go up soon, she thought. I'll just sit here for a moment.

# September 1935

Leonora half-opened her eyes. There was someone standing at the window, looking out at the garden. Rain beat against the panes, and the piece of sky she could see from the bed was horrid and grey and not blue and sunshiny, which was what summer skies were meant to be. The dark shape between her curtains wasn't Nanny. It was too tall and sort of thick. Nanny was small and skinny. Could it be Daddy? Was it? He'd only ever come into the nursery once or twice before, and he'd never been into the night nursery that she could remember. She felt a sudden chill and pulled the quilt up around her shoulders. Then she sat up on one elbow and her head hurt. She tried to speak, but only a faint noise came out of her mouth, and she coughed to clear her throat.

At once, the shadow at the window turned round and it *was* Daddy. He strode quickly over to the bed and sat down right next to her and took her hand. Leonora was so surprised at this that she fell back against the pillows. He was wearing a black suit and a white shirt and his eyes were rimmed with red. Leonora fixed her gaze on the shining gold watch chain that crossed his waistcoat. He said, 'My darling child, I didn't mean to wake you. You were so deeply asleep. And you need your sleep, do you not? You've been rather ill. Do you remember?'

'Have I had my birthday yet?' Leonora asked. 'Was it measles?'

'No, no, nothing like that. A fever, the doctor said, but we have been a little concerned. And yes, you are eight years old. Happy Birthday, sweetheart. We shall have to celebrate presently when you're feeling better.'

Leonora wanted to cry. How could she have missed her birthday and not even known about it? How could she? There were so many things she didn't understand. Why was he here? Where was Mummy? And Nanny? Why were all his clothes black? Something was in the room with them, and it was a sad thing and she didn't know how to ask about it. She said, 'Where's Mummy?' thinking that if she knew the answer to that, everything else would be much clearer.

'Don't you remember, darling, how ill she was?'

'Is she better now?' Leonora said. 'I don't remember.'

Her mother often kept to her room. She liked lying on the chaise-longue in the drawing-room for hours at a time. Sometimes she disappeared altogether and no one saw her and Nanny said she was 'indisposed'. That was like being ill, Leonora knew, although not with anything that had a proper name – measles or mumps or influenza. Suddenly, Daddy spoke.

'Are you a brave girl, Leonora?'

She nodded. Now that she was really eight, even though it felt just the same as being seven, she had to be *very* grown-up and being brave was part of that.

'I'm so sorry to have to tell you this, Leonora. So sorry.' Daddy started to cough, but it wasn't exactly a cough and he took his handkerchief out and wiped his nose and eyes before continuing.

'She's dead. My darling, my beloved Maude . . .' And then he was crying. Leonora stared at him, too shocked by his grief, his pain, to take in what he was saying. Daddy never cried. He was strong. He was the strongest, tallest, biggest, strictest person in the whole world and not this sobbing, wretched creature, whose shoulders were shaking and whose voice broke as he went on.

'I had no idea. No idea that she'd been so . . . so ill. So ill. She kept it from me, of course, not wanting to worry me. She was unselfish. Yes, without a doubt the most unselfish person. And then she was gone, and now I've buried her, and we must be brave, Leonora. We must take care of one another, mustn't we? So cruel. Such a cruel loss for you, my poor child. I will . . . you know I will . . . do my best, but it will not be the same. No, nothing at all will be the same. How will I bear it?'

He stood up, and squared his shoulders. Leonora looked up at him and said nothing because she didn't know what to say. Then he spoke again and sounded more like himself.

'Nanny will be here shortly, to see if you want to get up today. Perhaps we'll have tea together later. Would you like that?'

Leonora nodded. What would she find to say to him as they helped themselves to sandwiches and scones from the cake-stand? Daddy made his way over to the door and turned to smile at her.

'We'll survive, Leonora, won't we?' he said.

'Yes, Daddy,' said Leonora, wondering what he could mean. Was he, too, in danger of falling ill and dying?

As soon as he'd gone, she pushed back the covers and got out of bed. She felt wobbly. She remembered Nanny saying *only two more days to your birthday, dear*. So that was August the twenty-third. Now it must be after August the twenty-fifth. She'd been ill for days. How could that happen without her knowing about it? Tears filled her eyes when she thought of everything there was to feel sad about. Mummy's dead, she said to herself. Under the ground, and stiff and cold. Something dark and heavy fluttered at the back of her mind, and she shivered. She tried hard to remember the last time she'd seen her mother and couldn't think properly. Was it saying goodnight? Or maybe they were in the garden. Leonora knew what dead was. She'd seen Tyler, the gardener, carrying a rabbit once that a fox had killed and it was stiff and there was blood all round its head. She wasn't supposed to see it, but she had, and she'd dreamed about it at night for a long time after that. Mummy wouldn't be covered in blood, of course she wouldn't. She must have died in her bed because that was where people *did* die. They weren't a bit like rabbits. She imagined the body lying among the puffy pillows wearing one of her mother's lace-trimmed nighties and it was her and not her at the same time.

On the wall behind Leonora's bed there was a portait of her, painted by Daddy and she turned to look at it. It wasn't fair. Other people had mothers, and fathers and brothers and sisters. She was a little girl in this picture, and she was sitting on the floor beside the dolls' house, the very same one that lived in the nursery and that she played with every day. It was a tall sort of a house. Daddy had made it himself, and Mummy had decorated every room to look exactly like real rooms in a proper house, and everyone who saw it admired it and said what a labour of love it was and how lucky Leonora was to have it. Leonora could see every detail on the wallpaper; all the little lamps and pieces of furniture arranged in the rooms and even the tiny, tiny dolls that Mummy had made to be them: her and Daddy and Leonora. The light in the picture seemed to be pouring out of the dolls' house and it lit up the edge of the child's, Leonora's, cheek and made a golden patch on the dark carpet. I'll go and look at it, she thought. My dolls' house. The one my Daddy and Mummy made for me.

She went into the nursery and there it was, standing against the wall. Every door was shut and every window too. She looked down at the roof, painted with a pattern of overlapping roof-tiles. A memory, like the wing of a white butterfly, fluttered briefly at the edge of her thoughts. For the tiniest part of a second, she saw her mother's figure standing beside the dolls' house in a long, white nightgown and then she was gone. Leonora blinked and tried as hard as she could to bring the memory back, but it wouldn't return and it felt to her as though a light had been extinguished somewhere inside her. There was no light coming from the dolls' house either. No light at all. It looked as though no one had played with it for ages and ages. Suddenly, sadness filled her, like a flood of something cold rising up inside her, and she began to weep.

Leonora was growing fretful. Nanny Mouse had made her lie in bed and rest for what seemed like days and days. Perhaps it wasn't such a long while after all, but it felt like years. Because she'd been so ill, Nanny Mouse let Mr Nibs, the big ginger cat, come into her room. He wasn't usually allowed upstairs and the sight of him sitting on the end of her bed or curled up behind the curtains with just his tail sticking out from under the flowery material made her smile. He purred when she stroked him, and that made her feel happier, always. But sometimes the words *my mummy is dead* came into her mind and then her eyes filled with tears and her head started aching, but she couldn't think of Mummy all the time, and it was then she started wanting ordinary things. If only I could get out of bed, she thought, looking at the square of sunlight in the middle of the carpet, I could go down to see the swans. I wish Nanny Mouse had taken me into the village with her. I could have bought some sweets from the shop. Liquorice allsorts, or a sherbet fountain. Nanny Mouse always chose barley sugar in twisted sticks, and Leonora had had too much of that to think it exciting.

Where was Daddy? He came in every afternoon and sat with her for a while, but he was still sad and didn't want to talk very much.

Perhaps he was in the Studio, painting. The Studio was out of bounds. It was an attic really, the big attic that took up most of upstairs, next to the maids' rooms. The door of the Studio was always kept shut when Daddy was in there working, but he wouldn't be working now. She'd heard Nanny Mouse and Mrs Page the cook talking about it when Mrs Page brought up her supper tray.

'The poor man,' Mrs Page said. 'He isn't eating properly. And all he does is pace around the house like a caged beast.'

'He's not working, I know that,' Nanny Mouse said. 'He stands at the studio window and stares out of it. I saw him when I set out for church yesterday and he was still there when I came back. I swear he hadn't moved an inch.'

Leonora thought that perhaps he was up there now. I'll go and find him. I'll talk to him and that'll cheer him up. He won't mind. He can't. He's not working. She pushed back the bedclothes and put on her dressing-gown and slippers.

The silence in the house was so deep that Leonora could almost hear it as she tiptoed up the stairs. She looked down at her feet and not at the walls. The carpet here was a little threadbare, but that didn't matter because no one was allowed to come up to the Studio. The corridor leading to it had some paintings hanging on the walls, paintings which Daddy didn't really like, or he would have put them downstairs where everyone could see them. Leonora didn't stop to look at them, but made her way quickly to the baize curtain that hung across the Studio door.

She pulled it aside a little, turned the brass doorknob and stood for a moment on the threshold looking around her. In one of her books, there was a story about a magical country which had been frozen by a witch's spell so that nothing could move and no one could speak. This room was like that. Leonora felt that if she put one foot in front of the other here, something would break, or crack or disappear.

Don't be silly, she said to herself. That's a story. This is a real room in a real house. It's where I live. There's no such thing as magic. Nothing bad is going to happen in my very own house.

The studio was long and thin. There were canvases propped up facing the wall so that you couldn't see the pictures. The easel had nothing on it. Paints had dried to crusty flowers of colour on the palette. Leonora walked the length of the room, and went to stand at one of the windows. There were lots of windows up here; the biggest looked down on the garden and the lake, and she stared out of it, wondering if she could catch a glimpse of the swans. Her headache had come back, and she leaned her forehead against the glass. Her eyes filled with tears. Why aren't I better? she thought. Nanny said I was getting better but now I feel bad again. There's a ball of pain behind my eyes. Maybe if I go and sit down . . .

She stumbled to the chaise-longue that stood all by itself in the middle of the room and lay down on it. It was covered in pale green velvet, a colour Mummy used to call 'eau-de-Nil'. It was Mummy's favourite, but Daddy said it was wishy-washy. Leonora wondered briefly why he hadn't chosen his best colour for something that was only meant for him to sit on.

She closed her eyes and the lump of pain in her head grew smaller, weaker. She put her hand in the narrow gap between the seat of the chaise-longue and its wooden frame, and something soft caught in her fingers. She sat up to investigate. A small piece of cloth. She could see a corner of it now, sticking out a little, a white triangle of lace. She pulled on it and recognized it at once. Mummy must have been up here to talk to Daddy, because this was one of her hankies. Leonora sniffed it and the tears sprang up in her eyes. Mummy's smell. Lily of the valley, it was called, and all of Mummy's clothes smelled like that. Used to smell like that. Tears ran down Leonora's cheeks but she couldn't use the hankie to wipe them away. It would get dirty and crumpled. She tucked the precious square into her pocket and used the sleeve of her dressing-gown to dry her eyes. There was something foggy and dark inside her whenever she thought of Mummy. It meant she couldn't properly bring her to mind; couldn't remember how she really used to be.

'What are you doing up here, Leonora?' said a voice and there he was, Daddy, filling the doorway with his body, making the room suddenly icy with his voice. Leonora wanted to run away, to disappear, to melt into the floorboards, because she could hear his anger. Daddy was always quiet, very quiet when he was angry, and everything he said took on a special sound that made her tremble.

'I was looking for you, Daddy,' she whispered. 'I only came here to look for you.'

'And why would you think to find me here, may I ask?'

Because it's where you go when you paint, she wanted to say, but couldn't bring out the words.

'I don't know,' she said, hanging her head.

Ethan Walsh strode to the chaise-longue and Leonora, sitting frozen, unable to move, felt his hard fingers on her flesh, pulling her to her feet, leading her to the door, pinching her hard on the upper arm, muttering things above her head as they went.

'Never. You are never to come up here again, do you understand, Leonora? Never. You are quite forbidden to come into this room. Am I making myself completely clear?'

*Forbidden*. What a horrible word, Leonora thought. I hate it. It sounds like a wall of black ice. *Forbidden*. She looked at her father. He'd knelt beside her by now, bringing his face closer to hers. He put both his hands on her shoulders, and shook her slightly. His eyes were full of something Leonora didn't recognize. Something she'd never seen before and couldn't give a name to. All she knew was that the love she usually saw in his eyes when he looked at her had disappeared and this person, shaking her and pinching her shoulders with bony fingers, didn't like her a bit. Hated her, perhaps, and there was something else there in his face, too. Daddy looked scared. White and thin-lipped and frightened.

'Yes, Daddy,' she said, 'I understand. I won't come up here again. Not ever. Never. I promise. Cross my heart and hope to die.'

'Don't say that!' he almost shouted. 'Just go back to your room and stay there, please. Wait for Nanny to come back. I have to think.'

He turned away from her and blundered back into the studio, slamming the door behind him. It sounded like thunder in the empty house, filling the corridor and reaching down the stairs so that the whole building seemed to shake. Leonora looked at the closed door, imagining her father standing at the window with the blank backs of the canvases staring out at him and the dried-up paint flowers turning black under the fire of his rage. She ran all the way back to her room and flung herself face down on the bed. Stars and blossoms of scarlet and purple exploded under her closed eyelids. Never. She never would go there again. It was a horrid room, cold and unwelcoming and filled with a light that was too bright.

The hankie in her pocket. As soon as Leonora remembered it, she knew that she must hide it. If Daddy found she had it, he'd be angry all over again. She didn't know how she knew this, nor why it would be so, but she could feel in every bit of her body that it was true. Where could she put it? Nanny Mouse went through her drawers to make sure they were tidy, and if she left it in her pocket it would be found when her clothes were washed, and all the lily of the valley scent would be gone forever. Then suddenly Leonora smiled. She knew where it would be quite safe.

She got off the bed and went into the nursery. There, she crouched down in front of the dolls' house. She took her mother's hankie and folded it over twice. Now there was lace only on two sides of the little square. It can't be helped, she thought. It has to fit . . . like that . . . there. She tucked the fine cotton neatly over the body of the doll that her mother had made to look like the real Leonora, and for a moment she felt as though the lifeless stuffed body was indeed truly *her*, and that *she* was the one lying there, safe under a lace-trimmed coverlet that smelled like her mother. She sat back on her heels and looked at the doll's bed. They'll never see it there, she thought, because grown-ups don't look properly. I shall know about it, though, and I can come and sniff it whenever I want to. And when my dolls go to a dance, I can pin it around like a dress, and flowers of white lace will hang down over all the ordinary day clothes and make this doll really beautiful so that everyone at the pretend ball will want to write their names in her dance card. She'll look like a princess.

Both Freud and Leonora would have a word or two to say, Rilla thought, about my love of kitchens. Here she was again, with the whole house to choose from and her pick of family members available to chat to, sitting at the beechwood table and watching Mary peeling carrots for tonight's dinner. Her way with these unassuming vegetables was legendary, and by the time she finished with them, they'd have turned into golden circles, glazed and sweet and delicious, and fragrant with a green sprinkling of fresh herbs.

'Your scones, Mary,' she said, adding home-made raspberry jam to a thick layer of butter, 'are the eighth wonder of the world.'

Mary sniffed and got on with her work. Her silence wasn't unfriendly. She was simply a quiet sort of person, not given to gossip. Rilla didn't mind. Whenever she got a chance to sit about in the Willow Court kitchen, she felt as though she were on a stage set of some kind. It was Gwen's doing, this rather clichéd prettiness. There was a Welsh dresser against one wall, predictably loaded with willow-pattern plates and plump teapots and flower-painted jugs. The walls were butter-coloured and there was a small sofa in one corner. The colour of the curtains picked out the swollen pink roses in the sofa fabric, a typical Gwen-ish touch. The working part of the kitchen was through an archway and down two small steps. When she was tiny, Rilla liked sitting on these and watching Cook at work. Nowadays the cooker was what was known as 'state of the art', but in those days it was an ancient, blackened range, like something out of *Hansel and Gretel*. There was one time when she'd stayed away from the kitchen for about a week, after Gwen told her that yes, that oven was indeed the actual one from the fairy tale, transported magically to Wiltshire straight from the Witch's cottage.

'I might have known you'd be here, Rilla,' someone said, and she turned round with a mouth full of scone to smile at Efe.

'You are not,' she said, when she could speak, 'supposed to be rude to your auntie, Efe. Come over here and give me a big kiss. Gosh, you're gorgeous! I could eat you alive!'

'That,' said Efe, hugging Rilla, 'is what they all say.'

He sat down on the chair opposite her and smiled at Mary. 'Got a scone for me, Mary?'

'You'll spoil your supper, you know,' she answered, with a smile, getting a plate down from the rack and putting two scones on it for Efe. Even Mary unbends under his gaze, Rilla thought. It's amazing the effect he has on women. Dangerous, probably. He cut the scone neatly through the centre, and said, 'You cannot imagine what a relief it is to see someone tucking into food. Fiona is forever on some diet or another. Although now she's pregnant again, I expect she'll lighten up on that. Hope so, anyway. I've given up wondering why women are so silly.'

Rilla bit back a sharp comment. The reason Efe found women silly was because he wasn't attracted to the sensible ones. She adored her nephew, but he definitely made a beeline for the puppyish kind of woman, the sort who, in return for even one word of kindness, tended to lie down and wave her legs in the air.

'I should go and get ready for dinner,' Rilla said. Efe looked up at her.

'Get your glad rags on,' he said. 'Absolutely. Actually, Rilla, can I have a quick word with you? There's something I want to ask you. I want to raise something with Leonora but it's a question of timing. Have you got a moment?'

The scones had been put away in a tin. The tin was on the dresser, ready to go in the pantry. Rilla stood up, went over to it, opened it and helped herself to another one. She brought this to the table and sat down again opposite Efe.

'Go on, then,' she said, reaching for the butter. 'Tell me all about it.'

The back door opened as she spoke, and James came into the kitchen. Efe made a rueful face at Rilla and stood up.

'Hello, Dad, got to go, I'm afraid. Sorry about that, Rilla. Never mind. Catch you later, perhaps.'

'What was all that about?' asked James, as Efe left the room. Rilla looked up at her brother-in-law.

'I really have no idea. I think Efe was going to tell me something. Confess, perhaps. D'you think he has things to confess, James?'

'Shouldn't be bit surprised. Chip off the old block, wouldn't you say?'

In Rilla's opinion, James rather overdid the old roué routine. True, he looked the part, but he was altogether too moustache-twirling for comfort and that was without a moustache. She suppressed a giggle.

'What are you laughing at?' James asked her.

'Nothing, really,' Rilla said. 'Nothing important.'

'Jolly nice to see someone laughing, I can tell you. It's been quite tense round here lately. Gwen's so busy with everything to do with the party that we've hardly exchanged two words in the last couple of days. Still, I expect things'll go back to normal after Sunday, wouldn't you say?'

'You're never here, James,' Rilla said. 'I arrived yesterday just after lunch and it was breakfast today before I laid eyes on you. You can't altogether blame Gwen, you know.'

'Well, I was seeing people in town, of course. Couldn't be helped.' He pulled on his earlobe. Rilla had read a magazine article once called 'What your body-language says about you' and was almost sure that earlobe-pulling meant that person was lying through their teeth. He'd probably been knocking it back rather too much in a bar somewhere.

'You look very well, James,' she said, and was rewarded by his famously brilliant smile. It was true, too. He certainly didn't look like someone who drank too much. His skin was more lined, and his hair greyer than Efe's but they shared the stature and the charm. Such a shame, Rilla thought, that he knows it. He'd be completely irresistible if he was unaware of the effect his looks have. As it is, he's too fond of himself by half. He was the kind of person – and there were plenty of men as well as women who were like this – who couldn't pass a mirrored surface without checking to see whether their beauty was undimmed.

'And you are as lovely as ever, Rilla dear,' he said, automatically. Rilla smiled. He'd been saying the same things to her for all the years he'd known her, and once upon a time, might even have meant them. Still, it was kind of him to pretend she hadn't changed, and she appreciated the gallantry.

Fiona was feeling queasy. Pregnancy was the biggest drag going and part of her felt resentful that she had to go through it yet again so soon. Douggie was only two and a half, for Heaven's sake. Bless him! Her son was very busy on the floor at her feet, constructing a fort or something out of Lego bricks. She'd produced an heir, someone to inherit the Walsh Collection and everything that went with it, hadn't she? Surely now she could have a few years off to recover her waistline and have a bit of fun?

She wondered whether she was going to be able to get through dinner without throwing up. It wasn't fair. Some people only got morning sickness, but she had it at different times of day, and it ought to have been getting better by now. She listened to Efe, waiting for him to start humming in the bathroom, which he often did, but he was oddly silent. He'd been in a funny mood altogether for the last few days and, anyway, he was always a bit strange down here at Willow Court. Never mind, she thought, he knows I'll be here for him whatever. She wondered why it was that some women were forever running their husbands down. She always supported Efe. Some of her friends thought she was mad to be so submissive and she knew that Chloë certainly, and Beth too, probably, reckoned she was nothing but a living doormat. Fiona didn't care. She regarded obedience as a wife's duty. That wasn't a fashionable view, and privately she thought that was most likely why divorce was so common. Women just had no idea, some of them. Men needed to be jollied along, rather like children did, and it didn't surprise her at all that she got her own way much more frequently than most of her friends managed to.

Fiona knew very well that no one gave her credit for any intelligence, and there were, she acknowledged, many things she had no idea about. She'd left school with two GCSEs and they were in Art and Food Technology. But there was more to her than everyone thought. She may not have read many books, but she understood how to please a husband.

It wasn't hard for her, of course. Who in their right mind wouldn't adore Efe? She did sometimes wish that he could have been named differently. Efe was silly, really, like a lot of nicknames, and Fiona avoided it by saying 'my husband' when talking to others and 'Darling' or, more embarrassingly, 'Pie' when she addressed him directly. 'Pie' was a silly nickname too, short for 'Sweetiepie' and he frowned blackly at her whenever she uttered it outside their bedroom, so she tried hard not to let it cross her lips once he was fully dressed.

He emerged from the bathroom with his mobile clamped to his ear. She was used to that, but still, it was a bit much to be still talking just before drinks. His whole family was here, so it must be business. Fiona looked at him and tried to guess who he was speaking to and what exactly was going on. It was something to do with the Collection, she realized, but was a bit hazy about the details. All she knew was that her husband was preoccupied and she wished he'd go back to being his usual self again. She needed him to act as a sort of guard around her, to protect her from his family.

They'd taken some getting used to. Efe was the only one, for instance, who took after James and Gwen in any way that Fiona could see. Her heart still gave a little jump in her chest whenever she looked at him – handsome, well-dressed, successful – everything a man should be. His father was like that as well. Oldish now, of course, but he must have been a heartthrob when he was young. Gwen, too, was always expensively dressed, even if style wasn't exactly her middle name, so what had gone wrong with Alex and Chloë? Neither of them would have looked out of place lying around in a shop doorway with a thin dog on the end of a string.

Fiona sighed. Efe was worried these days, and it was because of the bloody paintings that were everywhere you looked in this house. She didn't understand the ins and outs of it all exactly, and in fact was rather bored by the whole subject, but they had been in Efe's mind. *They're my responsibility ultimately* was something he said quite often. *Leonora won't last for ever, and then they're in my hands.*

Even though she'd been a married woman for more than three years and had a baby and everything, the old lady made her feel about six years old, shy and tongue-tied and silly in every possible way. It wasn't anything she actually said, but just the way she looked at you. It drove Fiona mad, but she couldn't ever admit it. Leonora had cast a sort of spell on the whole family and criticism of any kind was strictly forbidden. She'd more than once pointed out to Efe that when his grandmother died, Willow Court would actually pass to Gwen, his mother. And Efe always laughed and said, 'Well, yes, of course, but that means me, really, doesn't it? Ma will do exactly as I say, because she knows I'm right.'

He said it perfectly seriously, and somehow it didn't even seem conceited, just commonsensical.

Fiona thought the terms of Leonora's will rather unfair, and had once dared to say, 'What about your aunt Rilla? Doesn't she get anything? She's Leonora's daughter too, isn't she?'

Efe had smiled and said, 'She'll get a fair old dollop of money, don't you fret. And she'd hate to be saddled with dealing with the paintings. Willow Court is not her favourite place in the world, and besides, she leads such a rackety existence. If it was left to her, it'd be some kind of commune within the decade. And although she works hard at looking like some kind of gipsy, she's actually not short of a bob or two. She still works, you know. In telly and sometimes even in movies.'

Ethan Walsh's paintings hung on almost every available wall at Willow Court. The entire art world, it seemed to Fiona, kept approaching Leonora, writing to her and telephoning her, wanting her to give permission for the Collection to be rehung somewhere a little more accessible to the Great British Public than the depths of Wiltshire. Leonora wouldn't hear of such a thing. The paintings stayed exactly where the first Ethan had wanted them to be. Fiona never breathed a word to anyone, but she couldn't really see what all the fuss was about. Everyone in the family, and crowds of other people, said the pictures were masterpieces. They spoke about the Walsh technique for laying colour on canvas, his method of depicting light; the strange imagination which lifted ordinary objects into some other, more surreal universe, but Fiona couldn't really warm to the paintings. They were troubling, that was true, and when she was actually here, she found herself not looking straight at them if she could help it.

Efe was still on the phone. She worked out from what was being said that he was discussing some boring thing about money. She knew, because he moaned about it so much, that things were hard for him at work, as far as money went. That was one reason he was so keen that Leonora should agree to his plan; he stood to earn a huge commission if the deal went through. Fiona would have been quite happy to give him as much money as he needed, because she had more than enough, but once when she'd dared to suggest it, Efe's eyes blazed at her and he'd sounded so enraged that she never suggested it again.

'Fine kind of a husband I'd be if I came running to my wife every time I had cash flow problems,' he'd almost spat at her, and she blushed and said nothing, which was silly of her. She ought to have fought back a bit, said that now they were man and wife her money was his, and so on, but she hadn't dared to utter a word at the time.

Now, she stopped listening to Efe's conversation and put it out of her mind entirely. Instead she thought about maybe being in this documentary that was being made. Leonora was a vain old thing, really. She couldn't resist the idea of being on TV and it was typical of her to arrange for filming to take place during her birthday celebrations. The house and garden would be looking mega-lovely and she'd be seen at her best, every inch the grande dame. Efe, she knew, would make sure he was in plenty of shots, and quite right too. She stared at her husband and thanked her lucky stars, as she did every day, that he'd chosen her, out of everyone else in the world, to be his wife.

Efe caught Fiona looking at him as he spoke and signalled that he'd be finished soon. And he smiled at her. Her heart melted. There were times when he went for ages without smiling at her and then she felt as though the sun had gone behind a cloud. He spoke unkindly to her, too, occasionally, but only when he was fed up with her, and Fiona resolved each time that happened to try as hard as she could not to annoy him. She'd worked out some of the things he didn't like her doing and saying, and whenever he frowned or showed his disapproval she made a note of what it was that had angered him, and determined to try to be more the sort of person he wanted her to be. She loved him too much, that was the problem. She knew all his faults and still loved him. Sometimes she wondered what it was about her that had attracted him in the first place. She knew she was pretty, but feared that prettiness on its own wouldn't be enough to keep him interested in her for ever. Her mind went back, as it often did, to the very best day of her life. Her wedding day.

They'd got married in December, and the snow was falling as they left the church, like confetti dropping down from heaven. Her dress was cream satin, its train stitched with snowflake-shaped jewels, and her veil was like a cloud of lace around her head. She'd carried a bouquet of white and pale pink roses, and in the photographs you could see the ribbons falling from the flowers and making three shining lines on the lustrous fabric of her skirt. Oh, she'd been beautiful then, all right, and Efe had looked at her with something like adoration. Not like now, when she felt bloated all the time and nauseous too. At home, there was a whole album of photographs, taken by Alex, which showed her looking her best and she wished she'd brought it down here to comfort her. There'd be so many people here on Sunday for the party. So many women, all dressed up. What if one of them caught Efe's eye?

Cold dread rose in her as she began to think about it. She found it hard not to worry about all those hours when he was at the office, away from her. Wasn't there a good chance that he'd meet someone else, someone cleverer than she was? Fiona made a huge effort not to think about it, and was quite determined to stay married to Efe. She would do exactly what he wanted in every way. He must never have anything to complain about, ever. If being pregnant was what was required, she would bear one child after another, just as long as he never left her. Her life, her house – everything – was absolutely as she wanted it to be, and that was how it must, must, must remain.

'Come on, Fiona,' said Efe, putting the mobile away. 'Let's get down there. Come on, Douggie. We're going down to the garden to see the others.'

'Piggyback!' the little boy said, but Efe replied, 'Tomorrow, old chap, okay?'

Fiona knew he was anxious not to crease his shirt. Well, so what? There was nothing in the world wrong with wanting to look nice. She followed her husband and child out of their room and down the stairs to the hall.

Sean came into the drawing-room and looked around rather tentatively. Leonora was waiting for him.

'Ah, Sean,' she said. 'Perfect timing! We've all started on the drinks, but you'll soon catch up.'

Gwen stood just inside the room, and smiled at him.

'Hello, Sean. Shall I introduce you to everyone?'

'I'll do that, darling,' said Leonora. She tucked her arm in his and led him over what seemed like acres of carpet towards the French windows, which stood open on this golden evening, letting the warm scent of summer flowers drift indoors. James Rivera, whom he'd only met briefly on his last visit, stood beside the drinks trolley looking debonaire. That was the word for him, Sean reflected. Rather flashily handsome. Hair silver at the temples and an air about him of a forties movie star. Not completely trustworthy, but maybe I'm being unfair, thought Sean as James called out, 'Sean, what are you drinking?'

'Dry sherry, if you have it, please.'

'Absolutely!' He turned to the bottles ranged before him and Leonora directed Sean's attention to the sofa.

'You haven't met my younger daughter, Cyrilla,' said Leonora. 'Cyrilla, this is Sean Everard from the television company.'

'It's exciting, isn't it? The film I mean. Only please call me Rilla,' said the rather plump, red-headed woman dressed in a long, purple silky blouse and black silk trousers. She indicated the younger woman sitting beside her and said, 'This is my daughter, Beth Frederick.'

'Stepdaughter,' said Gwen, coming to sit down on Beth's other side. 'Her father is Jon Frederick, do you know him?'

'The singer? Are you really his daughter? Gosh, yes, I remember him well. He was quite big in the seventies. Well!'

Sean was saying the first thing that came into his head. He had noticed the furious look that Rilla shot at her sister when Gwen had pointed out that Beth was not a blood relation. Even now, after he'd moved the subject to the music of the seventies, Rilla's mouth was still set in a line, and she was eating one pistachio nut after another from the small dish on the occasional table beside her, discarding the shells into an ashtray.

'Darling, do leave some of those for other people,' said Leonora. 'And Sean, we can't let you be monopolized, can we? You haven't met my grandchildren and you really must! Come out on to the terrace. I won't allow smoking in the house, so they all puff away out there.'

Sean followed Leonora outside. A young man and a very pretty woman indeed were sitting on white chairs at a white table whose surface was almost hidden by an assortment of glasses, an ashtray, little china dishes filled with nuts and cheese straws, and a packet of cigarettes. A boy of about three, who was surely their son, was rolling down the grassy slope beyond the terrace, then running to the top and rolling all over again. The young man leaped to his feet and said, 'Darling Leonora, how super you're looking. As usual. Sit down for a moment.'

'Yes, do,' said his wife. She blushed as she spoke and glanced nervously over her shoulder, just like a small child looking to see whether she's said the right thing in grown-up company.

'Thank you, Efe dear.' Leonora sat down, saying to Sean, 'You've spoken to Efe on the telephone, I believe? Beth, whom you met inside, called him that when she was very tiny. Childhood names do stick, don't they? Efe, this is Sean Everard. Do sit down, Sean. There are enough chairs for everyone.'

'It's good to meet you face to face at last,' said Efe. 'We're all very excited about the film. This, by the way, is my wife, Fiona. And that's Douggie, my son.'

'My son' Sean noticed. Not 'our son'. He wondered whether Fiona minded that excluding possessive pronoun.

'How d'you do?' said the young woman and stretched out a hand for Sean to shake. Her clasp was rather limp. She was like a doll, with long fair hair, and blue eyes fringed with ridiculously long lashes. Efe was almost too good-looking. Perhaps it was his clothes. His chinos were too clean and well-pressed, his shirt was casual, but obviously came from Jermyn Street. His loafers were certainly Italian. It was as though he'd just stepped out of an advertisement.

'Where's Chloë?' Leonora asked. 'Shouldn't she be down by now?'

'Oh, you know Chloë!' said Efe. 'She's never been on time in her life.' He explained to Sean. 'Chloë's my younger sister. She's a bit of a law unto herself. Anything she can do to cause trouble, she'll do.'

'Oh, Efe!' Fiona breathed. 'You are mean! Poor Chloë!' She smiled at Sean and elaborated. 'She's an artist.'

Leonora shook her head and Efe said, 'She calls herself an artist, but I don't know if I would. Anyone can hammer together all sorts of stuff and call it art, but that doesn't make it so, does it, Leonora?'

'Indeed it does not. You will understand, Sean, I'm sure, that it's quite a mystery to me that a descendant of a great artist such as Ethan Walsh should dare to call her student daubs "art".'

Just at that moment, a strangely-dressed figure came striding round the side of the house and made straight for the table. Chloë. It had to be. Sean half rose from his chair as she began shouting out while still approaching them.

'What's the betting you're already tearing me to shreds, Efe? How's it going, Gran? You're looking dead pretty as usual, Fiona. And vice versa.'

Fiona's brow wrinkled as she tried to work out what Chloë was saying, but Sean got it at once. Dead pretty and pretty dead. Clever but cruel. Had Efe understood? Just to make sure that a fight of some kind wasn't about to break out between the siblings, Sean stepped into the silence.

'I'm Sean Everard,' he said. 'Delighted to meet you. I'm directing a programme about Ethan Walsh and we're filming your grandmother's birthday celebrations for that.'

'Right,' said Chloë. 'They did say, only I didn't quite take it in. Great. Can I sit here? Philip's still upstairs, dressing. He'll be down in a minute. I'm Chloë, by the way.' She flung herself into the chair next to Leonora and grinned at her. 'Your face, Gran! Honestly! You should see it.'

'My face, dear, doubtless reflects my feelings about the clothes you have chosen to wear. And I dislike being called Gran, as you know very well.'

'Sorry!' Chloë said. 'And my personal appearance is out of bounds, don't you remember? You promised.' She turned to Sean. 'My mother and grandmother disapprove of the way I dress. They always have ever since I was a kid. Only they don't seem to realize that I'm all grown-up now. Every single time I see them, they do promise to butt out, not to say a word, because to be frank with you, it's none of their fucking business.'

'Chloë!' Efe and Fiona said in unison.

'I will not stand for such language!' Leonora stood up and swept away from the table and into the drawing-room, leaving an almost visible trail of anger in her wake. Sean, unsure whether to follow her or stay at the table, glanced at Chloë.

'Take no notice. She's in a huff. I don't care.'

'That's always been your trouble,' Efe said, frowning. 'You're selfish.'

'Me? You're calling me selfish? King Selfish himself? Bloody nerve!' She leaned forward, scooped some peanuts out of one of the china dishes, and tipped them into her mouth. She grinned at Sean as she munched.

'You could do with Tennessee Williams as a scriptwriter for any film you make about this family. Take my word for it.'

There was nothing, Sean thought, that he could say to that. He sat awkwardly for a moment, noticing how Chloë's arrival had disturbed the gathering. She had obviously been cast as the black sheep of the family, and seemed rather to be enjoying the part. Fiona had moved to the grassy slope to play with her son, Efe had followed Leonora into the house, and now Cyrilla – Rilla – had stepped out on to the terrace and was making her way to the table.

'Oh, God, pass me a cigarette, Chloë darling!' she said, sinking into the chair beside her niece. 'I was dying in there, by inches.' She smiled at Sean. 'Sorry, but I'm sure you know how it is. One does adore one's family in theory . . .'

'. . . but in practice they don't half get up your nose!' Chloë and Rilla burst into squawking laughter together. Sean hadn't been in the house more than an hour and already he was aware that the laughter, the closeness between the women, was at least partly designed to irritate Gwen. There was nothing wrong with Gwen, Sean reflected, but you couldn't exactly call her a barrel of laughs. But Rilla – she had a face that seemed familiar in some way. Could he have met her, at some gig in the seventies, perhaps, if she'd been Mrs Frederick? 'I hope you won't think I'm being rude,' he said, 'but I'm sure I've seen your face before, and I can't quite remember where.'

'In the movies. My Auntie Rilla is a movie star,' said Chloë. 'You must have seen *Night Creatures?*'

'Oh, Chloë, do you have to? I'm not not exactly proud of my work in films, Mr Everard. Shlock, really, all of it. Hammer Horror, that sort of thing. I'm sure you can't . . .'

'Yes! Yes, that's it! *Night Creatures.* Is that really you? Of course it is. You've scarcely changed at all, but it's not having the costumes and so on. And please call me Sean. I adore *Night Creatures.* It's a cult classic. You were marvellous.'

Rilla held her hand out for Sean to kiss. 'You've made my day,' she said. 'No one around here feels it's any sort of achievement.'

'My mum's jealous, that's all,' Chloë said. 'She's never even left home.'

And, Sean reflected, she's probably not best pleased that her daughter gets on better with Rilla than she does with her. It wasn't surprising, really. He could see that Rilla really didn't care what Chloë wore or what she said or did. In fact, she probably liked the way her niece looked.

Chloë said, 'Wait till you see what I've made Leonora for her birthday, Rilla. You'll love it. Beth was ever so impressed.'

'Chloë's amazingly gifted,' said Rilla. 'She makes the most marvellous things.'

'And Rilla's the only person who thinks so,' Chloë laughed. 'Rilla and Beth. And my dad is biased in my favour as well, but the rest of the Willow Court mafia wouldn't know a decent piece of sculpture or painting if it hit them between the eyes. I can't imagine that they understand Ethan Walsh's stuff either. Leonora will tell you she's an expert, but that's crap, really. All she means is she knew the artist, and that, she feels, gives her a sort of divine right to pronounce on the paintings. It doesn't. I don't think she knows that much about it at all.'

Sean looked at Chloë, slouched in the white chair, with her yellow hair sticking out clownishly all over the place and those enormous trainers incongruous at the ends of her long, rather skinny legs. Either she hadn't slept for months or else she'd applied dark eyeshadow with a particularly heavy hand, but in the white oval of her face her greenish eyes looked at him with a disconcerting directness. Her lipstick was almost black. Sean wondered whether she always dressed like this or whether she worked extra hard to annoy her mother.

He glanced towards the French windows. Efe was there, leaning against the frame and talking to Beth. Sean couldn't hear what they were saying, but Efe was gesturing earnestly with one hand, and Beth's eyes never left his face. Sean could see them shining, even at this distance. She was bending towards him, looking up at him with a glance of such naked adoration that he felt a little embarrassed and looked away. Had anyone else seen this? Had Fiona? He turned round to see where she and Douggie had got to, and there they were, coming up the slope of the lawn. It was impossible to tell if she'd noticed anything. She was carrying the child on her hip but she waved at her husband and he waved back. Instantly, Beth withdrew. She stepped away from Efe and stared for a moment at the ground, before walking along the terrace to where Chloë, Rilla and Sean were sitting.

'Hello again,' she said, and Chloë smiled.

'Hi, Beth!' she said. 'Beth is my friend,' she explained to Sean. 'You wouldn't think it to look at her, but we see eye to eye about a lot of things. Specially things about the family. Only she's got a bit of a blind spot where my brother's concerned, haven't you, Beth?'

Beth blushed. 'Shut up, Chloë! I'm sure Mr Everard isn't a bit interested.'

'Of course he is, aren't you? And it's Sean, Beth, not Mr Everard. He's an observer of the scene. Beth can't see that Efe is only after what suits him. Doesn't give a damn about anyone but himself, my beloved brother.'

'Leonora wants us all to go in now,' said Beth. 'That's the main reason I came out . . . to fetch you. Dinner will be ready soon. Philip's in there, too. Hadn't you better recue him from your dad?'

Chloë stood up. 'Oh, God, yes, I guess I'd better. Poor old Philip, Mum'll be after him too, I suppose. Well, Sean, see you at dinner, I'm sure.' She stomped over the flagstones and went into the drawing-room. The sun was low now, the shadows of every bush stretched black over the grass and the last of the light filled the sky with a glow of blue and rose.

'We should go in,' Rilla said, standing up. 'Mother hates being kept waiting.'

They walked together to the drawing-room. The lights hadn't been turned on yet in the room and, for a moment, Sean had the feeling that he was stepping into darkness.

It was nearly over. The curtain, thought Rilla, will come down soon and then we can all get up from this table and talk in smaller groups amongst ourselves and stop being so on show, so exposed. She sipped at her coffee and resisted the urge to reach out for yet another chocolate. She was sitting next to James, far away from Leonora, but you could bet your bottom dollar that, even with all the conversation and the to-ing and fro-ing of platters and glasses and wine, her mother would have been keeping tabs on Rilla's consumption of bittermints. Why does it have to be *my* mother who's sharp as a tack at seventy-five? she thought. Why can't she be a doddery old lady, not knowing what's going on half the time? Guilt at such thoughts made Rilla feel a little faint and she distracted herself by looking round at what she thought of as 'the cast'. What a fine drama they'd make, if they put their minds to it! Thank Heavens there'd been nothing like that tonight. Everything had gone quite peacefully and Mary's roasted chickens, her carrots and a strawberry sorbet to die for had been enjoyed by everyone. And now, the whole ritual was nearly over for another twenty-four hours.

Here we are, she thought. Leonora, at the top of the table, every inch the heroine in pale blue, had Sean on her right and Efe on her left. Rilla wondered why it wasn't Alex sitting beside his grandmother as he normally did, but supposed that perhaps Leonora had her reasons. Efe looked divine as usual. Those eyes were quite mesmerising and he wore his clothes so well. He was born out of his time. In the twenties, he'd have been a matinée idol for sure. Fiona didn't take her eyes from his face and it would have been funny if it wasn't so sad to see the way she always deferred to him, even to the point of only eating what he ate. She sat almost, but not quite opposite her husband, the perfect ingénue. Pretty, in buttercup yellow, but not a face you'd want to dwell on for very long. Darling Beth next to Efe, not saying much. Not eating much either, as far as Rilla could see. She'd left almost all her pudding. Could she be ill? She had dark rings under her eyes. Tomorrow, first thing, we'll have a proper talk, Rilla thought. We haven't had a heart-to-heart for ages. She sighed. Beth was so striking. Why on earth did she practically erase herself in public? She was wearing a white shirt and black trousers and might just as well have picked up some plates and taken over as a waitress! And if she was wearing make-up, Rilla couldn't see it.

Rilla smiled at Alex, who was making patterns in the sugar bowl with his coffee-spoon. He didn't fit in this family. He was tall and shambling, and had made some effort to dress up by swapping his khaki shirt for a navy blue one, which was either fashionably-creased linen, or unfashionably-creased cotton. Rilla would have put money on the latter. Alex was the least vain person in the world and yet, more than anyone she knew, aware of the look of things.

Rilla noticed Sean looking at her. Could her mother have said something about her chocolate consumption? He smiled at her. He wasn't a bit smooth, which was what she'd feared when the dreaded words 'TV director' were spoken. He was a craggy sort of man, with a lot of dark, grey-streaked hair and a very nice nose. Not a lot of people had nice noses in Rilla's opinion, so you paid attention when you came across one. Gwen was talking to Leonora, so she risked it, and put her hand out for one more chocolate.

Chloë and Philip sat together near James's end of the table. Philip was small and red-haired and gentle, and seemed to get on with Chloë, whom a lot of people found difficult. He also listened to her, which must have been part of the attraction. He was, Rilla thought, one of the quietest and most self-effacing people she'd ever met and made Alex seem positively garrulous. Rilla noticed that Gwen, in her beige silk blouse, had to stop herself from wincing when she glanced down the table at her daughter. How strange we are, thought Rilla. Gwen should have adored Fiona, who was exactly the sort of person she'd have wanted as a daughter, but, oddly, she didn't. Of course, no one in the whole world would ever be good enough for Efe, so maybe that was it.

Efe tapped his wine glass with a fork. Silence fell in the room.

'Thanks, everyone,' he said. 'I don't mean to stop the chatting or anything, but there is something I want to say. If you don't mind.'

A murmur went round the table. Much later, when she was staring at the ceiling and trying to sleep, Rilla thought back to that second, when everyone thought that Efe was about to make a toast to Leonora, or say how lovely the food had been. When everything had been untroubled.

'There's something I have to tell all of you,' he continued, when everyone was quiet. 'But mainly, of course, Leonora. And ask you, too, really. I wouldn't normally bring up matters like this at a party. Celebrations should be celebrations, I've always said, only time is important here and I'm afraid we don't have too much of it.' He paused. 'It's about the Collection, Leonora,' he continued, looking directly at his grandmother. He spoke very softly, very gently. 'I know what it means to you. It means a lot to all of us, but mostly to you, I know that. They're your pictures, in every way. But the thing is, they're not being seen at their best. The way they're hung isn't ideal – you've often said so yourself – and so many people out there would like to see them, to understand them better, and they can't. Now, I know you've turned down all sorts of offers before, but I have been in touch with Reuben Stronsky.'

No one said a word. They sat quite still, as though a spell had been cast, freezing them in their chairs. Rilla knew Stronsky was a millionaire financier from the States with a great interest in the arts. Efe went on. 'Stronsky is offering to buy the Collection and build a museum especially to house it. It goes without saying that he is offering a very large amount of money indeed.'

He picked up his wine glass and drank from it. 'That's it. We can talk through all the details tomorrow, but that's what I want you to consider, Leonora darling.'

No one spoke. Rilla looked at her mother, who had gone as white as a sheet and hadn't moved. Oh, please God, don't let her have a stroke, or heart attack or anything. Not now. Not just before her party! Leonora stood up and with both her hands resting on the table, she smiled at everyone, and particularly at Efe.

'Well now,' she said quietly. 'You've given us something to think about, Efe, have you not? It's been a wonderful day, and I don't intend to spoil it now. We'll speak further about this matter as you say, but I should warn you that my father's paintings leave Willow Court over my dead body.' She smiled. 'I'm very tired now, so you'll forgive me, I'm sure, if I retire to my bedroom. I wish you all a very good night.'

She turned, and left the room, and as always, every eye followed her as she went. The silence in the dining-room swelled and grew, as one by one, everyone stood up from the table and melted away. Some of them would go to their bedrooms, others would probably slope off to the pub in the village. Rilla sighed. That's it, she thought. No more peaceful family party from now on. And no quiet after-dinner coffee and liqueurs in the drawing-room, either. A well-known dramatic trick, she thought. The surprise just before the first act curtain. Who needed it? She walked into the hall, dreading another early night. Bloody Efe! Couldn't he have waited one more day? Hours and hours stretched before her, dark time, in which she would try to sleep and fail. Should she phone Ivan and see how he was getting on? She didn't really feel up to speaking to him. No, damn it, she thought. I'll leave it. And I won't go up to my bedroom and vegetate either. I'll make myself a coffee, even if it will only be instant decaf.

Gwen was in the kitchen bending over the sink and Rilla could see, just from a single glance at her back, that she was making a superhuman effort not to cry. There was no sign of Mary.

'Gwen,' she said, going over to her sister. 'What is it? What's the matter?'

'Oh, Rilla, honestly! As if you need to ask.' Gwen turned round to look at her, eyes full of unshed tears. 'I could cheerfully strangle him. Efe, I mean. How could he? After everything . . .' Her voice faded away. 'I told Mary I'd wash up. I'll go mad if I don't do something.'

Rilla spooned some coffee into a mug and switched the kettle on.

'I'm sure it'll be all right,' she said. 'We'll all talk to Mother tomorrow. Persuade her that this whole thing with the paintings is nothing we can't discuss next week.'

'But that's the whole point!' Gwen wiped her hands on a teatowel and sat down at the kitchen table. 'Efe insists that it's all got to be done now. God knows why. Something to do with cash flow in his firm. And all the work that I've put in for this weekend will just be wasted if everyone's squabbling and people are closeted in corners and Mother's sulking. You know how she can put a cloud over everything when she's not happy. Or maybe you've forgotten, as you're always in London.'

Rilla decided not to rise to this taunt. Gwen, she noticed, looked tired and had more grey hairs than Rilla remembered. She was twisting her wedding ring round and round.

'Sorry, Rilla, sorry. I'm feeling ratty. You cannot believe how much work I've put in, organizing everything and getting rooms ready and seeing to the flowers and the caterers and the invitations and even working out the place settings for each table in the marquee and now Efe's little bombshell just crashes on to the table and threatens it all.'

She sniffed. Rilla could practically hear the phrase 'it's not fair' hanging in the air. She said, 'It'll be fine. There's going to be the filming to take Mother's mind off things. And she's always got on so well with Efe. They'll have a chat tomorrow and she'll just put him straight. I think it's much more likely that Efe is going to be the one left sulking, because he hasn't got his way. Mother never does anything she doesn't want. And she's longing for this party, you know she is. She won't let anything spoil it, I'm quite sure.'

'Maybe you're right. I hope you are. And Efe in a sulk won't be much fun either, but I suppose he'll behave himself. I'll speak to him in the morning. God, I'm exhausted, Rilla. I haven't slept properly for days. I just lie in bed and go over lists of things in my mind.'

'Everything will be fine, Gwen. You're so organised and efficient. And of course if there's anything I can do to help you, just say. You ought to be able to relax a bit and enjoy the weekend, too, you know. Have a brandy or something. Have a cigarette. I've got one here.'

Gwen looked yearningly at the small, sequin-encrusted drawstring bag lying on the table next to Rilla's mug.

'No, no, I mustn't. It's nearly ten years since I gave up. Can you believe it? I'm not going to wreck all that just for a whim.'

'Well, I need one. Have you got an ashtray?'

'You can't smoke here,' Gwen said. 'Mother would have a fit. She's got a kind of X-ray nose when it comes to cigarettes.'

Rilla sighed. 'Okay, okay, I'll go and sit on the terrace. It's a lovely night and I could do with a bit of peace and quiet. You get a good night's sleep, Gwen. Everything will look better tomorrow morning. I've got experience of such things and I can tell you that everything really and truly does look brighter by daylight.'

Gwen squeezed Rilla's arm on her way out of the kitchen, and smiled.

'I'm really glad you're here, Rilla,' she said. 'Sleep well.'

Rilla stared after her, pleased and moved by her sister's unaccustomed gesture of affection. She picked up her handbag and made her way out of the kitchen.

Between the conservatory and the dining-room there was an alcove, a little like an outdoor room, with three walls and no roof. Rilla sat down on a bench which stood against the side of the house. The black silhouette of the marquee, down on the lawn, looked like an illustration from a fairy tale against the midnight blue of sky. To her left, dark windows glimmered in the light of a moon which kept appearing and disappearing behind clouds drifting slowly across the sky. There was a trellis to her right, nailed to the dining-room wall and the roses growing all over it were almost fragrant enough to mask the smell of her cigarette smoke. The particular varieties growing here were called *Mrs Herbert Stevens* and *Long John Silver*. Leonora knew both the popular and the botanical names of every single flower and plant at Willow Court, and so did Gwen, but Rilla could only remember the roses, some of whose titles reminded her of fine French ladies strolling through formal gardens in whispery long skirts. The flowers winding into the wood of the trellis were white with pale pink hearts, and they glowed in the strange summer darkness that wasn't really dark at all.

A noise on the path, someone walking along the terrace, made her catch her breath. Damn and blast! Even in a good mood, Rilla wouldn't have welcomed company at this precise moment. She wanted to think, to unravel the implications of Efe's announcement at dinner, and the effects it might have on all of them over the next couple of days, to say nothing of the long-term consequences, and lo and behold, someone had taken it into their heads to come out here as well. Probably Chloë or Philip or one of the other younger members of the family thinking to have a quiet joint. That'll test the air-freshening quality of *Mrs Herbert Stevens* all right, Rilla thought, and smiled.

'Oh,' she said as she caught sight of Sean. 'I thought it might be one of the kids.' She shook her head, ruefully. 'I must stop calling them that. They're all grown-up now, and Beth really hates it when I say "kids". But that's how I think of them. It's very hard to break bad habits, don't you think?'

I'm babbling, she thought. She put her cigarette to her lips, and sucked so hard that the tip glowed brightly. She exhaled slowly and said, 'Do sit down, Sean. I didn't mean to blast you with conversation. I expect you came out here for a bit of peace and quiet too, didn't you?'

'No, really, it's okay,' he said, and sat down beside her. He turned to look at her. 'I came to find you, actually. Everyone else seems to have disappeared.' He laughed. 'No, that hasn't come out quite as I intended. I didn't mean that I wanted to talk to anyone else. I was just stating a fact. I came to find you.'

'Really? Why?' (Oh, my God, is that too direct? Why the hell, Rilla thought, can't I *think* before I blurt out exactly what's going through my mind?)

Sean was looking, she noticed, straight ahead and not at her. Had she embarrassed him? She was just about to speak again when he said,

'I think I'd like to get to know you better.' He laughed. 'God, doesn't that sound awful? Like something from a magazine. Only what I said before is true. I am an admirer. I really did love you in *Night Creatures*.'

'Thank you,' Rilla said. He didn't have to say that. *I really did love you.* She was very gratified all the same. She stubbed her cigarette out under her shoe, then picked the stub up and pushed it into the earth around the roses.

'Leonora would kill me if she found a fag-end out here on the flagstones. I suppose to her *I'm* still a kid. I suppose we all are.'

She turned to face him and smiled. 'It's kind of you to say all that. I don't do enough work these days to be blasé about meeting a fan.'

'I can't imagine why not. They must all be mad, those casting directors, or whoever.'

'Let's change the subject, okay?' Rilla made sure to smile. 'How's the filming going?'

Sean sighed. 'Your family would fill at least a dozen films. I've got no idea how I'm going to fit everything I want to show into an hour. All the stuff about Ethan and the pictures of course, and also the family and the party, and most of all your mother. She's amazing, isn't she?'

'Amazing is only the half of it,' Rilla said, and then regretted it. 'I truly don't mean to sound catty, but she's hard work sometimes, that's all. She's got very high standards, and I sometimes fail to meet them. That's what I feel anyway. But every family has its things, hasn't it? It's not that we're not devoted to one another. We are, of course, but there's always some sort of friction around when we all get together. I just can't get steamed up about arrangements and lists and the day-to-day things that worry Gwen, and she thinks I'm rackety and disorganized. It's only to be expected, I suppose.'

'Of course it is,' Sean said. 'There isn't a family in the land that doesn't have its share of troubles, secrets and so forth. You all seem to get on rather well, actually.'

'Oh, we do. We really do. Only I suppose I'm not the best person to talk to about Willow Court and what goes on here. I haven't been a regular visitor for, oh, more than twenty years.'

Sean didn't say a word. He's waiting, Rilla thought, for me to say something else. To explain. She opened her handbag, looking for another cigarette. She said, 'D'you mind if I have another? Only it's so firmly banned indoors that I feel I have to puff away like a chimney the minute I step over the threshold.'

'Go ahead,' he said. 'I only ever smoke about twice a year, but I'll have one now, if you can spare one.'

Rilla shook two cigarettes out of the packet and held one out to Sean. She struck a match and he took hold of her wrist as the flame came close. He breathed in, then released her hand, which he'd held on to for a heartbeat longer than was strictly necessary. She lit her own cigarette, thinking, how many years has it been since I felt that small thrill? And am I entitled to be feeling any sort of thrill? It's the night, and the roses and the moonlight and all the bloody clichés getting to me, that's all. She said, 'I ought to explain, oughtn't I? Why I don't usually come here?'

'You mustn't feel you have to.'

'No, I don't mind.' She looked at him again. 'You're easy to talk to. You listen.' She paused and looked at her shoes.

'My son, Mark, drowned in the lake down there. Twenty years ago. He'd be about Alex's age if he'd lived. He was five when he died. So little. It was an accident, of course, but it's hard to live with, still. I manage to put it to the back of my mind when I'm in London. Most of the time, anyway, but when I'm here . . . well. The place is haunted, that's all.'

'It's difficult to know what to say, Rilla,' Sean said quietly. 'Thank you for telling me, and I'm so sorry. I think you're very brave to come back for an occasion like this. Very brave.'

'Not really,' Rilla said, grateful that he hadn't moved, hadn't tried to comfort her by putting his arm around her or, (and other men had done this on a couple of occasions), kissing her, as though their attentions would somehow make her feel better about everything, including Mark. As though a quick screw with them would be so fabulous that all thoughts of the death of her child would simply fly out of her head. She blinked back the tears that had suddenly filled her eyes. Oh, God, no, she thought. Surely I must be all cried out by now.

'I'm sorry,' she said quickly, fumbling in her bag for a tissue. 'I can't help it. You'd think that after all these years, I'd have found some self-control somewhere . . .'

Sean interrupted. 'You've nothing to reproach yourself with, Rilla.'

Rilla smiled and dabbed at her eyes. 'I think it's your doing really. I'm not used to having such a sympathetic listener. I'm all right now. Honestly.'

'Any time. Even if it might mean you bursting into tears.'

Rilla laughed. 'Thank you. It's been lovely talking to you, but I think I should go in now.'

'I suppose you're right. It's a little late and there's certainly going to be a lot going on tomorrow.'

Rilla stood up. 'Fireworks from dawn onwards, I shouldn't wonder, while Leonora hits Efe about the head with his own proposal. But please don't feel you have to come in if you want to stay out here.'

'No, that's all right. I'll call it a night as well.'

They walked together to the door of the drawing-room and went in. This is the second time he's come into the house with me, Rilla thought. She was surprised to realize that she found his presence at her elbow comforting; that she wanted him to be there. They walked into the hall, and made their way upstairs, just like an elderly married couple going slowly up to bed together. Oh, grow up, Rilla Frederick, she said to herself. What planet are you on?

He should have done as Rilla suggested and stayed outside. Here he was in his bedroom and it wasn't even midnight yet. Sean sat on the edge of the bed and ran a hand through his hair and sighed. He'd never felt less like sleep in his life, and wondered why Rilla should have had this effect on him. In his job, beautiful women were part of the landscape. But Rilla was different. Rilla's warm, he said to himself. Her flesh would be warm and yielding and comforting and she'd find it easy to laugh, too, even though there was something sad behind her eyes, which was not at all surprising.

Sean hadn't been flattering her when he'd told her of his admiration for her work. She was rather a good actor, with a screen presence that was both sexy and unthreatening, almost cosy. He wondered why she hadn't been doing so much lately. He knew that for women no longer in their first youth, there were fewer and fewer parts on screen and in the live theatre, but still. Rilla was not like other people. She had something.

He looked into the mirror. What conceit made him think that someone like Rilla would be at all interested in him? His figure hadn't changed much since he was eighteen or so, and from behind, in a good light, he looked like a tall, thin young man, but there was the pepper-and-salt hair and the thin features and the skin which had seen more sun than was good for it. Weather-beaten if you were being generous and wrinkled if you weren't. He looked like a poor man's version of Jeremy Irons.

It had been so long since he'd made a play for anyone. Tanya, his ex-wife, once accused him of being emotionally illiterate, though how she managed to find out anything at all about him when she was busy in so many extra-marital beds, he had no idea. But all that was in the distant past, and if anyone had asked him, Sean would have said his life was full and rewarding. Now he realized how lonely he'd been, and for how long.

He lay back on the bed and chided himself for being a fool. You're here to do a job. Fancying one of the daughters of the house isn't part of your brief. Apart from anything else, he thought, time is so short. You'll be away from here on Monday. Sean was uncomfortably aware that he'd never been a fast worker where women were concerned. He sighed. Do some work, he told himself. That'll get your mind off her.

He went to the table that Leonora had kindly provided for him. She'd smiled and said, 'So much more use to you than a dressing-table. There's a mirror in the wardrobe door after all.'

And she was right, of course. He'd spread his papers all over the surface and now went to find the shooting schedule for tomorrow. Above the table, there was a very small Walsh, which pleased him whenever he looked at it, a pastel drawing of Leonora aged about five, he supposed. She was facing directly out of the frame, peeping from behind the skirts of . . . who could it be? Nanny Mouse? No, Nanny Mouse would never have worn a skirt in such a delicate fabric. You couldn't tell much, really, from seeing only the lower half of the body. Perhaps it was her mother, Maude Walsh.

Sean sat down and stared at the picture. Something occurred to him and he shuffled the papers on his desk till he found what he was looking for – an inventory of all the pictures hanging at Willow Court. He'd spent hours subdividing the list into categories such as landscapes, still lifes, portraits, and so forth. He turned to the list of portraits and ran his finger down the column of titles. It couldn't be true, but it was. Amongst the fifteen portraits there were only two depicting Maude, and she was hidden in both. He knew all the paintings so well, had studied them for so long, that merely seeing their titles typed on a page brought them into his mind complete in every detail. One was a domestic interior in which Maude's figure was bent over some kind of needlework, her face turned away. The lamp on the table was the focus of the artist's attention.

In the other, she was walking down a path bordered with lavender bushes, which echoed the colour of her parasol. This gorgeous accessory made a most beautiful composition, like another flower growing near the centre of the canvas, but it hid the face from view completely. All the artist's skill had been devoted to depicting the lace of the glove on Maude's one visible hand and the silky texture of her skirt. How could that be? What sort of relationship did the artist have with his wife which prevented him from ever attempting a likeness? Ethan's portrait of his child and of Nanny Mouse were delicate and skilful and his self-portraits astonishing. There were several of these, in which Ethan could be seen glaring out of the picture, his eyes full of something Sean couldn't quite put his finger on. Was it unkindness? Cruelty? Why would someone paint himself so unflatteringly? Maybe it's me, he thought. Maybe everyone else sees a prosperous, handsome man with a firm character. Sean thought there was something chilly about the eyes; something off-putting. Young Efe had inherited the same look, and both he and Leonora had Ethan Walsh's green-blue eyes.

Maude, Sean supposed, was the one who'd passed down to Rilla her creamy skin, reddish hair and those hazel eyes with flecks of gold in them. I'll ask Leonora about her mother's looks tomorrow, he decided. He went over to the window and looked out at the black lawns. Someone slipped around the side of the house just too quickly for Sean to see more than a shadow, moving. He shivered. There was nothing to be afraid of at all, but still, who was it creeping round at dead of night? Drawing the curtains closed, he turned away from the window and started to undress.

Mark was calling her. Rilla felt herself coming up and up through fathoms of darkness, waking suddenly with everything in the room around her misty and her body cold with terror. I'm dreaming, she thought. It's a ghastly dream brought on by too much cheese at dinner. He still filled her dreams but silently, moving through the landscapes of her mind as she slept like a ghost, which, Rilla thought, was exactly what he was now. A beloved little ghost. She clung to her sleep whenever Mark appeared, knowing somehow even as the dream was unfolding that it *was* a dream and would vanish the moment she opened her eyes. Sometimes, afterwards, long after she was properly awake, she would lie very still in bed, willing the dream to come back as though it were a video in her head that could somehow be switched on again through the force of her love, her longing.

She sat up in bed, suddenly fearful. There it was again, that crying and a voice calling *Mummy, Mummy*. She hadn't imagined it. She pushed back the bedclothes and ran to the door and opened it. The blood-red carpet of the corridor stretched out silently in front of her. She blinked. She'd forgotten, totally forgotten about little Douggie. Of course, it was him crying for Fiona. Not Mark. Not even the ghost of Mark. Rilla closed the door and sat on the edge of her bed. Don't dare cry, she said to herself. Your eyes will hurt tomorrow and you'll look like death warmed up. She reached over to her handbag and scrabbled around for the chocolate she knew was there somewhere. Thank God for small comforts, she thought, closing her eyes and leaning back against the pillows. Would she sleep again? Two tears slipped out from under her eyelids and she brushed them away.

Friday,
August 23rd,
2002

Voices woke Beth. Men's voices calling, shouting out. Some big vehicle turning on the gravel of the drive. Hammering. She couldn't think what the noise was about and then she remembered hearing Gwen telling Efe that the lighting for the marquee was being delivered this morning and she realized that that was what they must be doing: working away inside the enormous greenish space, getting all the electrical stuff in and fixed up before the flowers and decorations arrived.

She got out of bed and went to the window to see what was happening. It was going to be another hot day, and she was now wide awake. It wasn't worth going back to sleep again, so she put on her dressing-gown and went to have a shower.

When she returned to her bedroom, she dressed in blue jeans, a white T-shirt and white trainers. There was a photograph on the wall showing her and Efe and Alex as children and she peered at it as she brushed her hair and pulled it into a pony tail. Why had Leonora or Gwen or whoever it was decided that this photo was worth mounting and framing? It looked rather dull to her – Efe and Alex in shorts, with their eyes crinkled against the sun, and a Beth she could hardly recognize, also in shorts but with a puffy-sleeved blouse and her hair in bunches. Where, she wondered, were we standing? She looked for clues and saw the corner of the gazebo, and the poppies hiding her shoes from view. We must have been in the wild bit of the garden. Probably on our way to play jungles, or explorers or something. Efe, she thought, could make whole worlds appear as if by magic. He just had to tell us, me and Alex, and we believed him. We believed every word he said. She went up to the glass and traced her finger over the small pale circle of his face. The young Beth was staring up at him and the older Beth smiled. Nothing had changed.

Breakfast at Willow Court used to be a formal meal. Almost Beth's first memory of the house, of her life with Rilla as her new mother, was Leonora, who didn't like being called Gran or Granny, telling her where she must sit, and how to slice the top neatly off her boiled egg. She even remembered the egg-cup, which was made of china and had a pair of feet in red and white spotted shoes to balance it on the plate. Beth was fascinated by it. It was one of a set of children's crockery in which all the cups had been given feet and different sorts of shoe. Efe's were brown and laced-up and Alex had green boots on his.

Nowadays, when the house was full of visitors, everyone came downstairs when they felt like it and helped themselves in the kitchen to whatever they wanted and took it through to the dining-room. Leonora herself was the only fixed point. She was always there in her usual place, at eight o'clock sharp every single day, eating her usual meal of a grapefruit, peeled and chopped into small pieces and sprinkled with a little sugar, followed by two small slices of wholewheat toast spread with butter and marmalade. Margarine reminded her of the war, she told Beth once, and though Gwen and James listened to the advertisements promising them lower choles-terol and a multitude of health benefits and went in for modern spreads and pastes, she wouldn't let the tasteless greasy stuff pass her lips. She always drank Earl Grey tea from a translucent china cup and saucer decorated with pale pink and blue flowers.

Beth took her mug of coffee and a banana into the dining-room. It was quarter past eight and there was no sign of anyone else. Gus, the laziest cat in the world, was in his usual place on the window-seat and she stroked him on her way to the table. He looked up briefly, made a purring noise deep in his throat and closed his eyes again. Beth sat down and peeled the fruit and ate it slowly. Where was Leonora? Was it possible that she'd finished already? Had her breakfast and gone out somewhere? Gwen had probably got up hours ago and started on one of the thousand things she claimed to have to do before the party. James, she knew, was out in the garden overseeing the electricians.

She sat by herself in the dining-room and stared at the banana skin on her plate, feeling something like a small whisper of worry in the back of her mind. Efe's announcement last night had obviously shocked Leonora. Maybe she was ill. Maybe she was . . . no, of course not, Beth, don't be so bloody alarmist. She shook her head to rid it of even the smallest vestige of the possibility that Leonora might have suffered a fatal heart-attack.

She picked up her dishes, took them through to the kitchen and washed them up. I'll go into the garden, she decided, and see what they're doing in the marquee. And maybe see Efe, go on, admit it. Maybe he'll be there. Surely Leonora's all right.

She'd almost stepped over the threshold into the warm sunlight that was beginning to filter through early mist, when her footsteps took her to the stairs instead and she found herself halfway up them before she knew it. I'll just go and check on her, she thought, and then I'll go out. She's never late for breakfast. Never ever.

At the top of the stairs, she paused. Douggie, still in his pyjamas, was outside the nursery with his hand on the doorknob. Neither Fiona nor Efe were anywhere to be seen, and Leonora, Beth knew, would have a fit if a toddler were to go into the nursery all by himself. He probably wanted to play with the dolls' house, but someone should have made it clear to him that it wasn't allowed.

Beth hesitated. She wasn't quite sure how she felt about Douggie. On the one hand she loved him because he was a part of Efe, but he was also a constant reminder of Efe's marriage, his relationship with his wife. Now that Fiona was pregnant again, Beth found herself thinking more than usual about the two of them together and had to make an effort to turn her thoughts to something else. Little Douggie didn't resemble Efe in the slightest, but seemed a quiet, grave sort of child, not given to wildness or much noise. As she approached him, he smiled tentatively and said, 'Going in now.'

Beth went up to him and knelt at his side. She removed his hand from the doorknob.

'No, darling,' she said as gently as she could. 'Not in there. It's not allowed. Come with me and I'll take you back to your mummy.'

'Don't want Mummy,' he said firmly and looked as though he might be going to cry. 'Want dolly house.'

'No one's allowed in there without Leonora,' Beth explained, wondering briefly whether Douggie knew who she meant. Perhaps

Fiona had given the child's great-grandmother another name alto-gether. *Leonora* was a bit of a mouthful for such a baby, she thought, before remembering that she and Efe and Alex and Chloë had all managed it perfectly well.

Just as she was hesitating about whether or not to knock on the door of Efe and Fiona's bedroom, it opened and Fiona herself came out, looking for her son.

'There you are, Douggie!' she said. 'Naughty boy. I've said, haven't I, that you mustn't go wandering all over the house without me. I'm sorry, Beth. He hasn't been worrying you, has he?'

'Not at all,' Beth said. 'It's fine. I was just going to bring him back.'

'Thanks so much.' Fiona made an effort to smile, but Beth was surprised at how washed-out and bedraggled she looked. She took Douggie's hand and pulled him to her. 'Come on now, lovey. Breakfast time soon, isn't it?'

Douggie could be heard complaining; whining that he wanted to see the dolls' house, but then Fiona closed the door behind them, and silence spread through the corridor. She was looking, in Beth's opinion, distinctly queasy. It must be early morning sickness. Whenever she thought about the new baby, it felt to Beth as though heavy weights had been attached to her heart. At one time it had been possible to imagine Efe leaving Fiona but every single thing that had happened to him lately (the engagement, the wedding, Douggie's birth, now this pregnancy) was like another steel ribbon thrown around him and Fiona, binding them together. I won't even think about this now, Beth decided, and made her way to Leonora's bedroom.

She hesitated for a moment. That was another unwritten rule at Willow Court: children didn't bother Leonora unless there was some kind of emergency. But I'm not a child, Beth thought. And maybe this is an emergency. She knocked firmly at the door and Leonora's blessedly strong voice called out, 'Come in.'

Now that she'd heard her, Beth felt like running away, but of course that was quite impossible. Go on, she thought as she went in, she's not going to eat you.

Leonora was standing by the window. She was elegantly dressed in pale grey trousers and a hyacinth blue cashmere jumper. Even at this hour of the morning, her make-up and pearls were immaculate. Rilla always called them *Mother's working pearls*, the necklace and earrings Leonora always wore when she wasn't making any particular effort. The bed was so neatly made that you'd swear no one had ever slept in it. Bertie, the upstairs cat, eyes closed and purring gently, was stretched out like a ginger bolster just under the slope of the pillows. He was quite devoted to Leonora and as long as she was in his territory, he always tried to position himself somewhere close to her.

'Hello, Beth dear,' Leonora said. 'What's the matter? You look a little worried.'

'I thought, I mean, I thought there must be something the matter with you because you weren't at breakfast.'

'That's kind of you,' Leonora smiled, and went to sit in the armchair near her dressing-table. 'To tell you the truth, I wasn't in the mood to talk to anyone and I didn't feel that I could ask Mary to bring me up a tray when everyone's so busy getting the party ready.'

'I'll go,' Beth said. 'What would you like? You should have said. I'd have brought a tray up, or Chloë would have.'

'I'd starve to death if I had to rely on her for breakfast. It wouldn't appear till teatime. You know she sleeps all day.'

Beth sat down on the window seat. 'I'm glad you're okay. I thought you'd be terribly upset. Angry. I don't know. Something.'

'I'm not best pleased with Efe, to tell you the truth. That young man sometimes forgets what I've done for him.' Leonora winced. 'I hate to hear myself saying that. I hate even thinking such things. It's exactly the sort of remark I promised myself would never pass my lips. I was never going to do that dreadful parental thing: look what I've sacrificed for you, and so forth.' She shook her head.

'I'm sure you don't mean it like that,' Beth smiled encouragingly.

'You're right, Beth. I don't. But don't let's talk about this now. Let's just go down and have some breakfast. I am rather peckish after all.'

Beth stood up and followed Leonora out of the room. Whatever did she mean? As they went slowly downstairs Beth asked, 'Are you going to talk to Efe?'

'In my own good time,' Leonora said. 'He does, after all, know my

97

response to his suggestion and I'm sure he's informing whoever it is in America who needs to be informed.'

In the kitchen, Beth said, 'Sit down, Leonora, and I'll get your tea and toast ready. I'll carry it through to the dining-room for you.'

'No, I'll have it here at the kitchen table. It's so late.'

Beth could feel Leonora's eyes on her as she filled the kettle and took the cup and saucer down from the dresser.

'You're staring at me, Leonora. Have I left something undone?'

'No, no, dear. It's only that you look so young. Just like you did when you came here for the school holidays.'

Beth laughed, 'Don't be fooled by jeans and a T-shirt! I'll be thirty in a couple of years, you know. On the shelf, that's what I am!'

'What nonsense, child! Thirty's still a girl, almost. On the shelf indeed! Though there's a lot to be said for shelves. Things may get dusty on a shelf but they don't get broken.'

Beth knew from the way she said it that this particular pearl of wisdom was one Leonora was fond of and must have used a million times, probably to console her unmarried friends. On another day, she might have considered giving her an argument, but now wasn't the time, so she put two slices of bread into the toaster and wondered what she could say to change the subject.

James stood in the middle of the marquee, aware that there was really nothing in particular for him to do. Everything was under control, but he did enjoy pretending to be something like a ringmaster. As he turned his head, he caught sight of Chloë, carrying a sketch pad.

'Am I seeing things?' he laughed. 'Surely it can't be you, sweetheart, at this hour? I didn't think the morning was your time of day.'

'Hello, Dad. It isn't,' said Chloë, sounding, James was glad to note, quite amiable. 'But I wanted to go and look at the willows.'

'Absolutely,' he said, as though this were the most normal thing in the world to be doing so early in the day. He would never have admitted it to Gwen, but he knew and Chloë knew that there was a bond between the two of them. They liked one another. James made no secret of his admiration for Chloë's work, and even had one of her less comprehensible sculptures displayed on a table in his office. He made a point of never commenting on her appearance, which was, he realized, a painless way of staying in her good books. Sometimes he could scarcely hide a smile as Gwen rose, predictably, to Chloë's bait, unable to stifle criticism of this or that outlandish fashion. He'd never discussed it with his daughter, but had a shrewd idea that a lot of what Chloë did was designed to irritate her mother. Once, when she was about ten, she'd said out loud what James had always thought himself but felt vaguely guilty about.

'Mummy's always on Efe's side, isn't she?' Chloë had asked him, and when he'd hesitated, she'd added, 'But it doesn't matter, does it, because you're on mine.'

'Well, yes,' he had answered. 'I suppose I am, but don't go saying so to your mother.'

'I'm not stupid, Dad.' And she'd smiled the smile that melted his heart every time. His sweetheart . . . that was what she was and James felt proud that she never minded him calling her that. She wouldn't have put up with it for a second from anyone else. What on earth did she want with willow trees, all of a sudden? She must have looked at them thousands of times.

'I expect we'll see you later, then,' he said.

'Suppose so,' she said cheerfully, and waved at him as she went off towards the lake.

Alex slung his camera over his shoulder and made his way back to the house. He'd been up for hours, and had gone out at what felt like dawn, but was actually only about seven o'clock, to photograph the men moving along the shining lengths of scaffolding, carrying stage lights to fix to the steel skeleton inside the marquee, ready for the party. Then he'd wandered down to the lake for some shots of the waterlilies. The swans were right over on the far bank and he didn't have the energy to go all the way round there without so much as a cup of coffee. I'll get some breakfast, he thought, and then go back later. It occurred to Alex that there were probably a hundred tasks his father would want him to take on, and he got his excuses ready as he walked across the terrace. I'll tell him I'm working on Leonora's present, and that won't even be an excuse but the plain truth.

As he approached the French windows of the drawing-room, he

heard Efe's voice coming from the conservatory. Tearing a strip off someone, by the sound of it. Alex stood quite still for a moment, wondering whether he should go away and leave whoever it was to their fate, or whether he should at least have a look to see what was going on. Perhaps Efe was shouting over the phone and no one was actually catching the blast full-on and in person. He looked in at the window.

Fiona was cowering – that was the only word for it – near the door, holding Douggie close to her. Her arm was hugging the little boy into her skirt, shielding him from the full force of his father's anger, though the poor kid was obviously terrified.

'I *can't*. Don't you understand how impossible all this is for me, Fiona? You're the first to spend all the bloody money I bring back, on top of everything your Dad sees to it that you have, so I don't think you're really in a position to give me all that shit about neglect and so forth. Jesus, the house is full to the rafters with doting fucking relatives. How come it's today I suddenly have to be the perfect new man? You know your trouble, Fiona? You're a fool. You can't help it. You always were and I daresay you always will be and it's just my misfortune to be married to you, but honestly . . . today. How *could* you? When you know how much this means to me? When you know how much hinges on this and how Leonora, just by being so fucking obstinate, can wreck my career for ever?'

He'd run out of steam. Alex looked through the window and it took all his self-control to stop from rushing in there and hitting Efe. Fat lot of good that would do. He'd been wanting to hit Efe from time to time for more than twenty years, but whenever he'd tried it he'd come off bruised and battered for his pains. He was ashamed to recognize that part of his reaction to this latest demonstration of his brother's occasional cruelty was surprise. Fiona was so self-effacing in everything that related to Efe, she echoed his every opinion so closely that Alex was shocked at this physical evidence of some sort of disagreement, or disharmony. His sister-in-law worked so hard to see that Efe got his way always that any bullying must have seemed doubly harsh to her.

Poor Fiona now looked as though she was about to burst into tears and it occurred to Alex that maybe he could create a diversion. He knocked on the glass and smiled, as though he'd only just glanced in at the window at that moment.

'What do you want?' Efe mouthed at him.

'Thought Douggie might like to go and look at the men putting up the lights in the marquee.'

Fiona ran to open the door from the conservatory to the terrace.

'Oh, Alex, would you? That would be super, wouldn't it, Douggie? Go with Alex to see the men working in the big tent?'

Douggie nodded gravely and put his hand in Alex's.

'Thanks, Alex,' said Fiona. 'That's so nice of you.'

She was wearing a long-sleeved blouse but the cuff fell back as she pushed a lock of hair away from her forehead and Alex noticed bruises on the lower part of her arm, dark, purple stains in a pattern like fingers, or was he just imagining it? Was Efe capable of that? Suddenly, Alex felt chilly, even though the sun was rising in the sky and it was going to be a hot day.

'Come on, Douggie. Got to grab some food from the kitchen and then we'll go. Bet you'd like a biscuit, right?'

Beth turned to walk up to the house. She'd left the kitchen and gone out to see whether Efe was anywhere near the marquee. She'd been hanging round it now for what seemed like ages and he hadn't appeared. Alex and Douggie (what was Alex doing with the little boy? Where was Fiona?) arrived just as she'd decided she'd had enough of pretending to be interested in the problems of where to put the spotlights, and although she could see that Alex would have been only too glad of a bit of help with childcare, her need simply to lay eyes on Efe was too strong.

'I'm off back to the house, Alex,' she'd said as kindly as she could, and could feel his disappointed gaze on her back as she walked away. I'm getting worse, not better, she thought. I have to see him. Why aren't I like this in London? She knew the answer. There, she had a whole life to distract her. There was work and there were other people. Other men who took her out and bought her dinner and shared her bed sometimes, too.

She hadn't dared to ask Alex where Efe was. She wanted to preserve her dignity and it was somehow undignified and schoolgirlish to follow someone round like this; to look for them all over Willow Court.

As she stepped inside, the shade of the hall felt cool and silent after the light and the bustle of so many people around the marquee on the lawn. She knew, quite suddenly, where Efe might be. Whenever he wanted to work here, Gwen let him use her laptop in the conservatory, where she generally had a table set out with all her things on it. He'd be there, probably e-mailing Reuben Stronsky to tell him about Leonora's reaction. Or else he'd be getting all the facts together to show her later. Beth felt rather sorry for him. He didn't realize quite how stubborn his grandmother was, and how adamant she was about her father's paintings.

She could hear his voice. Was someone in the conservatory with him? There was a place in the corridor where you could stand and look into the room without whoever was in there seeing you. She and Efe had often stood in exactly this spot, listening to conversations between Gwen and James or between Leonora and Rilla; often these were quarrels or disagreements of some kind, which had made the younger Beth blush and squirm, and want to run away and hide. It was Efe who made her stay and listen. Sometimes she burst into tears and then he was cross with her for hours.

Now, she looked to see who it was talking to Efe and saw that he was on his mobile phone. She couldn't quite hear what he was saying but she caught the tone. It was seductive, and occasionally he'd laugh in the way you only laughed at something a lover said to you. Beth found herself unable to move, and strained to catch a word, or a name. Who was it who'd turned Efe, on this morning of all mornings, into this loving, almost purring creature? His voice was a little louder now.

'Not long, my darling . . .' she heard. '. . . together . . . Me too . . .' Then a long silence, then, 'Not now, for God's sake, Melanie. I can't bear it. Stop. Please stop.'

Beth thought she could guess what Melanie was saying to him. The only Melanie Beth knew was a friend of Gwen's, who kept an antique shop in the next village. Melanie Havering, she was called. Efe couldn't possibly be talking to *her*.

She found herself as jealous of this Melanie person as she was of

Fiona. And more surprisingly, she was sorry for Fiona and she didn't understand that at all. The most surprising feeling, though, the one that lay over all the others, was disappointment. She'd never thought Efe was particularly moral or well-behaved, but something about this whispered conversation going on in a place where his wife and child might walk in at any moment struck her as tawdry.

Beth waited till he'd put the mobile phone back into his briefcase and then she went into the conservatory.

'Hello, Beth,' he said. 'You're up early.'

'It's ten o'clock, Efe. I've been up for hours. What have you been doing? I'd have thought you'd be in there ordering the workmen around.'

'Other fish to fry, haven't I? I spoke to Reuben last night and he's getting on a plane.'

'On a plane?'

'For God's sake, stop repeating everything I say, Beth. Fiona does that and it drives me up the wall. Yes, he's coming over here to talk some sense into Leonora. Don't say a word to anyone. Not a single word. I don't want to spoil the party or anything.'

Beth sat down in a cane armchair.

'Did I hear right? You don't want to spoil the party but you're not taking no for an answer and getting this Stronsky chap to come and put pressure on Leonora? Don't you think that's taking things to extremes a bit?'

'Reuben Stronsky isn't the sort of man to put any pressure on anyone. Not in the way you mean. He's quite charming and quietly spoken and Leonora will love him. In any case, I thought you'd be on my side,' Efe said, frowning, and looking so much like he did as a boy that Beth almost laughed.

'Well, I'm not. I think the paintings look very nice here. They're part of the landscape, aren't they?'

'You hardly ever look at them. And Leonora for all her talk about opening the house to the public doesn't exploit them nearly as well as they could be exploited. People are desperate to see them. Ethan Walsh is one of the most talked-about artists of the last century.'

'You sound just like a brochure. Haven't you thought that maybe it's the very fact that one has to make a bit of an effort to get here that adds to their desirability? Makes them fashionable?'

Efe said, 'I can't stay here chatting to you, Beth, if you're going to be as obstinate as Leonora! I thought I could rely on you, so I'm a bit disappointed, if you must know.'

Part of her longed to say *yes, Efe, please smile again and I'll agree with anything you want me to agree with, always.* But she remembered the conversation with Melanie and suddenly didn't feel so inclined to smooth things over.

'Oh, dear,' she said, still smiling. 'I'm so sorry, Efe. To disappoint you. I expect you'll get over it.'

He swept out of the room scowling and Beth blinked back tears. She'd always hated crossing Efe and being nearly thirty made no difference to that at all. I must find something to do, she thought. I must stop being so obsessive about him.

Beth sighed and left the comfort of the armchair. I'll go and find Rilla, she thought. See what she thinks about this plan of Efe's. And when Alex has finished being a nursemaid to Douggie, I'll ask him as well. Chloë's probably still asleep.

Alex wondered why he was finding it so difficult to concentrate. He was crouched down in the shrubbery, taking close-up shots of the parasol mushrooms growing around the roots of the rhododendrons. Mary used to fry them for breakfast when he lived at home, and Alex wondered whether he ought to pick these. In the end, he decided to let them grow, quietly where no one ever thought of looking for them. When he'd taken enough shots of the parasols, he moved to the roots of the shrubs themselves, and the leaves that had fallen during the summer. If you only looked carefully enough, there were entire worlds in nature that simply existed without anyone paying them any attention.

Alex was used to analysing his feelings. He did it more than most people he knew, going over and over things that people said and what they meant by them, and also what he felt about particular events and whether there was anything at all useful he could do to change things and, most of all, if he should speak out or shut up. Most of the time he kept quiet because he honestly couldn't see that anything he might have to contribute would be of any interest to anyone or of any use in making things clearer or better.

But he did have to talk to Beth, that was becoming obvious. Part of him had always known she loved Efe, but it was only yesterday that he got an inkling that this feeling might be more intense than he'd thought, and of a different order from the brotherly affection he'd always assumed was in her heart. At dinner last night, for instance, she'd looked at Efe all the time, not even bothering to turn and face whoever was talking to her. Also, she followed him around. Today, he could have sworn she was looking for Efe, ready to trail round after him just as she used to do when they were all kids.

There were two questions Alex kept asking himself. Would it do any good to tell her about Efe's behaviour where women were concerned? Warn her off? If he did that, she'd probably deny she felt anything at all. He reasoned that Beth must feel some sort of embarrassment about her devotion to Efe. They were cousins, for God's sake. A small voice so far in the back of Alex's head that he could easily ignore it and pretend that it hadn't spoken at all said *she isn't really. She's not related to you and Efe at all. There's nothing to stop her loving Efe. Nor Efe loving her, if he felt like it.* The next thought he had was so unexpected, so devastating, that for a moment he didn't even acknowledge it: *Beth isn't your cousin either. She's no relation of yours.*

He stood up. He put his camera back into its case and walked slowly towards the house. He was wondering why that thought, that relevation about Beth, which he'd known all his life and which hadn't affected him in any way at all, should suddenly, just today, burst in on him.

Fiona looked out of the window at everyone on the lawn. She'd finished crying now, and felt exactly like a wrung-out flannel. Her eyes were raw and her skin, her porcelain skin (that was what Efe called it, when they'd first started going out together) was blotched all over with reddish patches. You could see them even under all the make-up. I look hideous, Fiona thought in an anguish of self-pity. It's no wonder that Efe wants to hit me. She felt herself near to tears all over again, and blinked rapidly in an effort at self-control.

Stop thinking like that, she said to herself. It makes Efe sound like some common wife-beater or something, and he's not. It was just, she knew, that he'd been under tremendous pressure and things sometimes got on top of him. He wouldn't really hurt her. He loved her, and she was his wife. They almost never disagreed about anything, unlike some couples she knew who were constantly at odds, so there was really nothing to quarrel *about*. Last night he'd lost his temper with her, just for a couple of seconds, but it was no wonder after everyone had been so dismissive of his plan for the paintings.

Fiona sighed. She'd spent ages and ages with concealer and powder and foundation and now looked practically normal, if only the blotches would go away. She knew she should calm down because, apart from anything else, it wouldn't do the baby she was carrying any good if she got het up.

It was nearly lunchtime and she'd have to go down and face everyone, and the last thing she wanted was for people to know she'd spent half the morning in floods of tears. Over by the marquee, she could see Douggie on Alex's shoulders, his legs hanging down on either side of Alex's neck. Even from this distance, she knew he was laughing with joy. She could just tell. There was Chloë, walking towards them. Had she really only just got up? She certainly looked as though she were still wearing pyjamas. Fiona wrinkled her nose at the sight of her sister-in-law's royal blue floppy trousers, which looked, from here, as though they were made of satin. With these, she was wearing a man's shirt in some sort of garish checked fabric with the sleeves rolled up. The girl had absolutely no idea at all of how to dress, even if you made allowances for the fact that she was a student.

That TV man, Sean, was walking up the drive. Perhaps he'd been talking to Nanny Mouse. Efe did say he was going to film her quite a lot. Who was that with him? Was it Rilla? It was, and something about the way they were walking made Fiona look more closely. Were they holding hands? No, they weren't. She could see that as they came nearer but they *were* very close together, and Rilla had her face turned up to look at Sean and she was smiling and then they laughed together about something.

Where was Efe? She looked for him among the workmen and all over the garden and couldn't see him anywhere. Beth was just coming out of the house and walking towards Alex and Douggie. Leonora wasn't there either, so that was maybe where Efe was, talking to her. What would she be saying? Couldn't she see how fantastic it would be if the paintings were hung in some white, shining building in a city where lots and lots of people could come and see them, and where everyone could have a cup of coffee and a cake after they'd been round the exhibition, and then buy postcards and reproductions in the museum shop? A pleasant vision of herself at the opening of such a place, in some shimmering dress and shaking hands with all the important visitors, flashed into her mind. She could almost visualize the photographs in the magazines.

Fiona shook her head. That was a long way away, and if they weren't careful, Leonora would get her way and Efe would be permanently cross. Then there was the question of the money. It never seemed to last long, however much there was. Efe's work seemed to swallow more and more of it, and Fiona didn't really understand why. Then, of course, with the new baby coming, there were bound to be extra expenses. Perhaps there was something she could do to persuade Leonora? She could see that this was a bit unlikely, but she'd ask Efe about it at the very next opportunity. When he saw how eager she was to help him, he'd stop being so angry and irritated with her, she was almost sure of it.

She looked in the mirror to make sure that her hair was tidy and there was no lipstick on her teeth or anything like that. At least the shirt she had put on was exactly the right shade of pinky-red, which flattered her and made her look slightly less washed out. You got what you paid for, her mother always said, and she was right. This shirt had cost nearly two hundred pounds but it was worth every penny. Efe said once that she looked like a peach when she wore it, and it made her happy just to think about that. She opened the door and went downstairs, ready to face whatever there was to face.

Beth sat at one end of the table and listened to the conversation going on between Leonora, Gwen and Rilla. Everyone else had decided, mysteriously, to be somewhere else this lunchtime, and Beth rather wished that she'd joined them, wherever they were. Surely Chloë ought to be hungry by now? Efe and James had driven into town. They'd volunteered to talk to Bridget, the caterer, about last-minute arrangements, which Gwen considered was kind of them. Beth privately thought they wanted to be as far as possible from whatever flak Leonora decided to dish out today. Fiona had nibbled at something and made sure that Douggie didn't lay waste to all about him and then excused herself because she had to settle her son down for an afternoon nap. Alex could be anywhere. He never ate lunch and was probably in some corner of the garden, taking photos of bits of it that no one had ever thought of looking at before. Sean had joined his crew, who were setting up equipment in the studio. The plan was for Leonora to show him round the room where the pictures had been painted and for the cameras to film the interview. That leaves us, Beth thought, and decided to keep her head down and get out as soon as she decently could.

'I'm rather glad it's just us,' Leonora said, as though she'd been reading Beth's mind. 'I'm interested to hear what everyone has to say, but in the end it's my decision.'

'Yes, Mother.' Gwen took a sip from her glass of mineral water and looked for support from Rilla, whose attention seemed to be fixed on the asparagus quiche and bits of salad greenery on her plate.

'I do think,' Gwen continued bravely, 'that you should listen to Efe, Mother. He may not have set everything out properly last night. It was naughty of him to take you by surprise like that, but you might find it's not such a terrible offer as all that. And think of the money!'

Leonora looked scornful and sniffed in a way, Beth thought, that just showed she'd never had to worry about where the next penny was coming from.

'This has nothing to do with money,' Leonora said, mildly. 'I have – we all have – quite sufficient money for our needs and most of it has nothing to do with the paintings, as you know, but is the result of some rather wise investment by my grandfather and my late father-in-law. The house, these pictures, are a kind of separate world. Visitors like coming here. They enjoy seeing everything together. The place where the pictures were painted at the same time as the pictures themselves. If you can't see the value of that, and that it's far, far preferable to some concrete monstrosity somewhere in America then you're more foolish than I thought.'

Leonora looked at Rilla, who was still concentrating on her food, and spoke with some irritation.

'Darling, do lift your head from your plate for one second and tell us what you think.'

Beth watched Rilla swallow quickly, and pat her mouth with a napkin. She's embarrassed, Beth thought. How surprising to see your mother wrong-footed like that, made to seem no more than a child. That was Leonora's speciality: making everyone seem young and somehow *less* than they were. Much as she adored her grandmother, Beth knew that it was never a good idea to get into her bad books.

Rilla said, 'I think you're probably right, Mother, but I see Gwen's point of view as well. Maybe it would be good for the paintings to be more . . . well, to be seen by more people. I don't really know why it is, but somehow everyone seems to be more willing to visit museums in the States than a country house in Wiltshire.'

'Ethan Walsh was an English painter and his work is intimately bound up with this place,' said Leonora, and that sounded to Beth very much like the last word on the subject, for the moment at least. Leonora stood up and said, 'There can't be more than a dozen or so things by him in other collections, and those are very early works. All the rest is here, in one place, and here is where they should stay. I'm expected up in the studio but when Efe gets back, please tell him I want to speak to him at once.'

The moment Leonora left the room, Rilla helped herself to another slice of quiche.

'Phew!' she said. 'We can all come out of our foxholes now. That wasn't nearly as hairy as it could have been, was it, Gwennie?'

'Efe's the one,' Gwen said. 'He'll get it in the neck, I'm sure. And I don't quite know what you're looking so bloody happy about, Rilla.'

Gwen's right, thought Beth. She *does* look a lot happier than she's done for ages. Something good has happened to her. She waited until Gwen had finished her lunch and gone off on some errand or other and then she said, 'Come on, Rilla, you can tell me. What's happened? You look like the cat who's swallowed the cream.'

'I'm not saying a word at this stage,' Rilla blushed. She got up from her chair and smiled down at her daughter. 'There may be nothing in it.'

'It doesn't suit you to be enigmatic, Rilla. Do tell me what's going on.'

'The minute something goes on, as you put it, you'll be the first to know, my love. The only thing I'll tell you is that I'm not annoyed with Gwen. I expected to be. I thought her constantly looking overworked and yet not inviting me to help her in any way would get to me, but it hasn't.'

As she made her way out of the room. Beth stared after her, somewhat at a loss. Could she have had a phone call from Ivan? Beth doubted that it would have had this effect on Rilla. Gus wandered over to the table and twined himself around Beth's legs. She bent down and picked him up and buried her face in his fur.

'Gus, if you're looking for bits of ham, you're out of luck. They've eaten every last scrap.'

'My father,' Leonora spoke over her shoulder to Sean, 'used to spend hours and hours up here. I was never allowed across the threshold, of course. He hated anyone to see him working.'

'But what about all the portraits of you? You must have sat for him, surely.'

Leonora looked out of the window for a long time, and something made her shiver. A goose walking over your grave, Nanny Mouse used to say years ago. She wasn't going to admit it to Sean but the studio gave her the creeps and always had. She hated the silence up here, away from the life of the house. The place felt cold, even though nowadays it was centrally heated like the rest of Willow Court. She remembered her father's anger on the one occasion when he'd found her sitting on the chaise-longue that Sean was sitting on this very minute, making notes before the filming began.

'No,' she answered at last. 'I never did sit for him that I can remember. I suppose he painted those portraits from sketches.'

'Do you remember him sketching you?' Sean asked.

'No, not really. My mother did, sometimes. She never showed the sketches to anyone, though, and just stuck them into a kind of writing case she had. I have no idea what happened to them.'

'Could your father have used your mother's sketches?'

'I suppose he could, but I think it most unlikely. He . . . he didn't have a very high opinion of her, I don't think.'

'As an artist, do you mean?'

Again, Leonora thought for a few seconds before answering.

'Neither as an artist nor as a woman. I never . . .' she looked down at the floor, '. . . had the impression that he loved her very much. Although, naturally, I didn't know about their life together. Everything was different in those days, it really was. I didn't know my parents in the way young people do today. Or even in the way Gwen and Rilla know me. Life was full of rules. It was all very formal. And also, although no one spoke about it, Nanny Mouse always maintained that Daddy was never the same after he came back from France at the end of the War. The First World War, I mean. What I do recall, though, was how heartbroken Daddy was after Mummy's death. He certainly wasn't the same person after that.'

The crew was ready, gathered near the door, talking about technical matters. The lights were on already, shining too brightly. The sun was out, so why did they need them? Leonora wondered, but didn't ask because she supposed they must know their own business best.

'Right, Leonora, just turn to me a little. I'm going to ask you some questions and you answer and pretend it's only me you're talking to. I'm going to ask you a little about your mother's tragic death. Take no notice of the camera or the microphone.' He nodded at the crew and then said, 'Tell me a little about your mother. Did you have a good relationship with her?'

'I think I was rather irritated by her, to tell you the truth.' Leonora smiled at him. 'You know how uncharitable children are. I think I felt that her constant indisposition and the fact that she was so often laid up in her bedroom was in a funny way designed to avoid me, to avoid having anything to do with me. All nonsense, of course, as her early death proved. She was properly ill all along, it seemed.'

'Do you remember her funeral?' Sean said gently.

'That whole time is very hazy. I was ill too, at that time. I didn't go to the funeral because of that. She was buried up there, in the graveyard of the village church. Of course, I visit her grave when I go and . . .' Leonora closed her eyes and seemed to gather her strength.

'I go and see Peter's memorial of course, and so I make sure that . . . everyone else has a tidy grave as well. I see to the flowers.'

She turned the wedding ring round and round on her finger, lost in her memories. Then she squared her shoulders and turned her full attention to Sean again.

'I'm sorry, Sean. I was thinking about . . . never mind. We were talking about my childhood. When I think of it now, it's like peering through a misty curtain. I can make out some shadows and flickering things in corners but nothing's clear. Nothing at all. I do remember that it was shortly after my mother's death that I came up here for the very first time.'

'And what sort of life did you have after that? Was it a normal childhood?'

'I suppose so. I didn't really notice much difference, day to day. Nanny Mouse looked after me, just as she always had. I went to school and my friends were particularly kind to me for a while because of my bereavement. So were the teachers. And my father, well, he became like the person in the story about the Snow Queen. Chilly, as though a splinter of ice had entered his heart.'

'Cut!' Sean called out and to Leonora he said, 'That was wonderful, Leonora. Thank you so much. I think we've got enough now, from up here. May I escort you downstairs again?'

'No, no, thank you. I think I'll stay up here for a moment, if you don't mind.'

She couldn't have said why she wanted to do that. The words simply came out of her mouth before she'd thought about them. She watched the crew pack up the equipment and leave the room and then Sean was gone as well and she was alone.

It had been quite warm here while the interview was going on but now, as she sat down on the faded velvet of the chaise-longue, she felt chilly again. This room is cold because no one ever comes in here and because it's empty, she told herself. Nothing sinister about it at all. White walls, no curtains at the window, high ceiling. The easel empty, but standing in the corner as though someone were about to come in and start painting. The palette, Ethan Walsh's palette, on the table over there. Visitors to the house liked seeing that, with the colours dried on to it. They liked looking at the paintbrushes too, in a jar on the table.

Bertie the cat pushed at the half-open door and came into the room. He considered possible places to settle and chose Leonora's lap. 'Come on, then, Bertie,' she said. 'Let's sit here for a minute.' She stroked the pale orange fur and suddenly remembered Mr Nibs, the black and white cat who'd lived at Willow Court during the War and just after it. Nanny Mouse had named him. Leonora closed her eyes and listened to the silence. No one would miss her if she stayed here for a while. If only it weren't so cold.

# January 1947

The fire in the drawing-room was making no difference at all. Flames leapt and blazed and struggled to heat more than the space immediately around the hearth, but it was so cold that Leonora could see her own breath rising like white ribbons and drifting about in front of her face. Mr Nibs, the cat, hardly moved from the rug directly in front of the flames. He was elderly now, and spent most of his time asleep.

Leonora was sitting at the window, looking out at the snowy garden. The inside of every pane had a border of lacy frost around it, and she was wearing two cardigans and some woolly socks over her stockings, which made her feel like a child again. On her hands, the knitted gloves she wore in order to avoid freezing up entirely had their fingers cut off, but drawing was still rather difficult. She held the sheet of paper down on the hard cover of her atlas with one hand and sketched with the other.

The terrace steps, the stone urns, and the icy lawn in the background looked inadequate on the page, not what she wanted them to be like at all. Crosshatching. Perhaps that would help to make shadows appear in the right places, make everything seem more solid. She began to stroke the pencil again and again over the paper.

Just before lunch was the best part of the day for drawing. Today, a thin, pale light came from a sun that seemed drained of every bit of its warmth. Each blade of grass was crusted with white; the trees were stiff, and their leafless branches stood out black against the iron-grey sky. By tea time, darkness covered everything, and there was nothing to do except go to bed early and shiver under the blankets, trying to remember what spring was like, and praying for it to come.

Leonora's father sat very near the fire, wrapped in a shawl. She could feel his presence behind her, even though he wasn't saying anything. He spoke very little at the best of times and these times were certainly not the best. Not good at all, in fact. Daddy had grown more and more cross and quiet lately and whatever Leonora did to try and cheer him up didn't help. He stared at her sometimes as though he didn't quite remember who she was. His eyes were as blue as they'd ever been, but his hair was white now. When had it happened? Leonora wasn't quite sure. She still thought of her father as dark and handsome, and catching sight of him these days, stooped, and much slower on his feet than he used to be, shocked and saddened her.

We must be the only people in the whole country, she thought, who miss the war. Willow Court had been a convalescent home for officers, and for five years the drawing-room was a dormitory and the corridors had been full of soldiers, laughing, shouting, groaning sometimes because of the pain of their wounds, but in any case bringing some life to the house.

Leonora was fourteen in 1941 when the iron bedsteads were brought in. The servants had rolled up the carpets, and taken all the pictures off the walls, and moved them upstairs to the studio. No one had put them back, and now the drawing-room looked strangely bare and chilly with only picture-shaped spaces on every wall, and no colour anywhere. The carpets were in place, and some of the chairs and the sofa, but desert-like space stretched between one piece of furniture and the next. Leonora often mentioned the paintings and asked for them to be rehung, but Ethan Walsh was having none of it.

'Nothing but dust-traps, those pictures,' he'd say. 'Much better off where they are.'

'But Daddy, aren't you proud of them? Don't you want everyone to see them? To admire them?'

He would look at her most strangely then, and say, 'I'm better off without them. And so are you.'

Leonora sometimes opened her mouth to object; to say *how could anyone be better off with nothing to look at on their walls?* but her courage would fail her and she said nothing.

She herself had not been up to the Studio for years and years. Not since she was a little girl. She'd almost forgotten those days, but she remembered that Ethan had caught her up there and frightened her so much that she'd tried to put all thoughts of the room (and with it, her father's painting) out of her mind. Thinking about it now, she realized with a shock that he hadn't actually produced anything since that time. Could that be? Leonora racked her brain to think of something, some sketch or canvas – anything at all really – that would indicate her father was still working. She couldn't remember a single instance.

Of course, the war had stopped a lot of people from going about their normal lives, but surely she had some memory of her father working before the war? No, there was nothing. She was almost sure he was no longer painting. *Almost*, because of course it was possible that he crept up to the Studio when she was asleep and worked away there through the night, but she doubted it. One of the servants would have said something. No, the sad truth was that his wife's death and the coming of war had combined to end Ethan Walsh's career. He'd never *had* to paint for a living, because the money left to him by his father in stocks and shares made certain that he always had an income. He boasted occasionally that his pictures were worth a fortune, but as he never tried to sell any of them, Leonora suspected that this was one of his fantasies.

The war had been in the background for all the years that she was growing up. The fighting, the battles, the bombs and fires and ruined buildings were all far away, so far that it had been hard for her to imagine them, even though she'd listened every night with Daddy and Nanny Mouse to the news on the wireless.

At first, when the wounded soldiers arrived, she couldn't bear to look at some of their injuries. Missing legs and arms in particular brought horror to her dreams and she woke sweating and disgusted and ashamed that she could be so squeamish when the soldiers were so brave. They laughed a great deal and liked chatting to her whenever she came into the ward. That was what the nursing staff called the drawing-room, and where the men went at first while they needed most care. Later, when they were on the mend, they moved up into some of the bigger bedrooms.

There was a billiard table in the dining-room, and when the weather was fine the terrace was crowded with wheelchairs, and crutches propped up against the wall while their owners lounged on benches in the sun, getting better.

Leonora had loved the house when it was full of soldiers. They'd all liked her and made a fuss of her.

'You remind them of their own children, I dare say,' Nanny Mouse remarked.

'They're not much older than I am, some of them,' Leonora answered.

'Don't go getting ideas, young lady.' Nanny Mouse was frowning. 'They're far from home, most of them, and lonely. Don't go leading them on, now. Very easily led, young men are.'

'You're being silly,' Leonora said, blushing. 'They don't think of me in a sweetheart sort of way at all. Lieutenant Gawsworth said I reminded him of his little sister.'

Nanny sniffed and Leonora had changed the subject. Part of what she'd liked about the men was the admiration she saw in their eyes. She had gone to a girls' grammar school where she didn't have very many close friends, because of the shyness that her contemporaries thought of as stand-offishness, but she did have two special friends who lived nearby, Bunny Forster and Grace Wendell. They were forever grumbling about their looks (*my hair is too curly, my legs are too short, just look at my complexion* . . . ) and Leonora quickly realized that it was the done thing to pretend you weren't pretty even if you were.

And I was, she thought. A robin had appeared on the terrace, and Leonora quickly sketched it in. I *was* pretty and I still am. I have good skin and Daddy's blue eyes and my hair is as dark and shiny as his used to be. Perhaps pretty's the wrong word. *Gorgeous*. Peter used to say that. Quite ridiculous. Leonora blinked. I mustn't think about Peter, she said to herself. Not any more. He's not coming back. It's more than three years since I had a letter from him and it's five years since I last saw him. He could have decided he wants nothing more to do with me, because he's found someone more interesting. Someone he loves better than he loves me.

Leonora felt dreadfully guilty, but secretly she preferred the hideous option of Peter's death in action, and whenever the idea of that crossed her mind, she quickly prayed, oh, God, don't listen. I don't mean it. Please don't let him be dead.

She kept the letters he'd written to her, dozens of them, in an old biscuit tin, and every night before she fell asleep, she opened it and took out one or another of Peter's short messages to read to herself before she settled down to sleep. The letters were a secret from Daddy, of course. They would arrive in envelopes addressed to Nanny Mouse, who pretended to be slightly disapproving, but Leonora knew she thought the correspondence romantic. Perhaps Daddy wouldn't have minded a soldier writing to his daughter, but she hadn't felt she could take the risk of arousing his anger. What if he'd forbidden her to write back? She would never have been able to defy him.

She smiled as she read. Peter wasn't a very good writer, but she'd rather have had his words than anyone else's in the world.

*It won't be long before I come back to you, Leonora my darling . . . sometimes I close my eyes and imagine your face and that makes me feel better . . . can't say much but you know what I want to write, don't you?*

Three of the letters were different from the others. Leonora had no idea why this should be so, and thought sometimes that Peter had been drunk when he'd written them, but it was as though something had been loosened inside him. She knew these messages by heart and wondered if the sensible thing to do would be to tear them up or burn them, but she could no more destroy them than take a pair of scissors to her own flesh. She'd hidden them in the dolls' house, under the carpet that her father had laid in every room. No one would ever think to look there. Even Leonora had to work at the tiny carpet tacks with a nail file to lift a corner and pull out the tightly-folded paper.

*I want to kiss you all over your white skin. I think of touching you, your breasts, your neck, and your mouth open under mine. I think of this until I'm nearly mad with wanting you. We'll wake up together, Leonora, and we won't be able to tell where one of our bodies ends and the other begins . . . there are other women here, my darling, and I can't bear to look at them. It's you. Wait for me, Leonora. We will do nothing but make love all day long when I come back. All day long.*

Stop it, she said to herself, shivering. Don't think of that now. Think of something else. She closed her eyes and allowed herself the luxury of hearing Peter's voice in her head. The first time he'd ever spoken to her she was in the scullery all by herself, peeling a few potatoes that Tyler, the ancient gardener, had managed to dig out of the kitchen garden.

'I say, frightfully sorry, but I think I'm a bit lost. I'm looking for Sister Coleridge.'

'I'll take you, shall I?' Leonora could see that the young man at the door was struggling with his kit-bag. His left arm was in a sling and his head was bandaged. 'I can carry the bag, too, if you can't manage it.'

He'd smiled and his eyes that were somewhere between brown and grey looked straight into Leonora's and she felt something moving in her chest, a kind of fluttering under her ribcage. He had red hair. Leonora and Bunny and Grace had discussed red hair at great length and decided that it was lovely on girls but a little strange on boys. One look at this soldier had changed her mind for ever. He was tall and slim and he looked, Leonora thought, like a very handsome fox turned by some enchantment into a human being. His smile made his strangely-coloured eyes light up and his teeth really did shine, white in a rather sun-tanned face. His copper-coloured hair fell over his brow, and he tossed his head to push it back because he couldn't use his hand.

'No, I'll manage, thanks. Not such a crock that I have to have gorgeous young ladies carrying my kit. What's your name?'

'I'm Leonora Walsh.'

'And I'm Peter Simmonds. Delighted to meet you. Walsh. Isn't that the name of the chap who owns the house? Decent of him to turn it over to the Army. Jolly decent, actually. Don't know if I'd relish having the military running wild over my ancestral acres.'

'The men are very nice and don't run wild at all, really. They play the gramophone rather loudly, it's true, but I love the music. And sometimes they make rather a lot of noise at mealtimes, but I don't mind. Ethan Walsh is my father.'

'Then he's a lucky man,' Peter said. He'd smiled at her as Sister Coleridge came out of the drawing-room and made her way towards them.

'I hope you get better very quickly,' Leonora said, and went back to peeling the potatoes.

'Cheerio!' said Peter. 'Thank you for your help.'

Leonora knew from that moment that she loved him. It wasn't quite love at first sight. She'd taken about two minutes to decide. I shan't tell anyone, she thought, not even Bunny and Grace, because they won't believe me. They'll say I've got a crush on him, or something. Everyone thinks children don't know what proper love means, but they do. Puppy love, calf love – grown-ups gave the feelings silly names to make them seem less important, less interesting, less true. She longed for Peter Simmonds to stay at Willow Court for months and months, and immediately felt guilty at wanting such a dreadful thing. Fancy wishing someone wouldn't get better! How selfish she was!

I can't help it, she decided, and wondered what she had to do to make Peter Simmonds fall in love with her. He was so much older than she was. Perhaps it would be impossible, but she was going to try her hardest.

She'd made herself indispensible: reading to Peter when he was feeling low; playing card games with him and his chums, Georgie, Freddy and Mike; listening to him talk for ages about terrible things that he'd seen. They'd walked for hours in the Quiet Garden, where the pale roses planted by her mother grew against a sun-warmed wall, and the borders were crowded with pink and mauve and palest blue delphiniums and lupins, hollyhocks and snapdragons, and edged with white alyssum.

'My mother hated bright colours,' Leonora told him, and they sat on the bench built round the magnolia tree and breathed in the peace while he told her the hideous details of everything he'd seen happening all round him.

'I shouldn't speak to you about it, Leonora. It's not fair. You're only a kid and you ought not to hear about, well, about what goes on out there in the world.'

'I'm not a kid!' Leonora said, and nearly contradicted herself by bursting into tears because that was how he thought of her. How he still thought of her, after all these weeks. She'd wanted to tell him how she felt a hundred times and then funked it. Instead, she lay in her bed every night, too hot under the bedclothes, and daydreamed about kissing him and what it would be like. She'd kissed a boy last Christmas at a party – Nigel Drake, who was quite nice but who didn't make her tremble or blush when she thought of him. The kiss was all right, once she'd got into it properly, but Nigel was obviously not used to girls and hadn't known what to do with his hands, which just hung down at his side. Leonora knew from films she'd seen that he was supposed to put his arms around her, but she was so preoccupied with wondering what she thought about having his moist, rather rubbery lips clamped to her own that she didn't think she could mention it.

Peter's kisses would be different, she was sure of it. When she wasn't at his side, Leonora spent hours playing with her dolls' house. She'd stopped doing that ages ago, but since his arrival at Willow Court, it was a way of bringing her deepest and most cherished fantasy to life.

She pretended that the house was their house, hers and Peter's after they were married, and moved the dolls around it in a dream of what living with him would be like. One day, greatly daring, she put the man doll and the lady doll together under the covers on the biggest bed. As soon as she'd done it, she closed her eyes and imagined that it was them, her and Peter, naked under the bedclothes, then touching, and she felt a strange, melting, soft feeling somewhere inside her which she'd never ever felt before, something that nearly hurt, but didn't.

'You're a bit too old to be playing with that, I'd say,' Nanny Mouse said, coming into the room unexpectedly. Leonora's eyes flew open and she moved the lady doll from the bed to another room before Nanny spotted her.

'I'm not playing with it, not really,' Leonora said, getting to her feet. 'I was just making sure it was tidy, that's all.'

Nanny Mouse looked searchingly at her and changed the subject.

'Your father's expecting you for lunch,' she said. 'You know he doesn't like to be kept waiting.'

Then one day, while they were sitting in the conservatory, Peter said, 'I'll miss these times with you, Leonora. When I go. You've saved my life.'

She looked at him and wanted to say so many things but the words dried and shrivelled in her mouth. She couldn't speak. She ought to say something like *it's such good news that you're well enough to leave* and all she could think was *don't go. Stay with me. What if you're sent back to the war and killed? What'll become of me then? Oh, stay . . . please please stay!*

At last she managed, 'When? When will you have to go?'

'This evening, I suppose. Maybe tomorrow. My mother's sending a car to fetch me. I really ought to go and convalesce at home. I'm all she's got left now since Dad died, and she's not very well. I . . . I will miss you so much, Leonora . . .' His voice faded as though he couldn't think of the right words. They were sitting next to one another on the ancient sofa that had been moved into the conservatory from the drawing-room to make space for the beds. He turned to her. Leonora could see he was hesitating. Silence filled the space all around them and the sun beat down on the glass panes and made golden squares on the tiled floor. Someone looking into the room from the hall wouldn't see them, Leonora knew. The plants were in the way. They were quite alone. If she didn't do it now, if she hesitated for even a moment longer, he'd be gone and she'd never see him again. She put out both hands and pulled his face close to hers.

'I wish you could stay,' she said, and then, 'Please kiss me, Peter. Please.'

His eyes widened. His face was so close to hers that she could almost count his eyelashes. He kissed her, and she breathed in his smell, and tasted his mouth on hers and felt the hardness of his arms on her back, pulling her into the heat of his body. More. She wanted more. She wanted it never to stop, this kiss, but it did and she found she was crying. Peter suddenly pulled away from her, and sprang to his feet and moved towards the door.

'I'm sorry,' he said, and pushed his hair away from his forehead. 'So sorry. You're just a child, Leonora. I had no right. Please forgive me. I don't know what came over me. I'll say goodbye now. So sorry.'

He'd gone before she could answer and she rushed after him.

'Peter! Please, Peter, stop. Where are you going?'

They were in the hall. At any moment, someone — another patient, Sister, even Daddy himself — might interrupt them. She took his hand. 'Come on,' she said. 'Let's go to the gazebo.'

She almost pulled him out of the front door and they walked slowly over the lawn together.

'We might be seen, you know,' Peter said, out of breath and leaning against the glass wall.

'I don't care,' Leonora answered. 'You're going away and I may never see you again. I couldn't just let you go like that. Come inside.'

The moment they were safely in the gazebo, she flung her arms round Peter's neck and burst into tears.

'Oh, Peter, don't go. What will I do? I'll die. Can I come with you? Oh, please say you won't go. Please . . .'

She felt him breathing; felt his arms encircling her and they stood clinging to one another until her crying subsided a little.

'I'm sorry,' Leonora whispered at last. 'I expect you think I'm a dreadful baby. I know you have to go back to your regiment. Only it's awful because I love you so much. I'll never, ever love anyone ever again, so I can't bear it if you never come back.'

She stopped speaking and looked down at the floor. 'I shouldn't have said that, I expect. You'll think I'm very forward.'

'Oh, Leonora, if only you knew!' He turned her face up to his. 'If you knew how much I loved you. How hard it's been not to tell you, all this time.'

'You should have told me. Why didn't you? Oh, Peter!' She nearly started crying all over again.

'I thought that if I told you, it would be, well, like lighting a fuse. I don't know whether I'd have been able to keep myself under control. You're so young, Leonora. Not even fifteen, and I'm seven years older.' He laughed ruefully. 'I had to behave myself, don't you see? You're nothing but a child.'

'I'm not. I'm not a child and even if I am, I shan't always be one. I'll grow up soon. I'll wait for you, Peter. And I want to write to you. May I write to you?'

'Will you? Really? And wait for me, too? Oh, my darling, I'll come through anything this bloody war can throw at me if I can believe that. I'll write to you every day. I'll write from home and from wherever they're going to send me when I'm a hundred per cent fit. Oh, Leonora, kiss me again.'

They stayed in the gazebo until it was time for Peter to collect his bags and wait for the car. Leonora's mouth was swollen from their kissing and she went straight from the gazebo to her bedroom. When Nanny Mouse came to call her for dinner, she said she didn't feel well, and stayed in bed until she was sure Peter had gone. She jumped out of bed every time she heard a car, and she watched him leave. She only half-heard the song that someone was playing downstairs, but she registered the fact that it was Duke Ellington's 'Mood Indigo', and the tears she'd been holding back started to fall at last. She buried her face in her pillow and wept and wept. How would she ever be able to listen to those swooping sounds again without remembering? When at last she ventured downstairs, Georgie gave her a letter Peter had left for her. That was the first letter she learned by heart, and it was the first she'd hidden in the dolls' house. *No one knows what will happen, Leonora my darling. If I survive this war, I'll come back and we will love one another for ever and ever. I promise.*

She could bear time passing. She could face every day because of the letters. Then, three years ago they had stopped arriving. Leonora refused to think of why he might not have been able to write, and went through the motions of her life. She met other young men, but they all seemed dull and uninteresting by comparison with Peter. She went to dances, and tennis parties in the summer and found herself dreaming of Peter even while she was talking to other people. It was no good at all. There would never be another man ever again whom she could love, and she even said so once to Bunny, in an unguarded moment. Bunny was having none of it.

'Nonsense,' she told Leonora. 'Someone will catch your eye one day. It's ages and ages since you heard from Peter, and you ought to face up to it, you know. He may never come back. I expect it might take longer for you to find someone, because you're more particular than the rest of us, but I'm sure you will in the end.'

Leonora hadn't said a word, but she knew that Bunny was wrong. If Peter never came back, she would grow into a wrinkled old maid, never having known what it was like to make love to a man, to have children, to share a life with someone else.

She was so absorbed in her memories that she jumped when she heard Ethan speaking just behind her.

'What's that you're doing?' he said.

'It's dreadfully hard, Daddy,' she answered. 'I was just trying to make everything solid and rounded. I can't seem to make things look real. Maybe if you showed me . . .'

He turned away.

'There's no point, Leonora,' he shrugged his shoulders. 'You don't have the talent and that's all there is to it. The world is full, bloody overflowing actually, with amateurs. No point adding to them with your nonsense. You'd be better off learning how to cook and mend socks. Perhaps I ought to write to that young man of yours and tell him to come and take you off my hands. If he's still keen, that is.'

'What young man?' Leonora asked. Surely he couldn't mean Peter? He never knew, did he, how she felt about him?

'Peter Simmonds. Don't pretend you don't know what I'm talking about, Leonora. I wrote to him. I told him he was to have nothing to do with you till you were of age.'

Leonora felt heat filling her, in spite of the cold. She had to understand this, these words her father was saying.

'When did you write to him, Daddy?'

'More than three years ago, it must be.'

'Why did you feel you had to do that?'

'Why? Oh, don't pretend innocence, Leonora. I intercepted one of his letters. Nanny Mouse left it lying about. It wasn't the sort of letter a chap should have been writing to a young girl who wasn't of age and so I forbade any further communication. Any good father would have done the same thing.'

'You didn't say a word to me!' Leonora shouted. 'How could you do such a dreadful cruel thing! Oh, you're a monster. A tyrant. How dare you? If you read one of his letters, you must have known how much we loved one another.'

'You were too young to know about love,' Ethan said, dismissing her with another shrug of his shoulders.

'I hate you!' Leonora screamed at him. 'I'll never forgive you. Never. Peter may be dead. He may have died. How could you have done such a thing to your own daughter?'

'You're being silly, Leonora. I was looking after your interests. Just as I'm looking after your interests when I discourage you from a life devoted to art.'

'It's nothing to do with you. You can't tell me what I can and can't do.'

She turned and looked at the page on which she'd been drawing. Maybe he was right about that. She was a fool, setting herself up as some kind of artist when her father was Ethan Walsh, whose paintings were so beautiful that everyone who saw them stood in front of them amazed, and wondering how they'd never noticed the world looked quite like that. She picked the picture up and tore it across once, and then again.

'There,' she said. 'I hope you're satisfied. Now that you've ruined my life in every possible way, like a Victorian tyrant. It's all in pieces.'

The tearing sound of the paper went through her, her eyes misted over with tears and she went on and on tearing and tearing till her picture was reduced to a kind of confetti. She wanted to grind the white flakes she'd made under her feet, stamp on them, obliterate them, but gestures like that didn't go down well with Daddy. He's the only person in Willow Court, Leonora thought, who's allowed to behave like a spoiled child. She went over to the waste basket and let the paper drop into it like so many flower petals.

'I'm going out. I have to be by myself to think.'

'In this weather? You'll freeze to death. There's nothing to do out there.'

'There is. The lake is frozen. I'm taking Mummy's skates out of the trunk and going skating.'

Mentally, she added *and just you try and stop me, and see what you get!* Almost, she was longing for him to try and prevent her so that she could scream at him again; tell him that she was nearly of age and it was absolutely none of his business what she did and if he didn't treat her better she'd leave Willow Court and see how well he managed without her. He didn't say a word. Leonora sometimes thought that she could disappear from the face of the earth and he wouldn't even notice.

'He's not properly got over your mother's death,' Nanny Mouse used to say, whenever she needed an excuse for his bad behaviour and Leonora would answer, 'Well, he should have, surely. That all happened years and years ago. I've got over it, and it was worse for me. Don't you think it's worse, Nanny? Losing a mother?'

Every time she asked the question, she knew that it couldn't really be worse in her case, because her mother had hardly looked after her at all. Nanny Mouse had brought her up. Leonora could barely remember the person called Maude Walsh. They'd played with the dolls' house, and those times together were the only memories she had left. All through her childhood, she'd had to keep asking Nanny Mouse to remind her of things her mother used to do or say and she'd come to the conclusion that Maude Walsh had been a distant, rather quiet person. Leonora couldn't in all honesty say that she missed her. Her father, in spite of his infuriating ways, filled the whole landscape of her childhood and left hardly any room in her head for memories of her mother. When I have children, she thought, I'll look after them myself and we'll play together and talk to one another all the time. I shall love them more than anything. And I shall never, never, interfere with them when they're in love. I shall never meddle in their lives the way that Daddy has meddled in mine. Tears of rage sprang to her eyes once more as she walked into the hall.

She put on her coat, a pair of wellington boots, her gloves, a knitted hat and a scarf and, holding her mother's ice-skates, she made her way out of the front door. The cold was like another element, so sharp that breathing hurt her chest. Whenever she thought of what Ethan had done, fury boiled up in her. Then she grew a little calmer and wondered whether it would now be possible for her to find out where Peter was. She could write to the colonel of the regiment and find out if he was alive. The pale sun was sinking towards the horizon. Every blade of grass under her feet as she walked was iced white and the sky above the black branches of the trees was like a lid squashed down over everything. She could see the lake now, silver in the remaining daylight, with the swans huddled together on the far bank. The gardener's lads had to break up the ice near their nest each day so that the birds had a little open water to swim on. I must be the only person in the world who loves the lake all frozen, when it isn't like itself at all, Leonora reflected. She hardly ever came down to walk around it in the summer, and she couldn't really think why that was. Now that the water had gone to ice, though, it was transformed into a landscape that wouldn't have seemed out of place on the moon.

Leonora sat down on a tree stump to put on her skates. This took much longer than it should have done because she didn't dare remove her gloves. At last, though, she managed to do up the laces and went out on to the ice, sliding and skimming across the surface. She looked down, and saw that the lake water had turned into a mass of blueish-white bubbles, impenetrable and smooth. The only sound in the whole world was the ssshing noise of steel blades on ice, and the occasional cry of a bird.

I won't think about Daddy, she thought, and the cold was so intense that it was easy to put all other thoughts out of your mind except, keep moving. Keep your circulation going. If she went round and round on the ice long enough, her anger and disappointment would dissolve. That was her hope.

She wondered about her father and thought that even if his writing to Peter was inexcusable, perhaps he really did think he was acting to protect her. I don't care, Leonora thought. I'll never forgive him for it, no matter what his motives were. And he's trampled on all my dreams. Did he realize, she wondered, how much he would hurt her, and do it anyway, or did he truly not know what effect his words had on her? And what was she supposed to do with her life? She'd never wanted to be an artist, not exactly, but now that she knew it was out of the question, she felt a sort of emptiness she couldn't quite explain.

Something caught her eye, a figure coming towards her over the lawn, through the wild garden. Who was it? She didn't recognize the person at first glance but whoever it was was bundled up in a heavy coat and scarf and wore a hat. A man, that was certain, but no one from the house. Perhaps it was Daddy, coming to apologize. She dismissed that idea at once. Nothing would get him to stir from the fire. As far as she knew, he hadn't left the house for weeks, and she'd never heard him say he was sorry for anything.

'Leonora!' The figure was calling to her. 'Leonora . . . it's me!'

She slid to the nearest tree and stopped moving. There was a time between hearing the voice and knowing, feeling, who it was, that seemed to go on and on for so long that she had the sensation of falling into somewhere white and quiet and empty where an echo lived that came from years ago. A sound that had been here at the lake perhaps, trapped between the willow branches, trying to reach her, came to her now, flying through the cold, waking memories, filling her with hope and love and warmth: Peter's voice. She looked intently and recognized the set of the shoulders, the way Peter walked, his head held high always. It was him. *He's come back, he's not dead, he's come back.* Every other thought in her head disappeared, and she skated over to where he was now standing, beside another tree almost on the very edge of the ice, certain it was him yet hardly daring to hope.

'Peter? Is it you? Really?' Her breath as she spoke rose up in front of her face and she moved her hands to brush it away, so that she could see more clearly. Yes, it *was* Peter, older, his skin paler now in winter and the freckles more visible, his long straight nose, above lips a little chapped from the cold now. Otherwise, he was just as she'd remembered him all these years – that tawny gaze, something of the wild about him.

'I said I'd come, didn't I?' Now that he was there, in front of her, Leonora didn't know what to do, what to say, where to go, and she pushed off again on to the ice, faster and faster so that she could think, so that she could collect her emotions. His voice followed her:

'Leonora! Don't go. Come back to me. Please come back to me. Leonora!'

She came, sliding to a halt right in front of him. He had to catch hold of her to prevent her from stumbling.

'It's you. It's really you, Peter,' she whispered. 'I can't believe it. I've dreamed about you coming back so often that I expect this might be a dream as well. *Are* you real?'

Peter said nothing, but put out his gloved hand and Leonora took it.

'Come here,' he said. 'We can talk later. I can't believe that after everything I'm with you again. And you're so beautiful, my darling.'

'Oh, Peter,' Leonora wanted to say so many things, but all she could manage was his name over and over again. 'Peter . . . Peter . . . I thought you were dead.'

'No, I wouldn't have, couldn't have, died without seeing you again. I've been waiting, that's all. Waiting for you to be nearly of age. Your father wrote to me and told me to keep away till then. Not to write. I expect he told you all about it.'

'No. I've only just found out. I came out here because I was so angry that I couldn't even look at him. I couldn't abide him sitting there so smugly when he'd done that. Prevented you from writing to me. And I went on and on sending letters off, as I thought, for months. I expect he found those, too, and destroyed them. Oh, it's too horrible to think about! You must have thought I'd stopped thinking of you. But I haven't. I think about you all the time.'

'Oh, my poor darling. That's terrible, it's too ghastly for words.'

'It doesn't matter. Nothing matters now you're here.'

He hugged her to him. 'Kiss me, Leonora. Kiss me.'

'I'm a bit wobbly on my skates.'

'I'll hold you steady,' Peter said, and put his arms around her. 'I won't let you fall.'

They kissed for a long moment and then Peter stepped away from her.

'It doesn't matter any longer about the letters. You waited for me. And you're grown-up now, aren't you?'

Leonora nodded. 'Quite grown-up. I've been dreaming about you coming back for five years. I'm so happy.'

'You ought to take your skates off, Leonora. We should go back to the house or we'll freeze to death.'

He gave her his hand, and as she sat on the tree stump, he helped her to undo the laces on her skates, and put on her wellington boots again. He was kneeling in front of her, so that all she could see was the top of his hat.

He raised his head and looked at her and said, 'Now that you are grown-up, and now that I seem to be kneeling at your feet, I can ask you what I've wanted to ask you for so long. Will you marry me, Leonora?'

'Yes!' she cried. 'Of course I will. As soon as possible. Oh, Peter, I love you so much. Will you love me for ever and ever?'

'Absolutely!' he laughed and stood up. 'For ever and ever and even longer. We'll live happily ever after like those chaps in the fairy tales.'

A thought occurred to Leonora. 'My father doesn't know you're here, does he? You didn't go up to Willow Court first?'

'No, I came straight to the lake. I saw someone skating on it as I walked up the drive and I knew it was you. We'll go and find him now and I shall ask him formally for your hand in marriage. Sort of thing he'd like, I suppose.'

'Yes,' said Leonora, 'I suppose it is. But I'm still furious with him, and I'll marry you whether he gives us his blessing or not. I'll be twenty next year.'

They started to make their way together through the wild garden towards Willow Court. Their feet made a crunching noise in the snow, and they left prints side by side in the white space, her smaller ones keeping pace with his, right beside him every step of the way. There were so many things she wanted to say to Peter but she found she couldn't speak. All the words she wanted to shout out were blocking her throat, her windpipe, so that she could scarcely draw breath. Just before they reached the house, Peter bent down and kissed her again. She could feel herself thawing out, feel the years and years of waiting and holding herself together falling away. I haven't been breathing, she thought. For five years, I've not been living at all. Not properly. I'm going to be happy now. For ever. I'm going to be warm and happy for ever and ever.

On her way down to lunch, Leonora tried to remember where exactly in this house, whose walls were hung with paintings, she'd put the photograph cut from the pages of the *Illustrated London News*, all those years ago. It's in the downstairs cloakroom, she thought, feeling pleased at how quickly she'd recalled its exact location. She found herself hurrying, wanting suddenly to look at it again, and hoping that no one else would be around to whom she'd have to explain what she was doing. The downstairs cloakroom was normally reserved for visitors to the house, and Leonora hardly ever went in there.

She stepped into the small room and locked the door behind her. There it was, on the back of the door, a large sepia photograph showing some young men, smiling broadly, and all lined up in wheelchairs or standing on crutches or bandaged about the head. There were four nurses, two at each end of the row, and a couple of doctors, bending over their patients. Ethan Walsh, unsmiling, stood behind everyone else. The men, who were, Leonora knew, all soldiers, looked amazingly cheerful, which was the whole point of the photograph. It was posed around a bench on the terrace of Willow Court, and you could see the darkened drawing-room windows in the background. She brought her head close to the picture so that she could read the caption underneath: 'Artist Ethan Walsh pictured with some of the servicemen who are recuperating at his country home, Willow Court.'

One of them was Peter. That one, second from the left, and even after all the years, Leonora found tears springing to her eyes. Peter. Even in sepia you could see how he would light up a room just by coming into it. She remembered how Ethan himself, within twenty minutes of Peter asking to marry her, had seemed to change from the cross, silent old man she'd left when she went out to skate on the frozen lake into someone who almost resembled the kind father of her early childhood.

'I can quite understand, sir,' Peter had said, with a shy smile and pushing his hair back off his forehead, 'that my letters to Leonora must have been a little, well, I suppose not exactly the sort of thing a father would be happy to read, so I did understand when you forbade me to write again. But I promise you that in the fighting, when I didn't know whether I was going to be alive or dead the next day, I wasn't thinking about anything but how much I loved her. Reckless, you might call it. I can't apologise for my feelings, sir, though I confess I wish you hadn't seen them.'

'Where were you, during your service?' Ethan asked, pleased to be called 'sir'. He seemed more lively than he had for years at the casual mention of life and death and war and all the things he'd managed to shut out of his thoughts as he skulked around Willow Court. Peter sat down on the chair on the other side of the fire, and began to tell stories from the front line. Leonora listened and saw it all – the darkness and sudden flare of gunfire. She heard the screams of the dying and the wounded in Peter's measured and unsensational account.

'And it was Leonora who kept me sane,' he said. 'Thinking of her, of this house and the kindness we were all shown here, well, those thoughts were like stars above my head that I knew would bring me home.'

He smiled at Ethan and continued, 'I hope you'll allow me to marry Leonora and call Willow Court my home.'

'Certainly, my boy,' Ethan said. 'Of course. Wouldn't dream of standing in your way, both of you. I think this occasion calls for a bottle of the pre-war champagne, don't you?'

Naturally, once the novelty had worn off, Ethan went back to being as moody and grim-faced as ever, but if anyone could bring a smile to his lips, it was Peter.

She kissed her fingers and touched the glass and immediately felt irritated at her own sentimentality. You're an old fool, she said to herself as she left the cloakroom. It's all long ago, and gone for ever. Somewhere far away she could hear someone whistling 'I Can't Give You Anything but Love,' which had been their tune, hers and Peter's. Leonora shivered. Who would be whistling it today? She shook her head, to clear it. I'm thinking too much about those days, she told herself. No one's whistling. It's just that the tune is in my head, suddenly. Probably because I've been remembering Peter. Melodies did sometimes take up residence in the brain. She wished she'd never thought of looking at that photograph again and wondered whether she shouldn't perhaps take it down and put it right away where no one could see it. No, that wouldn't help. His face was always there, whenever she closed her eyes. Whenever she allowed herself to remember everything she had lost.

Leonora watched Efe coming across the grass towards her. She knew very well that he'd been looking for her all morning and she'd been deliberately elusive. She'd made sure to help herself to a light lunch before all the others came in, and then went out to her favourite seat under the magnolia tree in the Quiet Garden and stared at the book on her lap without seeing it. Efe would know where to find her and sure enough, here he was. He hadn't changed. He still had the same combination of bravado and shyness that he'd had as a boy and his smile was the same mixture of apprehension about the way she was going to react, mixed in with a lot of confidence in his own charm; his own ability to get out of trouble.

'I knew you'd be here, Leonora,' he said, and stood directly in front of her. Leonora smiled back.

'You like this bit of the garden too, don't you? Aren't you going to sit down beside me? You always used to when you were in some kind of trouble as a boy.'

'I'm not in trouble now, though,' he said. 'I've come to do a bit of persuading, really. I shouldn't have sprung it on you last night in front of everyone like that, and I apologise. I guess I'm just eager. But I do think you haven't thought the whole thing through. There would be so many advantages for you in this plan. You'd be the main person to profit.'

'Financially, I daresay I would, but that's not the only considera-tion, is it? Willow Court is my home. How can you imagine that at my time of life I'd be willing to see it stripped of all the Walsh paintings, which are, after all, not simply the Walsh paintings to me but all that was best about my father. They remind me of him. Is it sentimental to want to keep them here?'

'Well, since you ask, I think it is a bit.' Efe frowned. 'The art world hasn't exactly been beating a path to your door, has it? Even though there's always interest in Ethan Walsh's pictures. It's just too out of the way, and you've let the whole operation become too cosy and domestic.'

Leonora stiffened. 'If you're going to be rude, Efe, then there's nothing at all to discuss. Cosy and domestic, indeed! Just because I don't go in for the aggressive marketing techniques that I'm sure you'd recommend it doesn't mean to say I don't have the best interests of the Collection at heart. You forget that I've been running Willow Court for years. I've been on the boards of several museums and art galleries and I know what I'm talking about. My feeling is that anyone who is truly interested in Ethan Walsh manages to find their way here without too much trouble. Your Mr Stronsky knows enough to be keen, doesn't he? And who was it, after all, who arranged for a really quite prestigious documentary to be made about my father and his work?'

'Yes, that's fair enough, but I'm not just talking about those who are truly interested in Ethan Walsh. I'm talking about everyone who could discover him if only they were given a chance. I'm sorry, Leonora. Honestly, I don't mean to be rude but try to imagine how splendid a whole purpose-built museum would be! You know there's no room at Willow Court to hang all the pictures, and some real treasures are almost always packed away in the studio and only brought out for special occasions. Even the ones that *are* hanging here aren't exactly displayed to their best advantage. You'd be able to keep some of the paintings, I'm sure, and lend them to the new museum in a kind of rotation or something. We'd fix everything to suit you, you know. Reuben Stronsky is a very reasonable sort of man. Really.'

Leonora looked at Efe and burst out laughing. 'That's the expression you always wore when you were after me for something, when you were about eight or so. Enthusiastic. Nervous. Look, you're even biting your lip in exactly the same way.' She shook her head. 'I'm sorry, Efe darling. I know this means a lot to you, but I can't do it. My father made me promise to keep the pictures here, at Willow Court. I wouldn't recognize my own house if someone removed them. Also, they'd feel strange and unloved hanging in some other place. Do you think I'm being fanciful? I'm not a sentimental person, Efe, as you well know, but those painting are like living things to me and I just cannot imagine them far away in America, or even somewhere in London, where I can't see them every day. Please tell Reuben Stronsky that I'm sorry to disappoint him but my mind's made up.'

Efe took Leonora's hand and squeezed it. 'Will you wait? Will you just please wait and give me your final answer after the party? I didn't . . . I don't want to spoil that. It's your special day and I really do want it to be a day you'll always remember, but will you just do this one thing for me? Wait till after the party? Please?'

'I can't think what could possibly change in such a short time, but very well, if it's going to make you any happier, I'll tell you again on Sunday night. My mind won't have been changed.'

'You don't know, Leonora. Anything could happen.'

'Anything but that, really. I simply cannot imagine anything that would make me suddenly want the paintings going out into the world. I promised my father and if you're harbouring any thoughts along the lines of *maybe we can do all this when the old lady's dead*, then put it right out of your mind. The terms of my will are as clear as those of my father's. The paintings stay at Willow Court.'

Leonora looked at Efe and saw that his mood was darkening. He was someone who carried his unhappiness all around him like a personal cloud and managed to affect everyone with his mood. When he was a child, she sometimes adopted a firm, no-nonsense approach. Perhaps if she tried it now it would still work. She said, 'Efe, you're not to sulk. There's nothing to sulk about. Forget about the whole matter till after the party. Try to enjoy yourself a little. You know, don't you, that I've always done everything I can to help you. Once, as you know, I helped you when perhaps I shouldn't have done, and I've had more than a few sleepless nights about that, believe me, but I forgave myself because whatever happened, I could say *Efe'll be all right. I did it for him.*'

That day came back to her now. She could almost taste the horror and the pain. She could remember the tears she'd shed and how she'd wiped Efe's tears and told him over and over that she'd look after him. That everything would be all right and he was not to worry. She'd promised him then that she'd never mention what he'd done ever again. She would never, she'd told him, discuss that day either with him or with anyone else and now she'd broken that promise. She looked at him now with something like dread. She should have been more careful. He wasn't saying anything but she could see that within the mass of silence he'd built around him, he was furious, hurt, angry with her. He was also, it occurred to Leonora, reliving his version of exactly the same scene and finding it painful. She said, 'I'm sorry, Efe. I know I said I would never mention it, and I shouldn't have said a word. I didn't mean to . . . remind you.'

Efe stood up. 'Well, you bloody well have reminded me, haven't you?'

'Efe! Don't swear at me, please. You know I don't like it!' Leonora's voice was uncharacteristically shaky. 'I know . . . I know you're right, darling and you're quite right to be furious with me . . .'

Efe interrupted her. 'I can't stay here any longer. I don't know how to speak about that. And I don't want to. I don't ever want to. You promised not to remind me and you've done exactly that, and I don't know what to say.'

'I'm sorry, Efe. I really am.' Leonora spoke as gently as she could. A vein was throbbing in Efe's forehead and his hands were bunched up into fists. If I wasn't his grandmother, she thought, he'd probably hit me.

'Don't you realize how hard I try not to think about all that? Don't you? Most of the time I succeed, too, but of course it's harder to forget all that old childhood stuff when I'm here, and now you've put the tin lid on it.' He shook his head as though suddenly a picture he desperately wanted to get rid of had come into his mind. He sank down on to the bench next to Leonora and put his head in his hands.

'I used to want to thank you, you know. I used to lie awake and think of things I could do for you in return.' His voice as he spoke was full of suppressed tears.

Leonora put her arm around him, and he turned to her and buried his head in her shoulder, just as he used to do when he was a small boy. He used to come and find her whenever he had bad dreams, and she could remember him weeping and weeping, saying don't tell anyone. Don't tell them I was crying.

Now she said, 'You don't need to do anything in return, Efe. I did it for myself as much as for you. Let's say no more about it, shall we? Look, here comes your mother and she's got Douggie with her.'

As soon as the little boy caught sight of his father, he pulled his hand out of Gwen's and began a wobbly run across the grass towards Efe.

'Dada!' he called. 'Dada!'

Efe stood up and caught him and swung him up to his face and gave him a big kiss on the cheek. Douggie immediately settled into Efe's arms and began talking.

'Want to see doll house, Dada. Want doll house. Dada take Douggie. Now.'

'We need to ask Leonora, Douggie,' Efe said. 'It's her dolls' house.'

Douggie began to squirm and Efe lowered him gently to the ground. The boy went straight to where Leonora was sitting and began to pull at her skirt.

'Doll house! Please take me to doll house! Now!'

'Your son,' Leonora said to Efe, 'has inherited your demanding nature.' To Douggie she said, 'Come on, then, Douggie. We'll go and visit the dolls' house, if it'll make you happy.'

'Happy!' Douggie agreed, putting his small, pink hand into Leonora's. 'Let's go to doll house. Now.'

Leonora stood up and Douggie began to pull her across the grass towards the house. She said, 'I'm much, much older than you are, Douggie. I walk more slowly than you do, too, so you must wait for me. And when we get to the dolls' house, you must be a good boy and touch everything very gently. The dolls' house is very special. We have to look after it.' Douggie nodded solemnly and slowed down to keep the same pace as Leonora.

'D'you need any help, Mum?' Efe asked Gwen as she made her way carefully along the paths of the Quiet Garden. 'I'm not quite sure what you're doing, but I'm happy to help you. I'm at a bit of a loose end, actually.'

'I'm checking my flowers to make sure that all the ones I want for the arrangements in the house on Sunday are going to be ready. Not that there's much I can do about it if they're not.' Gwen smiled at her son. 'This dahlia is called Bishop of Llandaff. It's doing rather well, and it's such a wonderful colour. I love it.'

'Bishop of Llandaff? That's not very glamorous as a name, is it?'

'No, I suppose not, but names often aren't. Don't pay any attention, dear. I know you're not the one to consult about such matters, are you?'

'God, no,' Efe grinned. 'One flower's much like another to me. They're very pretty and smell nice and all that, but I can't see the point of them, really. One minute they're blooming and the next the petals are falling off or yellow or something. And okay, I don't really want to discuss floral arrangements but just to ask you to have a word with Leonora for me. It really does matter, Mum.'

'You can't imagine I'm on your side in all this, Efe? I think a museum far away from Willow Court is a dreadful idea.'

Efe kicked at the gravel angrily. 'You're not thinking straight, Mum. Honestly. D'you really want to spend the rest of your days as a glorified housekeeper to a lot of pictures? Imagine how much freer you'd be if you weren't a caretaker and a sort of nurse-companion to Leonora?'

'That's quite enough, Efe!' Gwen turned to face him. The satisfaction she'd felt a moment ago on seeing that her lilies were coming into flower in a mass of white and pink at precisely the right moment vanished at his words. 'You think of no one but yourself. I don't know what's so important to you about this arrangement, but it doesn't give you the right to . . .' She cast about for the right word '. . . belittle my whole life. This is what I do, Efe. It's what I've always done: look after Willow Court and my mother and the paintings, and that's a lot of work I can promise you, and I never complain because I love it. I love Willow Court and even though she's difficult at times, I admit, I love my mother. I never noticed you wanting me to travel and avail myself of this freedom when you were living here. It was fine, then, for me to be dancing attendance on you children.'

'I wouldn't have minded if you'd had a job away from home. I wouldn't have minded not living at Willow Court.' Efe sounded uncertain, and the moment the words were out of his mouth, he shook his head. 'No, Mum, that didn't come out right. I'm sorry. Of course I loved living here and I'd probably have minded dreadfully if you hadn't been taking care of us. I know how amazingly lucky we were, all of us, to have a childhood like that, but still, it's over now and we've all left home and you've got years and years when you could do all sorts of wonderfully exciting things instead of . . .'

'Boring things like seeing which flowers go with which and how many there are and whether this or that combination will look good in the drawing-room and will we need the crystal vases or the ceramic ones? Is that what you mean?' Gwen was angry now, and felt the blood rising to her face. 'Making sure that the meals are all organized for my family? Playing hide-and-seek with Douggie because Fiona is exhausted with her pregnancy and you're still on the phone or the e-mail to your work even though you're supposed to be enjoying yourself in the country?'

'Okay, okay. I'm sorry, Mum, I didn't mean it like that. I *do* know what you do for us, and I do appreciate it, and so does Fiona and Douggie loves it here. You're right. It's just that this deal means a hell of a lot to me.'

Gwen resumed her walk along the path, trying to pay attention to the condition of the dahlias, and checking how many of the roses still had blooms that merited a place in one of the vases. Quarrels with her children always distressed her and it took some moments before her heart was beating normally again. Efe walked beside her silently. She'd never quite worked out exactly what it was her elder son did for a living. He worked for a Public Relations firm but his role in the company wasn't clear to her. His working day seemed to involve a great many meals in restaurants and much speaking on a mobile phone. She said, 'I meant to ask you, actually. What's in this deal for you? Why are you suddenly so interested in the fate of the paintings?'

Efe frowned. 'I stand to make money, that's all. And I need it at the moment, I can tell you. We've got ourselves into a bit of financial hot water in the firm, and this would see us safely out of any trouble. Don't look like that, Mum. It's too boring to explain, trust me, and it's nothing for you to worry about. I'm not going to have my face splashed across the tabloids or anything but a bit of cash right now would be bloody useful. To say nothing of the fact that Reuben Stronsky would probably hire us to do the publicity if there *were* to be such a thing as an Ethan Walsh Museum.'

'I think it's a vain hope, darling,' Gwen said. 'I do really. You know how obstinate Leonora can be. And on this occasion I actually agree with her. You'd be better off approaching your father. From what he said to me last night, which wasn't a great deal, he's quite keen. I think he rather fancies the idea of jetting across the Atlantic every few months. You know what he's like.'

Efe smiled. 'Leonora's never going to listen to Dad, though, is she?'

'No,' Gwen said. 'She isn't. And she wouldn't listen to anyone about this, I promise you.'

'I shan't stop nagging her,' Efe said.

Gwen tucked her arm into his as they made their way back to the house. 'No, darling,' she said. 'I never for a moment thought you would.'

You could get out of practice, Leonora reflected, and forget just how to talk to very small children. Douggie didn't come to Willow Court often enough to make him completely familiar to her, and she was, she found, somewhat at a loss when it came to dealing with him. He was a strange child, with passionate demands. Efe had been like that, wanting everything *now, this minute* and making a great fuss and to-do if he was thwarted. But Efe had been a chatterbox and Douggie was the opposite. There wasn't a word for someone who kept silent for most of the time. Alex had always been quiet, but thoughtful, and he'd been the least demanding child in the whole world. Now she found herself keeping up an almost constant stream of talk to lighten the silence a little, and she had to make a great effort to keep from using the same tone she adopted when addressing her cats.

'Here we are, darling,' she said, as they reached the closed door of the nursery. 'Let's go in.'

The curtains had been partly drawn across the window and the afternoon sunshine was no more than a dim glow falling on the dust sheets that lay over every piece of furniture, making particularly black shadows among the folds of white. The dolls' house loomed against one wall and for a second Leonora thought she saw someone standing near it, leaning over it, touching the place where the roof lay hidden under its protective covering. A woman, wearing something long and white like a nightdress.

Leonora blinked and looked again and there was nothing there. Her heart was beating rather fast and she closed her eyes and took two deep breaths to calm herself. A shadow, that's all. There's nothing there at all. I'm getting old and my eyes are not what they were.

Douggie was pulling at her. 'Doll house? Where's it? Where?'

'Here.' Leonora was surprised to find her voice trembling. 'We'll draw the curtains. Isn't it dark in here? Like night time, nearly. Then we'll take the cloth off and see if the dolls are at home.'

As she spoke she pulled the curtains back and light spread to every corner of the room. Then she went over to the dolls' house and lifted the sheet right off it, laying it carefully down on one of the shrouded armchairs. Douggie knelt down on the floor and put his face right up close to the miniature rooms.

'This is the mother doll,' said Leonora, bending down to show him, wondering whether she dared risk kneeling next to him. Better not, she thought. All I need is to damage something just before the party. 'And that's father, and those are the children. Play gently with them now.'

Douggie hardly played with the peg dolls at all, not in the way that Gwen and Rilla had done. Leonora could remember how they'd discussed the dolls' actions and feelings and how they'd forever been desperately sick and being nursed back to health or else dressing up to go to parties. Rilla and Gwen had talked and talked about their goings-on. They hadn't even been able to agree what to call them. Efe and Alex and Chloë had kidnapped them, hung them by their feet from the roof and generally been much rougher than Leonora had liked. She'd had to keep her eyes on the house to make sure nothing was damaged. Beth was the only grandchild who'd played with the dolls in what Leonora considered a proper manner. She respected them and their history and was always asking Leonora to tell her the story of how her father had made the house for her, and how her mother had decorated it and made the very first dolls; the ones that she wasn't ever allowed to touch but which Leonora sometimes brought out to show her as a special treat.

Douggie just stared. From time to time, his plump little hand would snake into one of the rooms and he'd move a chair or stroke the face of one of the dolls.

'We should go now, Douggie,' Leonora said gently, preparing herself for an argument and wondering whether she could tempt him out of the nursery if she promised that they would go and find Bertie the cat. 'It's nearly time for your supper.'

To her surprise, Douggie nodded and stood up. He leaned over the dolls' house roof and said, 'Woof.'

'That's right, it's the roof. Clever boy!'

He ran his hand over the paper painted to look like tiles. 'Paper woof,' he said, and smiled up at Leonora. In that instant, she saw Efe in him, in his eyes and the way he looked at her. He had Efe's enchanting smile. How strange it was, this passing down of pieces of oneself, through the years. The smile wasn't only Efe's. It had been her father's as well and here it was now, on this small child's face. Just the same. Leonora picked up the sheet and arranged it over the dolls' house again.

'I'm covering it all up so that it stays nice and clean,' she explained as Douggie watched her without saying a word.

'Night-night, house,' she heard him whisper as the white cloth fell over the roof. 'Night-night.'

Rilla woke up late on Friday morning, after a night disturbed by dreams, and then spent a full half-hour trying on one garment after another in front of the mirror, tossing the rejects on to the bed in disgust like any teenager getting ready for a first date.

The pink blouse was too pink and looked tarty. The black was unnecessarily funereal for a warm summer morning. Should she wear a skirt? Or trousers? The main thing was to look stunning while giving the impression that she hadn't taken the least little bit of trouble with her outfit, that this was the way she looked naturally, every single day.

Rilla peered at herself, feeling fat and hot. Who are you kidding, she told herself. Who says Sean's even going to notice you? He's probably filming something somewhere, and middle-aged women with red faces from making too much effort are the last thing on his mind.

Everything was going too fast. I'm not used to it, Rilla thought. I'm surely too old for this love-at-first-sight nonsense that I used to go in for. I'm supposed to think and consider and turn things over in my mind, weigh the pros and cons and boring stuff like that. It occurred to her that perhaps she'd had a bit too much wine last night and that what she'd felt out on the terrace was nothing but an illusion. It wasn't, though. Thinking about Sean, about seeing him again, was definitely producing all kinds of suspiciously love-at-first-sightish feelings and fretting about clothes was part of it.

Also, she was getting hungrier and hungrier and every bit of breakfast would have been cleared away if she didn't get a move on. She flung on the very first thing she'd tried, a loose brown crepe blouse with a lovely swing to the fabric and floppy-legged trousers in a fabric patterned with an abstract print of autumn colours. Amber earrings. Hair down. Rilla decided that this was probably as good as it was going to get and made her way downstairs in search of food.

After she'd eaten, she quite unashamedly went in search of Sean. The idea was to come across him as though by accident, and at first Rilla thought it wasn't going to work, but then she heard the crew talking in the drawing-room. She left the house by the front door and walked nonchalantly round to the terrace. There, she looked through the windows at the cameraman and at Sean overseeing the filming of some of Ethan Walsh's pictures, and pretended to be surprised. She didn't have to pretend to look delighted, because her heart gave a little jump when he signalled to her to come in and watch the filming.

'I won't be long,' he said, as she sat down on a chair that had been pushed out of the way.

'I don't mind waiting,' Rilla said, and prepared to enjoy gazing at Sean as he directed operations. She marvelled at the fact that it wasn't just the young who could suddenly develop a passionate interest in whatever it was their boyfriends were involved in.

She looked at the Walsh paintings on the wall opposite her chair and all at once they became the most absorbing pictures she'd ever seen. She'd lived in his house for years and years, and now realized she hadn't properly appreciated them before, perhaps because she'd never really looked. She tried to avert her eyes from pictures of the lake, but this room was full of them.

They're only pictures, she told herself, staring down at her hands. It's not the real lake. You can look at the swans. Just raise your eyes and look at the swans. Rilla took a deep breath and concentrated on the painting directly in front of her. Two swans, half-hidden by willow leaves, and in the foreground the path that wound round the edge of the water, twisted into an s-shape and fading up into the top right-hand corner. Shimmering green and shadows and white wings and long necks appeared as though from behind a curtain of leaves. It's beautiful, Rilla thought, and I hate it. I can't look at it.

She searched the wall for something else to concentrate on. I'm not going to be driven out by a picture. I want to stay. She found herself looking at a small canvas, which showed someone – it must be Nanny Mouse – with her back to the artist, darning something by the light of a lamp. You had to hand it to Ethan Walsh, she thought. No one she'd ever seen painted light in quite the same way. It was so golden and comforting, this lamplight, that you could practically warm your hands at it. It seemed to be shining out of the picture, and the shadows in the background became filled with a sort of hushed menace, as though the tranquillity of the scene were about to be broken at any minute.

I'm letting my imagination run away with me, she said to herself. That'll teach me to try and be serious. She turned her mind to Sean. It was all very well sitting about here, but how long could she decently wait for him to be finished? She was just considering what to do when he came over to her chair and knelt down beside her.

'It's good of you to wait,' he said. 'I wanted to ask you whether you'd come with me to Nanny Mouse's this afternoon? Are you busy?'

'No, of course not. I'd love to. It's ages since I've seen her and I meant to go myself.'

'Terrific.' He stood up and pushed his hair back from his forehead in a gesture that made him look much younger. He smiled at Rilla. 'I've got some outdoor stuff to do now, but I'll see you at lunch, I'm sure.'

'Yes,' said Rilla. She watched him follow his crew out of the drawing-room, which suddenly seemed to be filled with an almost echoing silence. She went to the window and saw the men disappearing down into the wild garden. They were on their way to the lake and Rilla turned abruptly away from the window. She found herself all at once on the edge of tears, and feeling much colder than she should have done considering how warm it was. I won't think about the lake. I won't think about the past at all, she told herself. I refuse. I'm going to be happy. She went into the hall and wondered how to kill the time between now and half-past twelve.

The armchairs in Nanny Mouse's cottage seemed small even though they weren't really, Rilla decided. She wasn't at all keen on the sage-green Dralon pretending to be velvet and the button-backs, which looked very pretty but weren't a bit comfortable. The refreshment provided by Miss Lardner for Sean and herself were more suited to a dolls' tea-party or a teddy-bears' picnic or something: fondant fancies in pastel colours and Earl Grey tea, which should have been called Pale Grey, for that was its colour. The cups were pretty, but they, too, had something of the miniature about them, with their delicate handles and faded pattern of pale pink roses.

I don't care, Rilla thought, biting into an achingly sweet square of iced sponge. She was happy simply to sit here in Sean's company, happy that he'd asked her to join him, happy that what Chloë had whispered to her at lunchtime (*he really fancies you, Rilla. I can tell* . . .) might actually be true. She was reluctant at this stage to admit, even to herself, how attracted she was to him, but all the evidence was there and she considered it now, while Sean was gently speaking to Nanny Mouse.

When he stood within touching distance, she found herself short of breath. When he wasn't anywhere to be seen, she looked for him. When she was alone, she indulged on fantasies she'd thought were the exclusive province of the under-twenties. When she was with other people, her mind wandered. When she was near him, she felt as though parts of her were at melting point, and when she walked beside him she forgot all about her feet and could have walked for hours and hours and followed wherever he wanted her to go.

Oh, guilty as charged, m'lud, Rilla thought. I've got it bad. I've got it dreadful and what if nothing comes of it? Can I take the hurt? This was a sobering thought that made her put down the teacup she was holding. She helped herself to another fondant fancy, a mauve one, while she considered the ghastly possibility that Chloë was wrong and that the signals she'd been reading since last night were just . . . nothing. Only Sean being charming and nothing to do with liking her in particular. What if he was like that to every woman he met? The truth is, she told herself, you hardly know him and you're behaving like a teenager. And besides, she thought, what about Ivan? Thinking of him, trying to imagine him back in London, was like peering at something very far away. In her present state she could hardly remember what it was about him that she'd liked, and the moment he came into her mind, he slipped out again as though he was of no consequence whatsoever. I'll deal with all that stuff, she thought, when I have to, and I may never have to.

Rilla looked round at all Nanny Mouse's photographs. Christening ceremonies were well represented on her mantelpiece. There I am, she thought, in Leonora's arms, and that must be Leonora herself with Maude and Ethan Walsh. One image, framed and hanging on the wall, caught her attention. It's Daddy, she thought, with Gwen in his arms at her christening. She was a vision cocooned in white lace. Daddy looked so handsome. Rilla had never seen her father, but from the photos that she'd been looking at for most of her life, he did have a certain fox-like charm. It was a black-and-white photograph, of course, so that you couldn't see his hair, but she knew it had been reddish because hers was, and everyone had told her from her earliest days that she resembled him. She'd always envied Gwen her dark hair and uncomplicated colouring. Most people she knew thought that being a redhead was something of a mixed blessing, and although Rilla was used to her own auburn curls by now, it had caused her some problems when she was younger. Everyone expected her to be short-tempered.

Sean smiled at her from across the room and something in her leapt and glowed. Oh, act your age, she told herself. She turned her attention to what Nanny Mouse was saying. The old lady seemed to be more like the person Rilla remembered, managing to stay in the present for most of the time at least. Maybe that was because Sean was such a good interviewer.

'I remember the wedding. There weren't any relations on the bride's side. All empty the pews were in the church. They let me go. I was only a parlour maid then but Mr Walsh said I could be her lady's maid. Miss Maude's. I called her that before she was married and couldn't seem to get out of the habit. She was a pretty thing, but quiet. I'm as much of a mouse as you are, she said to me once. She was, too. Hardly opened her mouth.'

'And Ethan Walsh loved her very much,' Sean said, his voice making the words a statement rather than a question. He hoped that his remark would change the subject. Nanny Mouse was muddling her weddings. Ethan and Maude had eloped. She must have been thinking of Leonora's wedding to Peter, just after Ethan's death.

'Funny way he had of showing it!' Nanny Mouse said this with such firmness that it seemed to tire her. She stopped talking and began to stare at a point in the middle distance and pick at the fabric of her skirt with one hand. When she next spoke, her voice was quite different, wavering and uncertain, and her memory had gone sliding through the years from one wedding to another. Rilla listened for clues. *Mr Peter.* That was her own father, so she must be thinking of Leonora. Sean gently reminded her of Maude, and her early days at Willow Court.

'Maude? Yes, you'll find her in the garden most likely. She's planting a border. No yellow, she hates yellow flowers. I expect you're surprised because people like yellow flowers generally, don't they?'

Rilla felt tears pricking in her eyes. Poor old Nanny! God, I hope I don't live to be as confused as that! She's making polite conversation now. I wonder if she knows who Sean is?

'Leonora was very ill, you know,' Nanny Mouse said confidingly, leaning towards him and lowering her voice. 'She got soaked through, you see and took a dreadful chill which turned into pneumonia, I think the Doctor said. Such a high fever, for days and days I was washing her down with damp cloths. And when they had the funeral, I didn't know who to be with. I didn't know. It was so hard to choose, but I chose my baby, because she was still alive. Stood to reason that the living come before the dead. Oh, dear, but I didn't like to think of my Maude all closed up in that coffin.' Tears fell from Nanny Mouse's eyes and she blinked.

Sean handed her his clean handkerchief and muttered something about not distressing herself. Then he changed the subject. 'What did Maude do while Ethan was painting? Did she help him at all? Give him advice? She was an artist, too, wasn't she? Before they married?'

Nanny Mouse seemed frightened. She shrank back into her armchair and turned pale and began to mumble to herself under her breath, blinking and holding both hands up in front of her face as though Sean were about to hit her.

'Don't distress yourself, Nanny,' he said quickly. He laid his hands soothingly on hers and stroked them. 'It's all right. We won't talk about that if you don't want to. You can tell me whatever you like about Maude. You choose. Tell me about the garden again.'

Nanny Mouse looked at Sean as though she had no idea what he could possibly be referring to. She pulled her hands away from his and sat up straighter. 'He has to have her with him. Don't you think that's odd? I think that's odd. What sort of a man needs his wife there every minute while he works? Cook says she hears him throwing things. I'm not one to gossip, you know. I never speak ill of anyone without good reason. Only the way he goes into those long silences and doesn't even pass the time of day with her . . . well, is it any wonder she's got so thin and pale? She'll hardly look at the child. Unnatural, I call it. Well, she does look of course, she's looking all the time in a manner of speaking. Sits there with that blessed book of hers and scribbles and scribbles and I know what goes on. I don't dare say, though. He's warned me. He took me aside in the scullery last night and I've got his fingermarks on my arm, see . . .' She pulled back the sleeve of her dress and showed Sean her wrinkled forearm, marked with nothing more sinister than age-spots.

This outburst tired Nanny Mouse and her head drooped on to her chest.

'That's splendid, thank you very much,' Sean said. 'Don't worry,

I'll leave you to rest now. We'll come and see you tomorrow and bring a camera so that you can be on the television.'

Even the magic word television failed to rouse Nanny Mouse. Her eyes were closed and Miss Lardner, who'd been sitting quietly in a corner listening to the conversation, stood up and said, 'Miss Mussington needs to rest now, I'm afraid. It's all been a little too much for her.'

'I understand,' Sean said, and added, 'Don't worry, we'll see ourselves out.'

Rilla said, 'Thank you for the tea, Miss Lardner. Everything was quite delicious.' She went over to Nanny Mouse and bent down to kiss her.

'Goodbye, Nanny,' she said. The old lady's eyes opened and for a second they were out of focus as she struggled to understand who was crouched in front of her. Then she smiled. 'Rilla! How lovely to see you, dear! You're quite the lady now, aren't you? Not a little girl any more.'

'No, not a girl any longer. I'll come and see you again soon.'

Nanny Mouse plucked at Rilla's sleeve. 'She'd never have agreed to it if she hadn't been frightened to death. D'you understand? She lived in fear. All the time. Fear of him. Yes.'

Outside Lodge Cottage, Sean exhaled as though he'd been holding his breath for a long time.

'Well . . .' he said. 'Who do you think she meant? Maude? Or Leonora?'

'Maude. It has to be. Leonora makes a point of not being frightened of anything. And besides, my father died very young and she's been a widow for most of her life. What Nanny Mouse was describing sounded like a really brutal man.'

'I'm sure you're probably right. Ethan Walsh is beginning to emerge as something of a domestic tyrant.' Sean shook his head. 'Of course you can't learn very much about a person's character from the art they produce.'

They began walking together up the drive to the house, and the works of Ethan Walsh and his relationship with his wife were the last thing on her mind. She wished the avenue of scarlet oaks could stretch and extend itself and go on for miles and miles. She wondered what she could say next. If this silence goes on, she thought, it will become a proper silence and not just two people walking along quietly together. 'I want . . .' Sean began, just as she said, 'I think . . .' They laughed and Rilla said, 'You start.'

'Right. I wanted to say thank you for being there while I was filming this morning. I realized too late that some of those pictures in the drawing-room probably wouldn't be your favourite Walshes. All those lakeside scenes. I'm sorry if it was hard for you.'

'No, not at all. I can look at pictures all right.' Rilla stared at the tips of her shoes as she walked through the gravel, listened to the sounds that their footsteps were making. She looked up at Sean. 'It's only the real thing I can't take.'

'Still . . .' Sean stopped and took her hand. Rilla turned to face him, suddenly aware that her heart was beating very fast.

'I won't be at supper tonight,' he said. 'I've promised the crew I'd go and eat down at the pub with them. I wish I didn't have to.'

'No, that's all right. I understand.' Rilla smiled. 'It'll be another family circus I'm sure. I don't think you'll be missing much. Most of the time, we're all just talking either about arrangements for the party or else Efe's plan and what should be done about that.' She was aware that she was filling the air with sound to cover up how foolish she felt at being so disappointed.

Sean said, 'I expect you'll need to have another cigarette, though, won't you? Like last night?' Rilla felt his hand tighten on hers, and she found it hard to speak in a level voice.

'Oh, yes, I always do. This time, though, I might have my cigarette in the gazebo. Do you know where that is?'

'I do.' He grinned at her. 'I'll be there. At about midnight, say? Can you bear to wait up till then? It's awfully late.'

Rilla nodded, not trusting herself to speak. She could scarcely believe her own daring. How was she going to keep her excitement under control for another six hours? Where was Beth? She'd understand how thrilling this was, this assignation. Yes, Rilla decided, that was the proper old-fashioned word for it: assignation. They'd begun walking up to the house again, but he hadn't let go of her hand. He kept hold of it until they were almost at the front steps.

'Are you listening, Mum? And Dad too, I suppose, but mainly Mum.'

Gwen looked up from the large, hard-backed notebook open in front of her on the kitchen table and nodded absently at Chloë. James was sitting next to her, reading the newspaper. Where did he find the time to read when there was so much to do? She was too preoccupied with the current list (checking to see that arrangements were in hand for parking on the day of the party and had she let everyone know who needed to know) to take in the detail of what her daughter was wearing, but got a general impression of black hung about with metal and wished that Chloë would put on something more like what Beth was wearing. She felt that it was somehow unfair that Rilla's child looked elegant even in a T-shirt and jeans while hers would have done a good job stuck in a corn-field to scare the crows. She was instantly ashamed of this thought, and made an effort to smile at Chloë and not sound as though she were dissatisfied with her in any way.

'I'm just going over my lists,' she said. 'There are so many of them. I suppose after the party I'll reach the stage where everything is crossed off every one of them, and by then it'll be too late to do anything about disasters.'

'Won't be any disasters, Mum, don't worry.' Chloë stretched her arms out above her head. Philip had come into the kitchen with her and was now leaning against the wall. James put his newspaper aside.

'What are you after, sweetheart? I can tell you want something,' he said. 'You've got that look on. I know it well. All right for money, are you?'

'It's nothing to do with money, Dad. I just wanted to know what you've got planned for displaying the presents, that's all.'

Gwen ran a hand through her hair and sighed. 'To tell you the truth, it only occurred to me last week that they ought to be displayed. We're going to give her our presents, just the family, after dinner on Saturday, but as for all the other gifts, I've decided that as people arrive, someone can put the presents on the dining-room table or somewhere and then Leonora can open them after the party, when it's just us. Why?'

'Because,' said Chloë, leaning over the table towards Gwen for added emphasis, 'I've had a brilliant idea. A few parcels came today, and there'll be some more tomorrow, and everyone who comes will bring something and there'll be too many to go on the dining-room table, don't you think?'

'I don't really know. I hadn't thought of that.' A frown appeared on Gwen's face.

'What about this, then?' said Chloë 'Philip and I'll pick some willow branches and make a tree in the hall and arrange all the presents under it, just like we do with the Christmas tree. I'd decorate it really spectacularly, I promise. We can put the presents Leonora's already opened nearest the trunk and then all the wrapped ones can go in sort of circles all around it. It'll be great, really. Please, Mum, please, say we can do it?'

Gwen thought for a moment. 'I suppose so,' she said finally, and Chloë leapt up from her chair and ran round to the other side of the table to hug her mother. 'Fantastic! You won't regret it, I promise,' she cried and, grabbing Philip by the hand, she raced out of the kitchen, almost bumping into Rilla and Sean on their way in.

'Chloë seems on good form,' Rilla said. 'She looked as though she was on the way to something really urgent.'

'She's had one of her brilliant ideas,' James said. 'I don't think any harm can come of this one though.' Rilla laughed. Chloë's ideas had, over the years, led to some spectacular catastrophes. Once she'd decided to try and make a fountain in the middle of the conservatory floor and the whole room had needed recarpeting.

'Do sit down, Sean,' said Gwen. 'Would you like a cup of tea?'

'No, thanks, Gwen,' Sean said. 'We had tea not long ago.'

'What was Chloë suggesting?' Rilla asked, and James told her.

'That sounds gorgeous!' she said. 'It'll look splendid, Gwen.'

'I expect it will. And I'm pleased that she wants to do something special for the party. It's a bit last-minute of course, but that's typical of the young, isn't it? I wish she'd thought of asking me weeks ago what she could do to help, instead of springing all this artistic improvisational stuff on us at the last moment. A law unto herself, that girl is.'

'But she's very gifted, isn't she? It'll work beautifully, Gwen, you know it will.' Rilla stood up and went to stand near her sister beside the sink. 'You're just tired, that's all, and no wonder. You never stop working, that's your trouble. Come and sit down with us and have a chat. We've just been down to tea with Nanny Mouse.'

Gwen flashed a look at Rilla that she couldn't interpret. Is that envy crimping Gwen's mouth, she wondered? Could it possibly be that she's put out to see me and Sean together? Poor Gwen! She thinks of herself as Queen Bee of Willow Court; the main person in charge of all arrangements, including the filming, so that when anyone else wants to join in, or contribute in some significant way, like Chloë a moment ago, her nose is put slightly out of joint. Rilla felt irritated with her sister and sorry for her at the same time. She said, 'Nanny Mouse strongly implied that Ethan Walsh used to hit his wife.'

'She's confused,' said Gwen. 'She can't remember what she had for breakfast, so I shouldn't think she's to be relied on about anything like that. Maybe she's thinking of something she saw on television.' She turned to James. 'I need a long, hot bath after the kind of day I've had. I'll see you upstairs.'

'That sounds remarkably like a summons,' said James to Sean and Rilla as he followed his wife out of the kitchen. 'I'll take her up a nice cold Pimm's. Times like these, what would we do without alcohol, eh?' He gave one last wave in their direction and closed the door behind him.

It was still quite early, but James had already changed for dinner and was lying stretched out on their bed. Gwen sat at her dressing-table sipping the last of her drink as she patted some powder on to her nose. She said, 'I can't think how Rilla has the patience to go through her make-up routine every day. It would drive me mad. "Slap" she calls it. She says that's the theatrical word for it.'

'You don't need any help from powders and paints, my love. It would be gilding the lily.'

Gwen turned to look at him. 'Do you want something? What's all this flattery about?'

James laughed. 'Can't a chap pay his wife a compliment? You're looking particularly fetching tonight.'

'Thank you,' Gwen said and picked up her hairbrush. Before a silence could grow between them, she spoke again. Silences that went on too long were not a good idea because they gave her thoughts room to go back to the days when James could not be trusted. That was all long ago now, and he'd sworn to her then that he loved her, loved her best and passionately, and he'd never never never . . . and so forth. She had made it quite clear that one more infidelity on his part would mean that he never crossed the threshold of Willow Court again, nor exchanged another word with her. That had been the end of the matter. Neither of them had mentioned it since, but James knew that she was careful to watch him and monitor his comings and goings discreetly but thoroughly. Now she said, 'I think Rilla's rather set her cap at Sean. She seems quite smitten, doesn't she?'

'He seems a decent chap,' said James. 'And they're both adults and so on. Can't see the harm in it, myself.'

'I suppose you're right,' said Gwen, 'but I do hope Rilla isn't going to get hurt.'

'Good Lord, why ever should she? You worry too much, my darling.'

'I suppose I do,' Gwen said. 'I can't help it. Still, I expect it'll be all right.'

This was the best part of the day in summer: the hour or two before dusk, when the sun was low in the sky but not quite setting. Beth was on her way to the lake, and wondered why the pearly light and the warmth and the sight of butterflies hovering above the poppies in the wild garden which normally lifted her spirits were not having their usual effect. The day hadn't been what she'd dreamed of when she was back in London.

There, she'd found it easy to weave fantasies of herself and Efe walking together through the long grass, which she would soon be walking through all by herself. Also, in her dreams of the weekend she'd forgotten to include swarms of people moving chairs and tables into the marquee, and coming and going constantly over the lawns behind the house. She'd managed to leave the film crew out of her imaginings as well. They kept popping up wherever you went in the house, whenever you least expected it. And somehow she'd blanked out the rest of the family – Fiona smug about the new baby; Douggie running about everywhere; Leonora materialising in that quiet way she had; Rilla mysteriously hidden away in her bedroom for half the morning and then disappearing with Sean Everard; Alex nowhere to be seen for most of the time; and Efe, the main focus of her feelings and attention, not in a sunny holiday mood at all, but looking sulky and cross whenever she caught sight of him.

She hadn't known about the Reuben Stronsky plan before last night, and at the moment, she wished fervently that the American millionaire and all his works could have been delayed till after these few days. Efe wasn't himself. No, that wasn't quite true. When he wasn't looking like a thundercloud, he was being a sort of on-duty, business-like, superficially charming Efe and not the friend of her childhood. Beth hated admitting it to herself but it was a fact that the man who'd been on display over the last twenty-four hours wasn't the sort of person she liked at all.

He'd been visibly irritated with Fiona at lunchtime for some completely ridiculous little thing like not passing him the right sort of cold meat, and Beth was amazed to find herself wanting to stick up for the poor woman. If he'd spoken to me like that, she thought, I'd have taken the bloody ham and shoved it up his nose. Fiona had just blushed and said *Yes, Efe* in that silly voice of hers and done exactly what he'd wanted; followed his instructions to the letter.

Beth also noticed (how come she'd never noticed it before? Maybe she didn't see them together often enough) that Efe didn't so much as glance at his wife throughout the meal. He didn't address a single remark to her, though his charm was liberally scattered around the table at everyone else. If it were anyone but him, she thought, I'd think he was vile, but I make allowances. She'd looked at him across the table and he'd smiled back at her, as though they were in league together about something. A conspiratorial smile, it had been, and since they had no secrets as far as she knew, she could only conclude that he did it to annoy Fiona, who had intercepted the smile, gone white and stared down at her plate. Beth felt suddenly ashamed. She pushed back her chair and excused herself from the table.

She looked over to the marquee and there he was, deep in talk with his father. James was in charge of all the outdoor arrangements, but he'd torn himself away from the knotty problems of overseeing the arrival of the lighting engineers and the putting up and checking of lights because Efe had button-holed him about the Ethan Walsh pictures. Even from this distance, Beth could see James was longing to escape from his son and go back to the easier task of making sure the the tent was lined and weatherproof and ready for the arrival of the tables and chairs tomorrow morning. She stood still for a moment, wondering whether perhaps Efe might catch sight of her, realize that she was on her way down to the lake and run over the grass to join her. Fat chance! He didn't even notice that she was standing there, staring at him as hard as she could in an effort to make him turn in her direction.

She set off down the slope. Once she reached the wild garden, she knew no one up by the marquee could see her. She was safe to take out her anger and frustration by swishing through the long grass as fast as she possibly could, almost running, crushing flowers under her shoes, wanting to get out of breath, to put all thoughts of Efe out of her mind.

'Watch where you're going!' said a voice at her feet and Beth jumped.

'Alex! What on earth are you doing down there?'

He was lying full-length on the ground with his camera held up to his face, and for a few moments he said nothing as he pointed the lens in one direction after another before clicking off a few quick shots. Beth sighed and sat down beside him. 'Taking photos of the ground, are you? Or some amazingly beautiful blades of grass?'

'As a matter of fact, yes,' Alex answered, and rolled over on his back. 'I've got some good shots of the lake through a sort of frame of grass and flowers.'

'Sounds very artistic,' Beth said, and pulled a blue flower out of the ground by its stalk.

'Don't take it out on me,' Alex said.

'Take what?'

'You know very well what. You're not pleased with the way the weekend is going and it shows. I don't know what you thought was going to happen.'

'I didn't think anything in particular was going to happen,' Beth said, and wondered how much Alex knew. He didn't ever say much, but he paid close attention to everything and even though she'd never actually told him how she felt about Efe, she was sure sometimes that he'd guessed her true feelings. For a mad second, she considered telling him everything and then decided that life would be easier, at least for now, if she changed the subject.

'I love the lake,' she said. 'Doesn't it look great in this light? You should take some more pictures of it. Come down there with me. The swans are over on this side, look.'

Alex continued to stare at the sky. 'I've taken entire films of the bloody place,' he said. 'Because Leonora would expect it but . . .' His words were left hanging in the air.

Beth shivered. She kept trying and trying to forget the afternoon of Mark's death, but it was still as clear as clear in her head and came into her mind often, mostly at night. It had been a blustery day, and the wind had blown sharp and chilly over the water and she could see, as though it were yesterday, Efe bending down into the black lake to pick up Markie's body and how every part of her baby brother had been dripping and streaming as he was carried back to the riverbank. Alex was at the edge of the water, silently weeping as Efe kept on and on trying to bring some life back into her little brother's body, shaking it and turning it upside down. It didn't take much to make her recall the icy dread that had crept over her as she realized that Mark wasn't ever going to breathe again, not ever. She'd turned and run up to the house then, unable to bear it. Shrieking and crying.

'It was a long time ago, Alex,' she said gently, shaking her head to clear it of those images. 'My mother hasn't looked at the lake since then, d'you know that?'

'Don't blame her,' Alex murmured. 'Beth . . . ?'

'Yes?'

'May I tell you something? Nobody else knows I know this. I'm not sure I should be saying anything, but . . .' His voice died away.

Beth nodded. She knew that Alex in a confessional mood was like a bird poised on a branch. One loud noise, one hasty movement and he'd be gone.

'That day, the day Mark died, we were playing a special kind of game. Trappers. We used to play it a lot. Do you remember it?'

Beth closed her eyes. She could see herself as she was then, racing down through the wild garden towards the edge of the lake and then going further along the path. The boys were already in the water. They weren't supposed to be. Mark was sitting under a willow tree.

'You were on the far side of the trees,' Alex continued. 'Efe was shouting at Markie.'

*Shut up, Markie! I'm busy. I've got to get to my trap.* Beth shivered. She closed her eyes and Efe's clear voice came to her as though he was speaking now, calling Markie to him.

'Bloody hell, you two!' Chloë was all of a sudden there in front of her, her arms full of willow branches. 'What are you doing skulking about in the grass ready to trip up unsuspecting people? I nearly dropped all this lot.'

Beth could have strangled Chloë. Why on earth did she have to spring out of the grass just at that very moment? Alex was already sitting up and gathering together his photographic equipment and pushing it into a bag. He was frowning. Beth put out a hand and touched him on the shoulder. 'Don't go, Alex,' she said, and then, turning to Chloë, 'We could say the same thing. What are *you* doing?'

'I'm going to make a tree. Like a Christmas tree but of willow branches. A birthday tree. I'm going to decorate it and display all Leonora's presents under it. Good, idea, eh?'

'Super!' said Beth, trying to sound as enthusiastic as her cousin. 'It'll be great.'

'You coming up to the house?' Chloë said, already on her way up the slope towards Willow Court.

'In a sec,' Beth said. 'We'll follow you.'

Once Chloë was out of earshot, Beth turned to Alex. 'I'm so sorry, Alex,' she said. 'Do go on with what you were saying.'

'Never mind, it was nothing really,' he said, getting to his feet. Beth stood up too and he went on, 'Just forget about it, okay?'

'Not okay! You can't do that, Alex, it's cruel. You've left it all dangling and unresolved. I hate it when people do that.'

'It wasn't anything,' he insisted. 'I was just teasing you, right? I'm sorry.'

Beth looked at him, and immediately understood two things. First, she was quite sure that Alex was going to tell her something about that day, something important. But even more urgent than telling her about it was his need to backtrack, to pretend that he was kidding, that he didn't have any secrets to share with her. He was looking really worried about it, too. Practically sweating. She said, 'Fine, let's leave it and go up to the house.'

'I'll see you there, Beth,' he said. 'I've got a couple more places to shoot before the light goes.'

She could see clearly exactly how relieved he was. His shoulders relaxed and the whole set of his body altered visibly. She watched him as he strode over the grass, tall and thin, his blue denim shirt flapping loose over his trousers, the last of the sun making a kind of halo around his head. Poor Alex! He never could articulate his thoughts very well. If he'd been nearer, if he'd stayed still for a while beside her, she'd have hugged him. Hugged him, and wanted to hit him too, for being so vulnerable and so impossible at the same time. He knew something about that day, the day Markie had drowned, and Beth was willing to wait until he told her. He would tell her one day, because he couldn't bear guilty secrets of any kind.

Alex's head was filled with words going round and round in circles. Oh God oh God and bugger and damn and double damn and fuck and bugger and oh God why did I ever say anything at all? This thought went through his mind as though on some kind of manic loop, some sort of never-ending tape-recording that pushed every other idea out of his head. He walked as quickly as he could, wanting to be out of breath; wanting to exhaust himself, wanting to take back every word he'd said to Beth. What had possessed him? I must be crazy, he thought. What good would it do to dredge up all that old stuff?

He found himself outside Nanny Mouse's cottage, down by the gates. I don't want to be here, he thought. I want to be out of Willow Court and its grounds and away from every single person who lives here. He walked through the gates and strode down the road towards the village, and for once he was oblivious to the world around him. He saw nothing but Beth's face as he'd begun to talk about that day. He should never have done it. It would be perfectly natural now for her to want to know exactly what he'd been about to say.

The tumult in Alex's head subsided a little as he walked. Perhaps Beth wouldn't bring it up again. She must have noticed how distressed he was just before Chloë had popped up. Thank God she had! What he would have done, what he would have said if she hadn't, he had no idea. He could never, ever tell Beth the truth.

Alex didn't know whether Efe had ever spoken to anyone at all about what had happened to Mark. He was quite sure of one thing: his brother was convinced that Alex had seen nothing. He knew this because he'd lied from the very first moment. Even at six years old, some instinct told Alex that he had to do this.

*It wasn't my fault, Alex. Was it?*

*He shouldn't have come. He shouldn't have shouted.*

*I didn't notice. I was over there. What's the matter, Efe? What's the matter with Markie?*

*Nothing. Shut up. I've got to think. Where's Beth?*

*Gone to get Mummy.*

That was the very last time Alex could remember seeing his brother in tears. He'd been down on the ground next to Markie, cradling the little boy's head on his lap, weeping like a girl. Weeping more than any girl Alex had ever seen, before or since. Efe's face had been red and wet and his eyes swollen almost shut from all the tears.

Alex closed his own eyes to erase the picture of his big brother, his hero, the person he loved more than anyone else in the whole world, the bravest boy, stronger and more fearless than anyone else's brother, reduced to this soaked, snivelling, miserable wretch. He hadn't known what to do at the time and, even all these years later, thinking about how useless he'd been made him feel ashamed.

I was only a little boy, but still I wish I'd known what to say, Alex thought. What to do, to comfort him. We'd never been in the habit of hugging one another, but surely at a time like that I might have done. Maybe if I had, maybe if I'd told him then exactly what I'd seen and then still hugged him and told him not to cry, helped him or sympathized with him in some way, everything would be different. Efe himself might well have become a different sort of person. It occurred to Alex that perhaps it was *because* Efe had suppressed the events of that day that he had become the sort of person he was, someone who was comfortable with deception; someone who didn't allow himself to show too much affection, even to the people he loved.

As he walked, Alex worked out what he was going to do. If Beth asked him again what he'd meant to say, he'd make something up. He could invent something, anything really, as long as it wasn't the truth. There was also the possibility that Beth would say nothing, never ask him. If she suspected that the story he was about to tell her reflected badly on her beloved Efe, maybe she simply wouldn't want to know it.

He came to a sudden stop, beside an ancient elm tree. That's it, he thought. I started telling Beth about that day because I wanted her to think less of Efe. I wanted her to love him less than she does. Alex leaned his forehead against the trunk of the elm and closed his eyes. She loves Efe too much, he told himself. That's the truth. I've always known that, really, even though I may not have admitted it to myself.

He turned and started walking back to Willow Court, not exactly sure why he was so worried for Beth. Perhaps it was because he knew that nothing good could come of her love for Efe, who was capable of hurting her in so many different ways that Alex wondered whether he needed to warn her, or whether he ought to do what he generally did and keep quiet. He tried to think of a word to describe how he was feeling and the best he could come up with was 'uncomfortable'. Or maybe 'churned up' was nearer the mark. Whatever he did, it would probably turn out to be wrong. Oh, bloody hell, he thought. This isn't going to be easy at all.

Beth glanced into the conservatory on her way upstairs to change for dinner and was rewarded by the sight of Efe, typing something on Gwen's laptop computer. She hesitated in the hall, wondering whether she should go in and speak to him and decided against it. He hated being interrupted. More than once when they were children he'd shouted at her for butting in, as he called it, while his mind was on something else. And besides, she thought, as she made her way reluctantly to her room, I don't really want him to see me looking like this. Her hair was windblown; her T-shirt, after a whole day of heat, felt grubby to her and she was wearing no make-up at all.

I feel messy outside and inside, she thought. Alex talking about Mark like that stirred emotions in her that she mostly kept well-buried. There were nights when she still dreamed about that time, but for the most part she'd managed to overlay all thought of those days with other, better memories. It was all such a long time ago, she told herself. She'd learned not to mention certain things so as not to hurt Rilla, and what she'd done was not even dare to think of them herself.

She could hear splashing noises coming from the bathroom, just down the corridor from her room. It was Douggie's bathtime and the house rang with his shouts. Beth knew that normally she wouldn't have made the comparison, but this evening she was reminded of her and Mark's bathtimes, and of how Rilla sang them the Ugly Duckling song while they fought over the yellow plastic duck and who should play with it. Beth found that she had tears in her eyes. How silly, she thought. Surely we could have had a duck each? Or maybe I was too old for a toy in the bath, or thought I was.

As she approached the bathroom, she became aware of another noise altogether. Someone was crying. It's Fiona, she thought. She was trying to be quiet, but the door stood open, and Beth could hear suppressed sobs and sniffs and, rising above those sounds, Douggie's splashing and babbling. For a split second she considered walking silently past and closing her bedroom door, pretending she hadn't heard, but then curiosity mixed with some sort of impulse to be kind made her go in.

Fiona was sitting on the low stool beside the bath, dabbing at her eyes and nose with a wodge of tissues. Douggie was moving a little toy boat, red with a blue funnel and a jolly face painted on the prow, through imaginary waves. Fiona's face was pale and blotchy and her eyes were red-rimmed and filled with tears.

'Fiona . . . sorry. Only I heard a noise and thought I'd better come in and see . . .' Beth's voice faded away. She coughed and said more firmly, 'Would you like me to dry Douggie?'

Fiona nodded. 'Would you? I feel so awful. I'd better wash my face, I think. Here's his towel. Thanks so much, Beth. I don't know what's the matter with me. It's the pregnancy, I expect, though I wasn't like this before.'

'Come on, darling,' Beth said to Douggie. 'Time to go and put your pyjamas on now.'

The little boy looked as though he was going to object, then seemed to change his mind.

'Beff dry,' he said, standing up in the bath and sounding quite happy at his change in his routine. 'Want Beff.'

Beth picked Douggie up and as he stood dripping on the bathmat, she wrapped him up in a towel and hugged him to her. 'Yes,' she said. 'I'll dry you. And we'll go and get you ready for bed.' She looked over the wriggling little body in her arms at Fiona who was calmer now, and making an effort to smile.

'Thanks, Beth,' she said. 'Take no notice, really. It all just got too much for me. Let's go to my room.'

Fiona led the way down the corridor and held the door open.

'It's a bit of a mess, I'm afraid,' she said. 'I haven't felt like tidying it, and Efe gets so cross . . .'

'When I've dressed Douggie,' Beth said, 'I'll give you a hand with putting stuff away.'

She prevented Fiona from saying any more by talking to Douggie in a constant stream of childish chatter. He was so like Efe and so much like Markie that Beth felt as though someone were taking a huge wooden spoon to her feelings and mixing them together. She'd never allowed herself to love this baby wholeheartedly, unwilling to acknowledge the physical evidence of Efe and Fiona's relationship, but now she buried her nose in the soft skin of his neck and wished that this moment of closeness could last.

Beth realized that she no longer knew what she thought about anything. It was hard not to feel sorry for Fiona, but still she couldn't bear to imagine her with Efe, just over there in the double bed, without a sharp pang of jealousy and dislike. The more she tried to turn her mind to other things, the more vivid the pictures became. Think about something else, she said to herself. Talk to Fiona.

'D'you want to talk about it? Whatever's wrong, I mean?' Beth pulled up Douggie's pyjama bottoms. I'm not saying the right thing, she thought. I wish I knew how to do this. I'm useless at it. She'd be much better off talking to almost anyone else.

'I don't know what to say, especially not to you,' Fiona answered. 'I mean, you and Efe are so close. I feel quite jealous sometimes when you're chatting.'

Beth looked so amazed at this revelation that Fiona smiled. 'You didn't know that, did you? I'm sorry. It's not your fault, but I *am* stupid where Efe's concerned. I know that. I expect he'd like me to be a different sort of person, but I can't be.'

'No, I'm sure he wouldn't,' Beth said. 'He's devoted to you. I know he is.'

'Has he said?' Fiona asked, and Beth could hear the desperation in her voice. She found herself lying without any hesitation.

'Oh, yes,' she said, and then moved away from this untruth at once and on to something which made her feel more honest. 'I've seen the way he looks at you.' I'm such a cow, she thought. I'm not telling her *how* Efe often looks at her, as though she's a complete fool. Fiona seemed visibly to brighten at these words.

'I do try, you know. To do what he wants me to do. I try all the time.'

'Maybe you shouldn't,' Beth said, taking Douggie on to her lap and cuddling him as she spoke. 'Maybe you should assert yourself more.'

Fiona's eyes widened. 'I daren't,' she said. 'He gets so angry if anyone disagrees with him. Look.'

She pushed her sleeve back, up above her elbow, and held out her arm for Beth to examine. There were bruises on the white skin, blue marks of fingers digging into flesh. Efe's fingers on his wife's skin. Efe, being angry and showing it. An Efe she didn't want to know about. She was shocked and revolted, but amazingly not completely surprised at this evidence of brutality. Surely she ought to have been astonished?

She swallowed and said to Fiona, 'You should tell someone. He shouldn't be allowed to do this to you.'

'He lost his temper. He apologized straight away, really. He was terribly, terribly sorry. Really. I'm only showing you because you suggested I should stand up to him. It's just easier to agree, that's all.'

Beth stroked Douggie's hair. 'Has he ever hurt you before? Tell me, Fiona. I won't tell a soul, promise.'

Fiona nodded. 'Once or twice. It's always my fault. And he's always sorry. It doesn't mean he doesn't love me. That's what he tells me, over and over. It doesn't mean that.'

'No, of course not,' Beth said, feeling nauseous. She stood up. What could she say? You must never, ever put up with it? You must leave him? Suddenly, she wanted to be alone in her room, to think. I must be as stupid as Fiona, she told herself, if knowing that Efe is capable of such behaviour doesn't make me think of him differently.

'I must go and get ready for dinner now, Fiona,' she said. 'Will you be okay?'

'Yes, of course I will, Beth. Thanks so much for helping with Douggie. Everything just gets too much, all of a sudden, you know.'

'Of course I do,' Beth said. She went over to Fiona and kissed her on the cheek. 'You look after yourself.'

She glanced at the dressing-table as she spoke. What caught her eye was a photograph in a leather frame, which Fiona must have brought with her and put up next to her make-up. It showed them being a family, her and Efe and Douggie. The little boy was on his father's shoulders and grabbing at his hair. Fiona was looking up at them both, with her hair blowing across her face. She looked radiant. They were walking down a beach somewhere with nothing but blue skies behind them.

Late afternoon sunlight made diamond shapes on the raspberry-pink carpet. Leonora's bedroom was silent apart from a purring hum coming from Bertie the cat. He'd followed his mistress upstairs and was now curled up beside her on the bed with one paw resting in a proprietorial manner on her thigh. Leonora lay with her eyes closed, taking stock. That was what she called it to herself, and giving it this rather business-like name made her seem less like an old lady resting before dinner and more like a tycoon assessing the events of a day in the hub of an enormous business empire. Willow Court couldn't be called that, of course, but she did increasingly feel like a juggler, keeping her eye on several coloured balls flying through the air, making sure not one of them fell to the ground.

Her success as a juggler, she often thought, lay in not taking any notice of matters that did not concern her; things like the sound of someone crying which she'd heard before she lay down. She knew the acoustics of the house and whoever it was was in the bathroom, and because Leonora was aware at the same time of a child chattering away, she deduced that it must be Fiona in tears. Well, that was to be expected. She was pregnant, and Leonora remembered very clearly how weepy she'd been when she was carrying Rilla. Her first pregnancy had been bliss from start to finish, but that was probably unusual, she now realized. And Fiona had to deal with Efe. It would take a woman of considerably more intelligence than Fiona had so far displayed to be able to cope with him. He was, in all probability, like a bear with a sore head because of her own firmness about the pictures. He'd call it 'obstinacy' of course, but that was Efe all over. He couldn't bear not getting his own way, and in this he resembled his namesake, Leonora's own father. You needed to have your wits about you to deal with men like that. I knew how to and Fiona doesn't and that's all there is to it, Leonora thought. Efe's marriage was not, she felt, her business. She turned her attention to other matters.

She began by ticking a mental checklist of things that should have been done in relation to Sunday's party and every one of them had been. She congratulated herself on the way the marquee had been erected successfully and without fuss. It looked wonderful already, with the lights in place and the lining falling smooth and pale green from the central point, just like a circus tent only smaller. They'd started putting up the decorations, and she'd taken in the sight of what seemed like an army of young people swarming up to the roof of the marquee on ladders with a growing feeling of satisfaction and pleasure. Tomorrow the chairs and tables were arriving and the final touches would be added: flowers, and pale green tablecloths to match the lining of the tent. Leonora suspected that perhaps when you were seventy-five you ought not to be feeling this rising thrill at the idea of a party but she couldn't help it.

It's because my birthday parties when I was a child weren't anything to speak of, she thought. Ethan and Maude didn't have the knack. There was always an atmosphere of constraint about such occasions when she was very young, the notion that you had to keep things under control so as not to disturb Daddy in any way. Nanny Mouse and the other servants were often in charge, and Leonora felt retrospectively resentful. Surely her mother, at least, could have made the effort to come into the nursery. However shy she was, however much she hated appearing in public, being there for your daughter's birthday was a mother's duty.

Birthday parties seemed to stop after Maude's death, although Leonora could still recall that particular summer because she'd fallen ill and missed her birthday altogether. She'd made quite sure, when Gwen and Rilla were young, to give them parties they'd remember for ever. Efe and Alex and Chloë too; they'd had good times under her roof.

Juggling. There were other things to consider. Rilla seemed to be growing more and more friendly with Sean Everard. Perhaps she was getting into the relationship rather too quickly. Surely at her age she ought to be a bit more dignified? Leonora resolved to have a word with her later. She'd been surprised to find herself less irritated by her younger daughter than she sometimes was, maybe because Rilla was trying to impress Sean. Certainly she appeared quieter and more ladylike than usual, and hadn't displayed too much of what Leonora thought of as her Bohemian side. I must, she thought, be grateful for small mercies, and it's also possible that she's making a special effort to please me.

Chloë, Leonora was sure, was plotting something. Alex was nowhere to be seen for most of the time, but there was nothing unusual about that. Gwen and James were busy, busy, busy with all the domestic arrangements and Efe, well, she herself had rather spoiled his weekend. It couldn't be helped. She shouldn't have mentioned what she'd done to help him in the past, though. It was a mistake to break her promise; not like her at all. At the time, she'd been quite convinced that what she'd said was for the best, but now she was not so sure.

For a moment, as she lay on the bed and let the events of the day drift through her mind, she wondered why it was that she was so set against Efe's plan. Wouldn't it be sensible to take this oportunity of making Ethan Walsh even better known? He deserved to be, she knew that, but there was her father's will and the fact that she had promised him the paintings would never leave Willow Court. Other people might find it easy to make light of promises, but not me, Leonora thought. I keep my word, she said to herself, and then, remembering her conversation with Efe, she blushed. Well, I keep my promises most of the time; ninety-nine per cent of the time; certainly more than most other people. Still, there was a part of her (only a tiny part, naturally, but something) which rather regretted that she would never be photographed at the opening of a dazzling new museum in Ethan Walsh's name.

Bertie moved himself into a more comfortable posture, taking the opportunity to lick his back paws before he settled. Leonora stroked his head as he rearranged himself on the duvet, and thought of all the guests who would be coming to Willow Court on Sunday. One of them was the son of Jeremy Bland, the man who'd helped her so much with the paintings and what to do about them, after Ethan's death. The only person, she thought sadly, who won't be here is my beloved Peter. Rage at the unfairness of this swept over her suddenly and she closed her eyes. Peter. She tried not to think about him too often, but now she allowed herself to remember everything.

# June 1948 – March 1954

Leonora woke up very early on the day after her wedding. The sky was already light, the birds were singing from every tree in the drive and she was a different person from the one who'd gone to bed last night. She turned to look at Peter's head on the pillow next to her own and wondered how it was possible to be so close to another human being and still find them mysterious. Peter awake, Peter talking to her, or kissing her she could say she knew, but this sleeping man, whose white shoulder was within inches of her own; whose red-brown hair fell over his forehead as he slept and made him look much younger than he did with his eyes open, well, he was someone altogether strange and wonderful. She wanted to put a hand out and stroke his face. She wanted him to wake up and fold her body in his arms as he'd done last night.

She smiled to think how Nanny Mouse had tried – and completely failed – to tell her about what would happen when her new husband took her into bed. Leonora was the first of her contemporaries to get married. She and her friends had discussed sex often, even though none of them spoke as frankly as Leonora would have wished. Not one of us, she thought, had any very clear idea of what to expect, that's the trouble. We were all woefully inexperienced. The notion of the enormous importance of the act, and the transcendent bliss that awaited those who managed to work out what to do when first in bed with a man came from films and books. Detailed information, on the other hand, *practical* information, was much harder to find.

Nanny Mouse might have had some adventures of an amorous kind in her youth, but it was obvious to Leonora that her knowledge of the subject was hazy in the extreme.

'I think I have to mention these matters,' she'd said a few days before the wedding. 'I wish that your poor mother had lived and been able to talk to you about the duties of a wife.' Her head was turned to examine the piece of darning she was engaged in and she was careful not to meet Leonora's gaze as she spoke.

'I love Peter, Nanny.' Leonora tried to help her, tried to suggest that this conversation was quite unnecessary, really, but Nanny Mouse went doggedly on.

'Men have certain needs, dear. It's a wife's duty to submit to those needs, and I believe at first the act itself can be quite painful. Though they do say you get used to it.'

Leonora stifled a giggle. 'It's all right, Nanny,' she said. 'I do know all about that. Really.'

This wasn't altogether true, but Nanny Mouse relaxed visibly and even managed to look at Leonora and smile at her.

'Good, dear. I just wanted to make sure you wouldn't be frightened.'

'No, I could never be frightened of Peter. I love him.'

'I think everyone agrees that love is important,' said Nanny Mouse.

At least, Leonora reflected as she lay beside her husband, I wasn't shocked by the naked body of a man. There were advantages to growing up surrounded by books full of lavish reproductions of Hellenistic and Renaissance sculpture: you knew what everything looked like. She closed her eyes and thought of Peter, standing undressed in front of her for the first time. Perhaps if you weren't expecting it at all, the sight might be a little surprising! She hadn't had time even to think, and she was grateful for that.

Everything had happened both too quickly for her to be aware of any conscious thought, and also so slowly that she thought the world must have stopped turning. Perhaps she had a special talent for love because she'd felt no pain, or perhaps the blinding, breathless flood of feeling between her legs, and all over her – her skin, her hair, every nerve-ending – was what other people thought of as hurting. I didn't, Leonora thought. I don't.

For what seemed like hours, Peter had breathed into her hair, kissed her all over, touched her, spoken words into her ear that warmed and melted her. She'd never realized how close two bodies could be. One flesh. That was what they had become and that part of the one flesh that was entirely Leonora longed for those feelings all over again.

She turned her head to see whether Peter was awake yet, but he wasn't. His eyelids were pale blue and she could see veins in his forehead she'd never noticed before. She wanted to put out her hand and touch him, draw him to her, but she closed her eyes instead. If I go to sleep again, then he'll wake me with a kiss. I shall be like Sleeping Beauty.

Something like a half-sleep came to her and the words from yesterday's ceremony sounded in her head, weirdly entwined with those of the funeral service. *Who gives this woman . . . to love and to cherish . . . ashes to ashes . . . in sure and certain hope of the resurrection . . . let no man put asunder.*

When I'm old, Leonora thought, it'll be a story I can tell. How my father died on the eve of my planned wedding day. It was now three full weeks since his death, and still Leonora expected to see Ethan every day, and when she first woke up each morning, the fact of his not being at Willow Court any longer came to her like a blow.

Nanny Mouse said he was lucky. His death was badly-timed but painless. He died on the afternoon before Leonora's wedding was to take place. Mrs Darting, the cook-housekeeper, who'd brought the tea in at four o'clock, found him slumped in his favourite armchair. She'd just made brandy-snaps, which her father particularly liked. His newspaper had fallen on to the carpet at his feet. The doctor said it must have been a heart-attack, and he kept repeating, 'He won't have known what happened at all. All done in an instant.'

Leonora knew that this was meant to comfort her, but couldn't help feeling cheated of a farewell from her father. She had wept and wept, and felt ashamed that at least a part of her grief was mingled with anger at Ethan Walsh for spoiling her wedding. The church was booked; the strawberries heaped high in the kitchen ready for the celebratory lunch, and now everything would have to be rearranged. Guests would have to be warned to expect mourning rather than rejoicing. She herself would have to wear her dreary black suit and a hat instead of the dress that was hanging in her wardrobe, shrouded in muslin – white satin in the style they called the New Look; wide-skirted, ankle-length and with the tight bodice embroidered with tiny seed pearls.

'Never mind, darling,' Peter said. 'We'll have the wedding in a few weeks. You will be just as beautiful then. I'm happy to wait for you.'

And now here she was, exactly three weeks later, and she was married. The wedding, because she was still partly in mourning, was a quieter affair than she'd planned, but she had worn the dress and her friends had been there to celebrate.

With Peter's help, she'd begun to change things at Willow Court as soon as her father was buried. Mr Edmunds, the family lawyer, had explained about the money. She'd never paid much attention to such things while Ethan was alive, but now Peter helped her to understand matters she'd previously dismissed as boring, like investments and income. She was surprised to find that she was wealthy, even though, as Peter said, 'You must have known that you'd be inheriting all your parents' money and property.'

She *had* known, but the knowledge had never meant anything until now, when the money could be used to make Willow Court beautiful. There hadn't been time yet for renovations or decorating, but they'd talked and talked about the house and how they would take down the dowdy old curtains and put up new ones, and paint the rooms in pale pastel colours and re-paper the nursery and buy Turkish rugs and have new parquet laid on some of the floors, and replace some of the black and white tiles in the hall that had cracked over the years. Their plans were ambitious and thinking about them moved Leonora's mind away from the sadness, which was all mixed in with her happiness.

For the first time since Willow Court had stopped being a convalescent home for wounded soldiers, music was being played. As soon as Peter came into the house, he put a record on the gramophone in the drawing-room. Glenn Miller, Duke Ellington, Lester Young, Billie Holiday, and wonderful Louis Armstrong: they were the ones she loved best. The names on the labels were unfamiliar at first, but the melodies lodged in Leonora's mind and heart. 'String of Pearls', 'Mood Indigo', 'The Man I Love', and 'I Can't Give You Anything But Love,' the song that Peter used to sing to her, imitating Armstrong's gravelly voice very badly indeed and making her laugh.

The garden was already being improved. For the first few days after Ethan's death, Leonora found that working with plants and earth was a comfort. Because she'd always associated gardening with her mother, she didn't constantly hear her father's voice as she dug and weeded and looked at catalogues to choose new shrubs and flowers to order. She'd decided some time ago to undertake the redesign of the Quiet Garden. She would care for the neglected espaliered trees, and intended to uproot some of the less interesting things growing in the borders and restock them with azaleas and Japanese quinces and pink and white peonies.

Sometimes, when Peter was at work, or in town seeing to all the financial and legal arrangements, Leonora sat on the bench under the magnolia tree with Nanny Mouse, who had known Ethan even longer than she had. She said, 'It's funny, Nanny. Daddy wasn't the chattiest person in the world, and yet I feel as though I can hear his voice in my ear all the time.'

'Well, dear, he hadn't been himself for some while, had he? Not really. He wasn't the man he used to be.'

That was true. Since the end of the war, Ethan Walsh had grown increasingly moody and distant, and in the months leading up to his death, he'd become a brooding, silent presence in the house. During the winter, he would sit for hours staring at the fire, and in summer he walked for miles round and round the lake.

'I know,' Leonora answered. 'But I miss him, because he's always been there, all my life and . . .' She didn't know how to continue. He's my father, she wanted to say. My only family, and now he's gone, and there's me and no one else.

'You won't be on your own for long, dear,' Nanny Mouse said soothingly. 'You'll have a husband soon and children of your own. A proper family.'

'Wake up, my love,' said a voice in Leonora's ear. 'Wake up, Mrs Simmonds.'

'I've been awake for ages,' Leonora whispered. 'I've been thinking about all sorts of things and waiting for you to wake up.'

'What were you thinking about? Tell me.'

He started to kiss her then, and she wanted to say *I can't remember. I can't remember anything. You're the only thing I can think of. Just you.* But the words were starting to slip and slide about in her head and soon she had no thoughts that could properly be called thoughts at all.

Gwendolen Elizabeth Simmonds was born in her parents' bedroom at Willow Court on 7th February, 1952. King George VI had died the day before the birth, and all the papers carried photographs of the new Queen, who used to be Princess Elizabeth, together with her mother and grandmother, wearing black and heavily veiled at the King's funeral. Leonora's labour had only lasted for six hours and, even though she'd been in agony and shrieking like a banshee for what seemed to her like years, the midwife told her she'd had an easy time of it, and it was perfectly true that within minutes of the birth, every bit of pain seemed to have been banished and forgotten in the joy of meeting the daughter that she and Peter together had made.

The whole country was feeling sad, but Leonora and Peter were happier than they'd ever been and a little guilty at their own joy. Calling their baby after the new queen, even only as a second name, was their way of showing how sorry they were to lose the King, who'd been much too young to die.

Gwendolen's first name honoured Peter's late grandmother. Leonora had thought that perhaps she would name the baby after her own mother, but then they'd both agreed that, thanks to Tennyson, Maude sounded too old-fashioned and Victorian.

Towards the end of her pregnancy, Leonora had worried about being able to love the child when it was born. She and Peter were so bound up in one another that it seemed to her anyone else coming into their lives was sure to receive short rations.

They'd had three years together, and Leonora could truly say that she loved Peter more than she did when they'd first married. Not only that, but they still found it hard to restrain their desire. Leonora discovered almost as soon as she became a wife that the reticence which (combined with ignorance) had kept her friends from talking freely about sex disappeared as soon as they were married.

These days, everyone seemed quite happy to share the details of their personal lives. Bunny, who was married a month after Leonora, and who had given birth to her first child within a year, confessed to Leonora that quite often her mind was on other matters while she was, in her words, 'at it.'

'Or rather,' she said, only last week, when she'd come to tea 'while Nigel's at it, really. I don't seem to be *there*, to be quite frank.

D'you know what I mean? There he is, poor darling, going at it hammer and tongs, and I'm miles away, working out some domestic thing or another, like whether we'll have roast chicken for dinner when the Colonel and his wife come round on Wednesday. I can never stop myself from seeing it all from someone else's point of view. Imagine! It's such a ludicrous posture, when all's said and done. Don't you agree?' She smiled brightly and helped herself to another biscuit.

Leonora sat quietly when Bunny or one of her other friends went on in this vein. They all did, and she wondered sometimes whether it was just a pretence, and whether they said such things because they were ashamed to confess their real feelings. She herself was always noncommittal. She smiled back at Bunny and said almost nothing and made every effort to change the subject to something she found easier to discuss.

There were no words with which she could have expressed what she felt for Peter; no way of telling anyone of the transformation that overcame both of them when they were alone. How they turned from normal, quite ordinary people who went to work in a firm of insurance brokers, or managed the house and estate, or oversaw the decoration of the nursery, or had dinner and tea with their friends and drank gin and tonic and cups of tea, into panting, heedless creatures who bit and sucked and kissed every part of each other's bodies for hours and yet ended up wanting only more and more of one another. Their bed was a separate universe where none of the daily rules applied and where even speech was unrecognizable; where words and sentences fractured and splintered into a private, intimate language of their own.

Now here was this tiny creature with her waving pink fingers and her tightly-shut eyes and Leonora looked down at her and realized that the love she felt for this baby was different from anything she had ever felt before, but, miraculously, no less strong. Peter, she could see, was enchanted by his daughter and sat beside the bed staring at her, hardly able to speak.

'She's the most beautiful baby in the whole world,' he said, and immediately grinned. 'I bet every father says that, but it's true in this case. She looks just like you.'

'She looks like a baby,' Leonora said, gazing at her daughter, and literally feeling love flow into every part of her in exactly the same way as the milk was coming into her breasts. She glanced from Peter to Gwendolen and the thought crossed her mind that if she were to stop breathing now, at this very moment, she'd die completely and totally happy.

'I'm so happy, my precious darling,' Peter said. 'I love you both so much.'

Leonora's eyes filled with tears. 'I'm sorry,' she said. 'I love you both too, and I don't mean to be crying. I'm happy, too, truly. Nanny Mouse says that new mothers cry all the time.'

Peter leaned over the baby and kissed Leonora on the mouth. 'You're my darlings. I couldn't possibly love you more than I do, and now Gwendolen's going to be the most adored baby in the world.'

Leonora couldn't find any words to express what she wanted to say. She closed her eyes and leaned back against the heaped-up pillows.

Gwendolen Elizabeth soon became Gwen. She was a most untroublesome baby. She loved sleeping; she never stopped smiling; she didn't mind Nanny Mouse looking after her when her mother was otherwise occupied; she murmured and burbled at her father whenever he picked her up, and everyone agreed that she was the best-tempered child they'd ever seen. Bunny and Nigel's little boy, whose name was Richard, was a different sort of creature altogether and Leonora rather dreaded the times when Bunny came to tea, bringing her son, as she put it, 'to play'. Richard never did play, not really, and in any case Gwen was much too little to play with.

The work on Willow Court went on and on, and neither Leonora nor Peter ever tired of making things more beautiful. One day in May, just before the Coronation, Peter said, 'It's time now, darling. Let's go up to the studio and bring all the paintings down. Let's hang them everywhere.'

At first, Leonora didn't know what she felt about seeing her father's pictures all over the house, but after thinking about it for a while, she knew she would be happy to have them around her again.

'It's taken me a bit of time to realize it,' she said to Peter at dinner, 'but Willow Court didn't feel right without them, did it? And they deserve to be seen, don't they?'

Peter picked up his glass and took a sip of wine.

'Actually,' he said. 'I think it's a pity we can't sell just a few. There was that chap, don't you remember? The one who came to see you after Ethan died? He said they were very valuable, didn't he? He wanted to pay you a great deal of money, as I recall, for that portrait of you in the lilac dress.'

'I'm not allowed to, Peter. You know that. Daddy's will made that quite clear. The paintings are to stay at Willow Court.'

Peter knew very well why she couldn't sell the paintings. He understood better than she did the complicated legal clauses which meant that her children would have no claim on the estate if the paintings were sold. It was all too confusing, but she'd never made the effort to understand the detail for the simple reason that she had no intention whatsoever of selling the pictures her father had created. They were part of him, the very best part, and now that she could see them again, she realized how much she loved them. How much she would enjoy looking at them every day.

'I want to remember Daddy as he was when he made them, and to try and forget what he'd become towards the end of his life. Anyway, I gave him my word.'

She thought about her father while Peter poured the coffee. Being a widower hadn't suited him. He'd stopped painting altogether, and nothing Leonora said or did made any difference. She used to have to choose her moment carefully if she wanted to talk to him about this. If the timing was wrong, he was quite capable of flying into a black rage, which meant that he retired to his bedroom with the brandy bottle and everyone had to tiptoe round the house and pray that he wouldn't come out into the corridors to storm and rage at them.

When the sun came out: that was the best time for conversation. Walking in the Quiet Garden, sitting under the magnolia tree, Leonora would sometimes dare to ask gently, 'Wouldn't this make a painting, Daddy? Isn't it beautiful?'

'Sentimental nonsense, flowers,' he'd answer. 'Not my sort of thing. Not now.'

'But the waterlily pictures, Daddy! And the one with the roses on the table. You do paint flowers so beautifully. And everyone loves them. We could make a lot of money you know, if you sold some of them.'

A mistake. It was always a mistake to mention selling the canvases. He father frowned, but on this occasion, all he said was, 'Over my dead body. The pictures stay here, at Willow Court.' Suddenly, he leaned forward and stared into Leonora's eyes. 'Promise me, Leonora,' he said. 'Promise me they'll never be sold. Not even when I'm dead. Promise.'

And I did promise, Leonora thought. I had to. Daddy always got his way and here he was still getting it, more than four years after his death. She said to Peter, 'I kept that man's card. The man from the gallery. He left it and I put it somewhere. I shall telephone him, and ask his advice. His name is Jeremy Bland. I'll ask him down to have a look and tell me what he thinks of the paintings. We can make money from them, don't you think? We might let the public into Willow Court to see them. If they're as good as all that, everyone will be longing to come, won't they?'

'But would you want every Tom, Dick and Harry traipsing round the house? Think of the work! The mud they'll tread into the carpets. I don't know if I think it's such a good idea, darling. I don't really.'

'Nonsense, Peter! We'd become famous. You'd like that, wouldn't you? We don't have to open the house every day, either. We can choose when we let people in. Bunny's cousin knows someone who works for the *Tatler*. I'll telephone him and I'm sure he'll oblige. Imagine, there might be photographs of us in a magazine! Or an article perhaps. And I'll get in touch with the Women's Institute and offer Willow Court for their annual Garden Party. Maybe they'll let me give a talk or something about the paintings.'

'Oh, well,' said Peter, 'if it means that much to you, I won't object.'

'You're a darling.' Leonora smiled at him. 'I hadn't realized how much I've missed those pictures. Daddy would be pleased, wouldn't he? He'd have loved the idea of people walking round admiring his handiwork. I shall telephone Mr Bland once we've hung everything in a good place.'

After several hours of back-breaking labour, it was over. The paintings had been brought downstairs from the studio to the dining-room. Tyler and his two young assistants came in from the garden to help move things around. Gwen's playpen had been positioned in the hall and she was gazing round at everything with great interest. Peter was at the office, but Nanny Mouse was there to help matters along. The canvases were stacked against the wall.

'Just till we can sort out what goes where,' Leonora said. 'I've been trying to remember where things used to be. Nanny, you must remember, surely? There were pictures all along the corridor, upstairs, weren't there?'

'Yes, yes there were. I expect I might recognize some of them if I see them again, though to tell you the truth, after a bit you don't notice things on walls, do you? I don't, I'm sure.'

Leonora shivered suddenly. For what was probably only a split second, something that might have been a dream she'd once had (when?) passed into her mind and then out of it again before she'd had a chance to examine it. Herself running down the hall staircase, and the pictures looming above her, enormous, much larger than they were in real life. A portrait of someone she didn't recognize – someone with a hat on, shadowing their face. A landscape showing the drive as it was at this very moment, with every leaf on the scarlet oaks the colour of fresh blood, that was all she could remember clearly, but she was left with a sense of there being something else, something just out of sight that she might catch a glimpse of – but it was gone and all that was left was unease of some kind. Leonora shook her head to dispel such thoughts and said to Nanny Mouse, 'I must have walked past all these pictures a thousand times. It's like seeing old friends again. Here's the blue teapot . . . I love that! Surely between us we can find the same places for most of them, can't we?'

'I wouldn't trust my memory, after all this while,' said Nanny Mouse. 'I think you should just put everything where you think best.'

'It's a very interesting collection, Mrs Simmonds,' said Mr Bland, glancing over Leonora's shoulder at the painting on the wall behind her, a landscape recognizable as the view out of the window next to which she'd hung it. 'And I admire the clever way you've placed some of these pictures so that whoever looks at them sees the original, as it were, beside it.'

Leonora smiled. 'It'll only be a match for part of the year, of course, but I thought it might be amusing.'

'Indeed.' Mr Bland, who had not asked her to call him by his first name, was not much older than she was, but his formal manner and mode of dress kept her at some distance. Today, he was visiting Willow Court to gather some biographical information for a brochure his gallery was eager to produce. At first, Leonora couldn't understand why a dealership which was not strictly representing her father as an artist, not selling his pictures, should be so keen to do this, and she'd asked Mr Bland this question.

'It's the reflected glory,' he'd answered. 'We shall advertise our gallery in its pages of course. Also one never knows what the future may bring, does one? Perhaps things may change in relation to these pictures.'

'It's most unlikely,' said Leonora. 'The terms of my father's will are quite clear.'

They went into the small drawing-room, where Mr Bland took out a notebook and began to question her as she poured tea from the blue pot that was the subject of what he had confessed was one of the Ethan Walsh paintings he loved best.

'Your father was one of the generation of artists working just before and just after the First World War,' he said, and Leonora nodded.

'He died four years ago, I believe?'

Leonora smiled. 'Yes, and it was what they call an easy death, but of course death is never easy, is it? Certainly not for the people who are left behind.'

'Please accept my condolences,' Mr Bland said quietly.

Leonora looked at him. 'Thank you. My father's death was not only sad, it was also very inconvenient. It happened on the eve of my wedding.'

'How very sad!' Mr Bland managed to take a bite from one of the scones Mrs Darting had provided, while balancing his notebook on his knees. 'But I believe there's no work of his dated later than 1935. This means that for the last thirteen years of his life he did no painting at all. Is that correct?'

'Quite correct, I'm afraid,' said Leonora. 'My mother died in 1935 and he . . . well, he was never quite himself again, really.'

'Nevertheless, it is a considerable body of work. There are fifty-four canvases, and several dozen sketches and watercolours. A great deal more than many artists have left us. And I'm quite sure that people will be fascinated to come and see them. An added attraction . . .' he smiled at Leonora '. . . will be your good self, of course, *in situ* as it were. Visitors will enjoy meeting the original of the youthful portraits.'

Leonora smiled. 'I thought that I would look forward to that,' she said. 'But I find that I'm a little nervous after all. Will I know what to say? Perhaps there's someone who might do it better than I could? Who'd know more?'

'Probably,' Mr Bland agreed. 'But if I may say so, you are Willow Court's greatest asset. Your presence would make a visit to see these pictures something very special indeed.'

Leonora said, 'I expect I shall enjoy it really, but I do hope there won't be too many people to talk to at any one time. I don't think I'd be too happy coping with droves of visitors. Also, I have to consider my husband and daughter. This is their house too, of course.'

'Of course it is. Then we must make sure that no droves come to trouble you or your family, dear lady!' said Mr Bland. For someone as staid as he was, Leonora thought, he was looking rather excited. 'We will limit the numbers. It will make the whole thing more . . . exclusive. The general public will have to telephone our gallery in advance and make a booking for the days on which Willow Court is open. And in my opinion, there should not be too many of these. A certain difficulty, a certain rarity value will do nothing but good, I think.'

'I agree,' said Leonora, much more relaxed now that she knew she wouldn't have to spend every single day pointing out the beauty of Ethan Walsh's works to masses and masses of people. Showing small groups around the house at intervals throughout the year was a different matter altogether. 'I shall enjoy it. I think.'

Mr Bland stood up. 'It will be a pleasure to deal with the details for you, Mrs Simmonds.'

'Oh, Leonora, please,' she said. 'If we are to be such close associates.'

'I'm honoured,' said Mr Bland. 'And you must call me Jeremy.'

Later, she and Nanny Mouse would laugh as she described the blush that had risen from the stiff collar of Mr Bland's shirt and up into the roots of his greying hair.

'I'm going to be a proper business woman, Nanny!' Leonora said. 'Isn't that thrilling?'

'Most exciting, dear,' said Nanny, busy stitching smocking on to the bodice of a pretty dress for Gwen. 'Willow Court will be quite the centre of attention, won't it?'

Leonora and Mr Bland – Jeremy – had chosen Thursdays as Open Day at Willow Court. That would be throughout the year, and during the summer months, Tuesdays would be added as well. There might also be the occasional weekend but that was subject to what Jeremy called 'your personal availability'.

'He imagines we live a life of pleasure and idleness, Nanny,' she said. 'You know, guests every weekend, or else gadding about to parties and what not. When we're such homebodies, really. He doesn't realize that we prefer our own company to anyone else's.'

Nanny Mouse said nothing but privately thought Mr Bland was a clever gentleman who knew Leonora rather better than she did herself. It was quite true that she and Mr Peter were devoted, but they were also forever entertaining and going about to other people's houses. A life of pleasure was exactly the right term for it, in her opinion.

'Look! Look, Gwen, darling!' Leonora pointed at the tiny screen of the television where a grainy greyish picture of the coach (which she knew was golden in reality) carrying the new Queen back from Westminster Abbey was partly visible through what looked like a snowstorm. It wasn't really a snowstorm, just a rather unclear picture, but still, everyone had gathered in the drawing-room to watch the royal progress.

'Such a shame about the rainy weather!' Bunny said. Richard was on her lap. Gwen was on Leonora's lap, which meant that for the moment, she was safe from the little boy's clumsiness.

'Ween!' Gwen called out, and everyone laughed.

'She talks so well for her age, doesn't she?' Bunny looked less than pleased as she said this. Richard wasn't the most advanced of speakers, and Leonora thought this was probably because he used most of his available talent to go charging about putting people's ornaments in grave danger.

'Yes, it's the new Queen, sweetiepie,' Leonora whispered into her baby's ear. Bunny's attention was fixed on the screen. 'Can you see her crown?'

Gwen nodded gravely.

'It's been quite a day,' said Peter, who had come in from the office specially to watch the ceremony on the television. Nigel was there, too, and the occasion had turned into a party of sorts. It wasn't every day that a monarch was crowned, after all. In the end, though, when the tea things had been cleared away, Bunny and Nigel and Richard went home, and before long, Nanny Mouse took Gwen upstairs to have her bath.

'I know what you're going to say,' Leonora said to Peter, leaning back against the cushions of the sofa.

'No, you don't.'

'I do. You're going to say *peace at last*. Or something along those lines.'

'A good guess, but not quite. I was actually going to say *alone at last!*'

'You sound surprised. We're often alone.'

'Not often enough for me.' He came over to the sofa and sat down next to Leonora and put his arms around her.

'Oh, darling! We're an old married couple. We're certainly much too old to canoodle on a sofa. There's a proper place for such things, you know.'

She didn't mean a word of it. They would be undisturbed for a while, and they were both aware of that, and aware of the special festive atmosphere that had coloured the whole day. They'd had rather a lot of champagne at lunch (*we don't have a Coronation every day, do we?*) and Leonora's head was swimming a little.

All at once, everything was happening very quickly. Her skirt and the lace-trimmed silk slip she wore under it pushed up, and her knickers somehow (how?) on the carpet and Peter making love to her and kissing her hair and the delicious terror that maybe someone would overhear them or see them so that they had to be quick and it was easy to be quick because they couldn't stop, they could never stop, and all the sounds rising in their throats and being stifled, and then nothing but silence broken by panting as though they'd been running for a long time.

Afterwards, they arranged their clothes in silence and lay back against the pillows.

'Time to go and kiss Gwen goodnight, I think,' Peter said at last.

'You go first,' Leonora murmured, her eyes still closed. 'I'll be there in a minute.'

She could have gone with him, but she didn't want to. She wanted to sit on the sofa and remember this time. Remember how full of love she was for him. How heavy her limbs were. How very little she felt like ever getting up and moving again.

'Darling? Darling, can you hear me?' Leonora was speaking as clearly as she could into the telephone. It still struck her as a rather magical invention.

'I can hear you, Leonora,' said Peter. He sounded amused but Leonora was aware that he must have work to do and probably wanted to get on with it but was too kind and loving to tell her so. Never mind, she thought. He'll forget all about that when I tell him the news.

'I wanted you to know at once. I was going to wait till you came home, only Doctor Benyon's just been and I want to tell Nanny Mouse but I can't tell her before I tell you and so I thought I'd telephone. I'm so sorry if I'm disturbed you, my love.'

'Can I guess?' Peter sounded different now. He knows, Leonora thought. He must do. He can hear how happy I am.

'I expect you can. We're going to have another baby. Oh, Peter, I wish you could be here.'

'Darling! Oh, darling, that's the most wonderful news. The very best news. Oh, God, I can't stay here now. I shall comes home. Just give me an hour or so to sort out a problem I'm in the middle of and then I'll be as quick as I can. Oh, Leonora, you're my treasure. You and Gwen. I'll be with you before you know it. May I tell them here? They'll be so delighted. I expect they'll want to drink a toast to you, darling. But I won't be long.'

'Promise?'

'Promise. Kiss kiss.'

'Kiss kiss,' Leonora smiled as she replaced the telephone in its cradle. If anyone could hear us, she thought, they'd think we'd taken leave of our senses. Well, perhaps we have. She looked around and wondered what she should do between now and when Peter arrived. Nanny Mouse had taken Gwen upstairs for her afternoon nap. The September afternoon was warm and sunny. I'll go for a walk, she thought. I'll walk all round the lake and by the time I come back to the house, Peter might be here to greet me.

The trees know that autumn is nearly here, Leonora reflected, even though it's as warm as summertime. The scarlet oaks in the drive were beginning to turn, and there were already red leaves visible among the green. The late roses were good this year, and the hydrangeas better than ever. Most people thought of this shrub as being hyacinth blue but these carried enormous heads of pink and white and mauve flowers.

She walked slowly round the lake, smiling at the swans, and with all her attention focused on the person growing in her womb. She put her hand on her still completely flat stomach and wondered briefly whether the child she was carrying was a boy or a girl. She could never understand why anyone would care about such things. If the child was healthy and happy, that was quite enough. She knew that she was unusual among her friends in enjoying the state of pregnancy. Grace had spent six months, in her own words, 'bent double over the lavatory' and even Bunny hadn't been able to drink coffee and had quite gone off all sorts of other things. Both of them had swollen up, too, like barrage balloons, but when she had been expecting Gwen, no one could tell till she was nearly six months gone.

What time was it? Leonora looked at her watch and began to walk more quickly. She'd been out and daydreaming for over an hour. Even if Peter isn't home yet, she thought, Gwen must have woken up by now and she'll want me. She made her way through the wild garden and then up over the lawn to the terrace. There were two police cars parked near the front door and at first, Leonora looked at them and wondered rather idly (because her mind was on other, more important things) what they could possibly want at Willow Court. She stepped into the hall and saw them, two male police officers and a woman constable, holding their hats in their hands and standing in an unnatural way, it seemed to her, as though they were taking part in a tableau. Still, she would have found an explanation, some reason for them to be there that didn't affect her if it hadn't been for Nanny Mouse. She ran towards Leonora, her face wet with tears she was still shedding, and folded her in her arms, saying, 'Oh, Leonora, Leonora darling. Be brave, my love. Oh, it's so dreadful, my poor darling. Never mind, never mind.'

Leonora felt herself becoming ice cold all over. She pushed Nanny Mouse away rather roughly and part of her wanted to stop and turn round and say sorry, I didn't mean to push you but what's happening and the words stuck in her mouth, which was dry and full of something bitter and she could only make sounds, like a baby.

'Mrs Simmonds,' said the woman constable. 'Please come and sit down, Mrs Simmonds.' She took hold of Leonora's elbow and guided her to a chair. We don't have any chairs in the hall, Leonora thought. They've brought it in specially. She didn't want to sit down. How dare this woman tell her to sit down.

'I don't know why you're here, but if you are prepared to wait a little while, my husband will come home and I'm sure he'll be happy to answer any questions you may wish to ask.'

Behind her, Nanny Mouse uttered a cry, and then immediately stifled it. The most senior of the police officers – you could tell, because he was grey-haired and looked like someone's strict uncle – came to her and gently indicated that she should sit down.

'I'm afraid we have some very bad news, Mrs Simmonds. Very bad news indeed.'

Grief shrouded Leonora like a thick fog, and for days after that terrible afternoon when she'd listened with every appearance of calm to what the police had told her (*driving much too fast . . . a tree . . . instantaneous death*) and then fainted away at the feet of the woman constable, she had spent hours in her bed, weeping and weeping until she felt as though there was not a single bit of moisture left in her whole body. When the tears stopped, when she struggled from her bed, every single thing she laid eyes on filled her with a rage she couldn't contain. She walked for miles, unseeing, round and round the lake. She hid the records that he loved in a box in a corner of the studio. She took the love letters she'd hidden in the dolls' house years before and put them with all the others in the biscuit tin and pushed them into the depths of her bottom drawer. Maybe she would burn them. She couldn't even glance at his handwriting without wanting to burst into tears all over again. Looking at Gwen filled her with pain, because every single thing about the child brought Peter into her mind. It wasn't that she resembled him at all, only that her very presence in the world was a result of their love, their passion, and thinking about that, about Peter's physical body, and contrasting how it used to be with how it was now was literally unbearable, and she felt a howl of anguish rising and rising in her throat, filling her with such agony that the small moans she sometimes found herself uttering seemed ridiculous, inappropriate, not any kind of reflection of how much she was hurting.

Sleep had disappeared from her life. The best she managed every night was lying in their bed (*their bed!*) in a half-doze, her mind alive with memories, her body aching for Peter's touch, her whole being raw and sore as though someone had taken a knife to her skin and removed it. She lay staring at the ceiling, calling Peter's name in her head, and maybe aloud, and pushing aside any help from anyone else.

Nanny Mouse tried. She cajoled and soothed and stroked Leonora's brow with a cool damp cloth after hours of tears had turned her into a red-eyed, swollen-faced creature, who bore less and less resemblance to the elegant Mrs Simmonds. In the end, that was how Nanny Mouse made her pull herself together sufficiently to attend the funeral.

'Leonora, dear, it's Peter's funeral tomorrow morning. I've taken out your black suit and brushed it, and the hat with the veil. But now, you know, you will have to take yourself in hand a little.'

'How dare you, Nanny? Take myself in hand . . . how can you speak of such things? Don't you realize . . . don't you realize exactly what I've lost? Everything. My whole life, my whole happiness, everything.'

'Nonsense,' said Nanny Mouse. 'I will overlook what you've just said, because of course you're not yourself, Leonora. But I would remind you that you are a mother. Gwen needs you. She will need you even more now that she is fatherless, poor little thing.'

Leonora stared at Nanny Mouse and wondered whether to shriek and tear her own hair out or shout obscenities at this stupid, stupid woman who was telling her to cheer up and pull herself together when she knew, she just knew, that she would never, ever be able to face the world again. I don't have to, she suddenly thought. I can die. I can take pills with a lot of whisky and never wake up again ever. She closed her eyes and considered this for a moment but that voice, that Nanny voice that had been in her ears since the day she was born, went on speaking. It said, 'I know that you would never do anything foolish. You know, after all, better than anyone, what it is for a girl to grow up without a mother. And think of little Gwen, and how much she loves you. And think of what Peter would say if he knew you'd abandoned his daughter.'

It was that possessive pronoun that brought her to her senses. Gwen was indeed Peter's daughter. Leonora opened her eyes and sniffed and said, 'Thank you, Nanny. I will have a bath now. And yes, I will be perfectly all right for the funeral. I shan't disgrace you. Or Peter.'

Saying his name aloud – was this the very first time she had done so since his death? – was torture, but she gritted her teeth and continued, 'I wish I'd never told him. I wish I'd waited. Oh, God, it's too late to wish anything, but I do because if it hadn't been for me telling him . . .'

'Telling him what, dear?' Nanny Mouse looked genuinely puzzled and Leonora smiled.

'You didn't guess. I thought you might have guessed. I'm pregnant again. I'm going to have a baby next March. I'd phoned Peter to tell him. That was why he was hurrying home. I think he died because of that. Oh, Nanny, Nanny what will I do without him? How will I manage?'

'You will manage by getting through one day at a time. You

mustn't think of the future. And you must try not to think of the past either. Not yet. There'll be time for that later. Let's just get through the funeral.'

The small church at the top of the hill that overlooked the lake at Willow Court was full for Peter's funeral. All the friends they had made in the area since their wedding day, all his colleagues from work, and from his days in the army crowded into the pews. Leonora had left Gwen in the care of Libby, a young girl from the village who often came in to help when things were, in Nanny Mouse's words, 'at sixes and sevens'. Nanny Mouse herself, in her best black dress with a black felt hat pulled well down over her hair, stood beside Leonora, ready to catch her if she should faint. She was, after all, nearly three months pregnant.

Leonora had helped herself to some Dutch courage before the ceremony. A quick swig from the decanter that held the whisky and she felt a little better. A little less shaky. If Nanny Mouse finds out, she thought, she'll be cross. It's not good for you in your condition, she would say. And I couldn't say what I want to say, not to her and not to anyone. I wouldn't mind anything that happened to me. I don't want this baby. This baby made Peter die. I don't want it. I don't want to have it. I wish it would die. There, she thought, I've said it, even if I've only said it to myself. I wish it would go away and never be born. Maybe it won't. Maybe I'll have a miscarriage. Lots of people do, so why not me? I'll pray for one while I'm in the church. Oh, God, no. What am I saying? My poor little baby! Oh, Peter, don't listen to me. I'm not myself. I'm not. I'm mad with grief, and saying things and thinking things no one should ever think. But how I wish I'd waited to tell you. You would have driven home slowly. You'd still be alive, and so would I.

The words of the funeral service went past her ears like blown leaves. She followed the coffin out to the place under the yew trees where a hole was waiting. Peter in there. She bit her lips till she tasted blood. The veil, the black veil on her hat, was down and covered her face a little but she knew that they were all looking at her; watching her to see how she stood up; how brave she was. I'm not brave, she wanted to shout. I want to die too. I want to jump in and have earth filling my mouth and covering me up and then I'd never have to suffer ever again. Gwen, she thought. Think of Gwen. Think of her little hands, her voice, think of how much Peter loved her and how angry he'd be if he knew you'd left her. She closed her eyes. Let it be finished, she said to herself, as the vicar's voice blew away in the wind . . . *all flesh is as grass . . . dust to dust*. Oh, Peter, my darling. Where have you gone?

Leonora gave birth to her second daughter on a wild day in March 1954. The labour was long and painful, and by the time it was over and her baby was placed in her arms, she was exhausted. She looked down at a red-faced, crumpled creature wrapped up in a blanket, and began to cry, bitter tears of grief and complete weariness.

'What a bonny baby,' said the midwife. 'Have you thought of a name for her?'

'Not really,' said Leonora. 'I'm sure I'll think of something.'

Nanny Mouse brought Gwen to see her sister.

'Babba!' said Gwen, and put out a finger to stroke the fine reddish hairs on the baby's head.

Leonora closed her eyes and wished she never had to open them again. It was now seven months since Peter's death and everyone thought she ought to have got over it to some extent by now. She'd fallen in with what was required of her by her friends and Nanny Mouse. She'd looked after Gwen and read her stories and given her her own little patch of earth to dig in the garden and she'd waited for the arrival of her second child, all the while filled with white anger and resentment that she wasn't allowed to express.

Now she considered the baby and wondered what to name it. The doctor she'd consulted to help her with her grief, because she hadn't wanted to go to Dr Benyon, had been a kindly man called Cyril Rotherspoon, with a practice in Swindon. She'd only been to see him twice, because she realized that all she could do about the grief was live through it, but now he came into her mind. Why not, she thought. I don't want to call her anything, so it'll do. It's unusual at least. *Cyrilla*. It sounds like the heroine of a romance. The baby started to rootle around for the breast, and Leonora sighed, and allowed the greedy mouth to fasten on her nipple. There was nothing to be done about it. She was weeping all over again. She felt as though her sorrow would go on for ever.

❧

Sean stared down at the list in front of him and tried hard to concentrate. He'd spent hours before the shooting started at Willow Court walking through the rooms and deciding which of the canvases fell into the category of 'absolute musts'. Ethan Walsh hadn't been the most prolific of painters but still, there were at least fifty works on the walls here, to say nothing of the drawings, sketches and unfinished pieces up in the studio. Sean knew the pictures so well by now that their titles alone could bring one into his mind in almost its full glory, and he'd spent days before coming to Willow Court summoning them up at will, working out how he was going to include this one or that one and writing a shooting-script for the programme that would say everything he wanted to say about the artist and his life and work.

The more he learned, the less he actually liked Ethan Walsh. That stuff today about his physical cruelty was interesting, too. I'll have to speak to Leonora about it, he thought, and reluctantly put the inventory of Walsh's works back into its file. Can't rely on Nanny Mouse who's confused for so much of the time, poor thing. He summoned some of his favourite paintings to mind and marvelled at the contrast between what he was getting to know about the character of the artist and the quality of the work. The luminosity, the elegance, the singing colours, and the air of sadness that seemed to pervade even the sunniest of the canvases didn't match the hard, masculine character that was being revealed to him. Well, art was often surprising, and there were plenty of painters around who hadn't behaved themselves at all well.

Sean was conscious of having to make a particular effort to pay attention to work-related matters. Rilla, he thought, and as soon as he allowed her name to come to the forefront of his mind, he felt himself flooded with the kind of elation he dimly remembered from his teens, when a date with a particular girl would render him tongue-tied with excitement and longing. I haven't felt like this for years, he thought, and he smiled as he acknowledged his resentment at having to go down to the village tonight to eat with the crew.

He stood up and started to undress, ready to take a shower before

191

dinner. I want to be with her all the time, he told himself. What's she doing now? And how soon can I make my excuses and come back here? He thought of the wrought-iron and glass gazebo and of how it would look in the dark. He imagined Rilla waiting for him there, on one of the cane chairs, with her hair down. Would she have her hair down? He wanted to touch it. Would he be able to say all the things that he wanted to say? Maybe a failed marriage and a divorce and all the vaguely unsatisfactory relationships of the last few years would have turned him into a clumsy idiot who didn't know how to segue from gentle flirtation to the next stage and then the next. Through the window he saw the sun low over the trees behind the lake. Roll on, darkness, he thought, and wished that time could somehow speed up till he was with her again. Rilla.

Ever since she was first married, Leonora had always changed for dinner. It was the custom then, though hardly anyone insisted on it these days, but no one who came to Willow Court complained about it. Even the grandchildren, because they'd never known anything else, realized that when they were here she expected them to discard whatever outlandish outfit they'd been mucking around in all day and get into something more acceptable for the evening meal.

Leonora was honest enough to acknowledge that one of the reasons she enjoyed the ritual was because otherwise it would have been perfectly possible for her to go through her entire life dressed only in a series of skirts and trousers worn with either blouses or a jumper depending on the season. And I'm vain, she thought, even at my age. Is that normal? She relished choosing, every night, which of her many dresses she would wear, and with which necklace or brooch and which earrings.

She sat down at her dressing-table, still in her dark blue silk dressing-gown. On the wall to her left hung a framed photograph taken on the occasion of her first formal ball, and whenever she felt particularly elderly and tired, she looked at it to remind herself of the old days, when she'd been what was called a 'bobbydazzler'. The dress looked white in the picture but she remembered clearly that it had really been ice blue. Around her neck were the pearls she still often wore, a present from her father on her eighteenth birthday. And the shoes in the photograph made her smile. They'd still have been the height of fashion if she'd worn them today. And the tiara was beautiful but no one wore such things now, which was a great shame in her opinion. She'd been very proud of hers, which had been Maude's and now lay in a bank vault in town. She turned her thoughts back to the immediate problem of tonight's outfit. Maybe the beige linen with the jade necklace. Her reflection didn't displease her. She smiled to think of how surprised her daughters would be if they knew how often she still thought about sex. As though I've been old for ever and can't remember how it used to be. A vision of Hugh Kenworthy flashed suddenly into her mind. The afternoon she'd spent with him could so easily have become . . . well, never mind. It was one of the times which still had the capacity to make her feel guilty, and she made a great effort to push all thoughts of him to the back of her mind. What on earth had made her think of him?

She stroked blusher lightly over her cheekbones, anxious not to overdo the make-up. Nothing worse than mutton dressed as lamb. No, that was all right. Subtle enough to make her look healthy. Perhaps it was seeing Rilla in a state again. With all her feelings about Sean pinned very obviously to her sleeve, her mouth practically hanging open just as it had with Hugh. Funny how one's children never realize how completely transparent they are. Leonora paused with the silver hairbrush in her hand. Was it possible that parents were equally well understood by their offspring? The thought made her blush, because she'd been thinking of Hugh, and she began to brush her hair rather more vigorously than necessary.

Leonora wondered whether it was her imagination or whether the conversation tonight really *was* more tentative than usual. It seemed to her that everyone was guarding their tongues, as though they were afraid of what might come out if they allowed themselves free rein. Fiona didn't take her eyes from Efe's face. He smiled at her once or twice when she managed to catch his eye, and it was quite touching and rather sad to see her face opening out like a flower in the sun. For most of the meal, Efe had been uncharacteristically silent, only talking when someone spoke directly to him.

Beth had made the most efforts in that direction. She wouldn't dare to raise the subject of the offer he'd made the night before. That might have provoked a row and Leonora had categorically forbidden rows at dinner times. There were occasions in the past which would have been quite unbearable if everyone had allowed themselves to quarrel at the table. As it was, rows and unpleasantness were usually private matters between two people and not what she thought of as 'free-for-alls'.

Beth was trying to cheer Efe up. That was what it looked like, but she was not having much success.

Leonora turned to her elder daughter. 'You look a little preoccupied, Gwen, dear. Is something the matter?' She took a bite of apple pie. Really, they were very lucky that Mary had such a light hand with the pastry. It was quite delicious, and she could hardly blame Rilla for tucking in when she herself was enjoying it so much.

'No, Mummy, I'm just going over my list in my head. There are so many things I have to check tomorrow. I'm sorry. Did I miss part of the conversation?'

'No, not at all. I don't think we've had much of what you'd call "conversation" tonight.' Leonora noticed that every face was suddenly turned towards her and she smiled to show she wasn't blaming anyone. She said, 'Rilla, I believe you and Sean went down to see Nanny Mouse. How is she?'

'She was rather well, actually,' Rilla said, dabbing at her mouth with a napkin. 'She seemed to know who we were for most of the time. But . . .' she paused. 'There was one rather interesting thing. She seemed to be saying that Ethan Walsh was cruel to Maude. At one point, she actually thought Sean was Ethan and seemed to cringe back in her chair as if she thought he was going to strike her. She looked quite terrified, poor old Nanny.'

'I don't think you ought to put too much faith in Nanny Mouse, even at her clearest. I don't remember anything like that at all,' Leonora said quickly, but she found that her heart had started to beat rather fast and her mouth was suddenly dry. She took a sip of water.

Rilla's remarks had certainly got some conversation going, and that had been what she wanted. She was dimly aware of Chloë and Philip and Beth, even Efe, talking all at the same time. The subject of men's violence against women was obviously one on which everyone had strong opinions. Leonora let the talk flow over her, hearing only snatches of it. *They never reform . . . don't know why any woman stands it . . . can't help it . . . doesn't mean they don't love . . . funny way of showing . . . wouldn't catch me . . . I'd hit him right back . . . masochism . . . should be locked up . . . lost their temper and regret it . . . not good enough . . . no excuse . . . love . . . love . . . bastards all of them.*

She fixed her eyes on the shadows behind Rilla's chair at the far end of the table. The lights in this room were deliberately kept quite low because Leonora couldn't bear white dazzle and wanted to recreate a golden candlelight glow. She'd never really thought of herself as old before, but lately the physical world was behaving so strangely that she'd begun to think this was how things were when you were about to turn seventy-five.

Look at what was happening, for instance, to the other end of the table. Rilla – she knew it was Rilla though she couldn't see her properly – her shape, the shirt she was wearing, which was the colour of a heron's feathers, were dissolving. That was the only word for it. Rilla was shimmering and shifting and when Leonora tried to make her out properly, she wasn't there. She'd disappeared and someone else was sitting in her chair. Leonora trembled and blinked. It's Maude, she thought. She opened her mouth to say 'Mummy' and realized suddenly that she must be the only person in the room who could see what she supposed she ought to call a ghost of some kind.

'Are you all right, Leonora?' James was speaking to her, leaning towards her looking anxious.

'Yes, yes, of course. Nothing to fuss about. I just felt a little faint for a moment. Too much apple pie, I expect.'

'Let's go through to the drawing-room for coffee, Mother,' said Gwen. 'The others can follow us. I'll tell you about the flowers for the tent.'

Leonora pushed her chair back and stood up. 'Yes, a cup of coffee would be most welcome. Thank you, darling.' She tucked her arm into Gwen's and as they walked out into the hall, Leonora said, 'I've never really liked the dining-room, you know. It's such a cold place.'

'It used to be,' Gwen agreed. 'When Rilla and I were young. But you've made it look lovely now. Not a bit cold any more.'

When they reached the drawing-room, Leonora sat down in her favourite armchair while Gwen went into the kitchen to organize the coffee. I'd almost forgotten, Leonora thought, why I hate that room. Seeing Maude there – she was wearing her lilac dress with the lace collar – reminded me. They'd let me come in sometimes as a special treat and I couldn't bear it and couldn't tell them why. Maybe I didn't know myself, but I remember now feeling that at any moment Mummy might break into pieces and Daddy might shout, or be very cross. With me or with her.

Leonora closed her eyes. No wonder I don't like the dining-room. It used to be full of silences that weren't just people not talking, but huge icy gaps in the air, filled with resentment and anger and some other emotion that she couldn't exactly put her finger on, even after so many years. She sat up all at once, listening out for Gwen, and thought she heard someone sighing, and stifling a sob. Over there by the sofa. The room was in near-darkness.

'Fiona? Is that you?' Leonora whispered. Fiona had been crying before dinner, she was almost sure of that. No one answered her question, and there was a rustling of something in the dimness near her and a fragrance of lily of the valley.

'Here we are, Mother!' Gwen put the tray down and switched on the lamp. Leonora looked all around her. Magical electric light had scattered the phantoms. She said, 'Can you smell something? Scent . . . lily of the valley.'

'No, I can't, I'm afraid. Actually, it's not a perfume I like at all,' Gwen said, matter-of-factly. 'Maybe Fiona? She does lay it on a bit thick sometimes, but I must say I hadn't noticed it being lily of the valley.'

Leonora shook her head. 'It doesn't matter, darling. I expect I was imagining it.'

Gwen was busy arranging cups and saucers and didn't answer. *Could you imagine a fragrance*, Leonora wondered. Could a perfume linger in the air for more than sixty years? I'm becoming silly and fanciful in my old age, she decided. A cup of coffee will pull me together.

'Decaffeinated, please,' she said to Gwen and closed her eyes. There was something like a door in her mind which she felt she was desperately trying to keep closed while something, or someone, was pushing at it from the other side. Nonsense, she said to herself. Concentrate on tomorrow. And the next day.

Saturday,
August 24th,
2002

I'm Cinderella in reverse, Rilla thought, and giggled. Going out after midnight instead of coming home. It's Saturday already, and I've had too much wine, she said to herself. I'm unsteady on my feet, or maybe it's these shoes. She kicked them off, bent down to pick them up, and left them neatly side by side on the path. I'll collect them on my way back indoors, she thought. I don't need them now. The night was stiflingly hot and the moon, coming and going behind puffs of cloud, diluted the darkness and made it unthreatening. She could see the whole garden quite clearly, washed in a sort of grey, shadowy light. One of the cats – it was impossible to see which – was out and about, too, creeping around a corner of the house.

She set off again over the lawn towards the gazebo, wondering how many years it was since she'd felt the cool, springy grass under her bare feet. It was probably an indication of old age to think that there was something remarkable and strange about walking around with no shoes on.

When she was younger, she used to go barefoot at every opportunity. This was the very path she followed on days when Hugh came to stay and they couldn't get together properly because Leonora always had her eyes peeled for any kind of amorous behaviour. Rilla smiled. It was a miracle, really, the ways they'd found to outwit her; to go somewhere where she wouldn't be. One of their favourite trysting places was the gazebo. Hugh had called it that, a trysting place. Rilla always felt stupid even thinking it, like someone in a bad knights-of-the-round-table movie.

Thinking about Hugh now was strange. Up until the time she'd met Sean, whenever her first lover came into her mind she felt such resentment towards Leonora for destroying that relationship that there was barely any pleasure left in any of her memories. Now though, Rilla thought, it's as though a migraine headache has lifted. She found to her surprise that she'd been talking to Leonora without feeling angry, and she could say Hugh's name to herself and not feel overwhelmed by a rising tide of regret and fury. Rilla smiled when she thought how very little it had taken, after all, to banish Hugh, whom she'd always considered the love of her life, to the safety of the distant past.

She stepped into the gazebo. It was quite beautiful, and the one place at Willow Court that Rilla loved without reservation because the only memories she had of it were good ones. As a child, she'd taken no notice of it. There wasn't much point to the place, as far as she could see then. Because the walls were made of glass, it didn't even pass muster as a good spot to make a den, and there was nothing interesting in it, only cane chairs with white cushions in the centre of the room and a white-painted bench running all around the walls. The building was a hexagon made of wrought-iron and glass, too small to be used for anything other than quiet reading or thinking by no more than two people at once.

Quiet reading and thinking was what it was originally intended for. Ethan Walsh had it built for his wife on their second wedding anniversary. So Leonora said. She also said she remembered her mother doing exactly that, sitting there for hours and hours, just staring into space. The more Rilla heard about her maternal grandmother, the more strange she seemed.

We found different things to do here, she thought, Hugh and I. She opened the door and let herself in and knew that the velvet night was hiding her now as it had then. She sat down facing away from the lake. The moon was hidden for the moment behind thick cloud, but Rilla didn't want to risk glancing up to see a flash of silvery water somewhere beyond the trees. She closed her eyes. Where was Sean?

All through dinner she hadn't worried about it for a second. She'd known he'd be coming, and could hardly go through the motions of talking, or listening, because she was so longing to leave the table and get out – out and down here where he'd be arriving, he said, as soon as he could. But where was he? Maybe he'd changed his mind. Rilla shivered and firmly pushed this thought away. The silence that surrounded her in this little glass cage was like no other; you could hear yourself breathing and even the noise of insect wings and the movements of nocturnal creatures of one kind and another were quite inaudible.

He *will* come, she told herself. He must. I'm not going back to the house. Not yet. She closed her eyes, leaned her head against the back of the chair and made herself think about something else. Hugh. They'd come here once after swimming naked in the lake. It was about three in the morning and the weather was hot and airless then, too. He'd carried her up here, wrapped in nothing more than the shirt she'd been wearing. They'd barely got into the gazebo before he put her down and pulled the shirt away from her breasts and began to kiss her all over. They'd sunk into one of the chairs, oblivious to everything but the demands of skin and flesh and open, gasping mouths. Leonora herself, together with the entire household, could have been standing watching from the other side of the glass and they'd never have known it.

Rilla smiled. God, when you were young you didn't care about anything. Not comfort, not shame, nothing. The fire in the blood just burned through whatever was in its path and took no heed of any consequences. Hugh. She could practically taste him, even after all these years.

# July/August 1971

I hate her. I absolutely and totally hate her. I wish I didn't have to live in this horrible place with horrible people who don't know anything. Nothing at all. Not about me, or what's going on in the real world away from this ridiculous house with its endless grass and flowers and stupid lake that everyone thinks is so marvellous, and which is really so boring because all you can do with it is walk around it and once you've done that, well, there's nothing else really. I hate it. I hate everything. They don't understand anything, not any of them. Not Mummy, not Nanny Mouse, and not Gwen because she's never bloody here anyway but in bloody Switzerland most of the time, learning how to fold napkins or something equally vital, and only coming home for a couple of weekends over the summer with James in tow because she's two years older and she can do whatever she wants and not have anyone criticise her . . .

Rilla's thoughts went round and round in her head and she could hardly see through her tears. Nevertheless, she was marching down the avenue of scarlet oaks towards the gate and freedom. Everything would be all right once she'd got away from Willow Court. It was five o'clock on an afternoon that threatened rain and she hadn't even bothered to pick up a jacket. I don't care if I get soaked, she thought. She won't care either. She thinks making a fuss about what I wear and what I do shows that she loves me, but it doesn't. She just cares about what people will think. Rilla almost laughed, even though she felt so angry. What people? Where were they?

'You are not,' her mother had said, just as she was about to open the door and go out, 'leaving this house looking like that.'

'Looking like what?' Rilla had answered. 'I don't know what you mean.'

'Of course you do, darling. Don't be silly.' Leonora (Rilla always called her that when she felt cross) had a way of saying things that managed at the same time to convey that you were completely thick for not understanding what she was on about, and also that she was so far above you that you ought to be somehow grateful that she'd bothered to take any notice of you.

'I don't,' Rilla persisted, although actually she had a pretty good idea of what it was that had made her mother see red.

'Well, then, I shall tell you.' Leonora looked Rilla up and down. 'Your skirt is too short. Your blouse is too tight. You have far too much eye make-up on and high-heeled shoes like that are inappropriate for a trip to the village. Please go back to your room and put on something more suitable. You look quite ridiculous.'

'It's none of your business how I look,' Rilla said, and strode towards the front door. Unfortunately, it was so heavy that slamming it shut was never an option, but she did her best to leave in a way that would convey how furious she was. Her mother would be silent and distant when she returned, but for the moment she didn't care.

As soon as she had run down the steps to the drive, the tumult in her head began. Now that she was nearly at the gate, it had subsided somewhat and she was thinking more normally.

She slowed down a little on the road to the village and part of her had to confess that her shoes were killing her. I don't care, she said to herself. They're beautiful. And Hugh will love the way I look in them, I know he will. Her heart began to thump rather loudly in her chest. I shan't think about Mummy or anyone else. I'm going to meet him. Hugh. I'm going to meet Hugh.

Rilla was in love. She'd fallen in love at exactly eleven o'clock on a Tuesday morning, three weeks ago. She remembered this because while she was in the shop and speaking to him for the first time the church clock was chiming. He'd been behind her in the queue and as soon as she turned and saw him, her whole body leapt and trembled. She'd bumped into him as she turned to go and sort of stumbled over his feet. He'd had to grab her by the arms so that she didn't fall over. For a second or two he held her.

'Terribly sorry!' he said, and he had a voice like someone you heard on the radio.

'That's okay,' she said. 'It was my fault. I wasn't looking where I was going.'

He held out his hand. 'Hello. I'm Hugh Kenworthy. Just moved into that cottage over there. For a bit of peace and quiet.'

'I'm Rilla Simmonds,' she said. 'I live at Willow Court.'

'Then you're very lucky indeed,' he said. 'All those marvellous pictures. I went round Willow Court a few years back. Those Walshes are quite amazing.' He smiled. 'I didn't see you though. I'm sure I'd have remembered.'

Rilla made a face. 'I must have been at school. I go to Greenbanks. That's a rather posh prison outside Bristol. I'm a weekly boarder, which means I only come home for weekends. But Ethan Walsh was my grandfather.'

Hugh looked at her and his eyes widened.

'How completely astonishing! Really delighted to meet you, Rilla . . . and what an unusual name.'

'It's short for Cyrilla,' she said. What was she doing? She never, never told anyone that unless they asked specially. All she could think was, I wish we could stay talking like this for ever. The other people in the queue were getting restless. He took her arm, and before she knew what was happening, they were outside the shop, and walking together towards his cottage.

He wasn't a bit like the men she met usually, but more like someone who might be on the cover of the magazines she bought sometimes, so that she could stare at the strange creatures inhabiting a world of clothes shops and shoe shops, cinemas and theatres, restaurants and discos, and imagine herself among them.

His hair was long, falling almost to his shoulders. It was the colour of a lion's mane, a yellowy-brown, and his eyes were such a pale blue that they looked almost silver. He had long fingers, and wore a denim shirt and jeans. On his feet he had leather cowboy boots and round his neck he'd wound a silky scarf made up of thousands of differently-coloured stripes. Rilla had no idea how old he was, but one thing was certain: he was not a boy.

She knew all about boys. In fact, at school, she was a bit of an expert on the subject. She'd kissed more of them than most people in her class had done, and more than once she'd nearly gone all the way . . . that was how she and her friends put it . . . but something had prevented this happening. Now, walking beside Hugh, she was glad she'd waited. His skin would feel rougher. His hands looked almost weather-beaten. His body would be hard. Rilla breathed in and out slowly, so that he shouldn't see what she was feeling.

'Here we are,' he said, opening the front door of a cottage at the end of the village street, just up the road from the shop. 'Convenient, right? For the shops, I mean. The commercial centre of the village. Where all the action is. Come in for a moment, and have a cup of coffee. Or are you expected at home? Maybe you'd better phone your mum or something.'

'No, that's okay,' she said, angry with him for a second, before gratitude for his invitation flooded through her. 'I'm seventeen. Old enough to be out on my own.'

She said it flirtatiously. Rilla was good at flirting. She knew exactly what she had to do with her eyes and her head to make boys think that . . . well, that she was interested. He pointed to the sofa and smiled.

'Right. Fine. Sit down, then, and I'll see if I can find a couple of mugs that aren't dirty.'

Rilla had never seen a living room that was at the same time such a mess and so enchanting. It was crammed full of more things than she had ever seen together in one room, and they were strewn all over the place. Books were stacked on the floor, clothes heaped on chairs, records on the table next to an open jar of strawberry jam and, in the sink, used plates and cups and saucers in tottering piles that overflowed out on to the draining-board. On the mantelpiece there were invitations, postcards, a clock, and a vase containing an arrangement of honesty and peacock feathers. In the fireplace, instead of logs, the grate was heaped with stones of all sizes and colours. What were they supposed to be for? Rilla wondered. There was a huge mirror on one wall, its gilt frame decorated with fat cherubs and garlands of roses.

'I like that!' she said.

'My grandmother's,' said Hugh. 'D'you take sugar? In your coffee, I mean.'

'Yes, please. Two.'

He stirred the drink and handed it to her, then sat down on a chair opposite the sofa. Rilla took a sip and said, 'I like your cottage. It's quite unusual, isn't it?'

'A mess, you mean. I'm sorry. I didn't know I was going to be entertaining. I'd have made more effort, truly.'

'That's okay,' said Rilla. 'I like it.'

And it was true. You couldn't have found a greater contrast to Willow Court in the whole of the county, and that was what she liked about it. She would have liked it whoever had been living here, but of course it was Hugh's house and that made it extra special.

'Are you an actor?' she asked him and he shook his head.

'No, I'm a potter. I've got a kiln in a shed out in the garden. I used to work full-time in an advertising agency in London, but it all got too much, d'you know what I mean? The rat race, and so on. So I've gone part-time, and this cottage, well, it's a sort of bolt-hole. Somewhere to escape to, where I can really be myself. And see whether I can make a go of the pots.'

'I'd love to live in London,' Rilla said. 'I think I'd enjoy the rat race. After the holidays, all I have is weeks and weeks of school to look forward to. But I'm leaving next year and then I'm going to drama school. My mother didn't want me to at first, but now she's given in. Well, Gwen, that's my sister, she's doing a Domestic Science course in Switzerland, so Mummy couldn't really say no, could she? I'm just dying to get there. It's so dead round here. There's absolutely nothing to do and no one to talk to.'

Hugh made a sad face, and Rilla laughed. 'I mean, till I met you there was no one.'

'I hope you feel you can talk to me,' he said. 'Or I shall be as lonely as you are, and I'd hate that. Will you come and visit me sometimes?'

'Yes,' said Rilla. 'Of course I will. I'd love to.' She put her cup down in the tiny space left between a pot plant and three or four notebooks, which took up most of the occasional table next to the sofa. She'd hardly drunk any of it after all. Then she stood up.

'I ought to get home now,' she said. 'My mother will wonder where I am if I stay any longer. I'm sorry I haven't finished my coffee. It was lovely, really.'

'My pleasure,' said Hugh. 'Do come again soon.'

He'd stood in the doorway and waved at her as she walked to the gate. Mrs Pritchard, who lived next to the pub and who was one of her mother's bridge ladies, was passing by on the other side of the road as she left. She can stare all she likes, Rilla thought. I don't care if it's not the done thing to go drinking cups of coffee with men who live on their own. I don't care if Mrs P tells Mummy. I don't care about anything. For two pins, she'd have turned round and hammered on his door again and cried, Let me in! I want to stay with you. No one else, not ever.

That was how it began. Now, everything had changed, utterly. Now she was a totally different being and walked through her life in a kind of daze, her whole body throbbing and singing and longing for Hugh every second that they were apart.

She'd fallen into the habit of going to see him in the afternoons when he wasn't in London. To her mother she said she was visiting this or that friend from her primary school days . . . there were still a few of them living near the village. On her third visit, they went upstairs to the bedroom, which was surprisingly tidy, with lovely pale pink sheets and curtains printed with a pattern of ivy and white flowers, and Rilla lost her virginity willingly, happily and with considerably less pain than she'd been expecting.

'I've never spoken to anyone like this before,' Rilla said, turning to look at Hugh's profile on the pillow next to her. 'I didn't realize you could. I love you. I love this; just lying here like this with the sun coming in and everything.' She closed her eyes. The smoke from Hugh's roll-up had a wonderful smell. He gave her puffs from it sometimes and it made her feel swimmy and delicious, as though her body might melt into the bed. She giggled. What would Mummy say, or Gwen, if they knew that she was here, smoking pot? Would it be more shocking than the fact that she was in bed with a man? Or less shocking? The two things together would, she was sure, be the height of wickedness in Leonora's opinion. Rilla couldn't help smiling at the hypocrisy. She's fond of a gin-and-tonic, isn't she? Practically hooked on it, was the woozy thought that went through her head. She's got no right to tell me what to do. No right at all. She opened her eyes, and there he was, still looking at her and smiling.

'I think,' Rilla said, 'I must have been born into the wrong family. D'you know what I mean?'

He traced a line with his finger from where her hair ended, down her forehead and her nose till he reached her mouth. When she felt him touching her lips, she kissed him, and put out her tongue and licked the finger, tasting his skin.

'Little kids think they're in the wrong family, don't they?' he said. 'They've been kidnapped away from a king's house, or something like that. Is that what you mean?'

'No, nothing like that. It's just that in my family everyone's so, I don't know what to call it, stiff? Formal, maybe. My mother is always properly dressed. I've never seen her in a dressing-gown, for instance. She gets dressed as soon as she gets up. No chatting over cups of tea at the kitchen table for her. And my sister's nearly as bad.'

'She's older, right?'

'Yes. She'll be coming back to London soon, when her course in Switzerland finishes, and then she'll do even more cookery and stuff, which sounds just so boring. And she's got a proper fiancé and everything. When they're together, they do all the prim and proper engaged-couple things together, even though they're not going to get married for ages and ages. You know, choosing equipment for married people. Knives and forks.' This suddenly struck both of them as tremendously funny and they rolled around in the tangled sheets together, laughing.

'I haven't a clue what they talk about,' Rilla continued, when she'd recovered a little. They slept together, she knew that much, but Gwen refused to discuss it. She believed such things were personal and private and shouldn't be talked about. Perhaps, Rilla thought, she's got a point. I wouldn't like her to know about me. About this. She went on, 'He's foreign. Well, not really foreign, only his people come from Spain. He's called James Rivera. He's quite nice actually. Good-looking and everything. Can't think what he sees in Gwen.'

'If she's anything at all like you,' Hugh said, 'there's no mystery.'

Rilla shook her head. 'She's the good one in the family. She only ever does what Mummy wants her to do, and she's very quiet and not at all like me. I'm all over the place. You have no idea how hard it is at school with teachers going *oh, you're not a bit like Gwen . . . why can't you be more like Gwen . . .* till I'm sick to death of hearing it. She's one of those people, you know, reliable and kind and good with animals and that sort of thing. And she and Mummy get on much better than we do. Me and my mother, I mean. I don't really know why. I can see that I annoy Mummy sometimes. She does her best to hide it, really, but it comes out every so often.'

'I can't imagine anyone not adoring you. Just can't imagine it,' Hugh said.

'Oh, she adores me, I expect,' Rilla said. 'But she gets annoyed all the same. It's what I told you. I'm not in the right family. Maybe I'm a whatsit. A changeling. The fairies came and stole her real baby away and left me instead. They're often redheads, aren't they? Change-lings?'

Hugh stubbed out his joint and lay back on the pillows. Soon, he was snoring slightly. He was always doing that, Rilla reflected. Men just naturally fell asleep quickly after sex. She'd read about it in books. I'm good at it, she said to herself. I'm good at sex. The thought made her happy. She became a different person when she was with Hugh, and it wasn't just the sex, which, okay, was brilliant, and which nothing she'd ever read described properly at all. She liked it better than any other thing she'd ever done. She felt shiny all over, and as though her body had a slight electrical charge going through it whenever Hugh touched her. Even when she wasn't with him, thinking about what they did together while, for instance, she was sitting at breakfast across the table from her mother, made her blush and go hot all over. Once or twice, Leonora had actually asked her if she was all right and she'd had to find some excuse for the sudden redness flooding her cheeks and neck. While she was asleep, she dreamed about him, and woke up sweating. There was one night when she was longing for him so desperately that she could hardly catch her breath. She'd actually started up out of her bed and begun dressing, ready to creep out of the house in the early hours of the morning and run and run all down the drive and through the village and into his cottage and up the stairs and into bed beside him before he was even awake. But she sank back on to her own bed in a storm of desire and despair, knowing the row it would cause if she were not in her place at breakfast.

Also, maddeningly, some of the days when she could have been with him she had to spend mooching around at Willow Court because he was up in London. He came for two or three nights a week and occasionally for a weekend and that was all. Soon the holidays would be over, and then she'd hardly ever see him at all. How was she going to concentrate on her A-levels knowing he was just a few miles away? Perhaps she could leave now? Just never go back for the Michaelmas term? All she wanted to do was go to drama school, but even though she'd begged and begged her mother, Leonora was unconvinced that acting was a suitable career, and insisted that her daughter stay at school long enough to notch up what she called 'proper qualifications'.

On Hughless days, which was how she thought of them, she found that she was actually missing Gwen. There was no one to talk to, and she spent hours pacing the grounds, walking round and round the lake, sometimes reciting speeches from Shakespeare out loud.

' "Halloo your name to the reverberate hills, and make the babbling gossip of the air cry out Olivia!" ' she declaimed to the swans, who passed in and out of the willow branches that dipped into the water, but they weren't really listening. No one listened to her like Hugh did.

Rilla was quickly aware that she'd never before had conversations like the ones she had with Hugh. They talked about everything: books, music, his work. He told her things. He asked her opinion and often agreed with her. He thought she was clever. She loved to watch him as he made his pots. He would throw the clay on to the wheel and stroke it into beautiful shapes till she was nearly mad with wanting to touch him. He warned her off.

'I know what you're thinking, young Rilla,' he'd say, and go on stroking and stroking the wet shape, pulling it and pushing it till it became what he wanted it to be. 'Just be patient. It'll be good when it comes, I promise.'

And when he kissed her, there in the little shed behind the cottage where the wheel was, his hands – greyish and chalky from the drying clay – on her hair or her back, she sank into her own pleasure and felt herself falling and dizzy and maddened by wanting him so much.

Rilla got out of bed and went to the window. She drew back at once behind the curtain, because there was that nosy Mrs Pritchard again. It was almost as though she came past the cottage deliberately when Rilla was there. Is she spying on me, she wondered. Does she know anything? No, of course she can't. If I ever meet her and she says anything, I'll make some excuse. Tell her I'm buying a vase or something for Gwen's birthday. Silly old woman. She was actually looking up at Hugh's bedroom window. What a cheek! There wasn't anything wrong with what she was doing. Some people would say that Hugh was too old for her, but how could he be when they loved one another so much? When their bodies fitted together as though some creator had carved them from the same block of flesh, so that when they made love they became one person? Ten years wasn't much at all. In fact, her father was much older than her mother, so Mummy couldn't possibly object, could she? Of course she couldn't. So why didn't she take Hugh up to Willow Court and introduce him to Leonora? She didn't really know, but there was something specially wonderful about the fact that Hugh was her secret and she wanted to keep him all to herself, for a little longer at least. Of course, once he asked her to marry him, he'd have to be introduced to the whole family, but till that day he was just hers and no one else's. She slipped back into bed and began kissing the top of Hugh's arm, where it became his shoulder. His skin was golden and smooth. He opened his eyes and smiled.

'Know something?' he murmured.

'What?'

'You're a very greedy little girl, that's what.'

'You've no idea how greedy I am.' She could hardly speak.

'Show me, then,' he said, and turned over to kiss her, covering her body with his.

Hugh stopped being Rilla's secret on the day of the Summer Fête at the church. She'd tried to get out of going but she couldn't try too hard or her mother was sure to be suspicious. Perhaps, she thought, as they trailed round in the hot sun from one stall to the next, he won't come. Maybe he'll just think the whole thing is too stupid for words, like I do, and stay away.

She walked slightly behind Leonora and smiled and said hello to everyone they met as they made their way around the Vicarage garden. Mummy knows everyone in the village, she thought, and just *has* to stand and chat to them and let them bore us all silly with their ramblings. Who gives a shit about the size of Bill's marrows, or how *inspired* the White Elephant stall is this year?

And, wouldn't you know it, Mrs Pritchard was running the Cake Stall, which was Rilla's favourite. She stopped in front of it for rather longer than she ought to have done and was just about to pay Mrs Pritchard for a scrumptious-looking meringue when everything happened at once, as though the whole thing had been choreographed. Her mother came up on her left, Hugh came up on her right and Mrs Pritchard just had to say, 'Oh, Leonora dear, what an amazing coincidence! Here he is! The young man I was telling you about? The one who's taken the Albertons' cottage. You know Mr Kenworthy, Rilla, don't you?'

Then there were all sorts of clumsy introductions, with Leonora saying how pleased she was to meet him and Hugh likewise and lying through his teeth and muttering about having meant to ask Rilla to take him up to Willow Court because he was such an admirer of Ethan Walsh's etc. etc. till Rilla was dizzy. Then Hugh went off in one direction and Leonora and Rilla in another and she hadn't even had her meringue.

Typically, Leonora said nothing about Hugh till they were at home. Rilla didn't know what to do. Would it look better if she said something? Or should she just shut up and let Leonora wonder? She decided to leave it till suppertime and see what happened and, sure enough, she'd hardly taken one bite of her cold salmon salad when Leonora said, 'He's rather good-looking, isn't he, that chap who's taken the Albertons' cottage. I've forgotten his name.'

'Hugh Kenworthy,' said Rilla, thinking *liar! You've just done that to hear how I say his name.* She went on eating the salmon in a wonderfully nonchalant manner, awarding herself top marks for good acting. Leonora went on, 'D'you know him very well? You've not mentioned him, have you?'

'No,' said Rilla. 'I don't know him terribly well. He's a potter. He chatted to me about the pictures in the shop, and I've had coffee with him a couple of times, that's all.'

Leonora said nothing, but looked at her daughter searchingly for a moment. *She's putting two and two together,* Rilla thought. *All those hours and hours that I've been out of the house. Can she guess? I mustn't look nervous. I must change the subject.*

'You ought to ask him to come up here sometime,' Leonora said. 'Why don't you invite him for lunch next Sunday? Gwen and James might be coming up then, I think, and you could all have a game of tennis or something.'

'Right,' said Rilla. 'I will. That's a good idea, only I don't know if he plays tennis or not. I'll ask though.'

The rest of the meal passed without incident, and when it was over Rilla went to her room. Jeffrey, one of what she still thought of as the new cats, the ones who'd replaced their beloved Cinders, was asleep on the velvet-covered chair. He was a handsome tabby, and his companion and brother, George, was black all over. George was an outdoors sort of cat who never came upstairs at all. Rilla stood at the window and looked at the lake, silver in the early evening sunlight. She imagined herself and Hugh walking beside it, his arm around her waist, her head on his shoulder. She closed her eyes, picturing his mouth and how it tasted on her mouth. Turning from the window, she fell forward on to the bed and pressed herself into the counterpane, fancying his body was between hers and the silky fabric, almost conjuring it up, so fervently was she wishing it.

'It was vile! You were vile! I've never hated a day more in my life. Why did you have to . . .' Rilla was screaming at Hugh. Part of her mind registered the fact that this was their very first row, but that didn't matter. She was so angry that even her love couldn't stop her.

'Stop it, Rilla!' Hugh was trying his hardest to be soothing. It was making things worse. 'You're blowing this up out of all proportion. What actually are you so het up about?'

'You don't know? You're seriously telling me you don't know?' They were still in the lounge of the cottage. Normally, the moment she came through the door, they started kissing and were halfway upstairs before a word had been said, but not this time. 'I can't see straight. I don't know what to think. I can't believe you didn't realize.'

'Didn't realize *what* exactly?' said Hugh. He was sounding bored. How dare he sound bored?

'You didn't realize when you were swarming all around my mother and sister that you were hurting me? You didn't even look at me the entire day. We could have been strangers, just people who mean nothing to one another. I couldn't bear it. How you kept talking and talking to Mummy as though she was the most fascinating person in the whole world and I was nothing. You even disappeared with her for hours. What were you doing? How d'you think I felt? You didn't say a single word to me from the minute you arrived till when you left. I had to go through a whole day with you and not even touch you once . . .' Words failed Rilla and she burst into tears.

'Come here,' Hugh said, and gathered her into his arms. 'You are a silly thing, Rilla darling. Did you really want everyone to know what I feel for you? Did you? Don't you think your mother might be a little – what shall we say? – upset to discover what her little girl had been up to while she wasn't looking? Your mother very kindly took me up to see Ethan Walsh's studio because I'd expressed an interest in the man. That's all.'

'I wouldn't care if people knew about us!' Rilla said. 'I'd shout it out if I could. I'd *love* it. I'd tell Mrs Pritchard. Everyone. I'm not ashamed. Not a bit.'

'I know, I know,' he murmured, kissing her on the lips, on the neck, touching her breasts, distracting her from her anger, making it impossible for her to think straight any longer. 'I know you're not ashamed. Still, it's better not to rock the boat, don't you think? Aren't things good? Isn't this good?'

Rilla said nothing. She felt the fury slide away from her. Her body wouldn't let her keep it in mind any longer. Never mind, she thought. He was pretending to be nice to them. He loves me. I can feel that he does, oh he does, he does, he really does and I'm going to faint because I love him so much.

'Rilla, dear,' said Leonora. 'I think we should talk.'

Rilla was so surprised to hear her mother say this, actually *ask* to speak to her, that she stopped on her way to the door. Could someone have had an accident? She was going to see Hugh but still, maybe there was an emergency.

'Of course, Mummy, is anything wrong?'

'No, not in the way you mean. But come to the conservatory just for a few minutes.'

Rilla felt a little frightened as she sat down. All around her chair there were enormous pots and vases from which her mother's jungle plants overflowed and clambered, spreading their green leaves over the glass walls. What did Leonora want from her? It couldn't (could it?) be something to do with Hugh? No, surely not. One of the best things that had happened this summer was how well Hugh fitted into life at Willow Court.

Since his first visit, he'd come up often. Partly Rilla was pleased, because it meant that she, too, just like Gwen, had a boyfriend, even though hers wasn't recognized by everyone as being officially with her. The disadvantage of having him constantly at Willow Court was that they had less time alone together. Less time for sex, Rilla said to herself, although there was the night they went to the gazebo after swimming in the lake and stayed there till the dawn came up. She sometimes wondered whether it was normal to want sex so much. There was no one she could really ask, except Hugh, who always laughed at her and said something silly, like *you couldn't possibly be too eager for my liking* or something. Nothing that told her whether it was normal. She never asked about other girlfriends he'd had before he met her because she didn't want to hear about those. He hadn't said anything about marriage. In fact, he hadn't even said he loved her, which worried her sometimes although she'd heard that some men just didn't like saying the words, whatever their feelings might be. Rilla knew from her careful reading of magazines that weddings were not a subject to be broached lightly and so she never said anything either, but of course she'd already arranged the furnishings of their house down to the last detail, in her imagination.

'It's about Hugh, I'm afraid,' Leonora said.

'What's wrong? Is he all right? Has he had an accident?'

'No, no, darling. Nothing like that at all. Please sit down again.' Rilla had jumped out of her seat. She sat down and stared at her mother.

'What's the matter with Hugh?' she said.

'I'm going to ask you something, Rilla, which I wouldn't normally ask but please don't think I'm interfering. I just have to know, in the circumstances. Have you slept with him?'

Rilla blushed and knew that the blush had given her away. I'm not ashamed, she told herself. There's nothing to be ashamed about. She looked up at Leonora and said, as bravely as she could, 'Yes, yes I have.' She waited for lightning to flash, some sort of cataclysm to match the enormity of the news, but Leonora only sighed.

'Oh, dear,' she said. 'I thought so. This is going to be hard for you to understand, darling, but I'm afraid all that's over now.'

'What's over? I don't understand. How can it be over? I was on my way to see him. What? How?'

'He won't be there. He's gone back to London. He won't be coming down here again.'

A pounding started behind Rilla's eyes. *Don't lose control. Keep calm* . . . she told herself, over and over again. When she spoke, her voice came out in a strangled squeak that she hated, but it was such an effort holding on to herself, not crying. She said, 'Mummy, if you're going to say hurtful things, you have to explain. You can't just sit there and announce that he's not coming back. He wouldn't leave me. He loves me. I know he does. We love each other.'

Leonora shook her head.

'He's been taking advantage of you, Rilla. There's no easy way to say this, but he's . . . he's dishonest. He's not what he appears to be. Truly. For one thing, how old did he tell you he was?'

'I know how old he is. He's twenty-seven. And you can't say a word either because that's how much older Daddy was than you.'

'Hugh is thirty-four. He looks younger, that's true, but he really is.'

'That's not true. How do you know, anyway? Did he tell you? How d'you know he's not lying to *you*, about being older? Not that it matters. I'd love him anyway.'

'It was a remark he made about remembering a street party at the end of the war. You probably didn't even notice him saying it, but I did. I realised at once that he must be at least thirty-two. And then I made a few enquiries, from friends in London. He's thirty-four, Rilla, but that's not all. Are you ready for this?'

'Ready for what? I don't care what you've dug up. Is he a white slaver? A drug dealer? I love him anyway. We'll run away if everyone is going to be horrible about it. We'll go where no one will ever find us.'

'Nothing so dramatic, I'm afraid. Just the rather banal fact that he's already married. He has two children, one of them a girl, only three years younger than you are.'

Rilla felt as though a stone had fallen on her and crushed her so that all the breath left her body. She opened her mouth to speak, and couldn't. She tried again.

'Is . . . do they . . . I mean, maybe they're separated. That must be it. That must be why he comes to the cottage. To get away from her. They must be thinking of divorce. I'll talk to him. I'll ask him what's happening. He'll tell me the truth. He has to. He won't need to hide anything from me any more. He loves me.'

'That may be true. He may love you, Rilla, but it makes no difference. And of course he didn't tell you. Why should he? He was having a wonderful time with you, why should he spoil it? But he spoke to me, when I asked him to tell me the truth.'

'What did he say? Tell me every single word he said. Every word, mind. Please, Mummy, tell me everything. When did you speak to him? Where?'

'Here. The day before yesterday when he came for lunch. While you were out in the Quiet Garden talking to Gwen and James, I think.'

It was true. There was an hour — was it as long as that? — when she was not with Hugh. Gwen and James said that perhaps he was having another cup of coffee with Leonora, and actually remarked on how well he got on with her. Rilla closed her eyes. All the time that she was lying on the grass and looking up into the leaves of the magnolia, he had been telling Leonora all these hideous things. It was unbearable. Rilla felt pain all over her body as though someone had beaten her. It's never going to end, she thought. I'm going to hurt for ever. Always. I'll never stop hurting. She breathed deeply and looked at her mother.

'Please tell me everything,' she said. 'Every word.'

'He confessed to me that he was older, just as I'd suspected. He admitted that he should have had more sense than to fall under the spell of a young girl, but that he couldn't help himself. He said he was . . . susceptible. Susceptible to the charms of young girls. He seemed to know that this was not something to be proud of. He looked down a lot while he spoke to me, Rilla. I asked him about his wife. She knows nothing, it seems, of the detail of what he gets up to when he's not with her. They have one of those . . . what do you call them? Open marriages. He is a devoted father. His cottage here, well, that was for his pottery. That was what he told his wife. He begged me. Begged me to say nothing to her about you. Not because you were his mistress, you understand, because those are a constant in his life, but simply because you are so much younger than – and these are his words – *his usual lovers.* He is frank about those, if about nothing else. I told him that he must leave the cottage and he agreed. He left yesterday, I believe. He undertook never to get in touch with you, and you must never contact him again, Rilla. It's best that way, really it is. He assured me that you wouldn't become pregnant, because he's had a vasectomy. For which we must be deeply grateful.'

Rilla didn't say a single word. She got up from her chair and left the conservatory without really knowing where she was going. A whiteness filled her field of vision and her heart . . . what was happening to that? It felt as though someone, something, was squeezing it and she could imagine it, just behind her ribcage, throbbing and bloody and being torn apart, nothing more than offal, and not the source of all emotions after all. She stumbled upstairs and went straight to the nursery.

She sat down in front of the dolls' house and looked into the rooms where the small figures of Lucinda and Lucas still lived, even though she'd stopped playing with them years ago. Their lives were lovely. They lived in Paradise Mansions and no one came to hurt them and tear their little bodies apart. I'll never see him again, she thought. Her mother's words went round and round in her head. *Married. Thirty-four years old. Other lovers, other lovers, other lovers.* Bastard. He was a bloody bastard and she ought to hate him. How was it then that she still loved him with every single cell in her whole body? I will never forgive her, she thought, as she picked up Queen Margarita. It's all her fault. She shouldn't have asked him all that. It wasn't any of her business. He would have left his wife for me in the end. I know he would have. Rilla felt the first tears running down her cheeks and didn't care if they never stopped flowing. She meddled in my life and fucked it up for ever. Fucked it up, fucked it up, fucked it up.

❧

'Rilla? Rilla, are you asleep?'

Sean. Sean's voice. Rilla struggled to her feet, smoothing her hair down with one hand. 'No. No, honestly,' she said. 'I was just thinking with my eyes closed. I was on the point of giving up on you. Isn't it very late?'

'About one o'clock,' Sean said. 'I can't tell you how sorry I am. I've been like a bloody cat on hot bricks, I can tell you. One round of drinks after another and there was I just looking for an excuse to escape. You know how it is. I didn't want it to look as though I was longing to leave. Got to work with everyone tomorrow.' He laughed. 'Well, today actually.'

'It doesn't matter,' Rilla said. 'I'm not a bit tired. Are you?'

Sean shook his head. 'Not at all. And I've brought some wine.' He held it out to show her. 'I had the presence of mind to get the cork out before I came down here, but I forgot the glasses. Does it matter?'

'No, of course not. We'll just swig.'

Sean sat down on the bench and leaned against the glass wall of the gazebo. A silence began to grow between them. Should I speak first? Rilla thought. What should I say? She was casting about in her mind for some appropriate remark, rejecting one subject after another frantically, when Sean spoke. 'I've been rehearsing all sorts of things I wanted to say to you and now I'm here, I can't think of a single one.'

'Me too,' said Rilla, relieved. She sat down beside him and held up the bottle. 'May I?'

'Sure.'

She took a gulp of the icy, dry wine and thought that no drink in the world had ever tasted better. She handed the bottle back to Sean who set it down on the floor beside his feet.

'What have you been thinking about?' he asked. 'You said you'd been thinking. Don't say if you don't want to. If it's private.'

'It's not a bit private. I was thinking about a man I used to know. My first lover, actually. His name was Hugh.'

'What happened to him?'

'Oh, God, it was so boring and banal. Just like a bad book, to tell you the truth. I fell for him and it turned out that he was married all

219

the time. Very run-of-the-mill stuff, I'm afraid. Mother found out and sent him packing.'

'And I expect you never forgave her for that.'

Rilla laughed. 'How did you guess? Is it so obvious? No, of course she did the right thing but it didn't feel like that at the time. I sometimes think she still looks on me as the naughty little girl she thought I was then. I don't feel approved of, much of the time. Again, boring stuff. I'm sorry. Let's change the subject.'

'Nothing to do with you is boring, Rilla,' Sean said, and she found that his hand was stroking her wrist, gently, slowly and a shiver of pleasure went through her. 'You're sad, though. That's obvious. And I know why because you told me. I've spent the whole day thinking of you suffering like that, when your son died. There were so many things I wanted to know, to ask and didn't feel I could.'

'I don't mind. Ask anything.'

'Where was Jon Frederick when it happened?'

Rilla looked at the floor. 'He was there. Not when it actually happened, but he came at once. He did the best he could, but of course he was as hurt as I was and, quite honestly, I don't think two terminally bruised and torn people can ever get things back to what they were. We couldn't anyway. And he was angry with me.'

'That's unforgivable!' Sean said. 'Completely unforgivable. It wasn't your fault. It was an accident, surely. A tragic, tragic accident. Did he blame you? How could he?'

Rilla didn't answer for a while. She was struggling with a sorrow that seemed to have become lodged in her throat. Her eyes filled with tears and trickled down her cheeks as she spoke. 'He was right to be angry, really. That's what I think. That's what I've thought ever since that day. It *was* my fault. All my fault. I should have been here and I wasn't. I left other people to take care of my baby and I shouldn't have. I shouldn't have taken my eyes off him. Not for a second.'

Sean put his arm around Rilla's shoulders and she buried her face in the crook of his neck and cried as though she never intended to stop. At last, after what seemed to her like a very long time, the sobs subsided and she lifted her head and looked at Sean and smiled.

'Oh, Sean, I didn't mean tonight to be like this! Look at us. I'm bedraggled and snuffly and red-eyed and you're soaked to the skin.

And your shirt must be ruined. I'm so sorry. Oh, God, just thinking about how awful I feel about it makes me want to cry all over again.'

Sean removed his arm from around Rilla's shoulder, took a hankie out of his pocket and handed it to her without a word. She dabbed at her eyes and nose.

'No, that's no good,' he said gently. 'You need to have a good blow.'

'This conversation is getting more glamorous by the minute,' she said, but she did as he suggested. 'There. That's a bit better.'

'Have another sip of wine and we'll begin again,' Sean said. 'I'll have my turn. I'll tell you about my failed marriage. How my ex-wife said I was a complete and utter failure who would never amount to anything, and how right she was. How I suffered when she made her way through a list of my more famous colleagues with me being the last to know anything about it. I can probably beat you in the boring and clichéd story stakes any day of the week.'

'How could she?' Rilla was indignant. 'You're a well-known director. What did she want you to be?'

'I don't know. Prize-winning. Visible. Glitzy. All the things I'm not, really. I just like making the programmes I want to make, that's all. I have to be passionate about my subjects, as I am about Ethan. I've always loved his paintings, you know. Since I was a teenager, anyway. I fell in love with them the first time I saw them.'

Silence fell between them again. Then Sean said, 'There's never a proper script for this sort of conversation, is there? You know what follows, Rilla. You know what I want to say, only I'm not sure I can say it well. It'll sound contrived. I'm very good at spotting traps in what people say, me included.'

'What did you want to say, Sean? Tell me. I won't laugh. I won't think it's the wrong thing or that you've said it badly, I promise.'

'I was going to say that I fell in love with the paintings the first time I saw them and the same thing exactly happened when I saw you. There you are. That's the sort of sentiment that shouldn't really be expressed outside the confines of a Valentine card, don't you think?'

'I would think that,' Rilla said, and she was smiling as she spoke. 'Only I felt just the same. Like a kid. Silly and giggly and watching out for your tiniest action. Did it mean anything? Were you really looking at me like that or was I imagining it? That sort of silliness. And then I'd think, hang on a minute, you're going too fast. It's undignified in a woman of your age. You only met him the day before yesterday. Things like that.'

'What I think,' Sean said, taking Rilla's face on his hands and turning it gently so that she was facing him directly, 'is that we haven't been going nearly fast enough. We've been wasting time. We shouldn't waste any more.'

He bent his head. She closed her eyes and waited and then his mouth was on hers and she opened herself to him, and it felt to her as though something golden and warm . . . sunshine, honey, oh God, I'm losing my mind, she thought, I'm gone . . . was racing through every vein in her body, making her tremble with a pleasure she thought she'd forgotten, flooding her and filling her with happiness.

Much later, they walked up to the house together, hand-in-hand and in silence. I would have, Rilla thought. I would have let him make love to me, just like any randy teenager getting carried away on my first date. He was the one who behaved like a gentleman and a grown-up and said he had a better setting in mind for our first time. She smiled at how offended he'd seemed when she accused him of being middle-aged. *I am middle-aged*, he'd said. *And so are you. It doesn't make any difference to what I feel.*

They'd talked all night, nearly. The dawn was coming up as they walked over the dewy lawn, and the sky was streaked with pale apricot and pink. This must be, Rilla thought, the most beautiful morning there's ever been. And the day that stretched out before her would be full of amazing and wonderful things. Starting with a strawberry shortcake.

She stopped on the path to pick up her shoes and said, 'I've just decided. I'm going to make a strawberry shortcake for my mother's birthday.' She started giggling. 'Gwen'll have fifty fits. They've got Bridget coming in tomorrow, of course. She's the caterer. I don't care. I'm going to do it. I might do it now, this minute, before I go to sleep. I doubt I'll ever sleep again. Sean, do you realize? You've wrecked my sleep for ever. I shall just lie on my bed at night in future and long for you. What have you done to me?'

'Nothing,' Sean said, and they stood close together near the drawing-room door and kissed as though they never meant to stop. 'Nothing compared to what I'm going to do.'

Rilla closed her eyes and leaned against him and allowed herself to imagine it all. Everything they were going to be and do and say. Everything.

The kitchen was cool and quiet. Five o'clock in the morning was the perfect time, Rilla thought, for baking. She knew she wouldn't sleep if she went to bed now, so this was quite the most sensible thing to do. Whether she was elated or depressed, cooking took her out of herself, calmed her down, and gave her something to look forward to, even if it was nothing more than a perfect batch of biscuits.

This morning, she felt as though she were walking, or floating, at least six inches off the ground. She opened cupboards and drawers silently, conscious that the whole household was still fast asleep. Mary would be up in an hour to start the breakfast, but the shortcake would be baked by then. Later in the day, she'd put it together with cream and strawberries, and present it to Leonora tonight. I'll talk to Mary when she comes in and suggest having it for dinner, she thought.

Willow Court never ran out of ingredients. Whatever you wanted, it was always there. Sugar, icing sugar, cornflour, butter – all present and correct. Rilla put on Mary's apron, which she found hanging on the back of the kitchen door. Thank goodness, she thought, it's not one of those skimpy little things which cover one square inch of skirt and leave your top half waiting for any stain that's going.

Rilla mixed, kneaded, rolled out the pastry and slid the tins into the oven. She tried to put the night's events out of her mind, but her thoughts returned to Sean again and again. When she was with him, everything seemed possible but now, even after a mere half hour on her own, all sorts of doubts had crept into her mind. Perhaps it was just Willow Court working a sort of magic, she thought. Maybe real life, London life, would dissolve the enchantment, and the whole thing, whatever it was (she wasn't going to name it, wasn't going to risk calling it *love*) would evaporate away from this house, this party, these few days.

Rilla stepped out of the back door and looked at the Peter Rabbit garden, cool and green in the early dawn. She sat down on a bench that was pushed up against the wall and took out a cigarette. The shortcake was beginning to smell delicious. I'll just wait for it to be ready, she thought, and then I'll go to bed. There was going to be too much for everyone to do today for Rilla to opt out, and besides, any hour she spent sleeping was an hour out of Sean's company.

What would he do, she thought, if I opened his door and simply got into bed with him? The buzzer on the cooker sounded at that moment, and put such ideas out of her mind. Time to take out the shortcake. She went into the kitchen and removed the tins from the oven. Perfect golden buttery circles. She smiled, put them to cool in the larder, and made her way upstairs.

She was on the landing when a noise she couldn't identify made her start. She looked along the corridor and saw that the door to the nursery was standing open. That wasn't right, surely? No one should be there at this hour of the morning. She tiptoed up to it, her heart beating rather too fast. Don't be a wimp, she said to herself. It can't be a burglar. Maybe it's . . .

'Douggie, darling!' Rilla saw that the litle boy was standing by the dolls' house. He'd pulled the white sheet away and was holding something like a ribbon in his hand. It fell to the floor when he caught sight of her. 'You shouldn't be here, sweetheart. It isn't time to wake up yet. Not nearly. Come with me, and I'll take you back to bed.'

She went over to him and picked him up, and for a split second thought she would faint. How sweet he smelled! Markie used to smell just like this, she thought. Douggie turned half away from her and Rilla could remember how her child, too, had done that when he was struggling to leave her arms. Tears sprang into her eyes and she blinked them back.

'Come on, Douggie. Let's get you back to your room.'

'Want Mama!' Douggie began to cry.

'We'll go and find her, shall we? I'll take you, darling. Don't cry! Sssh! Everyone's asleep.'

Fiona was already up, and looking for her child. She was almost running down the corridor as they left the nursery, wearing only her nightie. Without her make-up, without her smart clothes, she looked young and fragile and very pale.

'Oh, Rilla, I'm so sorry. Did he wake you? Come on, Douggie. Come with me.'

Rilla transferred the child to his mother's arms. 'It's quite all right,' she told Fiona as mother and child were walking back to their own room. She wanted to say something about not having been to bed at all, but it didn't seem the right time for such confidences. 'No harm done.'

She went back to the nursery to cover the dolls' house again. How long had Douggie been in there? Could he have damaged anything? This was exactly the sort of thing that no one needed today. Leonora would be furious. Perhaps it would be possible for her never to know, but she did have a way of finding out what went on in Willow Court.

Rilla saw at once what Douggie had done. 'Oh, no . . .' she whispered. 'Oh, God . . .'

He'd stripped off a piece of the paper that was stuck to the roof. How many times had Leonora told Rilla and Gwen about how Maude had painted it to look just like roof tiles? Now a whole strip of it, about three inches wide, had been torn away from the wood along the whole slope of the roof. Rilla didn't hesitate. The paper Douggie had dropped lay curled on the carpet like skin peeled from a huge apple. She bent down, rolled it up tight, and put it in the pocket of her trousers. Then she took the sheet and spread it over the house, hiding the damage. She left the room and closed the door behind her, suddenly short of breath. I can't think about this now, she thought. I must sleep. She went into her bedroom filled with foreboding. What would Leonora say? Could the roof be repaired? The strip of paper stuck back again? I'll think about it all later. Sort it out then.

Rilla sat on the edge of the bed with her wallet in her hand. Now isn't the time, she thought. I'm happy. It's the best day and I should leave well enough alone, but I can't. Picking Douggie up was a mistake. Rilla could still feel that warm body in her arms, twisting away from her. He'd put his hands on her hair, just as Markie used to do. Years and years go by, she thought, and you manage to have nothing at all to do with small children and then this happens and you're back there, back in those days when you knew what a child's body in your arms felt like and you realize how much you've missed it.

She opened the wallet and looked in one of the inner pockets. There it was. She felt it with her fingers and hesitated for a second. Should she look at it? When was the last time she had? She couldn't remember. Before she had time to change her mind, she'd put the tiny photograph on the duvet beside her and seen him, just as he used to be; smiling, dark-haired, her child. Her beautiful son. He was sitting on Beth's lap in the photo booth, making a silly face. The day they'd taken that photograph, at Paddington Station on the way to Willow Court, came back to her at once. Mark had been in a bad temper for some reason. Beth had suggested the photographs as a distraction and Rilla had been grateful because he'd cheered up at once.

Now she felt tears running down her cheeks and she quickly put the little photo back into her wallet. What a fool she was, to spoil this most wonderful night! She turned her mind to Sean. Let me dream of him, she told herself. Let me not dream of Mark. Not tonight.

Rilla closed her eyes. Her last thoughts were of the curled-up paper Douggie had torn from the roof of the dolls' house. She pictured it rolled up in the pocket of her trousers and something like dread came over her. She was too exhausted to wonder why she felt like that, and her eyelids grew heavy and heavier until she was falling, plunging into darkness and sleep.

'You're up early,' Beth said.

'So are you,' Efe replied. 'Douggie woke me. That bloody kid doesn't know what sleeping in means.' He picked up the coffee pot and poured himself another cup. Black with no sugar. Macho coffee, Beth called it. He raised the pot in the air and smiled at her. 'Want a cup?'

'Yes, please,' Beth answered and pulled out a chair. She sat down opposite Efe, and decided not to mention that it was his son who'd woken her also. 'Where are all the others?'

'Mum's out and about with Dad. They're waiting for the chairs and tables people. In about an hour the whole place will be crawling with people fixing things up. Haven't a clue where Alex and Rilla are. Chloë won't get cracking till about noon, probably, but her tree's well on the way. Did you see it?'

Beth nodded. She cut herself two slices of bread and put them into the toaster. Then she sat down again and reached for the butter and marmalade. She'd noticed that most of the hall was strewn with willow branches and, although she believed that her cousin would transform it into something amazing, she wondered at Leonora allowing it. The person Beth remembered from her childhood would never have tolerated it. She was definitely getting softer in her old age.

The toast popped up and she went to fetch it. Efe was looking at the financial page of the newspaper, which gave her a little time. He was wearing chinos and a turquoise linen shirt and his hair fell over his forehead in a way that made Beth feel a little breathless. She turned her mind, with some effort, away from these unproductive thoughts. This opportunity had presented itself quite unexpectedly, and she was determined to seize the chance of a private talk with Efe. It was the first time they'd been alone together for ages and ages; too good a chance to miss. Part of her wanted to talk about something that would put Efe in a good mood, but there were simply too many questions she had to ask, even though she wasn't at all sure she wanted to know the answers to some of them. Okay, she said to herself. No hesitations.

'Who's Melanie?' she asked.

'Why? What do you mean? I don't know a Melanie.'

'Yes, you do. I overheard you talking to one yesterday.'

'You were eavesdropping!' A typical Efe answer, Beth thought. Throw the blame on someone else.

'I wasn't,' Beth replied, trying not to sound like her twelve-year-old self. The trouble with talking to someone you'd grown up with was that you soon reverted to your childish modes of speech. 'You weren't hiding yourself away, exactly. Anyone could have walked in.'

'You mean Fiona, don't you? By anyone.'

'Right. What if she'd overheard you instead of me?'

'I'd have pretended there was nothing in it. She always believes me. I can charm her whenever I want to.'

Beth said, 'You'd have *pretended*. That means there *is* something in it.'

Efe held his hands up, in a gesture of surrender. 'Got me there!'

'Okay. So who is she?'

Efe leaned towards her across the table, took hold of her hand and gazed into her eyes. 'I can't tell you that, Bethie darling. Not unless you swear not to tell a soul.'

Should I agree? Beth wondered. Should I tell him to go to hell? I don't need to know details. He's admitted he's being unfaithful to Fiona. That should be enough, but I want to know everything. She became aware that a most peculiar series of emotions was passing through her, like those constantly changing neon lights in big cinemas that keep flooding the screen with every colour of the rainbow in turn. She wanted to know about Melanie. She shrank from knowing. She wanted to shout at Efe and tell him how unkind to his wife he was being. She wanted him to say *Melanie is nothing to me. I want you and no one else, not Fiona or anyone. Only you.* She saw him suddenly as selfish and cruel, smiling at the thought of deceiving his wife. She wanted to stay alone with him for ever. She wanted to run away and never see him again. She said, 'Okay, go on. I shan't say a word.'

'It's Melanie Havering. You've met her, surely?'

'From the antique shop? But . . .'

'I know, I know. Don't say it. She's old!'

'I wasn't going to say that. Only she's a good friend of Gwen's.'

'So? Gwen's friends are allowed to be sexy, you know. And Melanie isn't that old, actually. She's only forty-five.'

'That's fine, then,' Beth said. 'That makes it all all right. God, Efe, what are you thinking of? Your mum's friend! Isn't it embarrassing? What happens when she comes here to see Gwen and James? And hasn't Melanie got a husband?'

Efe smiled. He was, Beth noticed, positively sparkling now, as though admitting to this affair somehow made him feel better. He said, 'She's divorced. And when she does come up while I'm here, it all gets fantastically exciting. We have to take chances sometimes . . .'

'I don't want to hear about it, thanks very much. It's revolting.'

'No, it's not. It's great. Oh, grow up, Beth! You know what goes on. My dad used to be a bit of a lad in the early days, apparently, and got up to all sorts of stuff. No one minds, surely.'

'I don't suppose Gwen was exactly ecstatic when she found out,' Beth said.

'She's stayed with him.' Efe picked up the second piece of toast

Beth had made for herself and started to butter it. 'She would have left him if she'd had any strong objections.'

Beth decided to change the subject. There was no point, she could see, in explaining to Efe about all the other reasons his mother might have had for deciding to turn a blind eye. Like the fact that she had three children to consider. Like the fact that she loved him in spite of his infidelities. In any case, he was a reformed character now. Men were such fools sometimes and Efe was beginning to irritate her.

If the conversation had gone differently, Beth thought she might have been brave enough to ask Efe about his violence towards his wife. While she was with Fiona, she'd felt a blind rage overtaking her, and if Efe had been in the room with them, she might very well have lost it and yelled at him, screamed at him for his unkindness and for not being the person she'd been dreaming he was for years and years. Now, though, faced with him across the table, smiling and looking just as he always did, it was hard to believe that he could be the man Fiona had described to her. She knew she should say something, do something that might possibly help the situation, but she could hear voices outside the kitchen. Chloë and Philip were coming, so that was that.

'Hiya,' Chloë said, and slumped down into the chair next to Beth, white as a ghost. 'This is what mornings look like, then. Glad I don't see too many of them. Pass the juice, Efe.'

She ran her hands through her hair and it stood up in spikes. She was wearing baggy jeans, and a T-shirt splotched with paint in various colours and torn in several places.

Efe said, 'Chloë, are you properly awake? Can you listen a minute?'

He can't, Beth thought. He can't start discussing Reuben Stronsky's offer now, with Chloë still half asleep and Philip already absorbed in the sports pages that Efe had discarded.

'It's about the Ethan Walsh pictures. Don't you think they ought to be seen by more people? Don't you think Leonora should accept Stronsky's offer?'

'Not sure, really.' Chloë was pouring milk on her muesli. 'A museum in the States would be cool. But Willow Court is part of the . . . you know . . . the image. You'd lose that.'

'Does that matter?'

'Does to Leonora.'

'But if you had to choose. God, Chloë, I want *someone* on my side. Tell me I'm not crazy.'

'No, okay. It's a good idea, I suppose. I wouldn't mind a bit of jetting across the Atlantic.'

'Brilliant!' Efe said. 'Thanks, really. That's you and me and Fiona and Dad I think. Mum says she's against the whole thing, but I bet she'd come round in the end. What about you, Beth? What do you think?'

Beth longed to be on Efe's side. If she said she was with him on this, Efe would be pleased with her, she knew that. But what would Leonora do if the paintings left the house? What would become of Willow Court? One thing she was quite sure of, it wouldn't be the house it always had been, a fixed point in her life for as long as she could remember.

'I don't want anything to change at Willow Court. I'm sorry, Efe. I want the pictures to stay where they are.'

Efe's face darkened and he shot her a look of such naked hostility that she felt herself growing pale.

'Right then,' he said, pushing back his chair and standing up. 'I'm going out to see if I can help with the chairs and so on. See you.'

He left the room without another word, and Beth immediately felt guilty and as though she'd done something wrong.

'Don't look like that, Beth,' said Chloë. 'It's not the end of the world. Not even the middle of the world, really. My dear brother likes everyone to eat out of his hand. You're allowed to disagree with him, you know.'

'I hate it when he's cross though. Don't you hate it, Chloë?'

'He can get stuffed,' said Chloë. 'Don't let him bully you, Beth. He's a bully. He's got Fiona completely under his thumb, but she's a fool.'

Beth was on the point of telling Chloë about her conversation with Fiona in the bathroom, when she suddenly thought better of it. If his sister didn't know about that side of him then maybe she shouldn't be the one to tell her about it.

'Chloë, there you are, darling.' Gwen came into the room, looking, Beth thought, like an advertisement for the Ideal Mother. Rilla

230

generally appeared at breakfast in London wrapped in an ancient silk kimono and with her hair all over the place, and Beth marvelled as she always did at the difference between Leonora's daughters. Gwen was wearing black cotton trousers and a pale pink shirt, but the earrings were on, the hair was neatly brushed and the powder and lipstick were in place.

'I hope,' Gwen said, sitting down opposite her and helping herself to more toast made by Beth, 'that you and Philip intend doing something with the mess in the hall this morning.'

Beth held her breath and waited for an explosion of some kind from Chloë, but all she did was stare witheringly at her mother before announcing, 'That's my tree. Remember my tree? We discussed it yesterday. That's why I've got up so fucking early.'

'Chloë!' Gwen's mouth was pursed in disapproval.

'Sorry, sorry!' Chloë said, looking entirely unconcerned. She pushed her chair back. 'I'm off.'

She stomped out of the room and turned at the door to make a face at Beth and hold up her fingers in a V-sign behind Gwen's back.

'My mother's a pain,' Chloë said. She was standing on a stepladder, holding two willow branches steady with one hand and binding them with thin wire to a stem made from what looked suspiciously like a broom handle encased in foil. 'You're lucky, really, not to be related by blood to this lot. They've all got something wrong with them, except me of course. Pass me another bit of wire, Philip.'

Beth laughed. The devoted and silent Philip stood next to Chloë handing her what she needed. 'Nothing wrong with Rilla,' Beth said loyally. 'I've always got on with her perfectly well. And Alex. Nothing to complain about there either.'

'You're unnatural. You get on well with everyone. Rilla's okay, though. Bet you don't know what time she came back last night from wherever she was.'

'I don't think she went anywhere.'

'Well, she was outside somewhere and she certainly came back at about five o'clock. I saw her and Sean Everard walking up to the house holding hands. They looked completely shagged out. But happy. Yeah, definitely happy.'

231

'What were you doing looking out of the window at five o'clock anyway?' Beth said.

'I got up to go to the loo. Douggie must have woken me up. He's always crying early in the morning. Have you noticed? I just glanced out of the window and saw them. Fast work, I call that. He's nice, though, Sean, isn't he? What'd you think if he became your sort of stepfather?'

'Bloody hell, Chloë, you're jumping the gun a bit, aren't you? They were just walking up to the house together, that's all.'

Chloë giggled. 'You didn't see them. I'm telling you, something's going on there. I dare you to ask Rilla.'

'I will, too. I'll ask her as soon as she gets up.'

'She won't be up for ages,' Chloë pulled the branch she was working on into position. 'She only got to bed a few hours ago. I reckon you won't see her till lunchtime. How's that looking?'

'Great,' said Beth, but her attention wasn't really on the creation of trees, however beautiful. She added, 'I'm going out to see what's going on in the marquee, Chloë. My head's reeling with all this relationship stuff. See you.'

The chairs and tables had been unloaded from the truck that brought them and several men were going into the marquee, setting them down, and coming out again in a kind of procession.

'Hello, there, Beth!' said James, who was enjoying overseeing this work. He looked rather like an army officer in his khaki trousers and a vaguely military looking shirt. 'Very efficient, these chaps, aren't they?'

Alex was beside the truck photographing the whole operation. He came quickly across the grass towards Beth as soon as he caught sight of her.

'Hi, Alex!' she said, and smiled at him. James had disappeared into the marquee to make sure that all the furniture was properly distributed. 'Your dad's enjoying himself, isn't he?'

'Thinks he's General Montgomery. Almost expect him to salute, in that outfit. Sleep well?'

Beth nodded. 'You're up early, aren't you?'

'Didn't want to miss this light. I'm finished now, though. Come for a walk?'

'Okay.' Beth fell in beside him and they made their way towards the drive. 'Where are we going? And do we really have to go so fast? I want to ask you something.'

'Sorry.' Alex slowed down at once. 'Let's drop in and see Nanny Mouse, shall we? I haven't been down there yet.'

'Nor me. It's a good idea. I always mean to go and see her, but I hate going on my own. I'm not sure if she really knows who I am and I can't think of what to say.'

'I find her quite restful, really. Doesn't matter what you say, she'll have forgotten it before you've left the room.'

The sun shone through the leaves of the trees along the drive and made shadows flicker over Alex's face. For a moment, Beth considered asking him again about that day by the lake, the day when Mark died, but thought better of it. He'd seemed so reluctant to talk about it and so obviously regretted bringing it up in the first place that she hadn't the heart to remind him. He might know about Efe, though, and Fiona.

'Alex, may I ask you something?' she said. 'You don't have to tell me if you don't want to.'

'Go on, then. What is it?'

'I caught Fiona crying in the bathroom yesterday. She showed me her arms and they were covered in bruises. She told me Efe sometimes loses his temper with her. Did you know that?'

'I saw them too. The bruises.' Alex said nothing for a few moments, then, 'He's capable of it, you know, Beth. He's my brother and I feel disloyal saying this about him but he does get kind of out of control sometimes.'

Beth sighed. 'I know that, really. I've seen him, occasionally, only I never thought . . .' Her voice faded away. 'Oh, Alex, what can we do? Shouldn't we say something? Maybe we ought to tell your mum and dad. Or Leonora. What do you think?'

'I could speak to him, I suppose,' Alex said. 'But I doubt he'd listen to me. He'd probably deny it. Fiona's the one who has to deal with it. You could maybe talk to her.'

'I hardly know her and . . .'

'I know. You don't think much of her, either.'

Beth looked searchingly at Alex. 'You don't miss much, do you? I have tried to keep my opinion of her to myself. Is it that obvious? I feel sorry for her now, though.' She stopped walking and leaned against a tree. 'I don't know what I think about anything any more. I don't feel the same today as I did yesterday about anything. What's happening, Alex? Why is Efe so different from how he usually is?'

'He's not different at all,' Alex said gently. 'It's just that this is the first time for ages that we've all been together for a few days, and so you get to see other bits of him. The bits that aren't on display when you go round to his flat for dinner for instance. He's always liked his own way, and has always managed to charm people when he wants something out of them. He's been charming you for years, hasn't he?'

'Alex! You sound as though you're jealous!' Beth started to laugh, but she stopped at once when she saw Alex's face.

'Of course I'm not jealous,' he said, 'but I have begun to notice certain things. The way you look at him, for instance. I'm surprised no one else has seen it.'

'He makes me angry, most of the time. And anyway, you're just as bad. We've both of us sort of worshipped him since we were kids, haven't we?'

Alex nodded and adopted a tactic Beth had seen him use many times. He changed the subject.

'When we last went down to see Nanny Mouse,' he said, as though he'd never mentioned Beth's feelings, 'she thought I was Efe at first. Then she got confused all over again and called me Peter. I hope we can get her to recognize us for a bit.'

'It'll be okay. She drifts in and out of real life, doesn't she? In and out of what's happening now and you have to catch those moments when she's making sense as they go past you.'

Alex smiled at her and Beth was surprised how comforted he made her feel. He was always the same. Always there and always reliable. He hadn't changed. Unlike Efe. For years now Efe had been the focus of all her dreams. It was only in the last few hours that she'd begun to realize that the person she'd been fantasising about for so long was perhaps not exactly who she'd thought he was, but someone quite different. Someone who was capable of violence, and who thought

234

nothing of being unfaithful to his wife. I still love him, Beth thought, but was immediately aware of a tiny doubt creeping over her like the thinnest of mists, dissipating almost at once but leaving behind some trace, some inkling, that she would never again feel quite the same about him.

Alex. Beth looked at him striding along beside her in silence, and found herself considering him for the very first time in her life as a man. As someone whom she might touch, might kiss, might be able to love. Greatly to her surprise, such imaginings, far from shocking her, sent a small thrill through her, as though an electric current had passed along her body. This is ridiculous, she thought. This is Alex. It's mad to start thinking about him like this. Quite mad.

'We're here, Beth,' Alex said.

'Sorry, Alex, I was miles away.'

Alex knocked at the door of Lodge Cottage and Miss Lardner opened it at once. She must, Beth thought, have been standing just inside, waiting for them.

'I saw you coming down the drive,' she said. 'How very good it is to see you both! You're just in time for elevenses.'

Beth caught Alex's eye and they smiled at one another. She knew that they were both thinking the same thing exactly: this was the only place in the world where everyone still believed in elevenses. She said, 'That'll be lovely, Miss Lardner. We'd love some elevenses, wouldn't we, Alex?'

'Can't think of anything I'd like better,' Alex answered. He sounded dangerously close to laughter. He followed Beth into the tiny drawing-room where Nanny Mouse was nodding in her favourite armchair.

Whenever he sat in one of Nanny Mouse's armchairs, Alex felt like Alice after she'd taken the magic potion and grown too big for the White Rabbit's house. He remembered every detail of the illustration from the book he'd loved since he was seven; poor Alice's arms and legs pressing against the walls, her head at a strange angle. He put his feet together and pulled them as close as he possibly could to his chair.

The cups and saucers at Lodge Cottage were probably the same size as crockery everywhere else, but because they were so dainty, and patterned with roses and edged with gold, it made him feel clumsy just to look at them, and he hurried to finish his coffee (instant and too weak) and put the saucer down on the tiny little table that Miss Lardner had placed beside him.

Beth was doing a grand job, talking to the old lady. What Alex had told Beth about how much he enjoyed visiting Nanny Mouse was true, but there were ways in which he sometimes felt uncomfortable in Nanny Mouse's company. Or maybe uncomfortable wasn't the right word. On edge, in case anything happened to her, perhaps, and he'd have to deal with it. That was nonsense as well. Miss Lardner was always on hand. Still, Nanny Mouse was so old that she had become almost translucent and, even at her best, there was a faint trembling about her which made him nervous. He turned his attention to the many photographs in ornate frames up on the mantelpiece.

Most of them were well-known to him because he'd seen copies of them in family albums that belonged to Leonora and Gwen. All the baby pictures were there in force. Leonora herself, as a baby at her christening, swathed in cascades of lace; Rilla's christening, wearing the same dress and carried by Leonora; Gwen and Rilla wearing smocked dresses and standing rather awkwardly against their mother's skirt. Not a very professional shot, that one, with Leonora cut off at the waist. You could see her hand reaching out to rest on Gwen's hair. It always surprised Alex, who spent ages working on the best shot, the right light, and some kind of interesting composition how the old photos, with all their imperfections, turned out often to be more moving than anything he could achieve. Or maybe he was just romanticising the past, which had a lustre of its own just because it had disappeared long ago and left behind nothing but this faint trace of itself.

Had Beth realized what he'd admitted to? He looked at her, chatting and smiling with Nanny Mouse and wondered. If she'd taken it in, she wasn't showing what she felt. Maybe she hadn't decided yet. I'm an idiot, Alex thought. I don't know how to do that sort of thing. Were you actually supposed to come out and say it? *I love you.* Just like that? Was he some kind of a freak because he'd never articulated the words before? All the women he'd known had picked up the signals without him needing to say a word. He reflected ruefully that maybe these affairs, lasting not more than a few months most of them, would have turned out more satisfactorily if he'd spoken of his feelings. You weren't supposed to lie, though, he knew that much. It dawned on him that the reason he'd never loved another woman properly before was that he'd been preoccupied with Beth all his life, without even being conscious of it.

I mistook it for something else entirely, he thought. A mixture of friendship and admiration. It's taken me all these years to recognize that it might be something more. To acknowledge the fact that I love her and there's nothing to stop her from loving me. Nothing but the fact that she's besotted with Efe. Alex sighed. Nanny Mouse was talking to him now and he made a big effort to concentrate. You had to keep your wits about you when you embarked on a conversation with someone whose focus kept shifting.

'She was very ill, you know,' Nanny Mouse confided. 'She should never have run out of doors like that. It wasn't allowed.'

'Wasn't it?' Alex said, and Beth smiled at him and came to his rescue.

'Who was ill, Nanny? Do you mean Leonora?'

'Yes, of course. She caught a dreadful chill which turned to pneumonia. I nursed her through it. Oh, she was burning up with the fever! She missed her birthday, you know. We had to give her all her presents later. There was a little boy who drowned too. Did you know that?'

Beth nodded. Alex could see her calculating whether it was worth explaining about Mark, and her relationship to him. She changed the subject instead.

'What lovely flowers, Nanny! You like roses best, don't you?'

'If you keep them for a very long time, they turn into beautiful dried roses. Did you know that? I used to do it. I used to make pot-pourri, which smelled better than the ones you get nowadays. All chemicals they are. Not real dried flowers.'

Alex raised his eyebrows. Life was definitely too short to discuss pot-pourri, chemical or otherwise. Beth winked at him and said, 'We must go now, Nanny. It'll be lunchtime soon. We'll come again.' She stood up and kissed the old lady, who suddenly turned and clung to her hand.

'She was wearing her best dress,' she said, near to tears, her voice wobbling. 'Lilac lace, it was. She looked beautiful. But it was ruined of course. Soaked and torn and quite, quite spoiled. I gave it to Tyler to burn with the garden rubbish. The master wasn't in a state to do anything.'

'Goodbye, Nanny,' Alex said, leading Beth over to the door. 'Thanks for elevenses.'

As Alex and Beth left Lodge Cottage, a car came to a screeching halt on the drive beside them. It was Efe's Audi, with Fiona and Douggie in it, too, and although Alex knew for a fact that they'd gone into the village on some errand for Gwen, they looked as though they'd all been out for a delightful jaunt. Douggie waved at them from his child seat. Fiona seemed prettier and more relaxed than she had for days, and after she'd wound down the window on her side, Efe leaned right over her to speak to them.

'Bloody hell, you two, you're a bit early with the duty visits, aren't you?'

'Not duty at all. We've had elevenses,' Beth said. Alex noticed that she was smiling. 'Remember those? We used to have them when we were kids.'

'Rich Tea biscuits and milky cocoa,' Efe said. 'Want a lift up to the house?'

'Love one, thanks,' Beth said and turned to Alex. 'Coming, Alex?'

Alex shook his head. 'No, that's okay. I'm going into the village myself now, I think.' He didn't really need to go there, but nothing would have made him get into the same car with Beth and Efe. A shadow had fallen over the day, and he realized as he saw her stepping into the car exactly how much he'd been waiting to talk to her again once they'd left Nanny Mouse. Now he had no idea when he'd be able to get her alone. Up at Willow Court there was so much going on and so many people coming and going that it would be almost impossible. Shit. Bloody Efe sailing in there at exactly the wrong time and snatching things away. It had always been the same. Throughout their lives, it seemed to Alex, Efe had been the one to push himself forward, but perhaps it wasn't like that at all. It's probably me, he thought. I hang back too much. It isn't Efe's fault. I don't speak when

I should. I don't volunteer. I'd never have had the nerve, if it is nerve, to put an arm round Beth just now and say, no, Beth's coming with me, I'm afraid. Sorry, Efe! What would she have done? She may have gone with them anyway. Alex stood by the gate wondering whether he had the energy to walk into the village. Perhaps he was imagining it, but Beth seemed relieved to be getting into Efe's car. Relieved to be getting away from me, Alex thought. A picture of her stepping eagerly into the car and leaning over to kiss Douggie filled his mind so that he walked down the road in a daze of jealousy. She hadn't even waved at him as they left, much less actually said goodbye. You've got no chance, Alex, he said to himself, and set off down the road, staring at the tarmac, seeing nothing.

Oh God, Beth thought, staring at the back of Efe's head. For a wild moment, she wondered what would happen if she stroked his hair. She had both hands firmly in her lap and was happy to submit to Douggie hitting her playfully over and over again with his cloth rabbit.

I shouldn't have just left Alex, she thought. I should have gone with him and let him say whatever it was that he wanted to say. I should have been braver. She knew that one of the reasons she'd seized the chance to drive up to the house with Efe and Fiona was to avoid confronting Alex and the declaration that she knew he was preparing to make. I'm cruel, she thought. He must have been struggling for ages to say as much as he did say, and now he'll have to start from scratch. She almost asked Efe to stop the car, but they were already at the door of Willow Court.

I'm not completely cured of Efe yet, she thought miserably, listening as they got out of the car to Fiona telling her about the way they'd had to go down to the shop and get Douggie some fish fingers, without which he apparently couldn't survive.

'Nearly panic stations, I can tell you,' she breathed.

Beth said, 'I can imagine.'

Efe had clearly made it up with Fiona. He'd been stroking her thigh as Beth was getting into the car, and now the two of them were going up the front steps together with their arms around one another, leaving her to take charge of Douggie. They were smiling, too, in an embarrassingly coy and revolting way. It was quite clear to Beth that they'd been making love earlier. When on earth had he found the time? He must have gone to find her straight after their conversation about Melanie Havering. Just talking about it to me, Beth thought, probably made him feel horny. You could practically smell it on them. How had they managed it with Douggie around all the time? Maybe Gwen had taken him off for a bit to play in the garden or something. Beth had a sudden vision of Efe and Fiona falling into one another's arms, unable to stop themselves, carried away, barely able to breathe for the passion that overtook them. By the time she'd followed them inside, she felt bruised and sore and breathless, as though someone had hit her hard. She peered down the drive to see whether perhaps Alex had followed the car, but he was nowhere to be seen and she was surprised at how disappointed she was.

'Come on, Douggie,' she said, trying to sound cheerful. 'Let's go and see where Rilla is.'

Rilla lay in bed and wished fervently that she hadn't drunk quite so much the night before. I'm getting too old for it, she thought, and debated the wisdom of opening her eyes. When she'd first told her mother that she wanted to be an actress, Leonora had remarked rather acidly, 'Well, dear, theatre work will be most suitable for you, won't it? You are an owl rather than a lark.'

That was one way of putting it. Rilla just thought of herself as not terribly good in the mornings. No one knew that every day since Mark's death she'd woken up with a new shock of pain that seemed to catch her just below the heart. She generally managed to push it down or put it away, or at least reduce it to manageable proportions before she got out of bed. Today was different. The weight on her heart was lighter and that was Sean's doing. She hadn't been so drunk last night that she had forgotten what had happened. It was coming back to her in every delicious detail and she stretched out under the duvet, wondering why it was that she wasn't completely, totally happy. I've been dreaming of something like this, she said to herself, longing for it, so now what's the matter?

A dream. She'd had a dream, and in the way that dreams have of floating in wisps across your mind, fragments of it came drifting back now to trouble her. Fuck, she thought. I can't even be properly happy for a few uninterrupted hours without some horrible nightmare coming and spoiling it all. What was this one about? Mark was somewhere in it, as he always was. Running out of the gazebo with his hands outstretched and there was a mirror behind him. How could that be? There wasn't any logic to dreams, Rilla knew, and she should put this one out of her mind on a day like today, that promised to be so happy.

There were things she should be doing. She ought to go and tell Mary about the strawberry shortcake. She ought to make a huge effort to look really beautiful for Sean. She ought to check that Gwen didn't need any help with the last-minute arrangements, even at the risk of being rebuffed. She ought to phone Ivan. He must think she'd vanished off the face of the earth. What she certainly ought not to do was lie in bed and cry and that was what she was doing. She could feel unwanted, uncalled-for tears trickling down her cheeks and gathering in the crease of her neck. I did it, she thought miserably. That's why I can never, never be happy, whatever good things happen. However well everything is going it comes down to this: Mark's death was my fault. I never should have left him and I'll never forgive myself.

# March 1982

Rilla tucked the phone under her chin, held her lighter as far as she possibly could from the mouthpiece, and clicked it into flame as quietly as she knew how to light the cigarette that was already in her mouth.

'Rilla? Rilla darling, is that you lighting another cigarette?'

My mother should hang upside down from a beam, Rilla thought. Your average bat is no match for her. She smiled and said, 'Cigarette? Of course not. Must be something you heard on the line.'

Was that convincing? Rilla was an actress and in normal circumstances would have sworn she could lie to her mother with the best of them. She'd been doing it for years. Just lately though, Leonora had been particularly sharp about tuning in to what her daughter was really feeling. Rilla's marriage was over. She and Jon had come to that conclusion weeks ago, but now it was going to be public property, and even though they were both determined to have what was known as 'a civilized divorce', the fact that Jon was a pop star meant that the whole world seemed to be interested in such gory details as there were.

There weren't nearly as many as the *Sun* and the *Mirror* would have liked, but trust Leonora to be the first to find out that the Fredericks' split had now made the front pages.

'Listen to this, Rilla!' she said. 'It's from the *Sun*, the front page. I thought I should warn you. I knew you wouldn't be up yet.'

Rilla wondered how the hell her mother had managed to get hold of a copy of the *Sun* at Willow Court first thing in the morning. One of the gardening lads must have brought it into the house. Surely she can't have ordered it from the shop in the village?

She said, 'Okay, go ahead. I'm listening.' She pulled her silk kimono from Hong Kong (heavenly turquoise embroidered with scarlet and gold dragons, a present from Jon in the days when he still gave her presents) more closely around herself and turned her attention to her mother's voice.

Anyone who knows anything at all about Jon Frederick and his wife, the luscious Rilla Frederick, star of *Night Creatures*, and seen on our TV screens rather less often these days than she used to be . . .

'Is that true, darling?'
'Yes, Mother, 'fraid so,' said Rilla, trying to sound nonchalant. 'Do go on.'
'Where was I? Oh, yes. Right.

. . . won't need reminding of the lavish partygiving lifestyle the couple have enjoyed since they tied the knot five years ago. But all good things are about to grind to a sticky end with the news of the couple's upcoming divorce. Jon, on the eve of his forthcoming European 'Feel the Heat' tour says, 'We're still the very best of friends, but can't cut the mustard marriage-wise any longer. I have to be free to pursue my artistic goals, and Rilla has her own irons in the fire.'

Jon and Rilla are the parents of five-year-old Mark and Jon has made it clear that they will share custody of the child. He adds, 'Not only that. Beth, my daughter by my first wife (the late Carol Edmonds), regards Rilla as her mother and has insisted on continuing to live with her. That's fine by me, because Rilla is a perfect mother, and me, well, I'm a bit of a rover and a rambler. Footloose and fancy free, that's my style. And what children need is security.'

Our showbiz reporter adds that Jon's fancy-free status is under serious attack from gorgeous starlet Chansonne Dubois, who wowed crowds at his last concert with her topless rendition of 'Tell Me How to Do It to You, Baby'.

'What do you think about all that, Rilla?'
'Actually, I think it's rather good. Accurate, in any case, which is more than you can say about most of the stuff that appears in the press.'
Leonora's sigh travelled down the line, and Rilla said quickly,

'Don't sigh, Mother. I'll be fine. I've got Mark, and Beth's with me for most of the time, and we're all here in my lovely house. I'm okay. I'll manage.'

'I'm sure you will, darling, but I worry about you. Why don't you come down to Willow Court for a bit?'

'I'll think about it, Mother, honestly. It's kind of you to ask us, but it's the middle of the week and there's school. And anyway, haven't you got your hands full with Chloë?'

Leonora laughed. 'Yes, she *is* quite a handful, that child. Makes her presence felt, you might say. But I wouldn't worry about Beth's school. She's such an intelligent child. A couple more children here will hardly be noticed, I promise you. Nanny Mouse will be in her element.'

'It's getting late, Mother. Markie'll be waking up in a minute and I must go and get breakfast for Beth and take her to school. I'll phone you tonight and tell you what I've decided. Thanks for ringing. 'Bye.'

'Goodbye, darling. Kiss Beth and that sweet baby of yours for me.'

'I will. 'Bye!'

She put the phone down, and there was Beth, standing quietly by the door. She was already dressed for school. At eight years old, she was self-possessed and self-sufficient, but shy. She had plaited her own long, dark hair (not as well as I would have done it, Rilla thought, but brilliantly considering how young she is) and was looking at Rilla now with a smile that lit up her serious, pale face and made her eyes shine. That smile was Jon's. It was the most attractive thing about him, and he'd gifted it straight to his daughter. Mark had it too, even though he was much more like her. The love she felt for her son seemed to Rilla like an ocean deep inside her, washing over her all the time, filling her with a pleasure that was the best thing she'd known in her whole life, ever.

No one warned you. There were thousands of books and poems written about love and scarcely any of them touched on how you feel for the flesh that is truly your flesh. Almost from the moment of conception, Rilla was aware of *someone*, a person, to whom she would always be bound. The notion of cells and nerve-endings and growing foetuses never entered her head. Her child was someone she had adored even before he was as big as a fingernail and, what's more, she had imagined throughout her pregnancy a complete character for him; she visualized him so clearly that when he was born she recognized his face. When the doctor put Mark into her arms for the first time, she saw how paltry, how incomplete, how inadequate all other love was and forever would be. This boy, this creature with enormous eyes and a pink mouth puckered like a small flower, was exactly the person she'd been expecting.

'Oh, Jon,' she whispered. 'Look at him. Just look.'

Every part of her ached with a love so strong that she thought the separate atoms of her body might fly apart at any moment.

As for Beth, she'd been Rilla's child even before Mark was born, and Mark's birth hadn't changed that. She loved Beth just as much as she ever would have loved a daughter of her own and no longer ever thought of herself as a stepmother. Beth was hers, and that was that. Now that she'd given birth, she realized the truth of what her mother and Gwen and countless friends had all told her. The feelings you have for each child are different, because each child is different, but the intensity of the love was just the same. She adored Beth and, strangely, this feeling grew stronger once Mark was born. She was constantly amazed and delighted that she (her body, her heart) could contain so many different strands of love, all at the same time.

'Hello, chicken!' said Rilla. 'I was just coming to get you. How long have you been standing there? Leonora's been chewing my ear off.'

'Did she say we could go to Willow Court? Please, please say we can, Rilla! I love going there.'

'I know you do,' she said. 'Yes, I expect we will, tomorrow. I daresay it won't hurt you to miss a couple of days of school.' Rilla went upstairs to dress Mark whom she could hear wandering around in the bathroom. Beth followed her up the stairs, skipping with happiness.

'I can play with Efe and Alex. We've got a den. Did you see our den? It's in those bushes by the lake. Right next to the bank. Efe said he's going to try and get a boat for us in the summer, so we can go out on the water.'

Rilla wasn't really listening. She was thinking about that part of what Leonora had read out to her that said something about her not being on TV as much as she used to be. It was true, too. She'd been trying to fool herself that everything was exactly the same, but it wasn't. She was getting less and less work. There wasn't anything now till after Easter, and that was only a voice-over for a toothpaste ad. She tried not to think about how long it had been since she'd had a proper part in a real movie or a TV play, but she knew exactly. There had been nothing since *Reasons of the Heart* six months ago and that was just a tiny part as the heroine's best friend. I'll make more effort soon, she said to herself. Get about more. Talk seriously to Dennis. He's a sweetie but he really isn't putting himself out for me as much as an agent should. I'll take charge of my career, and not leave it all to other people. I'll go out to movie premieres and first nights. I won't just sit here with the children, making gingerbread men with Beth after school, or pushing Markie in the swings in the park.

The truth, which Rilla had told no one, was that getting a 'civilized divorce' was not as easy as it looked. She'd loved her husband well enough, and they'd had a good enough life together while it lasted for her to feel let-down and miserable and angry with Jon and, worst of all, disgusted with herself. These days, she looked at her face in the mirror and saw nothing but ugliness and the signs of age and unhappiness. She'd cried so much at the beginning, when he'd first broken the news, that now her eyes seemed permanently red and there were shadows under them that on bad days looked like two black eyes. She slathered on the make-up, knowing she was doing no more than putting on a mask that would disguise from everyone else the fact that she wasn't coping. Not at all.

I'm good at disguises, she thought. *Isn't Rilla marvellous? So brave! So cheerful!* She'd overheard people saying so at the parties she was too proud not to go to, though they were torture, most of them, with everyone paired off; passengers on some ghastly ark or other, sailing two by two into the night. Any single men at these affairs were uniformly unattractive to her, and she knew it was her fault rather than theirs.

Nobody knows, she thought, that I am kept afloat by pills. Tranquillisers, which didn't exactly make her tranquil, but which dulled the pain a little and made it possible to go through the motions of her life. There were the children to consider. You couldn't crack up if you had someone else to look after. What did Mick Jagger call them? *Mother's little helper.* That was exactly what they were. They smoothed over the rough edges of her life well enough for most people, but not, of course, for Beth. She was sharper than everyone else, always looking anxiously at Rilla to make sure she was all right. She'd sit on the chair in Mark's room while Rilla sang her way through the six songs he had to have sung to him every night, watching carefully. And Beth often asked as they sat down to their supper, after Mark was asleep, 'We'll be all right, won't we, Rilla? Now that Dad's gone, I mean.'

Rilla tried always to answer with a lift in her voice, saying something like, "Course we will, honeybunch! And your dad's not gone. Not really. He'll come and visit us really soon. He'll always be your dad, you know. He'll always love you best in the world.'

Beth usually picked up her knife and fork and said nothing, but you could practically see the thoughts in her head: *Then why doesn't Daddy phone me? That person with the funny name. He likes her better than he likes me. He's always going off to different countries and he never takes me with him. He can't love me properly.*

Now that they were outside the bathroom, Rilla shook her head and tried to focus on what needed to be done. Dress Mark. Right. Take Beth to school. Okay.

'Come on, sweetiepie,' she said to her son, who was busy floating a family of four yellow plastic ducks in the basin. 'You put the plug in all by yourself, didn't you? That's clever, but you must put the ducks on the shelf now and brush your teeth and then we have to get dressed. Beth's going to be late for school if we don't hurry up.'

Rilla moved the ducks and before Mark had time to object, she wet a flannel and began to wash his face.

'NO!' he shouted, and then added with less conviction, 'I want ducks! I don't want dressing.'

'We're going to Willow Court, Markie,' Beth said from the door, where she was standing. Rilla smiled at her over Mark's head. Amazing how she always knew exactly what to say to please and distract him. He grinned and said, 'Willow Court! Now. Now today? Will I play with Jeffrey and George? Let's go today.'

Mark spent hours at Willow Court trying to persuade the two old cats to play with him. Sometimes he almost succeeded, and Jeffrey had been known to chase a tinkling ball for a few minutes before retiring to his customary snoozing. George was cleverer at putting himself out of reach of all children by hiding somewhere in the garden, but Mark could spot his black tail from a very long way away if he'd forgotten to camouflage that properly.

'Tomorrow. If you're good,' said Rilla, 'and stand quite still while I dress you, then we'll be able to pack everything up ready while Beth's at school and as soon as we wake up tomorow, we'll be off. Westward ho!'

'Westward ho!' both children shouted. It was what they always said in the car, as they set off for Leonora's house.

'Will Efe be there? And Alex?' Her son's eyes were bright and Rilla kissed the tip of his nose.

'Of course. And the baby. Remember Chloë? Efe and Alex's new baby sister?'

'Babies don't play,' Mark said firmly, dismissing his little cousin with a shrug that reminded Rilla of Jon. 'Will I see Nanny Mouse?'

'Oh, yes, Nanny Mouse is longing to see you. She always says so on the phone when I speak to her. She says, when's my little Markie coming to see me? And you too, Beth. She's always asking after you, too.'

Rilla pushed Mark's socks on to his feet, just a little way, so that he could pull them up all by himself, and while he was absorbed in this, Beth asked, 'Are you just saying that, Rilla? So I won't be upset? About Nanny Mouse, I mean. Does she really ask about me?'

Rilla put both hands on Beth's shoulders.

'Of course she does! What do you take me for, Beth, honestly. It's about time you got it into your head that they're all mad about you down there. Everyone. Leonora, Gwen, James. They all love you to pieces. They're dying to see you. All of them.'

'What about Efe?' Beth said.

Rilla grinned. 'You love him best of all, don't you?' she said. 'He's the real reason you like going to Willow Court, isn't he?'

'He thinks up good games,' said Beth, trying hard to sound grown-up and nonchalant. 'He's fun, that's all.'

Beth's blushing, Rilla noticed with some amusement, and looking everywhere but at me. It'll do us all good to get to the country for a bit. Forget our troubles. Have some fun. Be cosseted by Nanny Mouse. Heavenly bliss!

The adults sat in the drawing-room having tea while Efe, Alex and Beth played outside, with Mark trying his best to join in, getting left behind sometimes, but struggling to keep up with the others. Chloë was sleeping in a carrycot at Gwen's feet.

'There you are, Gwen,' said James. 'She's good as gold, my little princess.' He smiled at Rilla. 'Gwen always tells me Chloë's a difficult baby. Not a bit like either of the boys. I don't find her a problem at all, I must say.'

'All very well for you, darling,' Gwen said. 'You don't ever have to deal with her yourself.'

'And neither do you, really, do you?' said James. 'You'd be lost without Nanny Mouse. Admit it!'

'I know, I know,' said Gwen. 'You're right, but still. I do more for Chloë than anyone else *except* Nanny Mouse. There's always quite enough work for both of us, I promise you. And of course we have to keep an eye on Efe and Alex and Mark and Beth as well.'

Damn, Rilla thought. Damn and blast. Is Gwen really going to suck me into childcare? I only came here to have a bit of a rest from that. The last thing I need is droves of children rioting around, needing attention. She knew this was a selfish thought, but couldn't help it. She felt sorry for herself much of the time nowadays, aware of misery as an almost physical thing, sucking her down, muffling any small moments of happiness in a kind of grey blanket.

At least the kids seemed happy enough at the moment, running up and down the slopes of the terrace. There was Efe, directing operations. His voice was the one that you heard, always. He was tall for his age, with something in the set of his mouth that Rilla couldn't help thinking of as trouble for anyone who crossed him, but even at eight years old, he *was* very handsome. Rilla preferred Alex's gentle, rather long face. Two years younger than Efe, he was an almost silent child with a sharp nose, floppy hair that fell on to a high forehead, and grey eyes that took in everything and seemed to understand much more than he could express. Markie, bless him, chased after the bigger boys, screaming with laughter, but Beth was now sitting on the terrace, just looking at the others; grave, pretty, with her best blue hair ribbon on in honour of Efe who wouldn't notice it, or if he did, wouldn't think of saying how pretty it was. I'm a bloody fool, Rilla said to herself. No eight-year-old boy would dream of complimenting a girl on her hair ribbon. The pills are making me stupid.

Someone was crying. Rilla woke up suddenly and for a moment couldn't think what it was, that unending wail that set every nerve on edge. She sat up in bed and tried hard to sort out what was real from things she might have been dreaming. That was the trouble with sleeping pills. You fell into darkness the minute you got into bed, but if you woke for any reason, it was like struggling up from the bottom of a pond with weeds and scum filling your mouth and nose so that you could hardly draw breath. And once you were awake, falling asleep again sometimes didn't happen for a long time and there was nothing to be done but smoke, or go wandering down to the fridge to see if there was anything there that might cheer you up, even for a moment.

The wailing was, of course, a baby crying. At first, because of the strange disorientation that went on every time she opened her eyes these days, Rilla thought, it's Mark. I must get up and feed him. Change him. Then she remembered that the baby wasn't Mark but Chloë, who was notorious for making nights an absolute misery for everyone. Rilla sank back on her pillows. Nanny Mouse would be taking care of it. There was no need to get out of bed at all.

Nanny Mouse came into her own with new babies. She had a gift for them, knew how to make the right noises and do all the proper things that seemed miraculously to soothe them. There were people who were good with animals and whose dogs were always amazingly well-adjusted and docile, and Nanny Mouse worked her spell on any child she encountered. She was the best baby-tamer in the world.

When Mark was first born, Nanny travelled up to London to help Rilla 'establish a routine' for the child, and Rilla was endlessly grateful to her for that. She also, guiltily, was relieved that Leonora realized that her own presence wouldn't be nearly as useful. She'd arrived at the hospital in time for Mark's birth then, after giving out presents and making all the right grandmotherly noises, she went back to Willow Court and Nanny Mouse stayed with Rilla for two weeks, teaching her all the things she didn't know about feeding and bathing and swaddling. Nanny Mouse believed that babies felt more comfortable wrapped up like small Egyptian mummies, and because Mark never objected and slept very well from the start, Rilla dutifully wound a length of flannel sheet around his body every night for ages and ages.

It seemed, though, that even Nanny Mouse might have met her match with Chloë. She wouldn't submit to swaddling, and pulled her arms free every time from the confining cloth. She howled at the slightest provocation. She had her own agenda, James said, and was sticking to it. You had to admire the child, he said.

Rilla stared into the darkness. The wails had stopped now but she was wide awake. She got out of bed and pulled on her silk robe, deciding to go and see if Nanny Mouse was still up.

She opened the door and looked down the corridor. There was a golden line of light under the nursery door. Probably the silence meant that Chloë was being given a bottle. Nanny Mouse wouldn't mind if she came and chatted for a while. She'd be pleased.

Rilla tiptoed along the carpet and opened the nursery door. There was Nanny Mouse with Chloë in her arms, on the nursing chair by the window. She was wearing her camel dressing-gown. Could it really be the same one she'd had when Rilla and Gwen were children? It most probably was. All Nanny Mouse's garments lasted for ever, or else she had a stock of identical replacements that no one knew about.

'Rilla my dear, come in!' she whispered, smiling. The baby was sucking gently from a bottle. 'I shan't be long dealing with this little one and then I'll make us a nice milky drink.'

'Lovely!' said Rilla, sitting down at the nursery table, and trying not to think of how she longed for a good slug of whisky, or anything alcoholic. Nanny Mouse thought milky drinks were the elixir of life and in her opinion there was almost no problem a good cup of cocoa couldn't solve. Horlicks was her cure for sleeplessness and Ovaltine was just the ticket when you were feeling poorly. Her hair, white now, was done in a plait which hung down her back. She must be quite old, Rilla thought. Older than Mother even, and yet she doesn't change at all. You couldn't even say she was wrinkled, not really. Her skin seemed thinner, and she looked even more mouselike than she had as a young woman but, basically, she was always just the same. That was the best thing about her. Perhaps, Rilla thought, there was something in this milky-drink idea after all.

'How are you, dear?' Nanny Mouse said. 'You don't have to put on a brave face with me, you know. Are you managing?'

'Oh, yes, I'm managing,' Rilla said. 'But I do get lonely sometimes. Even though the house is quite small, I feel as though we're all rattling round in it, me and Markie and Beth. As though we're waiting for someone.'

'You'll get used to that, dear, don't you worry. It's bound to be difficult just at first. After a while,' she looked up at Rilla and smiled in a way you could only describe as knowing, 'it'll seem quite natural to be on your own and you'll be relieved not to have to consider the needs of a man. You'll be able to please yourself, Rilla, and that's always nice, isn't it?'

She had a point, Rilla thought. It *was* nice, that part of it. What wasn't so nice was having no one to share with; no one to chat to about everything that came into your head, no one to be there in the bed with you when you woke up every day, no one to see how lovely the children were and how they changed every day, every hour almost. There was also the small matter of sex, which had been fun and a pleasure and which had ceased for a while to be any kind of a problem. Nowadays, there was plenty on offer, but it came hedged about with difficulties – how involved did you want to get? Was this or that person suitable? Could you risk Beth or Mark seeing a stranger in the bedroom in the morning? They were the sorts of difficulties Rilla thought she'd put behind her for ever when she married. That'll teach me, she thought.

'I'm fine, actually,' she said to Nanny Mouse. 'Just from time to time, I get a bit weepy. Nothing that won't get better, honestly.'

'That's my brave Rilla,' said Nanny Mouse, and stood up to lower the sleeping Chloë gently into her cot. 'Now come downstairs with me, and we'll have a real treat. Hot chocolate tonight, I think.'

Suddenly, Rilla felt ridiculously happy. She followed Nanny Mouse down the stairs to the kitchen. Everything would be much better after a mug of hot chocolate. Everything was going to be all right. She'd work again. There had to be a part out there for her, somewhere. It was just a question of searching it out, and she was determined to do it. She'd manage, all on her own. And before she got back into bed, she'd look in on Markie and Beth, asleep in the room next to her own. Her children. Her reasons for being happy.

Rilla looked out of the window next morning and wondered why last night's hopeful mood had evaporated. The sun was calling attention to itself, shining far more brightly than it had any right to do in spring. A green mist of new leaves wreathed the branches of every tree. Daffodils and narcissi were scattered everywhere in the grass, and Rilla wondered as she did every year what it *was* about daffodils that people liked so much. They're boring, she thought. Yellow and boring. She noticed that the camellias had buds that were just on the point of opening into the white and deep pink and very dark red flowers which she loved. This was a day bursting with every cliché of happiness and hope, and the fact that she wanted to lie down on her bed and cry and cry made her feel even worse, guilty as well as unhappy. She sighed, and made her way to the bathroom, where she unscrewed the cap on her bottle of Valium. I'll feel better after breakfast, she told herself, making sure not to meet her own gaze in the mirror.

'What's going on? Nanny Mouse, what's happening?' Rilla stood on the bottom step of the staircase and stared. The grandfather clock on the landing struck nine as she spoke. Nanny Mouse was dressed in her travelling suit and dark blue felt hat, holding a small leather suitcase in one hand and her handbag in the other. She looked as though she were about to burst into tears, a most un-Nanny Mouse-like state of affairs Leonora had an arm around her, comforting her. Gwen and James were by the door. James said, 'Come along, Nanny, or you'll miss that train. Engine's running . . .'
'But I haven't said goodbye to the children,' Nanny Mouse cried. 'Nor to Rilla. I haven't explained . . .'
'Here I am, Nanny,' said Rilla. 'And I'll say goodbye to the children for you. You go and get your train. Mother'll explain everything, I'm sure.'

'I'm so sorry, dear, truly,' said Nanny Mouse as James guided her towards the door. 'I shan't be gone longer than a few days. I may come back tomorrow if all's well. If I can arrange for someone else to be with Gladys. Goodbye! Goodbye . . . thank you, James, dear. I'm just coming.'

When the car had finally driven off, Leonora said, 'Well, it can't be helped. Poor Nanny Mouse!' She led the way to the dining-room. The children were already up and about in the garden. Whatever emergency had overtaken Nanny Mouse and caused her to pack her suitcase and leave Willow Court, she'd managed to get the children washed and dressed and fed before she left. Rilla helped herself to cereal and a bowl of fruit and sat down next to Gwen.

'So,' she said. 'How come all of you haven't eaten yet? I thought I'd missed breakfast altogether, it's so late.'

'We've been at sixes and sevens,' said Leonora. 'Nanny Mouse had a telephone call early this morning. Her cousin Gladys, who's her only living relative as far as I know, has fallen and sprained her ankle rather badly, I believe. She can't walk and is rather at a loss as to what to do. Nanny Mouse is going to help her for a couple of days, and see if she can arrange nursing care and so forth.'

'Poor thing!' Gwen cut her toast into two neat triangles and spread one of them with butter and marmalade. 'She hates leaving the children. I don't think she trusts us to look after them properly.'

'We'll manage splendidly,' said Leonora. 'There are, after all, three of us to share the work.'

Rilla said nothing. Shit shit shit shit shit, she thought. This is all I need. We'll have to be on duty the whole time, watching the kids, and making sure they're all bathed and fed and amused. Shit. She blinked tears away, knowing how selfish, how rottenly spoilt she was, but not able to stop feeling like a child who's suddenly been robbed of a treat. Pathetic. She was being totally and completely pathetic. Of course Nanny Mouse had to go and look after her cousin. And she wasn't one of those mothers who was always dumping her kids on someone else. I'm not like that, she thought. I love playing with them, reading to them, being with them, but just this once, I felt like a real rest. Just for a change. Some time for myself. Shit. Before she had come downstairs, Rilla had practically decided not to have toast today, but what the hell. She took a piece from the rack and covered it with a thick layer of butter. If Leonora says a single word, Rilla thought, I'll chuck the butter dish straight at her.

By Saturday morning, Rilla was determined to escape Willow Court and play truant. She outlined her lips with a more than usually firm hand and filled them in with a shade of lipstick that was darker than she normally wore. She dressed in the best approximation she could manage to a business suit, a pair of black wool trousers, a white silk shirt, and a moss-green velvet jacket, which she would have to leave hanging open because of her rather-too-generous bosom. Never mind, the thing was to get a costume that would reflect the new Rilla, the one who wasn't going to ask permission to go down to the village for a while, but was simply going to announce her intentions at breakfast and go.

The door to her bedroom opened and Mark came running in.

'What you doing, Ma? You're pretty!'

Rilla gathered him into her arms and put her face into the crook of his neck, smelling his warm skin, and kissing him in the tickly way he loved, batting her eyelashes against his cheek. 'A fluttie kiss' they called it, because that was Mark's word for butterfly.

'Not as pretty as you,' Rilla said.

'No! I'm not pretty!' Mark was indignant and Rilla laughed. Surely four was a bit young to be so macho?

'All right, not pretty, but my best, loveliest wonderboy.'

That met with Mark's approval and he beamed at Rilla and began pulling her hands. 'Come to breakfast. Breakfast time. Come on.'

'I'm going out after breakfast, Markie,' Rilla said, following him out of the room and wondering whether her determination would stand up to objections from her son. But there were none.

'Efe and Alex got a den. I seed it,' he said.

'I *saw* it, Markie.'

'No, you didn't seed it. I seed it.'

Rilla gave up. This wasn't the time to correct Mark's speech. It was okay. Everything was going to work out splendidly. He'd be fine without her and she, for her part, would be much better off away from Willow Court for a bit. Only a tiny part of her was willing to admit, even to herself, her real reason for wanting to go down to the village – she was curious to see what had become of the cottage Hugh had lived in all those years ago.

She could think about those days now without much nostalgia, and perhaps looking at something that would remind her of another awful time in her life would help her see her divorce, her lack of work or any prospect of it – the whole ghastly scenario she seemed to be caught up in at the moment – as purely temporary. Things pass. Every pain fades. You forget. That was what seeing the cottage would surely prove to her. For the last few years, on visits to her mother's house, she'd avoided going to the village at all or, if she did, she made sure to stay down this end of it and not venture up past the shop. Well, now she was going to be grown-up about the whole thing, and enjoy revisiting the scene of her first love affair. She would also try very hard not to think about why that first love affair was still the one she regarded as real, the best, and so forth. It was a bit like Method acting, she decided. She would *pretend* to be in control, and maybe true control would follow.

At breakfast, she spoke clearly, firmly, and in a way that she hoped made it impossible for anyone to make any childcare demands on her.

'I'm off down to the village this morning. I'll be back before lunch,' she said, looking at Leonora and trying not to see Gwen tightening her lips. 'I'm sure you'll all manage for a while without me, won't you?' An extra bright smile at this point was evenly distributed round the table and Rilla followed that with a lie. 'I noticed that new antique shop, what's it called?'

'The Treasure Chest,' Leonora said.

'That's the one! I need to buy a birthday present for a very dear friend who's just mad about such things. You don't mind, do you, Gwen?'

'No, of course not. Have a good time.'

Rilla smiled. How could Gwen possibly have said anything else? She couldn't, not without making herself look ungenerous. Laying down the law and presenting everyone with a *fait accompli* worked a treat, Rilla saw. She should do it more often. As it was, she wasn't going to risk something unforeseen coming up, so she bounded out of her chair and made for the door.

'I'll see all of you later,' she said as brightly as she knew how. 'Goodbye, Markie darling, and you too, Beth. Be good for Gwen and Leonora now. Thanks so much, Mother!'

The cottage was a disappointment. Rilla looked at it and felt a little let down by the complete absence of ghosts. A children's slide took up most of the tiny front garden, and two noisy toddlers were shrieking as they played on it. Postman Pat curtains hung at the bedroom windows, and the whole place looked so different from what she remembered that she felt not even the slightest tugging at her heart. She walked towards the antique shop and stepped into a small, shadowy room.

'May I help you?' said a rather angular woman from behind a mountain of ancient crockery heaped on a table. The till in front of her could have come from the TV version of some Dickens novel.

'I'm just browsing, thanks very much,' said Rilla. She peered around at the stock, so closely packed together that if you really did want something specific, you'd have had a hard time finding it. Something caught her eye. Light from the door bounced off a mirror, half-hidden behind a rocking horse with no mane. As she approached it, she noticed that her heart was beating rather too loudly in her chest. Could it be? Was it? The corner of the frame that she could see looked exactly like . . . she pulled it out and managed to prop it against the edge of the table. It was. It was Hugh's mirror; the one that had hung in the cottage, the one that had belonged to his grandmother. What was it doing here? Why did he not take it with him when he left? Rilla thought she probably knew the answer. The tale of the grandmother was probably another of his lies, but here it was. Surely finding it like this was some kind of omen? She peered into the glass and saw her face younger, happier, reflected more kindly.

'How much is this mirror?' she said, holding it up with difficulty.

'A hundred pounds,' said the angular woman.

'I'll take it,' Rilla said. 'Only I'll have to collect and pay for it later, if you don't mind. I came out without my cheque book. I live up at Willow Court.'

'I know,' said the woman. 'You're Rilla Frederick. I read about your divorce. I *am* so sorry. I loved *Night Creatures*.'

'How kind of you to say so! Thank you!' Rilla smiled. That was donkey's years ago, she thought. No one remembers me in anything else. She made her way to the antique till, glancing out of the window and saw . . . no, it couldn't be. Could it? Yes, it was Mrs Pritchard, still walking around after all this time. The old busybody! She wasn't that much older than Leonora but still, it was a shock to see her. Rilla took a step towards the window and caught her foot in something, some hanging thing, and in a split second that seemed to go on for ever, the mirror slipped out of her hand and fell to the floor. She cried out, 'Oh, oh my God! Oh, it's cracked. The mirror's cracked. I'm so sorry. Of course, I'll pay for the damage. I don't know what happened.' She burst into tears. 'What an awful thing to do. I can't imagine how I could be so careless. Do forgive me.'

'That's quite all right, dear,' said the woman, coming to comfort her. 'You can have the glass replaced. The frame isn't broken at all. And it's beautiful, isn't it?'

'Yes, yes of course it is.' Rilla sniffed, and wiped her nose with a tissue. 'And yes, I *will* replace the glass. It'll be almost as good as new, won't it?'

'It will,' said the woman. Rilla didn't even look at the gilt cherubs and garlands on the frame. Her gaze was drawn to the broken glass, and she was filled with foreboding. *Bad luck. Bad luck for ever.* The mirror had shattered into an almost perfect spiderweb pattern. She looked into it and saw her own face broken into splinters edged with silver; her skin was almost green in the dim light, the dark reddish mass of her hair fractured into a thousand separate pieces.

Rilla, walking up the avenue of scarlet oaks towards the house saw three things almost simultaneously and knew, knew at once, that something unspeakably dreadful was about to engulf her. She felt it, she could almost see it: a black wave bearing down on her. Three things. Beth, running full tilt down the avenue towards her and screaming and screaming. Leonora kneeling down, clutching someone to her breast. Who was it? Rilla couldn't quite see and in any case she was hearing the screams, Beth's screams. Someone was hurt. Beth was hurt. Who had hurt her? Where? The third thing she saw was two cars, one of them a police car and the other Dr Benyon's black Daimler. The doctor often came to play bridge at Willow Court but you don't play bridge on Saturday at lunchtime.

'Rilla! Oh, Rilla, please, please . . . I can't . . . I can't . . .'

'What's wrong, chicken?' Rilla's voice came out a squeak, her words slurring into one another, tumbling into nonsense as Beth threw both arms around her waist and went on and on, howling like a wounded animal. 'Are you hurt, Beth? Has someone hurt you? Tell me. Tell me what's wrong!'

'Markie,' Beth cried. 'It's Markie.'

Rilla heard the name and it was all she needed to hear. She knew. She said not one word to Beth, but began to run towards the house, stumbling in her haste. As she came closer, she saw everyone, outlined in a shimmer of black, standing on the front steps of Willow Court. Her mother . . . why did she look like that? When had she ever looked like that with a mouth twisted out of shape from pain? Gwen was cuddling Alex, hiding his head in her skirt and James was carrying little Chloë.

'Oh, my darling, my darling child, oh Rilla,' Leonora said, and came to hold her daughter. 'There's been an accident. A terrible, terrible accident. Markie . . .'

'He's dead, isn't he?' Rilla said. Her voice became something separate from herself. She heard herself shrieking. 'Markie, Markie, oh my God, my baby. I can't . . . Markie, oh God . . .' over and over again. Making no sense. Keening. Howling. She fell to the ground and tore at the crumbling stone of the steps with her bare nails. Shrieking. 'No, oh, God no. Not this. Please no. Please. Oh, Mummy, Mummy, I can't bear it.'

All she heard was her own pain. Somehow, in the darkness that fell over her vision, she sensed someone lifting her to her feet, helping her, taking her into the house. She struggled away from the hands, the loving hands that burned on her flesh.

'Where is he? Where's Mark? I want to see him, Mummy. Mummy, take me to see my baby. I want to. Please. Take me now. Please. Please let's hurry.'

'Yes, my darling,' said Leonora, and every word was thickened with tears. Her eyes were red-rimmed. She'd been crying for a long time.

A voice somewhere in Rilla's head said *If I get there quickly, maybe it won't be too late. Maybe I can save him. Breathe life into him. Maybe they're wrong, and he's only fainted and I'll hold him and he'll come back to me, open his eyes, smile . . .*

She started to run upstairs, Gwen and Leonora behind her. *Where is he?* she wanted to say, but the words wouldn't come. *Where have you put him?* She leaned on the doorframe of the nursery and hands took hold of her and led her to one of the spare rooms.

Mark was laid out on the bed. He was pale. His hair was wet. Someone had undressed him and his body was covered with a sheet. He looked the same as he always did when he slept. Rilla thought that the pain she felt must break her, split her in two. Almost, she expected to see it, to see something like a lightning flash cutting through her, but of course that was nonsense. She bent down to kiss her boy, her baby, and his skin was cold. She put her mouth near his ear and whispered sounds, moans, cries into his neck. She kissed him. Real kisses, and the fluttie kisses that used to make him laugh with pleasure.

'Come away now, Rilla,' said Gwen, who was weeping as she held her sister up, carrying almost all her weight. 'Come and lie down now. Come.'

'What happened, Gwen? Tell me what happened.'

'An accident. Mark wandered away and fell into the lake. He drowned. Oh, Rilla darling, Rilla . . .' Gwen was weeping as though she would never stop. Rilla, frozen into silence, walked slowly along the corridor to her own room, leaning on her sister. It was too late and she couldn't bring him back and he was dead and it was her fault. *I wasn't here. When my baby died I was somewhere else, far away. I wasn't here.*

She lay down on her bed and there was Dr Benyon suddenly, leaning over her.

'Take this pill, my dear. Just to calm you a little. To ease the pain.'

Rilla swallowed the pill and thought what a fool Dr Benyon was. Nothing could ease the pain. Nothing. Not ever. Never never ever.

There would just be more and more of it, heaped up on her head until she was very old.

'Thank you,' she said, acting calm because that was what they all wanted and she was such a good actress surely she could act calm? She sounded almost normal to herself. There was a bitter taste in her mouth and a rage that frightened her somewhere far away, under the pain. Where were her mother and her sister when her son went into the water? What were they doing? How could they take their eyes away from such a small child? How could they? As soon as this thought came into her mind, her agony hissed back. *But where were you? You were the mother. You left him. You didn't think. You didn't look back. You should have been there. Not Gwen. Not Leonora. You, his mother.* Rilla closed her eyes. If only she could find a way to stop trembling, to stop everything looking blurred and shapeless, she'd be fine.

Rilla woke up in the middle of the night. Someone had given her a strong sedative on top of Dr Benyon's pill and perhaps she had slept a little. Moonlight was coming in through the curtains and a blueish light filled her bedroom. She suddenly became aware of someone there, at the foot of her bed. She sat up and saw Efe staring at her.

'Efe? Is that you? Is anything the matter?'

'Rilla?' It *was* Efe. Why wasn't he asleep? He ran to her side, flung himself on her, clutching her round the neck, crying into her ear. 'Oh, Rilla, I'm sorry. I'm so sorry, Rilla. I am. I should've believed him. I should've tried harder, before it was too late. I'm sorry for everything.'

'Yes, Efe, I know. I know. Don't cry, darling.' She could feel his tears on her face. He let go of her then, and ran out of the room and Rilla sank back into darkness and anguish.

In the morning, she was in too much agony to know whether the events of the night were real or something she'd dreamed.

※

Rilla sat at the dressing-table wondering where to begin. It was practically lunch time and if she didn't get a move on, Leonora would be knocking at her door demanding to know what had happened to her. She disapproved strongly of Rilla's habit of turning up late at meals, regarding it as not only rude but a sort of indication of moral decline. Gwen had never been late for a meal in her life and what's more, when she did sit down at the table, she ate a moderate amount at all times. Rilla smiled. Moderation was not something she knew much about.

She felt, unexpectedly, a little better now, and thought that perhaps Gwen and all her friends had been right when they'd begged her to go and speak to someone after Mark's death. *I wouldn't hear of it then*, she thought, smoothing moisturizer over her neck. *All I wanted to do was work and eat and try to forget about it and it was buried deeper and deeper and that made it hurt more and more.* She peered at herself in the glass and wondered whether the fact that she'd been crying was obvious.

'Not too bad, old thing,' she said aloud to her reflection, which, she noticed somewhat to her surprise, was actually smiling a rather smug smile.

'What have you got to be so smug about?' she asked her mirror-image. 'As if I didn't know.'

This was getting silly. *Grow up, woman*, she told herself sternly. *You're middle-aged. You need to lose weight. Your hair would be grey if left to its own devices. There's absolutely nothing for you to feel so happy about. Oh yes there is* said another voice in her head, a sing-song pantomine voice. *There certainly is.*

She hurried to get dressed. Quite apart from Leonora demanding to know why she was so late, suddenly Rilla felt ravenously hungry. She picked up the trousers she'd worn yesterday and went to hang them up in the cupboard. Her hand felt something through the thin cloth — had she left something in her pocket? She felt for whatever it was and brought out the rolled-up strip of wallpaper. *I must be losing my mind. How could I possibly have forgotten that?* she wondered and sat down quickly on the bed. *The dolls' house. The roof, stripped of some of its paper. Douggie. Oh, my God, what is Leonora going to say? Should I tell her at once, or wait till after lunch?*

Rilla knew suddenly exactly what had to be done. *I must dress quickly*, she thought, *and go and find Gwen. She'll know what we should tell Mother. Oh, please, please don't let anyone go into the nursery till I've told Gwen.* She took a pair of black trousers from the nearest hanger, pulled them on, and thrust the roll of wallpaper into one of the pockets. Then she pushed her arms into a loose silky T-shirt and went to find her sister.

Gwen looked down at her watch and was amazed to find that it was only quarter to twelve. She'd done enough this morning to fill two whole days. That was how it felt, anyway. The inside of her head was like the drum of a washing machine lately, with all sorts of things whirling around inside it in no particular order. Every so often someone would fling another item into the mix. For instance, she still hadn't worked out the origin or meaning of three enormous circles of shortbread, which had materialised in the larder overnight. Could someone really have been baking while the rest of the household was asleep? Who would want to and why?

Gwen pushed these questions to the back of her mind. She'd already added them to the mental list she kept in her head at all times, which was a version of the written list she kept in her notebook, but with added worry. Bridget, whose small firm was catering for the party, wouldn't be best pleased to have rogue shortbreads appearing out of nowhere and spoiling her plans. The menu for the three-course birthday lunch had been carefully planned, and she knew it by heart: *Mozzarella and basil fritters served with a tomato and roasted garlic sauce; Crêpes filled with smoked salmon, cucumber, créme fraîche and chives; Persian omelette (for non-fish-eating vegetarians) made with leeks, walnuts, raisins, watercress and fresh herbs; dark chocolate mousse cake and raspberries and strawberries marinated in elderflower cordial, served with whipped cream; coffee and birthday cake.* Just thinking about it made her feel hungry. The dessert in particular would be spectacular. Bridget was famous for this cake, and Leonora had always loved chocolate.

Today had started very promisingly. She had arranged for the cleaning firm that looked after Willow Court to come in this afternoon for a final dust and polish. The marquee people were efficient and well-organized and what was more they could be left to their own devices and didn't need constant supervision. This, of course, didn't prevent James from strutting around as though it were his idea to have the nine tables in just that formation: a central table seating a dozen for the family, with the others each seating eight people arranged around it. Every table was to have its own theme flower and the guests would be given that same flower to help them find their places. This was the idea of Jane, the pretty young florist in charge of the arrangements for the tent. She had come for a chat and promised to be at Willow Court almost before dawn tomorrow to see to the individual table ornaments herself and hang the baskets from the specially designed brackets, which were even now being put up. These would be filled with freesias, roses, ferns, orchids and small lilies in shades of cream and white and pale pink. It would all look heavenly and therefore Gwen had to make sure that the flowers in the house and the plants in the garden for which she was responsible didn't let the side down.

The begonias were beautiful. Double blooms in every shade of pink and orange you could think of spilling out of the stone urns along the terrace. Gwen felt properly happy for the first time in days. The Quiet Garden was glorious, too, with the late roses looking quite presentable. The hydrangeas were spectacular this year, huge flowerheads heavy with blooms. The dahlias looked better than she'd ever seen them, the lilies were terrific, and there were plenty of Oriental poppy heads, which would be good in the vases as a contrast. If the weather held, it would be all right. Everything she'd laboured over for weeks would work out and tomorrow would be a day for them all to remember with pleasure.

Efe's suggestion for the paintings had put something of a spanner in the works for a while, but thank goodness Mother was being sensible and not sulking about it. After the party was over there'd be plenty of time to talk about what should happen to the Collection. She made a note to check for dust on the frames later on this afternoon. Even though every picture had been cleaned to within an inch of its life, Chloë's tree-decoration going on in the hall would doubtless be creating dirt of some kind. You couldn't be too careful.

The presents would have to be put under the tree tonight as well. The postman this morning had delivered more parcels from those guests who weren't able to come to the party. Gwen thought that perhaps Alex and Beth could see to the unpacking of the gifts that Leonora hadn't had time to open yet. They didn't seem to have too much to do. She'd seen them walking down to Lodge Cottage earlier and thought how kind it was of them to visit Nanny Mouse, but now they ought to muck in with the rest of the family in getting things ready. And what about Rilla? Gwen felt a stab of irritation. She was hardly ever about. Had she even got up this morning? Typical of her, she thought, not to offer to help when she must see how busy I am.

No sooner had Gwen thought of her sister than she came round the side of the house, almost running. This was unusual. Rilla had never, ever run in her life. Gwen felt a chill come over her.

'What's wrong, Rilla?' she said, and as she spoke, she suddenly realized that it must have been Rilla who'd made the shortbread in the middle of the night. It was exactly the crazy kind of thing she might take it into her head to do. She said, 'Are those shortbread circles yours?'

'Yes, they are. I was going to tell you about them but something's happened, Gwen, which I have to ask you about.'

'Oh, God, don't tell me. Is it Mother? Is she okay? I knew this news of Efe's was worrying her more than she was telling us.'

'It's nothing to do with Mother. Well, it is in a way, but don't worry. No one's ill. Can we go somewhere a bit private? I've got something I want to show you.'

Gwen opened the door which led from the terrace into the conservatory. The room was empty, and she sat down at the table.

'What is it? You're being very mysterious, Rilla.'

'Here you are. It's a piece of the wallpaper from the dolls' house roof.'

Gwen watched as Rilla took something out of her trouser pocket. She unrolled a long strip of the familiar paper on to table, and as soon as she let it go, it curled up again.

'Where did that come from? How could it possibly . . .'

'Douggie got into the nursery. I found him there early this morning.'

'What were you doing up early in the morning? That's not like you at all.'

'Doesn't matter now, Gwen. I'll tell you about that later. I hadn't been to bed.'

'So *that* was when you made the shortbread, though I can't think what for. There's going to be so much food here that we'll be up to our ears in the stuff. Why on earth d'you want to add to it with your shortbread? And why those huge circles?'

Rilla sighed and sat down opposite Gwen. 'Talk about irrelevant, Gwen, honestly. We've got a crisis here, don't you see? If Mother finds out that the dolls' house has been wrecked, she'll be livid and you know what that means. The shortbread is for strawberry shortcake, for your information. I'm going to see if Mary will let me make it for dessert tonight. I just felt in the mood for baking, that's all.'

Gwen was used to her sister's moods and, apart from raising her eyes to the heavens, said only, 'Have you seen? There's something written on the back of this. It's very faint but you can read bits of it. Look.'

Rilla picked up the strip of wallpaper and peered at it. 'You're right,' she said, 'but the main thing is, what are we going to tell Mother? Do you think we should just run up there now and see if we can somehow glue this damn thing back on in some way that she won't notice?'

'No, of course not. Don't you remember the time you broke that dish and threw all the pieces away, hoping she'd never notice?'

Rilla laughed. 'Yes! Bloody silly of me to leave one piece behind, wasn't it? God, she let me have it, didn't she? I'll never forget how she said *it's not the loss of the dish I mind, it's being deceived by my own daughter.*'

Gwen smiled in spite of herself at the accuracy of Rilla's mimicry.

'I do think we might leave telling her till after lunch, though,' she said. 'It'll wait till then, and at least we can have one meal in peace.'

'Fine, but I want you there when I tell her, Gwennie. I can't face her alone. I wouldn't know what to say.'

'All right. We'll get her on her own somehow. She'll be going upstairs for her rest anyway and to get changed for this afternoon's filming. Sean's taking her down to talk to Nanny Mouse.'

Rilla didn't answer. She was holding the strip of paper in her hand, very near her face. Gwen said, 'What are you doing? What can you see?'

'The things that are written here are rather strange. The way it's been torn off makes it look as though there's more.'

'Of course there's more. You can see that it's part of a letter or something. I noticed that there were half-words there at once. Can you actually read any of them?'

Rilla nodded. 'Yes. There's *didn't touch* and then later on *crying for me* and *Solace. Comfort.* Then here's *glow and shine and leap out* and *fragile* and what's this? Can you read these words?'

Gwen frowned and tried to decipher the very faded sepia ink. *Paint never lies.* 'That's what it looks like, anyway, though goodness knows what it can mean. Any of it. And who do you think wrote it?'

'I've no idea,' said Rilla. 'But it's mysterious, isn't it? The dolls' house roof is quite big, of course. If there's a lot more of this writing . . .' She left the sentence unfinished. Then she said, 'We've absolutely got to see what the rest of the letter, or whatever it is, says. We'll have to piece it together otherwise I'll die of curiosity. This little strip on its own is no good at all. It's just mystifying without actually telling us anything.' She rolled the wallpaper up again and put it back into her pocket. 'I wonder whether it'd be possible to peel off the rest of the paper, and then we could read whatever else is there.'

'We can't do that before we've told Mother, though,' said Gwen. 'She'd never forgive us if we did that.'

'But what if she just wants to patch the roof up again without reading any more? She might care more about the condition of the dolls' house than about reading some faded words on a scrap of paper. If we got it off before she saw it, then at least we'd know what there was to know.'

'No.' Gwen shook her head. 'We can't do that. We'll have to leave it to her, but she always wants to know everything that's possible to know about everything, so I doubt very much she'd be able to resist reading the rest.'

'Yes, you're right, of course,' Rilla said. 'Are you coming in to lunch now?'

'I suppose I might as well. This has rather driven other things from my mind. I don't know, whatever you do, nothing ever does seem to go completely smoothly, does it? Don't you find that? You've just dealt with one problem and another three crop up in its place.'

'Food helps,' Rilla said. 'Come and have some lunch.'

'My appetite's left me,' Gwen said. 'I'm dreading telling her, you know.'

'Me too,' said Rilla, 'but that doesn't affect my appetite. I'm starving!' She gave Gwen her hand to pull her out of her chair and linked arms with her as they walked along the corridor to the dining-room. 'United we stand!'

Gwen smiled gallantly. They'd always said that when they were girls. It was comforting that Rilla hadn't forgotten.

Silence filled the nursery and Rilla closed her eyes for a moment. When would Leonora speak? Waiting for her to do so was like counting the heartbeats between the flash of lightning and the dreaded clap of thunder. Telling her mother about the damage to her beloved dolls' house was one of the hardest things she'd ever done. All the way through lunch she'd been distracted, working out the best form of words. She'd hardly noticed the food, and everyone at the table seemed shadowy to her. Conversations taking place between Beth and Chloë, Fiona and Douggie, Efe and James, drifted over her head like smoke. Gwen was miles away too, Rilla noticed. She's as nervous as I am, whatever she says. If she wasn't careful, Leonora would cotton on to the fact that all was not well, so Rilla deliberately asked Gwen a question and tried to flash her a warning. Fortunately, she realized what she was being warned about and immediately turned to Leonora and engaged her in animated chit-chat.

Oh, my God, Rilla thought, she's useless at deception. Several times it looked to her as though their mother was about to ask why both her daughters were behaving so strangely, but the meal finished at last. As they were leaving the room, Rilla went over to Leonora and took her arm and tucked it under her own.

'Mother, would you mind coming up to the nursery with Gwen and me, just for a minute?' she said.

'Now?' Leonora looked put out. 'I have to rest, you know. Sean is coming to fetch me at three and we're going to be filming down at Lodge Cottage. Can't it wait, dear?'

'No, Mother,' said Gwen. 'It's really important. There's something you ought to see.'

'In the nursery?' They were on the landing as she said this, just outside the nursery.

'Yes. Let's go in, Mother, and then Rilla will tell you . . .' Gwen stopped speaking and opened the door. Leonora stepped into the room with her daughters close behind her. Rilla went straight to the dolls' house and took off the sheet that was covering it. Leonora crossed the room quickly and went to run her hands over the roof.

'Who did this?'

'I wanted to tell you before you saw it, Mother. It was Douggie. He got in here early this morning. I've got the strip he tore off . . . look.'

She held out the roll of wallpaper and Leonora took it from her, without looking at it. Her gaze was fixed on the tear, on the damage. She was breathing rather loudly and Rilla wondered whether that meant anything. Was she about to collapse? Have a heart attack or something?

'Maybe you should sit down, Mother,' she said.

Leonora ignored her and went on staring down at the dolls' house. On the right hand side of the roof where Douggie had torn off the paper, there was a snake-shaped white space. When she spoke at last, her voice was falsely bright, as though she were making a special effort not to cry. 'Matters could be even worse,' she said. 'Perhaps we could mend it, stick the piece you have on again, if that hasn't been ruined.'

'Someone's written on the back of the paper,' Rilla said.

Leonora sat down on one of the covered chairs and said, 'Let me see it, please.'

Rilla handed her mother the rolled-up strip, still tightly curled from being in her trouser pocket for so long.

'Thank you,' Leonora whispered, her eyes wide. She began to unroll it. Rilla, looking at her, couldn't believe what she was seeing. Her mother was shrinking, becoming smaller and weaker by the second as she stared at the writing. Her mouth was trembling and there were tears in her eyes.

'Mummy.' Leonora's voice sent shivers up Rilla's spine. 'My mummy's writing . . .'

'Are you all right?' Gwen said, kneeling beside her mother. 'Get your breath back.'

It was true that Leonora's breathing had become ragged. She blinked and Rilla could see that she was making an enormous effort to regain control.

'I'll be all right in a minute,' she said, sounding tearful. 'I will . . . in a minute.'

She wiped her eyes with the back of her hand, like a small child, and this shocked Rilla more than anything. Leonora, the Leonora she'd always known, would never wipe her eyes with anything less than a handkerchief. Even tissues were only for dire emergencies. She had a hankie in her pocket, Rilla would have bet money on it.

Now she was holding the strip of paper up to her eyes.

'Shall I get your reading glasses, Mother?' Gwen asked.

'No,' said Leonora, after a long pause. 'I can see enough.' She was sounding more normal. She sighed and seemed to gather herself together a little. She looked in the pocket of her trousers, found her handkerchief and patted at her eyes. She said, 'My mother wrote this. Can you make out what it says, one of you? It's such faint handwriting.'

'I think so,' said Gwen. 'I think I can.'

'Read it to me,' Leonora said. She had her eyes closed now, listening.

'Very well, if you're sure, Mother.' Gwen spoke gravely, and Rilla wondered why she was speaking in a tone of such reverence. What if it turned out to be some shopping list or something that Leonora's mother had scribbled on the back of this off-cut of wallpaper. Gwen began to read.

'It won't make much sense, Mother. There are only a few words on each line. But I'll have a go. It says: *won't blame me / Have darling, darling / rified me* . . . could that be horrified? Or terrified? . . . *small bones / so didn't touch. / Never even / rything a mother should do / calculating how painful it / up again, but down forever into / 'd hurt to breathe the water into / u were crying for me and was / all. Went up to the studio / day. Solace. Comfort. / under another name. / was coming to life /* then there's just the letter *m* then it goes on: *the window, brushing / getting that highlight / s: object (or subject) had / mories of what it was. / nished, wanted it to be like a / glow and shine and leap out / to do that / and they didn't / than saw that. Even while / than his. Also, he / ever. He is, clever and / for years. He said doesn't /*

then there's a letter *s. Paint never lies. You* . . . and the next three letters are *ngs*. Could that be something like 'longings?' *and not ask for fame/said you we're fragile. You'll/away from my door, and he/ed to say this to him, but it is* . . . that's it. That's all. I'm afraid it doesn't really make much sense.'

Rilla looked at her mother, who was stiff and upright in her chair. Tears came from her eyes and ran down her cheeks unchecked.

'Mother?' she said, feeling suddenly afraid. 'Mother, please. Don't be sad. What is it? Tell us. We're here. Aren't we, Gwen. Please stop crying, Mother.'

'I'm sorry, darling,' Leonora answered, visibly pulling herself together. 'It's just that it's been very many years since I saw my mother's handwriting. It brings back memories. Nothing for you two to concern yourselves with, I promise. I'm perfectly all right really, but of course I shall need to see the rest.'

'The rest?'

Leonora's hankie was now a ball held tight in one hand. She relaxed her hold on it and wiped her eyes. Then she took a deep breath and said nothing for a few moments. Finally, she spoke. 'What Gwen's just read is only a part of something. I think my mother must have written it just before her death, because the dolls' house roof was a present for my birthday . . . and . . .' Her voice faltered. Rilla knew all about that terrible time, even though Leonora rarely referred to it.

'Can we get it off, though?' Gwen said. 'Without damaging it, I mean. What if it's impossible?'

'Nothing's impossible. Didn't you tell me that young man of Chloë's is a picture restorer? He'll know what to do.'

Gwen looked relieved. 'Philip. Of course. How clever of you to remember, Mother! I'll go and find him at once. I'm sure he'll be able to help.'

She left the room quickly and Rilla could hear her going downstairs, calling for Chloë.

Leonora stood up and made her way to the door. 'Will you find Sean, please, Rilla? Tell him I'll see him at four o'clock if he'd be good enough to delay the filming for a while.' She left the room before Rilla could answer.

Rilla picked up the sheet again and spread it out over the dolls' house. She looked at the sharp edge of the roof outlined against the wall. The sun was coming in at the window, and she could see the motes of dust drifting and floating in the golden air. Rilla felt a small shiver of apprehension at what might be hidden under the fall of white material.

A noise was coming from her own mouth which Leonora didn't recognize at first. It sounded like a wounded animal, something caught in a trap, not like a person. Not like me, she thought. She must have walked along the corridor to her room, and decided to lie on the bed. She closed her eyes and saw suns and stars and purple streaks exploding behind her closed eyelids. *Oh, Mummy, Mummy* she heard herself cry out like a baby, like a weak, small child, but the cry was in her head and the real noises were sobbing and gasping and she couldn't, whatever she did, stop herself from trembling. She tried to breathe steadily. To think of ordinary things.

Rilla and Gwen would arrange for the filming to be postponed for a while. Chloë's young man, Philip, would see that the words her mother had written were revealed. It will be better when I know, she thought, and she was aware of something dark and heavy, like a piece of stone lodged somewhere within her. She had carried that weight inside her all her life she now saw, and had always thought of it as the natural pain that any child who loses a parent at an early age has to bear and learn to live with. Now she was beginning to wonder whether it might be something else entirely. She opened her eyes. There's something, she thought. Something my mother's words may tell me. If only I could know, she thought. If I could read my mother's words, this heaviness, this lump of darkness in my heart might dissolve. I should think of something else. The party. Leonora tried to fix her thoughts on tomorrow's celebration but what came into her mind was another day, long ago. I have been like something buried underground for a long time, she told herself. Something struggling to wake up after a long sleep.

# August 1935

Leonora hesitated as she came into the drawing-room. It was the grandest room in the house and usually she only went in there if Mummy or Daddy invited her to. Daddy's paintings hung all over the walls, and there were rugs on the polished wooden floor with complicated patterns all over them. When she was very little, she used to sit and follow the lines of colour, tracing them with her fingers.

Mummy didn't look round when she came in, though she must have heard her walking across the floor. She was standing at the window looking out at the garden and you could tell, just from her back, that she felt sad. Even though Nanny Mouse often said that a trouble shared was a trouble halved, Leonora didn't really know how to break into the silence that surrounded her mother most of the time. Mummy spoke very little, and Leonora was always unsure what to say to her. She felt that it was babyish for someone who was going to be eight soon not to know how to speak to her own mummy, but she didn't. Not really. Mummy used to speak to me more, she thought, when I was very, very little, but maybe I'm not remembering properly.

It wasn't that she didn't love her mother. She did, with a passion that she didn't know how to express to anyone, except sometimes when it was very dark in the night nursery and she was whispering to her teddy bear, Mr Worthing. He knew all her secrets. He knew that Leonora sometimes wondered whether she was really and truly the daughter of Maude Walsh. Perhaps she'd been exchanged at birth. This sometimes happened in stories, and Leonora was almost sure it didn't in real life, but she would still have believed it were it not for the fact that she looked so much like her father. Looking in the mirror, she could see it – the same dark hair, the same blue eyes, and exactly the same ears – that was funny. Leonora thought it was magical the way things like your ears came out as though they'd been

273

copied somehow, but however hard she looked, she couldn't find a trace of her mother in her own face.

'You're your father's child, and no mistake,' Nanny Mouse used to say.

'I know that!' Leonora was impatient. 'But am I my mother's child?'

'Silly goose! Of course you are. I was there in the room with her when you were born. Just because you're not very like her to look at doesn't mean she's not your mother.'

Maude . . . that's my mother's name, Leonora thought, staring at the small figure. It fits her. It's a gentle sort of name. She hasn't even turned round to see who's come into the room. If I wasn't looking for her, it would be easy not to see her, because she's so still and small. Her clothes are plain, and her hair is almost the same colour as the curtains: a sort of goldy-brown. But she's pretty, Leonora thought. I think so, anyway. She's like a cat, with a pointed chin and greenish eyes and a small mouth with lips that often tremble. She speaks so softly that you have to lean forward to hear her. Not like Daddy. Daddy is tall and speaks in a loud voice and everyone says he's handsome, but I can't say that, because I look just like him. Leonora crossed the carpet and made her way towards the window.

'Mummy! Tyler's making a bonfire in the garden. May I go and look?' Maude moved her mouth into a smile.

'Yes, dear, I suppose so. I was just thinking about the bonfire myself. I can see Tyler out of the window, look.'

Leonora came to stand beside her mother. There was their gardener, shaping wood and logs into a pile. Near him in a wheelbarrow was a heap of assorted papers, small sheets like letters and bigger sheets with drawings all over them. Those were Daddy's sketches. Every so often, Daddy had told her, the paper all got too much and had to be burned. Leonora was used to this, and she loved the bonfires; loved the leap and the gold and the scorching heat of the flames and the way the paper shrank into curling grey ash and how sometimes a glowing fragment went up and up, carried by the wind, like a fiery butterfly into the blue air. Sometimes, too, there were little showers of sparks, just like tiny fireworks.

She wanted to ask her mother something but had to think before she spoke to make sure that the question wasn't too upsetting. She knew that lots of things upset Mummy. Nanny Mouse said she was sensitive, which meant that she felt everything more than other people. It also meant that she was often ill, and kept to her room. Sometimes, Leonora didn't see her for days, because even when she wasn't ill she spent hours and hours keeping Daddy company in the studio where Leonora wasn't allowed to go.

'Why can't I?' she would ask Nanny Mouse. 'Why can Mummy go up there and not me? I wouldn't disturb him. I'd be very quiet, really.'

Nanny Mouse shook her head. 'It's not the noise. It's just that your father likes to be alone when he's painting, apart from your mother, who's a sort of muse to him.'

'What's that? What's a muse?'

'A muse is a person who inspires artists to do good work. Like a guardian angel who watches over a painter or a poet and makes their work better.'

'I could do that,' Leonora said. 'I could be a muse. Couldn't I?'

'I expect you could, dear, but your daddy has chosen your mummy and there's nothing to be done about that.'

Leonora brought her attention back to her immediate surroundings and took a deep breath.

'You don't like bonfires, Mummy, do you?' she asked.

'No. No, I don't. They're so . . .'

'So what?'

'So final. Once a thing has been burned, there's really no getting it back at all, is there?'

'But if you make sure that you don't want the things that are going on the fire, then you don't mind, do you? Not getting them back, I mean.'

Maude smiled at her daughter and touched the top of her head briefly, stroking her hair.

'I never know, you see. Whether I really want something or not. I change my mind. You can *think* you don't want something and then wake up in the middle of the night and want it most desperately. *Most* desperately.'

Mummy's voice is wobbling, Leonora thought, and looked

sideways at her mother. She had tears in her eyes and for a moment, Leonora felt impatience surging through her. Her friend Bunny's mother was full of energy and strode about the village in her divided skirt, saying hearty hellos to everyone in her bright voice and smiling all the time. If only she had a mother like that!

Leonora blushed at the disloyalty of this thought and said, 'Is it all right if I go and watch Tyler? Watch the bonfire? Nanny Mouse said I was to ask you or Daddy.'

It wasn't until she spoke the words that she wondered why Nanny had sent her to ask permission. *She* was usually the person who told Leonora what she might and might not do.

'Yes, darling, of course it is,' Maude said.

'You could come with me if you like. We could watch it together.'

'That's very kind of you, sweetheart, but I think I must go and rest now. I have a headache this afternoon. I expect it's the thunder in the air. Run along, now. I shall go and lie down upstairs.'

Once she was outside, Leonora could feel the heaviness of the air, which seemed to be pressing down on the earth. The heat was so thick that you could almost see it and there was no wind at all, and everything looked as though it were holding its breath. Tyler had set light to the bonfire by the time she reached the kitchen garden. Everything that had been put out for burning had been fed into it and fire had already touched every sheet of paper and crisped it into glowing red and gold.

'How do, Missie.' Tyler was shouting a bit. The noise of the flames always surprised Leonora. They really did crackle and spit and roar.

'It's a lovely fire!' she cried. 'It's bigger than ever.'

'Months and months' worth of rubbish, that's what Mr Ethan said, but it didn't rightly look like rubbish to me, some of it. Proper lovely, some of it was.'

A sheet of paper blew off the bonfire and leapt towards the sky. Leonora followed it with her eyes. It was a funny shape; not a whole sheet of paper but part of something that must have been torn up. A triangle of white, a corner of something, which somehow had escaped and was being carried away across the lines of growing vegetables. Leonora ran after it as it blew into the Quiet Garden, right over to

276

where an apple tree grew like a fan against the pinkish bricks of a high wall.

She found it where it had drifted down to the earth, near some delphiniums, and picked it up. The paper had scratchy pencil marks on it and Leonora couldn't see exactly what they were, however hard she looked. Some of the marks were words. She could just make out 'light' and 'window' and 'ora'. Maybe that was a bit of a word but the rest had been torn away. She knew her father's spiky handwriting very well from staring at letters he'd put out for the post, and she also knew her mother's sloping, tiny script. These words, these parts of words, were written by her. Why had she scribbled on the edges of Daddy's paper? Daddy hated anyone fiddling with his things. Surely he wouldn't let Mummy write words on something that belonged to him. Maybe she was allowed to do that because of being a muse, but still, it was a mystery. Leonora tucked the piece of paper covered in faint pencil marks into the pocket of her cotton dress. Later, she would take it out and put it with the collection of secret objects that she kept in a biscuit tin, which had a picture on it of a ginger kitten who was just like Mr Nibs must have been when he was young. She knew she shouldn't say anything about having this scrap of paper, though she couldn't have said exactly why not.

She went past the bonfire again on her way indoors. Most of the flames had died down a little and grey ashes were all that was left. Leonora glanced towards the house and Mummy was still there, standing by the window. She hadn't moved at all. Her face, which Leonora couldn't see very well, looked blurred and indistinct because of the shimmering heat and because it was half-hidden by the curtain. She looked sad. Small and sad and pale.

Leonora was a good reader, but she loved those nights when her father came into the night nursery to read aloud to her. He would sit on her bed and pick up whatever it was that she had started and just go on from where she'd got to for a few pages. Tonight, Leonora knew, he'd come specially because of the storm. It wasn't that she was exactly *frightened* of the thunder and the weird lightning which lit everything up in a shiver of white; or that she really worried that the rain was too hard and driving to be held back by the glass of the windows, which was dreadfully thin if you looked at it carefully, but still. All the weather swirling and whirling around Willow Court made her feel a little nervous, and if Daddy came with his strong voice and comforting presence to sit on her bed and show her that *he* wasn't in the least bit worried, well, that made her feel better, always.

She leaned back against her pillows with Mr Worthing tucked into the crook of her arm and listened while Daddy read from *Little Women*, which was her very favourite book. They'd got to the part where Beth was most awfully ill, one of the bits Leonora liked best of all. Daddy was sitting up and leaning forward, about halfway up the bed. Suddenly he stopped reading and put the book down on the eiderdown.

'What's this, Leonora? Where did you get this?'

The scrap of paper! How could she have forgotten to put it away when she came in from outdoors? The storm had put it out of her mind. The clouds had gathered, puffed-up and purple as bruises all across the sky, and just as she came into the nursery the first crash of thunder shook the house and she'd left the piece of paper (which she'd taken out of her pocket and was already holding in her hand ready to go into the box) on her bedside table, and forgotten all about it. Now, here it was and Daddy had seen it. He looked very angry, but why ever should he be? She said, 'It flew off the bonfire this afternoon and I picked it up, that's all. May I keep it, Daddy? It doesn't look very important.'

It crossed her mind to wonder why it was that she wanted it so much, but she didn't really know the answer to that question, only that she did. Ethan Walsh stood up with the scrap of paper still in his hand. He seemed taller than ever because she was lying down, and his head was just in front of the light where it hung down from the ceiling, blocking it, which made his face almost black. You couldn't see his features properly. He said, 'No, I'm afraid you can't keep it, Leonora. It was wrong of you to take something that didn't belong to you. I must go now, I'm afraid, dear. Goodnight.'

He left the room before she could say a word in her defence and the injustice of the whole thing brought tears to her eyes. How could he? She hadn't done anything wrong. No one wanted those papers anyway or they wouldn't be putting them to be burned on a fire. They were rubbish, that's all, and rubbish didn't belong to anyone. In fact, that was what rubbish *was*, if you thought about it: things people didn't want any more. Two tears crept down Leonora's cheeks and she brushed them away angrily. She almost never cried. She prided herself on being brave and more grown-up than any of her friends but she couldn't help it. Daddy was such a bully sometimes. He made people do what he wanted. He *always* made Mummy do what he wanted. She never liked coming to pour tea for the London Men for instance, but he made her. He said it would look bad if she didn't, and Leonora had seen her, sitting stiffly in one of the smaller armchairs in the drawing-room, looking down. The London Men was Leonora's name for the gentlemen who came to Willow Court from time to time, trying to persuade Daddy that he was such a good artist, he really ought to exhibit some of his paintings, but he never would. He explained it to her once.

'People like things better if they can't have them,' he told her one day as they were walking round the lake. Mummy wasn't very well, and had to stay indoors all afternoon. Leonora loved the lake and often went down there, either with Nanny or with Daddy, to visit the swans and look at the willow trees that grew on the bank and leaned over with their branches dipping into the water. If you walked round it, it took nearly a whole hour to get all the way back to where you started.

'Everyone loves talking about paintings they can't see,' Daddy explained. 'They wonder about them. Wonder whether they're really as good as everyone says. Occasionally, I sell a couple, so that the art world knows what it's missing, but most of them will stay here. And when I'm dead, Leonora, they'll be yours and you will exhibit them and everyone will flock to Willow Court, because they've not been allowed to see them for so long, do you understand?'

She didn't, not really, but she said only, 'I suppose so. But I'm sure everyone would love to come to Willow Court now and have a look, wouldn't they?'

'They most certainly would,' her father said. 'But that would disturb my muse.' He meant Mummy, probably, and this was even more peculiar, because he didn't usually think about what she would like.

Leonora lay in bed and wondered whether she should wait to speak

279

to Nanny Mouse when she came to bed. She used to sleep in the night nursery when Leonora was a baby, but two years ago she'd moved into the little bedroom next door. She was still just behind the wall, and she never minded being woken up if Leonora had a nightmare or found it hard to get to sleep. She closed her eyes and hugged Mr Worthing closely.

Suddenly, she was quite wide awake again, and for a moment didn't know whether she'd been asleep or not. She crept out of bed and opened her door quietly. She couldn't see any light coming from Nanny Mouse's room. It must be terribly late, which meant she must have slept. The house was quiet all around her, but Daddy was working still, because a faint glow filtered down the corridor from the Studio. He must have not quite shut the door, which was most extraordinary. That door was like the one in the story about Bluebeard, so firmly closed that you felt something dreadful must lie beyond it. She knew this was a silly thought, but she couldn't help it. Daddy was always so cross when he found her on the next landing down, as though whatever he was keeping behind that door was monstrous and shouldn't be seen, which was exactly the opposite of the truth. His paintings were there and they were meant to be seen because they were beautiful.

Leonora tiptoed downstairs to look at the grandfather clock in the hall. It was nearly two o'clock, which was the very latest she'd ever been up in the night. She wasn't afraid of the dark, not really, only everything looked different in the dimness and all the furniture seemed to her on the point of moving. Even the pictures on the walls, Daddy's own pictures, had changed. There were no colours at night, she discovered; instead, every frame held shadows and gleaming spaces full of whiteness and shapes that seemed to shift and move as she passed them. She found herself unable to face them properly, and turned her head away as she fled up to the safety of the night nursery and closed her door tight. Should she go and wake Nanny Mouse?

She heard a noise and went to the door and opened it. Something heavy had crashed to the ground. That was what it sounded like. She put her head out into the corridor, and heard some more bangings and bumpings from upstairs. What was Daddy doing there? She listened, trying not to move, stiffening in terror as the voices came to her.

Daddy was shouting. You could hear that he was trying to be quiet, but some of his words reached Leonora and she wondered who he could possibly be so angry with. *Bloody careless . . . what we agreed . . . you can't do this now. I shan't allow it . . . Stop it. Stop that snivelling, you know I won't have it . . . tolerate it, Maude and that's all there is to it . . . if I hurt you, of course, but . . . get out of my sight . . . tomorrow . . .*

Was it possible? Was he shouting at Mummy? She'd definitely heard him say her name. Maybe he was just talking about her to someone else, but who? Who'd be up there in his Studio in the middle of the night? Leonora heard footsteps and ran back to the safety of the night nursery. She stood, trembling, just inside the door and kept it open a crack. Someone was coming down the stairs and she'd see who it was. Did she want to? Should she hide her eyes? Maybe it was a monster. Too late. She could see too clearly now. There she was, Mummy, in her nightgown. She was sobbing. She was making noises that sent shivers through the whole of Leonora's body. Animal noises. She knew she ought to close the door and not see this; not see her mother changed into something she didn't recognize, but her fingers wouldn't move and she *did* see. There was only a split second when Mummy was exactly level with where she was and in that moment she saw it clearly: a cut under Mummy's eye that was bleeding so that two thin lines of blood that looked black were scribbled on her white cheek. She must have fallen over. That must be why she was crying. She'd gone now, into her bedroom.

Leonora stood for a few minutes, waiting for Daddy to come down from the Studio, but he didn't. Perhaps she was in a nightmare, and if she pinched herself, she'd wake up in her own bed, safe and sound. She nipped hard at her arm and almost cried out with the pain. No, she was definitely not dreaming.

She tiptoed to Nanny Mouse's door and opened it. Nanny Mouse always slept very tidily, on her back with her hands folded on her chest, and for a moment Leonora wondered whether she should wait till morning, but there were too many frightening things in the house tonight. She went over to Nanny Mouse and touched her arm.

'Nanny Mouse? It's me . . . wake up, Nanny. I'm scared. Please wake up.'

Nanny Mouse opened her eyes at once.

'What is it, my love? What's the matter? Have you had a bad dream?'

As she spoke, she pushed back the sheets and got up. Her hair, normally carefully done up in a neat bun, hung down her back in a long plait and her nightdress was blue with embroidered flowers near the neck. She put a soothing arm around Leonora's shoulders.

'Come, I'll tuck you back into bed and bring you a warm drink. Then you can tell me all about your dream and it won't seem nearly so dreadful, I promise.'

She put her dressing-gown and slippers on and took Leonora by the hand. Together, they walked quietly into the night nursery and Nanny Mouse, talking in a soft voice all the time, made sure that Leonora's night light was on.

'I'll be back before you can blink,' she said. 'With a nice mug of warm milk and a biscuit as a special treat. We won't tell a soul we've been having midnight feasts. It'll be our secret.'

As she waited for Nanny Mouse to come back, Leonora wondered again whether perhaps she'd dreamed it all. Maybe she'd imagined her mother with a bloodstained face and those horrid noises she was making. She slipped into a doze for a while, but woke up again when Nanny Mouse returned.

'Now then, Leonora, I'll sit down here and you drink this and tell me all about your nightmare.'

Leonora felt a little silly and wondered whether she ought to say anything after all. Everything was quite safe and comfortable now, and it was hard to recollect the terror she'd felt earlier. She said, 'I heard something banging about. I thought it was coming from upstairs, and I went out into the corridor to listen and then I saw Mummy. She was crying. Well, not exactly crying, but sort of sobbing and whimpering and she ran right past me and there was blood on her face. On her cheek. I felt so frightened that I couldn't go back to my bed in the dark so I came to get you.'

'Poor little pet!' Nanny Mouse took the mug out of Leonora's hands and put it on the bedside table. 'Never you mind about things that the grown-ups do, my love. That's between them and it's not for us to wonder what goes on between a man and his wife. Best to forget all about it now. What I always say is what you don't know can't hurt you. This isn't anything for us to meddle with, Leonora, and it'll be all right. You'll see. In the morning, you'll most likely have forgotten all about it. It'll just be like another bad dream. I promise. And look at you now, child. Your eyes are closing. I'll wait here till you're properly asleep. And don't forget what I said. Most probably you didn't see anything, really, and you don't know anything and what you don't know can't hurt you.'

Leonora felt herself falling into darkness and silence and as she fell she could hear Nanny Mouse's voice, saying the words, saying them over and over: *what you don't know can't hurt you what you don't know can't hurt you* until they faded to silence.

And then all at once she was wide awake, and it was morning and there was Nanny Mouse drawing the curtains open.

'Wake up, sleepyhead! It's a lovely day and not a sign of the storm. Rise and shine. It's nearly time for breakfast. I've put out your yellow skirt today, as you're visiting Bunny later.'

Leonora sat up and rubbed her eyes.

'I went to sleep quickly last night, didn't I? After you'd brought me a drink.'

'I didn't bring you a drink, dear. You've been dreaming again.'

Leonora frowned. 'You did, Nanny! I know you did. I saw Mummy, don't you remember? With blood on her face? And I came and woke you up and you brought me a drink and then I fell asleep.'

Nanny Mouse came and sat on the bed and took Leonora's hand.

'Now, Leonora, you know you have a vivid imagination, and that brings on very vivid dreams, dear. I slept like a log all through the night. What's all this about your Mummy? I shouldn't tell her about it if I were you, she wouldn't like to think of herself there in your nightmares with blood on her face. Now jump out of bed and go and brush your teeth, dear. It's quite late already.'

Nanny Mouse left the room walking briskly, and Leonora stared after her, amazed. It *wasn't* a dream, she thought. I saw her. I heard her. I even pinched myself to make sure I wasn't dreaming. I can't have been, but Nanny Mouse would never say I didn't wake her up if I did. Would she?

Leonora got dressed slowly, thinking hard all the time. She could remember every single thing that happened, and every word that

Nanny Mouse had said. *What you don't know can't hurt you.* That's what she'd told her, but dreams were funny things and sometimes they were as real as anything and you thought you were awake when you weren't at all. Never mind, she thought, I'll know when I go down to breakfast. I'll be able to see whether Mummy's hurt her cheek or not. I'll see her and then I'll know.

She almost ran into the dining-room and when she saw that her mother's place was empty, tears of sheer disappointment came to her eyes. She blinked them away before Daddy could look up from his newspaper and notice her. Daddy didn't like people crying. He went cold and stiff if he ever caught her in tears, and she'd learned to stop herself. Lots and lots of girls in her class at school cried at the least little thing, but not Leonora. Now she waited for her father to look up and when he didn't, she said, 'Good morning, Daddy,' and sat down at her place and pulled her napkin out of its silver ring.

'Ah, Leonora! Good morning,' Daddy said, but he only lowered his newspaper for a second and then it was up in front of his face again like a shield.

'Where's Mummy?' Leonora asked, pouring milk over her cornflakes. 'Is she still asleep?'

The silence that followed this question went on for so long that Leonora thought perhaps Daddy hadn't heard her. She wondered whether she ought to repeat it, and decided to wait just a little while longer. Maybe he was reading something very important. She gazed at the black lines of type on the back page with the spoon halfway to her lips, and then with a rustle he lowered the newspaper again and stared straight at her.

'Finish that spoonful, Leonora, please, before we continue our conversation.'

The crunching of the cornflakes sounded very loud in her ears. She put her spoon down when she'd finished and looked across the long table at her father. He was very pale this morning and there were purple shadows under his eyes. He said, 'I'm afraid your mother is not very well today. She'll be keeping to her bed for the next couple of days and you must try not to disturb her.'

'But can I go and see her? Please? Just for a second. I won't be noisy, I promise, only I want to see her, please.'

Leonora watched her father pushing his chair away from the table. He stood up, and when he spoke to her she heard that coldness and anger in his voice, that tone which frightened whenever she heard it, the one that froze the air all round her head when he used it. He said, 'You haven't understood what I've told you, Leonora. Your mother is unwell. What that means is that she does *not* wish to be disturbed. Not by anyone. You will see her all the sooner if you allow her to return to health. You are not to visit her, is that clear, child?'

'Yes, Daddy,' said Leonora. 'I'm sorry.'

I'm not sorry, she thought, as she ate one spoonful of cornflakes after another. I'm only saying I am, because you have to say you're sorry with Daddy and then his voice gets less icy and he's cheerful again. Sometimes. Today, though, the magic word didn't work and he walked out of the room so crossly that even Mr Nibs, who was asleep on the window-seat, looked up as he swept past. Leonora felt that her whole head was in a muddle and besides, her eyes felt sore and itchy, as though she'd been crying. Now she'd have to wait till Mummy was better before she could see if her cheek was all right and every time she thought about what she'd seen in the night, it was getting less and less clear in her mind.

She took a piece of toast from the toast rack and nibbled it without bothering about butter and marmalade. She was going to spend the afternoon at Bunny's house today and soon it would be her birthday and she was going to have a party with a special birthday cake. She went over to sit next to Mr Nibs, who opened his green eyes briefly and then went back to sleep again with his head resting on his paws. Mummy wasn't well. She was often ill, but she always got better. Maybe I did dream everything, Leonora thought. The memory of what she'd seen was fading and the image of her mother howling in anguish grew paler and paler every time she thought about it. *What you don't know can't hurt you*, Nanny Mouse said in the dream. What did that mean? And why were those words still there in her head? They hadn't faded. They were as loud as could be. She didn't seem to be able to stop hearing them.

Her birthday was a week and a half away now. Leonora had been longing for it for ages and ages. Time had slowed down so that each day seemed to last far longer than it should have done. The fine weather meant long walks with Nanny Mouse, and she'd been to visit all her friends and they'd come to Willow Court, but even so there was still a very long time to wait. Mummy had been in her room for three days, and surely, Leonora thought, today she'd have to get up. The doctor hadn't come, and now Daddy was in London talking to some important gallery people. He'd gone off this morning in the car with a picture all wrapped up and leaning against the back seat. He wouldn't be back till tomorrow, so she could go and see if Mummy felt better without worrying about what he would say if he caught her. It'll be all right, I'm sure, Leonora thought, if I just creep in and say hello to her. Nanny Mouse was busy in the kitchen, chatting to Mrs Page, the cook, and Leonora very much hoped they were discussing her birthday cake and when it ought to be made and what it ought to look like.

She walked to Mummy's bedroom, past the closed doors of all the other bedrooms on that stretch of the corridor. There were more doors on the other side of the house as well. She never used to think about what was in those rooms, but Bunny had asked her once, when she'd come to play, who slept in them.

'No one,' Leonora answered. 'They're empty. When visitors come, they sleep in there, but we don't have visitors very often.'

'May I look?' Bunny had her hand on one of the handles and was turning it. Leonora wanted to stop her, but couldn't think what to say. She followed her friend into a space echoey with silence, where all the furniture was draped in white sheets.

'Why is everything covered up?' Bunny wanted to know.

'Well, Nanny Mouse calls the sheets dustsheets,' Leonora said. 'So I expect it's to keep off the dust.'

The girls left the room and closed the door. Bunny never asked to peep into a closed room again, but Leonora thought about them quite a lot after that and promised herself that when she was quite grown-up she would invite lots and lots of people to Willow Court and take off all the dustsheets and put vases of flowers everywhere.

Mummy wasn't in her room after all. Leonora knew she should have left at once, but instead she crossed the carpet and looked out of the window and then she saw her, down there in the gazebo, which was one of her special places. Leonora loved it too, because every bit of it was made of glass, even the roof, and when it rained you could sit in it and watch millions and millions of drops of water streaming around you and never get wet. Leonora ran out of the room and down the stairs. Nanny Mouse was just coming out of the kitchen.

'Where are you off to, dear?' she said.

'To the gazebo, to see Mummy,' Leonora said over her shoulder, and she could hear Nanny Mouse calling out to her, telling her not to disturb Mummy if she wanted to be all by herself. She took no notice, but ran down over the lawn till she reached the small glass and wrought-iron house with the pretty roof that ended in a sharp point. Maude looked up as she came in and smiled and held out her hands.

'Hello, darling. Have you come to talk to me?'

'Oh, yes, Mummy! I've been longing to see you. Are you feeling better?'

Maude didn't answer the question but said, 'Come and sit by me and tell me what you've been up to. It's so hot, isn't it?'

Leonora made sure to sit in the chair on her mother's right. That was the side that had been bleeding. She began to talk, telling stories of seeing the new cygnets down on the lake and playing croquet with Bunny and her brothers, and all the time she kept glancing up at her mother's face. She saw it at last, even though there was a lot of foundation cream and powder over it. Mummy must have tried to hide it, but it *was* there, underneath – a small bruise with a thin, long scab right in the middle of it. That meant that Nanny Mouse *had* been lying to her, and only pretending that she'd been dreaming. She would think about that later; what it meant, and why Nanny had done such a thing.

'You've hurt your cheek, Mummy,' Leonora said after a pause.

'Oh, that was silly of me,' Maude answered. 'I walked into your father's easel, up in the Studio. Can you imagine how foolish I felt?'

'Was it at night? In the middle of the night? I heard some noises. They woke me up.'

'No, no.' Maude shook her head. 'In the morning. I remember distinctly. It happened on Wednesday. Quite early in the morning.'

Leonora looked up and saw the blue sky through the glass striped with white. She worked backwards in her head. Today was Friday.

Monday night was when the storm was, and when she'd had her dream (but it wasn't a dream. There was the scar, on her cheek). Mummy was still in her room on Wednesday. Could she have gone upstairs to see Daddy? And bumped into his easel? Maybe she could have. Or maybe she wasn't telling the truth either. Leonora felt confused – baffled – and a little frightened, too. Should she ask? Tell Mummy about the dream? Should she say she'd seen her? She was just about to open her mouth to speak when Maude said, 'I'm busy making a little surprise for you, in time for your birthday.'

'Tell me about it, Mummy! Do tell me.'

'I can't, Leonora,' Maude smiled. 'If I told you, it wouldn't be a surprise, would it?'

She sounded almost happy; almost like other people. Leonora didn't really know what it was in her mother's voice, but there was always an edge of sadness and sighing in whatever she said. She looked up and saw tears in Maude's eyes.

'You're sad, Mummy!' she burst out, and put her arms around Maude's body, which felt thin and trembly. She buried her face in her mother's lap. 'Don't be sad. Please don't be sad,' she said into the fabric of Maude's dress. 'Please be happy.' She wasn't sure if her words could be heard, but she kept clinging to her mother, till Maude gently disentangled herself from Leonora's arms and lifted her face up and kissed it.

'Oh, my darling child,' she said. 'You must forgive me. I'm so sorry. Please say you forgive me, Leonora. Please say it.'

Leonora felt a cold terror creeping over her. She didn't know what the words meant. What should she forgive? Had Mummy done something bad? She must have done, or why would she want to be forgiven? Was this something to do with the crying in the night? Should she talk about that night again? Or did forgiving Mummy mean she mustn't speak about it any more? She saw the tear-streaked face looking down at her and wanted more than anything to be gone, to be safe with Nanny Mouse and away from Mummy whom she didn't understand, and whose crying made her feel embarrassed and awkward and nervous. She said, 'I forgive you, Mummy. Please stop crying. Please be happy.'

'I will, I will, darling.' Maude had let go of Leonora and was dabbing at her eyes with a white lace handkerchief that smelled of lily of the valley. 'I'm all right now, darling, truly. You can go and play if you like. I'll be perfectly all right, I promise.'

'Will you? Will you really?'

'Yes, I'm going to the Quiet Garden for a little walk now. I want to have a look at all my plants and flowers. There isn't much to do in the garden but I do love it so. Can you feel autumn in the air? I always feel it in August. Even when the sun's burning down, I know that autumn's coming. You run along now, Leonora.'

Leonora made her way towards the house, feeling guilty. Should she be so happy to leave her mother's company? So relieved? There must be something wrong with me, she thought. I'm a bad daughter, and maybe that's why Mummy's sad. Maybe if I loved her better, she'd be happy. This was such a dreadful thought that she nearly ran all the way back to where Maude was sitting, ready to fling herself at her mother and swear she loved her best of anyone in the whole, whole world, but she stopped herself, and glanced behind her first, just to see if Maude really *had* stopped crying. She was sitting exactly where Leonora had left her, turning her lace hankie round and round in her hands and looking down, clearly visible through the panes of shining glass that made up the walls of the gazebo.

Nanny Mouse came across the lawn towards Leonora just as she was turning to run back to her mother.

'Come along, dear,' Nanny Mouse said. 'It's nearly time for lunch.'

'Yes, Nanny,' Leonora said. I'll make sure to tell Mummy how much I love her later, she thought. There'll be time later on. She went into the house, feeling a weight fall away from her, feeling happy.

'I had such a funny dream last night, Nanny,' Leonora said as she was getting dressed the following morning. 'I was lying in my bed and I wasn't properly asleep. My eyes were half-open, I think, because I could see things, only not very clearly. Anyway, what I saw was a person in a long white dress with long hair hanging down at the back going into the nursery. She stood by the dolls' house, just over there and I could smell wallpaper paste and she was sticking something on the dolls' house roof. Then she went away again and I can't remember anything after that.'

Nanny Mouse went on plaiting Leonora's hair. She came to the end of one braid and tied a blue ribbon round it, making a pretty bow. She was very good at making bows look pretty – not too droopy and with both loops exactly the same size. She said, 'That wasn't a dream, dear. Your mummy came in last night and did some work on the dolls' house. That's part of your birthday present. She did tell me she was going to make it a surprise for you, but I suppose something must have happened to change her mind.'

'May I go and see? Please, Nanny! Let me go and see.'

'Sit still and let me finish your hair, Leonora, and then you can.'

Leonora looked over to where the dolls' house was standing against the wall. There was nothing different about it that she could see. She thought of her dream. The figure she'd seen was putting paste on the roof. As soon as her hair was plaited to Nanny Mouse's satisfaction, she raced to see what her mother had done.

'Oh, it's the roof, Nanny! Look!'

Where before there was nothing but plain paper in a reddish colour, now the whole roof was covered in pale grey and yellowish tiles, not real tiles, but painted ones. Mummy must have taken ages to paint them. She'd covered two large sheets of paper with watercolour images of proper tiles. Leonora looked at them carefully. Every single one seemed different from the one next to it, and from the ones above and below it.

'It looks just like a real roof, doesn't it, Nanny? It must have taken her hours and hours, mustn't it?'

'It's most beautiful,' Nanny Mouse said. 'You make sure to thank her now.'

'Yes, I will,' Leonora said. She could never say anything, of course, and she knew Mummy must have taken enormous trouble over painting pictures of roof tiles, and they *were* exactly like real tiles and very beautiful if you thought about it, but she couldn't help feeling a little disappointed. It wasn't what *she* would have called a birthday surprise, not really. A new doll for the house, or perhaps some new clothes for the dolls she already had would have been more exciting. You couldn't really *play* with a roof. All you could do was look at it, and she'd scarcely paid any attention at all to the old one, so why did Mummy think she'd like a new one?

She could feel her mood darkening as she went down to breakfast, and tried to cheer herself up by thinking that maybe this wasn't the whole surprise, but only part of it. Yes, perhaps that was the answer. There was something else to come, something much, much better. That must be it. After all, it wasn't even her birthday yet and she was being allowed to see it. By the time she reached the dining-room, she'd almost persuaded herself that the new roof paper wasn't her present at all. But, she said to herself, if Mummy is there I shall thank her very much and give her a kiss as well.

Mummy and Daddy were both sitting at their places when Leonora came into the dining-room, but she could see from the way they were sitting, from how they weren't smiling or talking to one another, that something was wrong. They didn't even look at her and Nanny Mouse as they came into the room and took their places at the other end of the table. Silence fell over everything, so that the noise of spoons on cereal bowls and cups being put down on saucers sounded really loud. That was what it felt like to Leonora.

She glanced from her mother to her father. Daddy was frowning. His lips were pressed together, as if he wanted to shout but was holding himself back. Mummy's gaze was on her plate, but she hadn't touched her toast. There was a lump of butter right next to it, and some marmalade as well, but she made no attempt to pick up her knife.

'Nanny,' Daddy said, not quite looking at Nanny Mouse. 'I'd be most grateful to you if you kept Leonora occupied outside today, if you don't mind. It's a fine morning. We have matters to discuss, Mrs Walsh and I, and wouldn't want to be interrupted.'

'Of course, sir,' said Nanny Mouse. 'We'll go to the village, and for a walk in the fields behind the church. Perhaps we'll take a picnic, Leonora. Would you like that?'

Leonora nodded. She didn't trust herself to speak. How *could* Daddy be so beastly? She never interrupted them when they were busy. She never went up to the studio because she knew she wasn't allowed to. She wasn't a baby to be taken off on a picnic so that the grown-ups could talk in peace. She was nearly, very nearly, eight years old. She bit into her piece of toast and glared at her father but he was looking out of the window and didn't see how cross she was. I'll say something to Mummy, Leonora thought. I'll thank her for repapering the dolls' house roof. She took a deep breath and said, 'Mummy, I love the new roof for the dolls' house. Thank you for making it for me.'

To her astonishment, Mummy's eyes filled with tears and she turned so pale that Leonora thought she might be going to faint. She bit her lip and looked across the table at her daughter with something like terror in her face. She was trembling too. Leonora wished fervently that she'd never mentioned the roof paper, never opened her mouth. Before she could think of what to say next, Daddy spoke.

'Maude, my dear,' he said in a voice that was icy and soft at the same time, 'what paper is this? Have you shown it to me?'

'No, dear,' her mother answered. 'I painted some paper to decorate the dolls' house roof. It's of no consequence, really.'

'A waste of your time, I'd have thought. You could have used some off-cuts from old wallpaper rolls, couldn't you?'

'Yes, but this was a special treat for Leonora's birthday. I enjoyed painting the tiles.'

'They're beautiful, Daddy, really,' Leonora cried, hoping that she could divert the force of her father's displeasure away from Mummy. 'I love them. The dolls' house looks so much nicer now. Thank you, Mummy!'

She left her place and ran round the table to her mother's chair. She flung both arms round her neck and hugged her. Mummy's body, she thought, is stiff and trembly at the same time.

'Nanny, please take Leonora away now,' Daddy stood up. 'This scene has gone on long enough.'

He left the room, and Leonora could hear the sound of his footsteps on the marble floor of the hall and then going up the stairs.

'I love you, Mummy!' Leonora cried, not sure what was happening, not knowing what anyone had done wrong, nor why everything felt so horrible this morning.

'And I love you, my baby,' said Maude and burst into tears. Leonora didn't know what to do, or what to say.

'Go to your room, Leonora,' Nanny Mouse said. 'And wait for me. Your mummy will be quite all right. I shall look after her. Don't worry, dear.'

Leonora made her way slowly to the nursery, wanting to scream with rage and weep with anguish, both at the same time. Stupid, stupid Nanny Mouse, she thought, kicking with the toe of her foot against every step of the staircase. How can she tell me not to worry? My mummy's sad and I don't know why. They won't tell me. She slammed the nursery door behind her and flung herself on to the bed to wait for Nanny Mouse. Why, she wondered, does Daddy want me to be out of the house? What is he going to do?

Leonora came in from outside, and stood in the hall. Nanny Mouse had stopped in the drive to talk to Mrs Page who was on her way to the village, and she'd told Leonora to run on ahead. Daddy and Mummy were quarrelling. She could hear loud, angry voices and stood quite still to listen, even though she knew she wasn't supposed to. Mummy was screaming. She usually spoke quietly, and to think she could shriek like that made Leonora feel sick and frightened. She knew at once that Daddy and Mummy wouldn't want her to hear what they were saying, so she shrank against the wall, but she didn't run away. In spite of herself, a longing to *know*, a desire to understand for the very first time exactly what it was that was troubling her mother, kept her standing there, trembling, with her mouth half-open and her eyes wide. They were in the drawing-room, and she could hear almost every word.

'No more. I utterly refuse. And if you lay one more finger on me, I swear I'll tell. And then what would your fine friends in London think of the wonderful Ethan Walsh? Will they still come here and drink your gin and admire your pictures . . .'

Then there came a laugh from Maude that chilled Leonora's blood: shrill, horrible, not really laughter at all, but a sound that set her teeth on edge and made her wince. '. . . well, I've had enough, that's all. The worm is turning, and that's what I am. A worm, and I've been in the dark long enough, and now everything will change. I'm warning you, Ethan. I'm tired of being the one you take everything out on. Tired of it.'

Her mother's voice faded to a whisper and Leonora didn't catch the next murmured remarks. She could hear her father's voice, too, but not what he was saying. Could it be that he was calming Mummy down? Making her feel better? Leonora was just beginning to feel more normal, when she heard her father say, 'I don't want to hear any of this again, d'you understand? If I ever discover that you've told anyone, anyone at all, then you'll be very sorry. Very sorry indeed. And remember. I, too, can speak. I can have Doctor Mannering up here in twenty minutes and tell him that my poor dear wife has gone insane. It's well-known all over the country that your health is what they call "delicate". You'd be in the asylum within the hour. And I shan't hesitate. D'you understand? Hesitation is not in my nature. Are we agreed?'

Tears started from Leonora's eyes, and she tiptoed as quietly as she could to hide behind the curtain near the hall window before her parents came out of the drawing-room and caught her. Too late! There was Daddy, striding across the marble tiles, and he'd seen her. She knew he had. She closed her eyes, sure that something dreadful was going to happen. She didn't understand everything she'd heard but she knew this – Daddy made Mummy cry by hitting her, and he was going to call the doctor and pretend that she was mad if she didn't do exactly what he said. That was cruel, and terrible. Surely Daddy, who could sometimes be so kind and amusing and friendly, wouldn't behave like a monster in a fairy tale? Surely he wouldn't.

'Come here at once, Leonora,' he said to her. She went to him and he gripped her arms. 'What are you doing? How long have you been in the hall?'

'I've only just come in, really. We've been in the village, and then we went for ever such a nice walk . . .' Leonora knew that she had to keep talking, as though she'd really just come in and hadn't overhead anything. He'd be so angry if he thought she'd listened to him and Mummy having an argument. She went on babbling, the words spilling out of her mouth and, gradually, her father's hold on her arms relaxed.

'Go to the nursery, Leonora. I have work to do now.'

He went up the stairs two at a time. Leonora listened hard and heard the door of the studio slam shut. She let out a breath that she felt she'd been holding for ages. Now that he'd gone, she wanted to run to Mummy and make sure she was all right, but Nanny Mouse came into the hall just then and she couldn't. Nanny Mouse said, 'What's the matter, child? You look as though you've seen a ghost.'

'Mummy and Daddy were quarrelling. It was horrid. He was saying terrible things. He said . . .'

Nanny Mouse interrupted her. 'Don't say a word, dear. Don't you remember what I told you? What you don't know can't hurt you. All this grown-up arguing is none of our business.'

'When did you tell me? When did you say that what I don't know can't hurt me?'

They were walking up the stairs. Nanny Mouse answered, 'Why, the night you came and woke me with stories of blood on your poor mother's face.'

'But you said it was a dream! You did, you did.'

Nanny Mouse sighed, and took her hat off and turned it round and round in her hand. She was looking down at the carpet outside the nursery and blushed.

'Yes, I'm so sorry, dear. I did say that, and it was very naughty of me, but I was only trying to make you feel less frightened, that's all. I shouldn't have done it, I know, but it's difficult to know what to do for the best sometimes. There are so many secrets in this house. It's very difficult. Never mind, you just stay in the nursery for now, till bedtime. I'll bring your supper up for you tonight. You just keep out of the way for now. It'll be all right, you'll see.'

Nanny Mouse made her way downstairs again. Leonora listened for a while, and there was nothing but total silence hanging over the whole of Willow Court. She went into the nursery and stood by the window for a long time, not moving. Yes, she thought. That's right. The house is full of secrets, but what I don't know can't hurt me. It isn't time for bed yet. Everyone is busy doing something somewhere else. I *do* know some things, but I must pretend I don't. I must pretend that my daddy is a good daddy who loves my mummy and not someone who shouts at her and makes her cry and makes her cheek bleed and tells her she's mad. I must pretend that what I saw was only a dream, but I know it wasn't. I want to be far away, out of the front door and away from Willow Court, where all these secrets live that I don't want to know. The lake. I'll go down to the lake.

Leonora looked out of the window. The shadows of trees were

black on the lawn and every rose was edged with gold. *What I don't know can't hurt me.* She said it over and over again, as though it were a magic spell that would keep her safe. *What I don't know can't hurt me.*

⁂

Gwen's tea had gone cold and she didn't have the energy to get up and make more. Rilla was busy whipping cream for the strawberry shortcakes. Mary wasn't due back in the kitchen for another couple of hours and had reacted rather better than Gwen had expected to the news that Rilla wanted to be in charge of dessert for tonight. The plan had been for a fresh fruit salad and cream, but when Rilla said, 'This'll save you all that cutting and chopping, won't it?' there wasn't much Mary could do but agree.

Gwen had hulled the strawberries and cut them into neater slices than Rilla herself would have done. She was, in Gwen's opinion, an inspired rather than a careful cook, and she did go in for rather a lot of tasting of anything she happened to be mixing in bowls, but still, Gwen felt herself relaxing more than she had for a long time in the kitchen, warm from the sun coming in at the window. The back door was open; she could hear Douggie and Fiona in the Peter Rabbit garden and hoped, selfishly, that they'd stay away for a while and let her enjoy these few minutes, which took her back to when she and Rilla were little girls allowed to help make cakes as a special treat.

She said, 'Chloë's tree's worked out rather better than I thought. I was a bit worried that it would all be hideously modern and not look right in the hall, but it'll be lovely, won't it?'

Rilla nodded absently. She wasn't really listening, being absorbed in spreading the shortbread with cream, arranging strawberry slices in concentric circles on the lustrous white and admiring her own handiwork. She said, 'Mmm. Lovely.'

'You're miles away. Honestly, I don't know how you do it.'

'Do what?'

'I don't know. Be so relaxed about everything. I can see you've not even given a thought to what Philip and Chloë might be uncovering up there in the nursery.'

'That's not true, actually. I have thought about it, but I've decided that it might be nothing at all. A shopping list or something,' Rilla said.

'It didn't look remotely like any list I've ever seen. You don't seem to be in the least worried.'

'I've stopped worrying because I don't know exactly what I'm supposed to be worried about. Your problem is, Gwen, that you go searching out the difficulties instead of waiting for them actually to happen.' She was now eating left-over slices of strawberry.

'Well, one of us has to be prepared,' said Gwen. 'And you seem to be in a sort of private cloud-cuckoo land.'

Rilla smiled enigmatically. 'I'd forget all about it, you know, until you have to deal with it. And in any case, it would have to be quite something to ruin the party, surely?'

Gwen frowned. 'I give up, I do really. You don't even admit to the possibility of a catastrophe.'

Rilla looked at her sister. 'My idea of what constitutes a catastrophe is a bit different from yours. The cancellation of a party doesn't come anywhere near it, I promise you.'

'Oh, God, Rilla, I'm sorry!' Gwen was near tears. 'I don't know what I'm saying any more. Of course I didn't mean. Don't think I . . .'

'It's okay, Gwen. Don't start crying, please. That's all we need.'

'I'm sorry. Really I am. And I know it's nothing like your feelings, but we haven't forgotten Mark's death either. You don't ever get over something like that, do you? I feel guilty, too, for not talking to you about it enough. I know you said at the time you didn't want to discuss it, but I should have persisted, shouldn't I? I couldn't believe it when you said it wasn't our fault, mine and Mother's. You'd left Mark in our care after all. If I'd been in your position, I'd never have spoken to us again.'

'I didn't think it was your fault, Gwen. I still don't. Either of you. I should never have left him. My fault, the whole thing. And how could I not have spoken to you? You and Mother and Beth were all I had in the world. I couldn't have managed without you.'

Gwen was silent, remembering the funeral. A grey March day and the wind like a knife and she and Leonora holding Rilla up, one on each side of her, their arms linked through hers as the tiny white coffin was lowered into the hard earth and Rilla, pale and breathless with grief, dazed and full of pills. If you were close enough to her, and

Gwen was, you could feel her whole body trembling. The trees were just beginning to come into leaf, and yet that day Gwen felt that spring, proper spring, with warmth and sunshine and new flowers, was a complete impossibility. She wiped a tear away while Rilla was moving the plates into the larder.

'Did you notice,' Rilla said as she came back into the kitchen, 'how great that tree of Chloë's is? She's really talented you know.'

'That's what I was saying before,' Gwen laughed. 'That's precisely what I was saying while you were doing the strawberries, only you weren't listening. I thought it would be a disaster, and I was wrong.'

'You ought to tell her. She'd love it if you admired it.'

'Would she? I find it so hard to talk to her, Rilla. You've no idea how envious I am of the way you and Beth seem to just, you know, chat like real friends. Chloë hates me.'

'What rubbish! You shouldn't think that, Gwen, honestly. She's young, that's all. You ought to try pretending that she's not your daughter, but some stranger who's just wandered into your house. A guest.'

'Would that work? Worth trying, I suppose. She's so prickly, though. And all sorts of things she does irritate me, like the way she dresses, for instance. You don't know how lucky you are. Beth's so elegant and *together*. Chloë's all over the place.'

'Speaking as someone who's often just as all over the place as she is, it doesn't matter a bit, Gwen. There's all sorts of other things that are more important, and if you let stuff like that get you down you'll never be happy. Never. Now come on, enough of all this. Let's go and find James and see how the marquee's coming on. It's going to be the best party, whatever they're in the process of finding up in the nursery.'

Gwen followed Rilla out of the back door, and shut it carefully behind her. I wish, she thought, that I shared her optimism. There were altogether too many unknowns in the situation for Gwen to feel easy in her mind.

'There was a time,' Leonora said, addressing Sean's profile as he drove, 'and not so very long ago either, when I would have scorned the idea of going down to Lodge Cottage in a car. I used to run up and down the drive as a girl and think nothing of it, and it's really only in the last couple of years I've become lazy.'

'I was born lazy,' said Sean, 'so it suits me to take the car for even the shortest of distances. The crew have gone down already, so we should be all set to film when we get there.'

'Miss Lardner will want to give us a cup of tea,' Leonora said. She hoped that she was sounding normal. She felt as though an earthquake had taken place inside her, and it surprised her that Sean couldn't see it. She felt confused, mystified, and uncertain of what she remembered. Something – she was not sure what it was – hovered at the edge of her memory, just out of reach. She had dressed most carefully for the filming in a silk dress of a particularly deep raspberry pink that flattered her skin, with pearl studs in her ears and her pearl necklace. It was becoming harder and harder to disguise things with make-up and she hoped that her eyes did not give away the fact that she had shed tears earlier.

'Are you all right, Leonora?' asked Sean. 'Has something happened?'

'No . . . no, nothing at all. Thank you for asking. I'm feeling a little tired, that's all.'

For a wild moment, she considered telling Sean everything. He was such a sympathetic listener. But then there they were, at Lodge Cottage, and the sound man was standing outside the open front door waving at them and the moment passed. A good thing, too, Leonora said to herself as she got out of the car.

'We're all set, Sean,' the sound man said, and they went into the house. Miss Lardner had set tea in the front room, on a table that had been polished to such a dazzling shine that the lighting man had asked for a cloth to cover it up a little.

'Nanny Mouse, how lovely you look!' said Sean, going up to the old lady as though she were his own grandmother and kissing her on the cheek. Nanny Mouse smiled, and Leonora thought she was blushing. Certainly, she looked as well as she had for a long time, and she sounded firm in her own mind today, as she greeted them all and told them to sit down.

'Leonora,' Sean said to her, 'if you could sit down there . . . that's right, by the window. Then if you don't mind pouring the tea, we can just talk naturally. I'll be out of shot, but of course the whole thing will be edited as you know. I'll get the ball rolling by asking a question, and we'll see where we go from there, shall we?'

Leonora nodded. She picked up the rose-patterned teapot and said, 'No sugar for you, Sean, is that right?'

'Yes, thank you. Now, Nanny Mouse, shall we get started? Do you remember whether Ethan Walsh ever came into the nursery when Leonora was a little girl?'

Nanny Mouse was silent for a while, and Leonora wondered whether perhaps it would be necessary to prompt her, but then, like a bottle suddenly uncorked, she started talking, 'The Master loved the nursery. That's what he told me. No nonsense in here, Nanny Mouse, he'd say and he'd laugh heartily. And he liked to read to Miss Leonora at bedtime. *Little Women* was her favourite book. I remember that. Of course she could read perfectly well herself, but it's not the same, is it? Not the same as having your daddy reading to you.'

'What about her mother?' Sean asked. 'What about Maude?'

'Oh, no, she never read to her. She wasn't that sort of mother really. She was always very shy, was Miss Maude. She had one layer of skin missing, that's what I told her. Thin-skinned. She wasn't very strong, you know and she bruised very easily. I knew about the bruises of course, though she thought I didn't see them. I did. I saw everything. It was my job really, to see things. I had Miss Leonora to think about and the Master was most particular that she shouldn't know.'

'What?' Leonora asked, hearing her own heart beating. 'What was it that Daddy didn't want me to know?'

'Oh, he didn't want you to know anything, dear,' said Nanny Mouse, as sunnily as though they were discussing nothing more important or interesting than the day's shopping list. She ticked items off on her fingers one by one. 'Not about the bruises. Certainly not about how Miss Maude died, but of course you don't remember about that at all, do you? The Master told me you couldn't possibly remember. He assured me you didn't and you've never said a word so I suppose he's right, though I must say I've always thought it strange that you could put such a thing out of your mind. Still, it's a mercy, for who'd want to remember anything like that?'

The air in the small room seemed all at once to thicken and darken round Leonora's head. She took a deep breath. What was Nanny Mouse saying? She closed her eyes and saw an image on the inside of her eyelids, as clear as any photograph: the lake and something in it, floating under the willows. Something dark spreading on the surface of the water. A skirt, that was what it was. Leonora opened her eyes and spoke to Nanny Mouse in a voice that sounded to her ears not like her own voice at all, but that of a small child, hardly daring to make a sound. 'Mummy drowned in the lake, didn't she, Nanny? She was in the water, wasn't she?'

'Leonora found her,' Nanny Mouse said confidentially, as though she were addressing a perfect stranger. She had slipped from recognising Leonora to not having the least idea who she was. 'Poor little mite. She'd run down to the lake because everything in the house was crosswise; out of sorts. Dreadful atmosphere for a child, and they never paid her the least mind, you know. Quarrelling all around her and worse. Much worse. I don't hold with children seeing all that. Never have. My children don't see such things if I can help it. I told her. I said, what you don't know can't hurt you, and I believe that.'

Somewhere, very close to her shoulder but also so distant that it might have been in another universe altogether, Leonora was aware that the camera was still turning, but she could feel the tears starting up again somewhere in her head. She could hear Sean saying something, asking her something. She pulled her attention over to where he was sitting and tried to listen.

'Leonora, I've stopped filming. Are you all right?'

She nodded, not caring, wanting to say, 'Do whatever you like', but not finding the right words. All the words she ever knew seemed to have left her and for a second she wondered whether perhaps she'd had a stroke. I'm seventy-five tomorrow, she told herself. I'm old. Maybe this is a stroke. Or some kind of heart attack. She made herself breathe slowly, in and out of her nose, and count at the same time from one to ten. There. That was better.

'I'm perfectly all right now, thank you,' she said at last, and lifted her teacup to take a sip of Earl Grey, lukewarm now but still a comfort. 'Please continue filming.'

'Tell me about the routines of the house,' Sean was saying to

Nanny Mouse. 'Did Ethan Walsh have a particular time when he liked to paint?'

Leonora only half-listened to the answer. She was somewhere else. She was down by the lake and it was hot and there was her mother, floating on the water, her face all white and her eyes staring. I found her, she thought. I found her and she was all wet and dead and I ran back to the house to get everyone to save her and they couldn't and then I fainted, and I was wet and cold, and after I went to bed there was nothing but fever and more fever and bad dreams all the time, and pain in my chest, and when I woke up, they told me a lie. They told me my mother had been very ill and had died from her illness and I believed them. Nanny told me and Daddy told me and I believed them because I wanted to. Because I didn't want didn't want didn't want to know that I'd found my own mother with water filling her mouth and dragging at her skirt and making her skin all pruney and white and horrible. I didn't want to know that, so I forgot it. Pretended I never ever knew it at all. Pretended that she'd died neatly in her bed and I'd never seen her floating in the lake with willow leaves caught up in her fingers. But I remember now.

'I'm so sorry, Sean,' Leonora said, putting her glass down on the saucer beside her. 'I think I'm quite recovered now.'

They were in the conservatory, where leaves of plants and branches of small trees formed a canopy of dark green over their heads. Sean had fetched a drink for Leonora and now they sat facing one another in the two cane armchairs. One of the cats – Gus, it had to be – was lying next to one of the gigantic Chinese pots in the corner, slumbering in the warmth. Sean could see that Leonora's hands were still trembling and that, although she was doing her best to appear in control, she was obviously still trying to come to terms with what Nanny Mouse had been speaking of. He said, 'I think you're being very brave. There's no need for any apology. That kind of discovery would knock anyone sideways.'

'I've always tried not to let things get the better of me.' Leonora attempted a smile but didn't quite succeed. 'With every single thing that's happened to me – my father's death, my husband's death, other things – I've always felt that if I could keep my head, everything would be all right.'

'You don't mention your mother's death,' Sean remarked. 'That must have been the most traumatic thing of all, for such a young child.'

Tears sprang into Leonora's eyes. 'But it wasn't. That's exactly why I feel so terrible now. I wasn't close to my mother. Not close at all. I loved her very much, of course, but I always felt that I could never really get near her. Nanny Mouse was more of a parent to me than she was, and for years and years what I most remember from those days was being ill and missing my birthday. The fact that my mother was gone when I came to myself was sad, of course it was, and it troubled me, but not in a way I could understand. And after a while I seemed to recover. But isn't it funny? For the last few months, I've felt – I don't know how I can express this – that there's some kind of darkness in my head, and that if only I could see into it, or over it or beyond it, I'd understand all sorts of things that I've never understood before.'

'Like why it is,' Sean said, 'that you seemed to suffer so little from such a dreadful tragedy?'

'Exactly. Yes, that's exactly right. It's as though all my life I've been stifling something. Covering it up. And now I feel as though I've opened a door into some dark space in my heart or my mind. I'm not at all sure which, but it's as though I've walked into this blackness carrying a candle. I feel as though I'm holding it out in front of me and different things are catching the light.'

Before they'd come up to Willow Court after leaving Lodge Cottage, Leonora had made him drive towards town ('Anywhere, anywhere, please, as long as I don't have to face anyone now. I'll be myself in a moment, I promise.') while she sobbed like a child, with her handkerchief held up in front of her face, covering her eyes. For several minutes, her crying had been the only sound in the car. Sean hadn't concentrated at all on where he was going, but stared at the road in front of him with all his attention on the old woman beside him, her anguish. In the end, the weeping had stopped and she turned to him and said, 'We can go back now, Sean. I'm sorry to land you with all this. By the time we get home I ought to look more or less all right.'

As they drove up to the front door, she'd turned to him and said, 'Actually, I'm very glad it was you who saw me like that, and not one of my children or grandchildren. Do you mind me saying that?'

'Not at all,' he'd replied, quite sincerely. 'I completely understand. Sometimes this kind of thing is easier to reveal to a stranger.'

'Actually, I don't think of you as that.' She'd smiled at him then, with the full force of her charm back in place: all the coquettishness, all the style. Paradoxically, it was only when he'd seen her crying that Sean understood how brave she was and how much he admired her courage.

'What do you see now?' he asked her gently. 'In the light of this candle you're taking into the dark place?'

'Almost the worst thing of all is what I've come to realize about my father. The person I thought he was is nothing but my own picture of him. A childish illusion as it turns out. He was a bully, Sean. I've been thinking about him a great deal in the last few days, and I see that my love for him, and I loved him very much, blinded me to all sorts of things he actually said and did, which were at best unfeeling and at worst, cruel. In those days, when I was a child, we were kept out of the way of adults as much as possible, and my father deceived me. That's what it seems like to me now, after all this time. And yet it's him I'm weeping for as much as my poor mother. More even. I feel I've lost more where he's concerned. Isn't that dreadful? I feel guilty about it, and also guilty about something I've discovered in my own behaviour. I hope I haven't been unkind, but I think I've kept things covered up all my life. Protecting people, including myself. I always thought that was for the best, but it isn't. Not really. You have to know the truth of things, even though sometimes it's painful and hard to understand. And I hope I can ask you not to speak about this to anyone.'

'I shan't say a word. But has it all come back to you, Leonora? Do you now remember everything?'

'I think so. I can remember running down to the lake. I can see the dark thing on the water very clearly. The next part is still very hazy. I can remember seeing my mother's face but after that everything is unclear. Did I pull at the skirt and stare into her face? Or did I run up to the house at once and call my father and Nanny Mouse? I can't bring it back into my mind properly, but it doesn't matter. Nanny won't be able to tell me details like that. And I don't really want to know, Sean. I can imagine. From when little Mark drowned. I did see him. I don't need anyone to remind me of that.'

She placed one hand over her eyes again, and Sean spoke into the silence that grew between them.

'Rilla feels responsible, you know,' he said at last. 'Because she wasn't there when Mark drowned.'

'Does she? Oh, no. I had no idea. How terrible. That is *so* terrible. Does she still? Oh, God!' Leonora's voice shook. She took her hand away from her face and Sean could see how white she was, how deep the shadows were under her eyes. 'I knew she did at first, but after all this time? Oh, how dreadful, how unforgivable of me. I never knew that. Am I stupid? Don't tell me, Sean. I know I am. I'm selfish and stupid not to see my own daughter's pain. Maybe because of my own. You cannot imagine what a terrible time that was. There's nothing, is there, in the world worse than the death of a child? I blamed myself. And thought Rilla blamed me too, because after all she'd left her child in my care. Mine and her sister's, and you'd think you could do that, wouldn't you? You'd think a grandmother and an aunt would be responsible enough to take care of one small child. I've never forgiven myself, not really, but Rilla always said, right from the start, that she didn't blame us. I didn't realize that that was because she still felt herself to be at fault. Stupid, stupid. Blind and stupid.'

'Perhaps Rilla hid her pain from you.'

Leonora nodded. 'Yes. Yes, there's been a great deal of hiding of things, one way and another.' She bowed her head and sighed. 'I'll have to do something about it, if it's not too late. I should have spoken to Rilla more frankly. About many things. I always let myself criticise her, when I disagree with things she does, but we don't really talk. Her way of life is so strange to me, but I shouldn't let that come between us. I will. I'll talk to her. I don't know where I'll find the right words but I'll try.' She leaned against the back of the chair and closed her eyes. For a few moments she sat there and Sean was aware of her gathering her strength together. He felt, ridiculously, that he could almost see the struggle that was going on in Leonora's mind in the reactions of her body: the twitching of the muscles round her mouth, the way she kept turning one of her rings round and round on her finger, and a trembling that came over her from time to time, as though a sorrowful memory was washing over her body like a wave.

'Rilla? Rilla wake up!' Beth touched the shoulder that stuck up out of the sheet covering the sleeping body on the bed. Rilla turned over and opened an eye, groaning slightly.

'God, Beth, must I? I was having such a lovely nap. What's wrong?' Rilla's voice was fuzzy and sleepy and Beth grinned.

'You only just got up before lunch, Rilla. Honestly! This is what comes of burning the candle at both ends. You're obviously tired, and we all know why, don't we?'

Rilla swung her feet to the floor and pushed her fingers through her hair.

'A little less sarcasm, miss,' she said. 'I'd have you know that it was well worth losing a night's sleep. Well worth it.'

'Spare me the gory details, please!' Beth said. 'And go and wash your face or something. You've been summoned. Leonora says would you mind coming to the conservatory.'

She watched as Rilla washed her face and hurried to brush her hair and get back into her clothes.

'Have I got time to put my make-up on again?'

'No, you haven't. You look fine.'

'I look,' said Rilla, 'like a rather plump ghost. And why on earth does she need to see me now, anyway? Do you have any idea?'

Beth shook her head. 'Not a clue. She just told me she wants to see you and Efe and me for what she called "a quiet chat".'

'Right, let's get it over with then. Whatever it is.'

They made their way downstairs to the conservatory, where the door stood open.

'Is that you, Rilla?' Leonora called out. 'Come in, darling.'

Rilla went in and Beth followed her. Tiny pieces of sunshine made their way into the room through the thick network of intertwined greenery that spread all over the walls and ceiling. Gus was lying in a shady corner, and Efe was there too, taking up most of the sofa. Beth hesitated. Leonora said, 'Beth, come in. Come in. Shut the door behind you, please. You can sit over there by the window. Rilla, why don't you take the other cane chair?'

Beth took the hard chair Leonora had indicated. This is bizarre, she thought. Why on earth does she want to talk to us? And why does the door have to be shut? She looked at Efe who was staring down at his shoes. He hadn't even glanced up when they came in, but the force of Beth's gaze made him aware of her and he met her eyes briefly, without smiling. Well, sod you too, then, she thought. If you're going to be all stiff and unfriendly, you can get stuffed. Before she had a chance to do any more wondering about anything, Leonora spoke.

'You must all be asking yourselves why I've asked you to come in here like this. It's all rather cloak and dagger and I don't mean it to be, only the house is upside down what with the cleaners and the film crew and so forth and I wanted a quiet word.'

Rilla, right on cue like the actress she was, said, 'Has anything happened? Is something wrong?'

'I suppose,' Leonora said slowly, 'that something has happened. And something *is* wrong, but I'm going to try and put it right. Yes, that's it.' She smiled, almost triumphantly. 'I'm going to put it right. I've felt for some time that I owe both you, Rilla, and you, Efe, an apology.'

Rilla looked anxious and Beth knew she would have loved to light a cigarette. Leonora was twisting the rings round on her fingers and her hands were trembling slightly.

She said, 'When I was a little girl, there was something Nanny Mouse used to say to me. I was brought up on it really. *What you don't know can't hurt you.* It was a — what do you call it nowadays? — a mantra. I believed it. I really did. Now I see that what you don't know *can* hurt you almost more than any other single thing.'

Efe, Beth could see, was getting bored. She could almost hear him thinking, cut to the chase. What was it with most men, that they needed the abridged version of any story? He was trying, Beth could see, not to make it obvious that he'd rather be doing anything other than sitting here with three women, listening to a whole lot of what he'd doubtless call ancient history.

Leonora obviously sensed his discomfiture as well. She looked directly at him and said, 'Efe my darling, the reason I wanted to see you is because we've been keeping something hidden, you and I, for many years. It's time to talk about it now, Efe. Don't you think?'

Efe turned white suddenly and clenched his hands into fists.

'I don't believe this,' he spat out. 'Are you seriously telling me you've brought me here for this? After all this time? You're going to make me tell Rilla?'

'Tell Rilla what?' said Rilla. 'What do you want to tell me, Efe?'

'I don't want to tell you anything. Nothing.'

'If you don't,' Leonora said, 'then I will. I want you to know about Mark's death. I want Efe to tell you exactly what happened that day.'

'I know what happened. You told me, Mother. I don't think we should . . .' Rilla's voice was shaking. Beth looked at her, wondering how long it would be before she burst into tears or ran out of the room.

'I think we must, my dear. I've had quite enough secrets and evasions for one lifetime. This is all my fault, I know, but you must see that I'm trying to put it right. Because I was protecting *you*, Efe, I hurt my own daughter, and I'll never forgive myself for that. But I did it because you were so very young, Efe. I thought, he's a child and his whole life might be ruined, but look what I've done. Look at Rilla, Efe. Can't you see how she's suffered? How she still blames herself?'

Beth could feel her heart thumping in her chest. Rilla was sitting quite motionless, very upright, with her mouth tightly closed. Leonora was still speaking. 'And it's not just Rilla, Efe. It's you, too. I think that living with this thing, this weight on your conscience, has altered you. I should have encouraged you to tell the truth right from the start, instead of helping you to bury it.'

All the time that Leonora was speaking, Efe had his head hidden in his hands. When he lifted his face, his whole demeanour had changed. He seemed younger, somehow. More vulnerable. Different.

'I tried to,' Efe said and his voice had lost its confidence. Beth had never heard him sound more tentative. 'I tried to that night. I went to Rilla's room and I wanted to tell her. I really did, but she was . . . well, she was upset and the doctor must have given her something because she was sort of asleep and not asleep and I didn't know what to do so I came to you, Leonora and you said it would be all right. I believed you. You said no one ever needed to know and that it was a hideous accident. Not my fault.'

Efe covered his face again. Rilla coughed, breaking the silence.

'Tell me what happened, Efe. I'm not going to blame you for anything. I promise,' she said, in a small, gentle voice. The kind of voice, Beth thought, you'd use to speak to a child.

'We were playing down there. By the lake.' Efe wouldn't look at any of them. He directed his words straight to the floor, so that Beth had to lean forward to catch what he was saying. 'Alex and Beth and I. We were playing trappers. I didn't want Markie to come, but he did anyway, and I thought it wouldn't matter. He was okay, for a little kid. We didn't mind him tagging along. He wasn't any trouble, really.'

Efe looked up suddenly, and Beth saw that he was crying. He'd hung his head, she thought, because he didn't want anyone to see him in tears. His cheeks were quite wet. He said, 'Rilla, I could have saved him. That's what I came to tell you. I could have. I didn't take any notice when he called out to me over and over again. I thought he was messing. Alex was about to find the secret trap and I had to stop him. It was the most important thing in the world that my trap, which didn't even exist, shouldn't be found.'

He buried his face in his hands, and started crying quietly again. 'It wasn't even a real trap. I was more caught up in a pretend game than in a real little boy shouting something that I wasn't paying attention to somewhere behind me. I didn't even ask myself what he was doing in the water. Alex was in the water and so was I, so I didn't think anything of it. It wasn't very deep, the lake. He must have lost his footing somehow. Alex was down by the willows and Beth was even further away. She was being a trapper's wife, getting the dinner ready.' He laughed without mirth. 'We made Beth do all those girly things. She didn't mind. Did you, Beth? You always did what I told you to, didn't you?'

Beth nodded. She didn't trust herself to speak. That day, the day she'd spent years and years pushing to the back of her mind was here, in front of her, and Efe was reminding her of how she felt.

'I heard the shouting,' she whispered. 'I didn't know who it was, and when I got back to where Efe and Alex were, there was Markie, all wet and lying at the side of the lake. I went to fetch someone. Efe sent me. I couldn't see because I was crying so much. I could see that Markie was dead. I never asked what happened. I didn't want to know, I think.'

'I turned round and saw him,' Efe said. 'I saw his arms waving and I didn't go back to help him and then I couldn't hear him any more and Alex was screaming and it wasn't till I heard Alex that I went to look for him, for Markie. It was too late, though. I didn't go when I should have, that's the truth. I killed him. I thought I'd killed him till you told me I hadn't, Leonora. You said it was an accident and I should never say anything about it to anyone. And I never have. Rilla, I'm sorry. It's a pathetic thing to say, and I don't know if you'll ever speak to me again, but I'm sorry. I shouldn't have listened to you, Leonora. When I was a kid, there was a reason for it, but lately, well, I knew how you blamed yourself, Rilla and I still never dared to say anything. I wish I could go back and do it differently. I don't know what else to say.'

Efe went and half-knelt down next to Rilla. He said, 'Will you ever be able to talk to me again? Rilla, speak to me.'

'Oh, Efe,' Rilla said. 'What's there to say?' She put both arms around him and drew him to her. His head was on her shoulder. 'I still blame myself. I always will, because it was *my* business to look after Markie and not yours or Mother's or Gwen's or anyone's. But I'm glad if you can feel less bad now, Efe, because you've spoken about it. I suppose we all ought to have spoken about it straight away and comforted one another, but we didn't, and I couldn't have at the time and then it just grows, the silence, doesn't it? Once you've started not saying things, it's so easy just to carry on. It was brave of you to speak now, Efe, and of course I forgive you. You were still only a child. I'd never have blamed you.'

Efe sat up and took a handkerchief from his trouser pocket. He said, 'I'd better go and wash my face, hadn't I? I don't want anyone to see me like this. Leonora, will you excuse me?'

'Yes, Efe. I'll see you at dinner.' She turned to Rilla as he left the room. 'Rilla, I owe you an apology, darling. You've said you forgive Efe, but I want to know whether you can forgive me. I should have told you. I see that now. I did think I was acting in everyone's best interests, but now I see that I protected Efe at the expense of your happiness. I think I felt that you could cope with tragedy rather better than he could. I'm so sorry, Rilla. So dreadfully sorry.'

Beth could see that Leonora wanted to touch her daughter, gather her up in her arms and didn't know how to. The struggle was visible in her face, in the way she was wringing her hands in her lap. Oh, God, she thought, please let Rilla do it. Let Rilla reach out to her. Please.

'No need, Mother,' Rilla said, and she put her arms round her mother. Leonora made a sound that was something between a groan and a sigh and Beth covered her eyes with her hands. Thank Heavens, she thought. Everything will be easier now.

'Beth, dear,' Leonora said, sounding almost like herself again. 'See that your mother rests a little before dinner. That's why I asked you to come with her. So that you could look after her. I'm going to my room now.'

She left the conservatory and Beth could hear her slow footsteps as she made her way to the hall.

'Are you all right, Rilla? Would you like a drink or something?'

'I don't know. I don't know what I want. Oh, Beth, it's so hard to forget things, isn't it? I've been so good at pushing bad things away all my life but now here's Leonora bringing it all back. Am I ready for this?'

'Of course you are, Rilla.' Beth knelt down beside her and took her hand. 'You're so brave. I've always thought you were. You always help me when I feel bad. I can't bear it that you're feeling bad now and I can't do anything to help you. Please say something. Please smile. Oh, Rilla, I hate it when you're sad.'

'I'm not sad, my love. Honestly. Just a bit shaken up by all this. That's all. And the heat doesn't help.' Rilla smiled as though she were trying out something new, something she hadn't done for a while. It was rather a wobbly smile at first, but it seemed to Beth that it quickly grew stronger; wider and more normal.

'Have you ever,' Rilla said, 'seen a run of hot weather like this? I feel as though I'm about to melt. I'm going to have a long, cool bath. And that's the first time I've heard Leonora call me your mother. Ever.' She was looking much happier now, Beth was glad to see. 'I'll be okay now. Go and get me a stiff gin and tonic and bring it to the bathroom.'

Beth made her way to the kitchen, feeling relieved, as though a crisis had been averted.

Philip stood on one side of the dolls' house, which he'd moved carefully away from the wall. A bathtowel from the linen cupboard was spread out under the window for the wallpaper to lie on when it came off the roof.

'Right,' he said to Chloë. 'We've got to make it just wet enough to peel it away from the structure, without going through and wrecking the writing on the other side. A bit tricky, but we'll do it, I think. I'll do the watery stuff.'

He smoothed a moist sponge over the paper. It had been Beth's idea to get sponges from Rilla's make-up bag. There were always, she was quick to explain, a couple of spares in case something happened to the ones currently in use. Beth had been only too pleased to let Philip have them in the cause of discovering what else Maude Walsh had written. Chloë had brought a knife from the kitchen and was busy inserting the long, thin blade under the damp paper on her side.

She said, 'Look, it's coming away, I think.'

'Okay, if you're sure. Take care.' Philip looked on anxiously.

'Of course I'll bloody take care. You don't have to tell me.' She pulled a face. 'I know what to do as well as you, you know.'

Chloë pushed the knife a little further under one edge of the paper. 'It's coming off beautifully, look,' she said and lifted one corner. The paper peeled away cleanly in a long strip, parallel to the one that Douggie had taken off.

'Brilliant,' said Philip. 'Now I think you could get a piece from this side. This is, incidentally, a really beautiful piece of work. Ethan Walsh's, is it?'

'He made the house, but his wife painted the paper, I think. My great-granny, that is. Leonora's mum.'

'She was an artist too, then.'

'Don't think so. Not really.' Chloë was working away with her knife again. 'I think she went to art school but didn't do much after she got married.'

'Shame,' said Philip. 'It's beautiful. If we can dry it out properly, I might be able to put it back, you know. Almost as good as new.'

'You're a gem and a treasure,' said Chloë. 'But what if Leonora wants to keep what's on the back?'

'She could make a copy, surely?'

'I don't know.' Chloë sounded as though she wasn't paying attention. She placed the second strip she'd managed to peel off beside the first, which lay with its painted side face down on the towel. She knelt down and peered closely at the writing.

'It's hard to make out, this writing,' she said. 'But I think . . .'

The only sound in the nursery was the faint noise of Philip's sponge, sweeping over the remaining section of wallpaper. Chloë was right down on the floor now, stretched out so that she could look more closely at the handwriting.

'You're very quiet,' Philip said. 'Is anything the matter?'

'Oh, my God! I don't believe this,' she said quietly, and then, 'Philip. Come over here. If this means what I think it does, it's unbelievable. It can't be, but I'm sure I've read it right. Come and see what you think.'

Philip went over and crouched down beside Chloë to read. After a minute or two, he pushed his hand through his hair and grimaced.

'Bloody hell,' he said shaking his head. Then he said it again, 'Bloody hell, Chloë. We'd better tell Leonora.'

'I'll tell her, Philip. She was down at Nanny Mouse's I think, but she must have come back by now. I'll go and find her. But don't say a word to anyone, Philip, promise? No one at all.'

'Okay.' Philip nodded. 'I shan't say anything.'

Chloë sat down on the floor by the dolls' house and read what was written on the back of the roof tiles all over again.

Leonora and Alex sat close together on the bench that ran round the walls of the gazebo, looking through the photograph album open on Alex's lap. During her conversation with Sean in the conservatory, it came to Leonora that there wasn't a single photograph of Maude on display in Willow Court. She had to rack her brains for several minutes before it occurred to her that there was an ancient album in the bottom drawer of her chest of drawers. Alex had been coming in at the front door as she was on her way upstairs to find it, and she'd sent him for it, to spare, as she put it, 'my ancient legs'.

Alex said, 'Are you sure you're okay, Leonora? You look a little tired. Don't you think you ought to lie down before dinner?'

Leonora shook her head. 'No, darling. I'm fine, really. Not a bit tired. Still, you know you're old when your grandson starts wanting you to lie down. No, I simply felt like looking for pictures of my mother, and I thought you'd be interested in seeing them too. It's hard for other people to understand, but I hardly knew her, you know. That's why I asked you to get this album. I want to look at some photographs of her. There must be some, I'm sure, though I can't actually remember any.'

'I'm always happy to look at old pictures,' Alex said. 'Though there are some things in your albums which I wouldn't really like to see again.'

Leonora wondered whether Alex was referring, indirectly, to Mark. It struck her suddenly that poor Efe was exactly the same age when Mark drowned as she'd been when Maude died. She said to Alex, 'I think my mother must have been the most camera-shy person ever. We've been all through this album and what have we found? Not very much, is it?'

'Two quite good shots of her in the Quiet Garden,' Alex replied. 'And that one by the piano.'

Leonora peered at the page Alex was holding up for her. There was her mother in the distance, but if you didn't know what she looked like, this photo wouldn't have told you. The tiny, tiny, figure of a thin woman far away down a garden path. In the foreground, a bank of white flowers. Shrubs against the garden wall taking up the side of the photograph. Quite a lot of sky filled with puffs of cloud. That was the first snapshot. The second showed Maude beside an espaliered fruit tree in full bloom. She'd evidently wanted to show off the blossom, spread like a fan all over the wall, and her face was turned away from the camera. Both photographs were, of course, in black and white and very small indeed.

'The piano one is better. Bigger, too. It was taken by a photographer, I'm sure,' said Alex. 'I wonder who took the garden ones. Ethan Walsh, I suppose.'

Leonora considered what she now knew of her father and shook her head. She could not, however hard she tried, imagine her parents snapping happy family pictures in the garden.

'It was most probably Nanny Mouse,' she told Alex. 'Or Tyler, the gardener. Let me see the one at the piano.'

Alex passed the album over to her and she took it in her hands and brought it up to her face to look at more carefully. She took a deep breath and let it out again.

'Are you all right, Leonora?' he asked.

'You still can't see her face properly, can you? She's pretty, isn't she? In a rather faded, quiet sort of way. She reminds me of a startled creature of some kind. A deer, or a bird, perhaps.'

'Yes, she's very pretty. But as far as one can tell, she doesn't look like you at all, Leonora. Though it's not the clearest image I've ever seen. You take after Ethan, don't you?'

'I suppose I do,' Leonora smiled. 'I look like him, and so does Gwen a little and Efe is very like him. You're not, though. Maybe it's you, Alex, who look the most like my mother. You have the same long, thin nose, look!'

'I can't see it myself,' said Alex, and at that moment, the door of the gazebo burst open and Chloë came in, holding a folded sheet of paper in her hand.

'I'm sorry to interrupt, Leonora, when you're chatting to Alex, but I'd like to speak to you, if that's okay.'

'Of course, darling. Alex and I were only looking at an old album. Come and sit down here by me.'

'D'you mind if I speak to you alone, Leonora? I'm sorry, Alex.'

Alex looked puzzled. 'No problem,' he said. He closed the album and stood up. 'I'll take this back to the house with me, should I?'

'That would be very kind,' said Leonora. 'We won't be long, I'm sure, and then we'll come back as well.'

'Ta, Alex,' said Chloë. She closed the door of the gazebo behind him as he left and went to sit next to her grandmother. 'I'm sorry to send Alex off like that, but you'll see why in a minute. I've typed out the message that we found on the dolls' house roof. This is it. I thought it ought to be just us. You'll understand why in a minute.'

Leonora squeezed Chloë's hand. 'You're a kind child, aren't you? I'm so glad it's you who's deciphered it all.'

'And Philip. He was the main one who got it off the roof without damaging it. He's brilliant.'

'What does it say? I'd better know what it says.' Leonora sighed and put out a hand for the paper.

'Here,' Chloë said, and handed it to her grandmother. Then she positioned herself with one arm stretched out along the back of the seat, poised to go around Leonora's shoulders. She was sure that such comfort was going to be necessary and she wanted to be ready to provide it when it was needed. She found that she was holding her breath as Leonora unfolded the sheet of paper and began to read.

Beth had spent much of the afternoon dealing with Leonora's presents. When Gwen had asked her to be in charge of those that had come by post she'd said yes at once. It would be good to be occupied with something. All the gifts, apart from those from the family, would be displayed under Chloë's tree. Beth had also undertaken to see to it that Leonora came to the hall at the proper time after the party to open the parcels she hadn't seen already, and to make a note of who had sent what, so that thank you letters could be written without too much trouble. These few days, she reflected, were not turning out to be the idyllic time she'd dreamed about in the weeks leading up to Leonora's party. Things hardly ever did live up to expectation and she ought to have learned that by now. Still, the gulf between her imaginings of strolling through the garden with Efe, or sitting on the terrace with him talking and talking, and what she was actually doing, was so huge that it almost made her laugh.

She couldn't have got out of helping in this way. Gwen had suggested it and also said that she intended Alex to help her but couldn't find him at the moment. Beth didn't object. The house was now full of young women with dusters and floor polishers cleaning the house before the party even though it looked perfectly fine to her. Everyone, it seemed, was running around hairless getting things ready, and doing her bit like this at least gave her mind a chance to wander as she wrote her notes.

She hadn't realized that Leonora had so many friends and

acquaintances. Nearly seventy people were coming to the party tomorrow and on top of that there were all these things from those who for one reason or another couldn't make it. Their cards said things like 'To dear Leonora wishing you many more happy years', or 'With great affection', and some of the gifts were worth displaying. There was an antique bon-bon dish, luxurious soaps and talcum powders, hand-made chocolates, and extremely expensive pot-pourri. Someone had sent fur-lined slippers, too, and Leonora would pretend not to love those, protesting that they were the height of old-ladyishness, but Beth knew she'd wear them every night. Another person had sent a special tray mounted on a cushion that settled round your knees as you watched television, but whoever it was clearly didn't know Leonora at all well. She'd never eaten a meal in front of the television in her whole life and wouldn't dream of falling into such lax ways merely because she was seventy-five. Beth smiled and stood up to take the first batch of gifts into the hall.

The tree that Chloë had created there was like something out of a fairy tale. Beth found Douggie and Fiona looking at it, entranced. As she approached them, the front door opened and Gwen came in from the garden. She was carrying a bucket full of flowers for the vases waiting in the scullery.

'You're going to catch flies in your mouth, Douggie darling,' she said, 'if you keep it open like that.'

The little boy took no notice at all, and Fiona laughed. 'You can't really blame him,' she said. 'It's the most beautiful tree I've ever seen.'

'It *is* lovely, isn't it?' Gwen said. 'I'm so pleased Chloë thought of it. It'll be quite a talking point, I'm sure.'

Beth suddenly realized that the trunk of the birthday-present tree was the old hatstand that had been thrown out into the shed by Leonora years ago on the grounds that hardly anyone wore hats these days and even if they did, most people weren't tall enough to reach the hooks on a piece of furniture which seemed to have been designed for giants. Efe used to like to use it in all sorts of pretend games when they were younger – as a barrier, or a cannon of some kind, or even, she now remembered, as a tree. He'd tied her up to it once when it was raining and they couldn't go out into the garden.

She looked carefully to see how Chloë had achieved her effects. There were handmade bows of tinfoil tied among the willow leaves, and these alternated with thin ribbons of gold tape, hanging down like small tassels. It really is, Beth thought, like something out of a dream. The metallic decorations caught every bit of light, sparkling and glittering and making tiny tinkling sounds as they moved in the air. Leonora would be overwhelmed, Beth was sure of it, and the guests would love it. Sean would almost certainly want a shot of it in the film.

'I'm going to do the flowers for the house now,' Gwen said, and then caught sight of the tray that Beth was putting down on the floor. 'I see you're all busy with the arrangement of the presents.'

'What're we going to do about our presents, Gwen? Are they going under the tree as well.'

'No, I don't think so. Mother's going to open them tonight of course, quite separately from all the others. It looks as though you've got quite enough to go under the tree without worrying about the family presents as well.'

'Okay,' Beth said. She started to take the gifts one by one off the tray and caught sight of Douggie out of the corner of her eye, staring longingly at her. 'Would you like to help me, Douggie? Give me a hand with putting the presents under the tree?'

Douggie nodded solemnly and Fiona said, 'That'll be fun, won't it, Douggie? Only you'll have to be extra careful, won't you? Here, I'll help you give them to Beth and she'll put them all in their proper places.'

'It's going to look amazing,' Gwen said. 'I'd better get on with my flower arrangement.'

Beth wondered where Efe was, and how Leonora's revelations had affected him. Where was he now? Maybe Fiona would know. She said, 'Where is everyone? Have you any idea?'

'Carefully, Douglet,' said Fiona in the rather silly voice she often adopted to talk to her child. 'Give them to Beth and let her put them down. It would be so awful if anything got broken. That's right.' She turned to Beth. 'I've no idea where they've all got to. Alex went into the garden. Chloë and Philip were up in the nursery but I don't know where they are now and Rilla's in her room, I think.'

No mention of Efe. Beth said nothing and turned her attention to placing Leonora's birthday presents in the sort of arrangement that you sometimes saw in shop windows at Christmas, where parcels were artistically disposed under the decorated branches. She said, 'There are going to be so many presents, aren't there? No one's going to arrive empty-handed, are they?'

'Hello, ladies!' said a voice, and Efe crossed the hall, picked Douggie up and kissed him. 'What are you doing and can anyone join in?'

'Of course, darling,' said Fiona. 'We'd love you to join in, wouldn't we, Beth?'

Beth nodded. Efe, quite amazingly, considering the state he'd been in while they were in the conservatory, looked altogether nonchalant, and she marvelled at his ability to hide his true feelings. Surely he hadn't been completely unaffected? He was wearing a khaki T-shirt and khaki trousers with rather more pockets than were strictly necessary.

'I've been helping Dad in the marquee. It looks great. Really excellent. Have you seen it, Beth?'

'No, not yet. Douggie, bring that bottle you're holding back here right this minute, please. I need it to go on this little pile.'

Douggie trotted obediently over to her and Beth took it from him and put it down before any harm could come to it.

'I see you're being about as useful as a chocolate teapot, beloved,' Efe said, looking directly at his wife, Beth noted with a shock, for the very first time since he had come in. He was smiling as he spoke and Beth felt suddenly furious with him. However troubled he was, there was no excuse for him to be so unkind. He was clever, too. If Fiona objected, he'd say at once that he was joking. That light tone allowed him to insult her and there was absolutely nothing she could do about it. Beth was wondering whether she should say something herself and if so, what it should be exactly, when Efe spoke again. This time, he addressed his remarks to Beth.

'My wife is very silly, Beth. I'm married to a moron. That sounds like a movie title, doesn't it?'

Fiona had tears in her eyes. Beth looked at Efe and opened her mouth, about to say something, when she saw that Alex had come in and was standing silently beside the door. He said, 'Apologize, Efe. That's an insult to your wife and if you weren't my brother I'd hit you. I might hit you anyway. Take it back. Now.'

Efe smiled. 'Oh, right. You've become some kind of knight errant, have you, Alex? A bit late in the day, isn't it, to morph from Wimp Number One into Bruce Willis? Having kept your mouth shut your whole life, don't you think this is none of your business?'

'It *is* my business. You think you can get away with everything. That's your problem.'

'Oh, fuck off, Alex. You're boring, d'you know that?'

Fiona said, 'Douggie, come on now. We'll go and find the kitty.' She picked her son up in her arms and left the room, almost running, frantic in her haste to get away from there. Beth followed her, wanting to see what Alex would do next, but knowing that someone had to look after Fiona. By the time she'd left the hall, though, there was no sign of her, and Beth sighed. She positioned herself in a part of the corridor which she knew wasn't visible from where Efe and Alex were standing, even though she could see them both perfectly well.

'You are a fucking arrogant bastard,' Alex shouted, and before Beth knew what was happening he had gone right up to his brother and punched him in the face. He caught Efe by surprise, so that he stumbled back for a moment against the banisters, but he recovered quickly and hit out at Alex, almost reflexively and his fist connected with the corner of Alex's mouth. Efe was pale with fury. 'Shit, man, what's got into you?' he shouted. 'Lay off, will you?'

'Apologize, then. Go on. Go and find Fiona and say you're sorry.'

Efe scowled. 'What I say to my wife is none of your damn business.'

'I don't care. Say you're going to apologize or I'll hit you again. Harder this time.'

'Ooh, I'm scared,' Efe said, in the voice he had always used when they were children specifically to tease Alex. 'Okay, okay, I'll apologize, Okay? I will. When I see her.'

He stalked away towards the staircase and took the steps two at a time. When Beth saw that he was safely upstairs, she came out of her hiding place and went over to Alex, who was leaning against the doorframe, touching his bottom lip, which was already swollen.

'You didn't see that, did you? Could've been worse,' he said to Beth. 'One of us could have landed on all those dainty presents and crushed every piece of glass and china. Look on the bright side.'

'Let me see how badly you're hurt, Alex.'

'I'm not hurt at all.'

'Yes, you are. You're going to have a huge lip and a bruise.'

'It was worth it, though.' Alex grinned suddenly. 'I haven't had a fight with Efe for years. Can't remember the last time, actually. I always avoided it as a kid. Scared of getting flattened, I guess.'

'That wasn't the only reason,' Beth said. 'You mostly agreed with every word Efe said.'

'I suppose so. So did you, though. Go on, admit it.'

'I admit it. Come into the kitchen and I'll fix you up.'

'Do I need fixing?' Alex said, but he followed her willingly enough and sat down at the kitchen table.

'You do a little. You've got a bit of a cut. It's not bleeding much, but still, I'd better mop it up. I've never done this before but I do know you have to have tea with sugar in it for the shock.'

'I hate sugary tea. Give me a Coke instead. That's full of sugar. In the fridge.'

'Times have changed,' Beth said. 'Leonora wouldn't have given house room to a fizzy drink in the old days.'

'My dad's been working on her, I believe. She's quite fond of rum and Coke on a hot day, it seems.'

'Wonders never cease.' Beth put the glass down on the table and went to find a clean tea-towel. She turned on the cold tap and wet a corner of the towel, then wrung it out as hard as she could.

'Okay, don't move,' she said, leaning over Alex, who turned his face to her. His eyes were shut and he looked suddenly, ridiculously, vulnerable. Because he was a little younger than she was, she always thought of him as needing care, but now for the first time ever she saw him as her equal. A man. She noticed the blue veins in his eyelids. She could smell his hair, and his skin. The sore lip was swollen and cut and one side of Alex's lower face was already showing bruising. There was something turning over in her stomach, a kind of fluttering, like the feeling you might have before going on stage. A sort of thrilled nervousness she hadn't felt in Alex's company before. What was wrong with her? Everything she was used to feeling, all her preconceptions, were being subjected to something like an earthquake. She was meant to be in love with Efe, wasn't she? So why was being so close to Alex having this effect on her. She felt hot and cold at once and closed her eyes because she thought that if she didn't she might faint. Above all, she knew that what she was feeling now was *true*. It had nothing to do with fantasy or imagination or dreams. Beth was almost overcome by a fierce desire to kiss Alex, to comfort him by wrapping her arms around his shoulders, but hesitated in case she was wrong about how he felt.

'Beth?' he whispered.

'Mmm,' she said. She couldn't speak his name in case her voice wobbled or gave away her feelings somehow. Everything she had previously felt, everything she'd believed for so long, all her emotions and desires, were like the translucent, brilliantly-coloured pieces in a kaleidoscope, and having Alex so close to her was shaking and rearranging them into strange shapes she didn't recognize. She lost all sense of who she was, where she was. There was nothing in her whole world but this mouth, which was on hers before she could find a word to say that might stop it, and her own lips were opening and she closed her eyes against the light and the heat that was running through her veins.

'Alex,' she murmured. 'Oh, Alex . . .'

'Don't say anything,' Alex whispered. 'Kiss me again.'

He stood up then, and put his arms around her. Beth could feel everything changing. Nothing would be the same again. This . . . this person who was kissing her was not the one she'd always known.

'Alex,' she said. 'What's happened? What's happened to us?'

'It's me,' Alex said. 'Something's happened to me. I've been stupid and slow and haven't admitted it to myself.'

'What? What haven't you admitted?'

'That I love you. I think I always have, only there was Efe and I could see how you felt about him, and I didn't want . . . I couldn't . . . oh, Beth, you know what I'm saying. I didn't think you'd ever, you know, be able to feel the way I want you to feel.'

'I didn't think I could either,' Beth smiled. 'But that was because Efe was dazzling me. I wasn't seeing or feeling anything properly.'

Alex stroked her hair, pushing it back from her forehead. 'And you were right, I *was* jealous. You noticed it, remember? On the way to see Nanny Mouse. When I thought of the two of you together, you and Efe, I became quite unlike myself; murderous, suicidal, pathetic. Just jealous, I suppose.'

'You don't have to be any longer, Alex. I promise.' She stood on tiptoe to kiss him and then drew back, leaning away from him a little, breathless from the force of what she had begun to feel.

'Alex, we can't,' she said. 'Not here. Anyone could come in.'

He sat down shakily on the kitchen chair again and grinned at her, and at that moment the kitchen door opened and there was Rilla.

'What's going on, darlings?' she said, coming in and sitting down immediately next to Alex. 'I saw Efe just now looking like a thundercloud. Have you two been fighting? Whatever about? Tell all, go on. Alex, sweetiepie, what *has* happened to your lip?'

'It wasn't anything, Rilla, honestly,' Alex said weakly.

'Nonsense, of course it was.' She turned to Beth and gave her a smile. 'Could I ask you to get me a Coke, Beth? Thanks, darling. Alex's looks delicious. And I wouldn't say no to a biscuit, either, if you'd pass that tin from the dresser. I can't possibly last until dinner.'

Beth went to get Rilla's drink and put the biscuit tin in front of her.

'I'll leave you two to it,' she said. 'I'm going out for a bit of fresh air.'

She knew as she stepped out into the Peter Rabbit garden that Alex would have given anything to come with her, to be rescued from Rilla's interrogation, but she wanted to be on her own.

She needed to think. She needed to think about Efe, because every single thing she'd thought about him before this weekend had changed. And now, because of Alex and what had just happened, even the strongest of her sensations, the physical attraction that often made her breathless and incoherent, had changed. It was as though by kissing her like that, Alex had woken her up, made her aware of him for the first time.

For about thirty seconds, Beth wondered whether this was what was known as the rebound. Whether she was making do with second-best because she had accepted that she couldn't have Efe, and even as she thought it she knew it wasn't true. This new emotion, this revelation, had nothing whatsoever to do with Efe and what she had once felt for him.

Oh, God, what a lot of time I've wasted, Beth thought. I could have saved myself so much anguish. So much unhappiness. I could have been spared loving Efe altogether if I'd had any sense. I never noticed Alex before because I wasn't looking properly. She sat down on the bench near the shed, which was out of sight of the house, and let the late afternoon sun fall on her face.

# December 1998

Beth sat quietly in front of the enormous three-sided mirror in the spare bedroom of the McVie house, having her hair arranged by Jules, Fiona's hairdresser. The other bridesmaid, Fiona's cousin Rowan, waited for her turn wearing a satin dressing-gown that looked as though it had cost more than a month's salary. December was a ridiculous time for a wedding. Efe was marrying Fiona McVie this afternoon, less than a week before Christmas. The happy couple were leaving tonight on a skiing honeymoon, and Beth could hardly bring herself to think about it. Any of it. Jules said, 'You're going to look perfect, Beth, just trust me, but you have to do your bit, too, you know. Smile, darling, smile! You've got a face on you more suited to a funeral.'

Beth moved her lips dutifully, and hoped that Jules would be taken in by her efforts. She had never felt less like smiling. The make-up they'd slapped all over her face was thicker than she was used to. The lipstick she'd been allocated was too pink. She'd asked Fiona why they had to have a make-up artist (Fiona's name for a young girl called Mirabelle) to do their faces. Surely they were all old enough to do it themselves? Fiona had explained patiently that it was 'for the photographs'. Make-up had to be more dramatic than usual if you didn't want to look like death warmed up for ever and ever in the wedding album.

'But Alex is doing the photos,' Beth tried again. 'He never makes people look awful. You know that. He's brilliant.'

'Oh, I know,' Fiona had answered. 'He's marvellous, of course, but it's never a bad idea to give Nature a bit of a helping hand, is it?'

Very latest light-reflecting miracle or not, oily-feeling make-up in the wrong colour seemed to Beth like defacing Nature, but she said nothing. It was, after all, Fiona's wedding day and everyone was having to do things her way.

Like getting married in December, when it was going to be too cold, really, for the kind of silly dresses the bride had decreed. While Jules scraped her hair back from her brow and fastened it into an immensely complicated arrangement at the nape of her neck, she thought of the dress she would soon be wearing: pale pink silk, edged with two layers of frilled lace around the scoop neck, which didn't really suit her. The colour wasn't flattering to her skin, either, but never mind. Everyone would have eyes only for the bride, and Fiona had been working hard at this day for the last six months.

She'd decided to have the wedding in London instead of at Willow Court. Fair enough, Beth conceded, considering that her parents had been limbering up for this day practically since Fiona was born. And it *was* more convenient for the airport. Also, most of the couple's friends were London-based. It all made perfect sense, and even Leonora, who would have loved to have had the whole shooting-match under her roof, had entered into the spirit of the thing. Fiona had enlisted the services of the best designers, the most fashionable caterers, and people like Jules and Mirabelle in order to leave nothing to chance. This was going to be the wedding of the winter season or she would know the reason why.

Jules stabbed two ornaments into the tight knot of Beth's hair.

'Absolutely darling, honestly! These snow-crystals. Just divine! Such a wonderful sparkly contrast against your dark hair. You look gorgeous. Truly gorgeous.' He made the 'o' of gorgeous last for at least three seconds. Beth said, 'That's lovely, thanks so much,' and got to her feet. It was Rowan's turn now and for her there was nothing to do but wait for the moment when the ghastly dress would be put on for her by someone else; wait for the whole pantomime to begin. The white limousines would be here in half an hour. She sat down on the chaise-longue and leaned gingerly against the blue velvet, making sure that her head was well clear of the back. It would never do to spoil Jules's handiwork. She frowned. Efe was getting married. Their whole relationship would change. It was bound to. His first loyalty would be to Fiona now. It wasn't always so. There was a time when he was closer to her than to anyone.

Everyone was busy somewhere else, and Beth was happy because she was doing what she liked doing better than almost everything else: looking after Chloë. The Easter holiday had just begun, Efe was back from his school, and Rilla had sent Beth to spend a week with her cousins. She herself hardly ever came to Willow Court since Mark died, but she knew how much Beth enjoyed it. At first, after Markie's death, Beth hadn't wanted to go back to Willow Court either, but as time went on, she began to pine for her cousins. Rilla noticed this at once, and persuaded her to visit whenever she could. She had said, 'I don't see why you shouldn't go down there just because I find it difficult. I know you love going, and they all look forward to seeing you so much.'

Chloë was five, and known in the family as a bit of a handful. She had firm opinions and a wide vocabulary.

'Where does she hear such things?' Gwen used to wail when her little girl, looking just like a cherub, came out with something awful she'd picked up from the television or the adults she observed so closely.

'From us, Mum,' Efe told her. 'From all of us.'

Chloë adored Beth, and clung to the older girl every time she came to Willow Court. She would take Beth's hand and pull her this way and that, to the Peter Rabbit garden to look at the carrots coming up; to the Climbing Tree, which was an enormous ash that leaned against the back wall of the Quiet Garden, and to her bedroom, which was a mess of toys, books, crayons and clothes, in spite of the combined efforts of Nanny Mouse, Gwen and whichever nursery maid was currently 'helping out' with childcare. She made her join in elaborate games with Sissy, the fluffy white cat, who was quite obliging and sometimes allowed herself to be pushed along in a miniature pram meant for dolls. She'd once let Chloë tie a bonnet on her head until Nanny Mouse put a stop to such behaviour and forbade the little girl to dress up her animals ever again. Tom, Sissy's black and white brother, was never in danger from such attentions. His particular talent was for running away and disappearing before anyone could catch him.

On this day, though, Beth had decided that Chloë was allowed a treat. She'd asked special permission from Leonora to play with the dolls' house in the nursery.

'I'll look after everything, I promise,' she said. 'Chloë won't touch anything without asking me, and we'll be very gentle with the dolls. Won't we, Chloë?'

Chloë nodded gravely. Leonora thought for a moment, and said, 'Very well, Beth dear, but you're responsible. Take great care, please. I know I can trust you.'

'Oh, yes, you can! We'll be ever so good. Come on, Chloë!'

The girls hurried up to the nursery. The rain was coming down hard now, beating against the windows and streaming down the panes diagonally, making what light there was watery and dim. Beth knelt down beside the dolls' house. She breathed a sigh of pure pleasure. This was, it had to be, the most beautiful toy in the whole world, and even though she was twelve years old and the playing was supposed to be to amuse little Chloë, she felt herself slip back and back till she was her own younger self again, believing in the dolls; creating lives for them and joining in those lives, sharing their dreams and emotions.

'Can I play?' Efe had opened the door so quietly that the girls heard nothing.

'With us?' Efe pretended to be too old and too much of a boy to be interested in dolls' house games, but he used to join in when they were much younger, speaking for Mr Delacourt and Lucas while Beth did the voices for Queen Margarita and Lucinda.

'Yeah, why not?' He came and sat cross-legged on the floor beside Beth. She could smell him. He had a particular fragrance of grass and soap and his own skin, and she remembered it from the days when they shared bathtimes. She blushed now to think of that. He was in a bad mood. You could always tell with Efe. His face grew stiff and frowny and he wouldn't talk properly. He mumbled something if you asked him a question, but his eyes were sad and he always looked as though he were about to hit out at something. Sure enough, he began kicking the skirting-board that just happened to be near his foot. Beth said, 'What's wrong, Efe?' She didn't really expect a reply, but her words had the effect she was looking for. He stopped kicking the wall.

'Nothing. Well, nothing different anyway. I'm fed up, that's all. A whole fortnight here with them bickering all the time. I hate it. Mum nags Dad and he goes all silent and then he goes out and doesn't come back for ages and then Mum starts nagging all over again. You're lucky your parents have split up, I can tell you. It's murder.'

Beth, who would have given a great deal to live at Willow Court with her mother and father still together said only, 'Come and play mothers and fathers with us, then. Chloë, look, Efe's going to play.'

'Efe!' Chloë flung herself on top of her brother and started to tickle him. 'Efe can be daddy. I'll be baby. I'll cry, listen . . .'

'No, Chloë, don't be a crying baby. Be a sleepy baby, please!' Beth began, but it was far too late. Chloë was enjoying her new role and was lying in Efe's arms, wailing and howling in a convincing imitation of what she did quite a lot of the time naturally.

'Stop it!' Efe said to her, and she stopped at once. It always astonished Beth, this gift he had for getting people to do what he wanted. 'We're playing good babies, Chloë, and if you utter a squeak I'll chuck you out of the window into the garden.'

Chloë treated this threat as the joke it was meant to be and started laughing. She wandered away to the window, to look down and see how far she'd fall if Efe did what he said.

'I'm never going to be a dad,' Efe said to Beth. 'It's too much trouble. My dad's never here. Your dad's gone off with someone with a ridiculous name. They're all crap. I'm not going to be crap.'

'But if you fall in love with someone, you'll want to marry them,' Beth said.

'No, I shan't. Girls are silly. Not you, Beth, but most girls are. Just silly. They can't play properly. They giggle.'

Beth was glowing from Efe's compliment. He didn't often say nice things, but when he did, she stored them away in her mind to take out and think about later when she was alone.

'I expect,' she said, 'that you'll change your mind when you grow up.'

'Shan't. I'm not marrying anyone but you.'

His expression was not one she'd ever seen before. He looked different. Sad. Sad and older. He was staring at her almost like a grown-up. She shivered. He put his hand on her arm.

'You wouldn't mind marrying me, would you, Beth?'

She felt a funny sort of melting feeling in her stomach, and wondered for a moment whether she was going to be sick. When she tried to speak no words came out of her mouth.

Efe continued, 'You're the only girl I've ever liked, so I think I ought to marry you. You're my cousin, but you're not properly related to me, are you? Not by blood.'

Beth shook her head. Efe stood up suddenly.

'I know,' he said. 'Let's become blood brothers . . . well, blood brother and sister. Or blood cousins.'

'If we do that, become blood cousins, then you won't be able to marry me.'

'Yes, I will.' Efe always sounded so definite about everything. 'We won't really be blood cousins. It's just like a promise, that's all. That we'll be loyal for ever. I have to come and rescue you if you get captured. That sort of thing.'

'Can I rescue you, too?'

'I won't need rescuing, don't worry,' said Efe. He looked around for something they could use to prick their fingers. Beth said, 'Queen Margarita's got a hatpin, look!'

'I'd never have seen that. It's absolutely tiny. How did you know?'

'Your mum gave it to me last time I was here, when I told her I wanted Lady M to have a hat. Leonora made the hat specially.'

Neither Efe nor Beth referred to Rilla. It was simply understood that she didn't come to Willow Court any longer, had only come once or twice since Mark died, and then just for a day or two. She still, even after four years, could hardly mention her son without tears filling her eyes, so Beth tried not to talk about him. She remembered him every day and missed him, and wondered now whether she might speak to Efe about what happened that day, which had become mixed up in her head with the nightmares she kept having, but it was too late. He'd already taken the hatpin out of the doll's hat and was holding it up so that the tiny piece of glass that was glued to the top and pretending to be a diamond, caught the light and flashed white.

'Here, give me your thumb.'

'Will it hurt?' Beth shrank back a little.

'Course not. Not a bit. We're always doing stuff like this at school. Really. Don't be scared.'

Beth closed her eyes and put her arm out. She could feel Efe taking hold of her hand and then a prick, less painful than an injection.

'Okay, open your eyes. It's all over. Look.'

Chloë chose that moment to come and see what her brother was doing.

'I want!' she said. 'I want to play, too.'

'No you don't, Chloë. This is a game for big children,' Efe told her.

'DO!' Her lower lip was beginning to wobble. Efe pushed the pin into his own thumb.

'See, Chloë? Blood. It's not a nice game. It'd hurt.'

'Does it hurt, Beth?' the little girl asked. Beth nodded, because Efe wanted her to say that, but it wasn't sore, really. Or if it was, she didn't notice the pain. Efe was holding his bleeding thumb over hers. Their blood was mingling. She thought that maybe she could actually *feel* Efe's blood, entering her body. He held her hand and gazed into her eyes with an expression she couldn't fathom. His face was serious, grave. He was very close to her. She could feel his breath on her hair.

'Friends for ever, Beth?'

'Friends for ever and ever.'

They'd got to the 'just cause and impediment' bit, and for a wild moment Beth wondered what would happen if she jumped up and objected to this whole wedding. Almost her favourite book in the world was *Jane Eyre* and she loved the part where Jane's wedding to Mr Rochester was interrupted. What would Leonora, Gwen, Rilla, Mr and Mrs McVie, all of them, say if she ran to the altar and flung herself at Efe, shouting that no, no, he mustn't marry Fiona. He was hers. They had exchanged blood, hadn't they? Didn't that mean anything? She sighed and turned her attention to the bride. Fiona looked beautiful. Beth would have liked to think differently, but was too honest to deny that all the work that had been put into the organization of this wedding had paid off. The dress, plain cream satin, flowed like liquid over Fiona's remarkable body; the jewelled snow-crystals currently poking viciously into Beth's scalp every time she moved her head were just an echo of the cascade of similar glittering shapes stitched all over Fiona's train. Her bouquet gathered together white and pale pink roses and there were roses all over the church. This was quite an achievement at Christmas time. They must have been flown in from somewhere abroad. What a waste of money! Still, money wasn't a problem Efe and Fiona had to worry about. His job as a something vaguely financial in an advertising agency was well paid, and he was also, of course, one of the eventual heirs to the Ethan Walsh estate. And the McVies were wealthy, too.

The family was out in force. They'd all come, dressed to the nines. Leonora would have made sure that everyone on Efe's side of the church was present and correct. She herself looked amazing. She was over seventy, and still stood straight and slim in a peacock blue suit and matching hat that suited her perfectly. Gwen wore pale yellow, some kind of dress with a jacket over the top, with a dark brown and yellow hat. Rilla had decided to pull out all the stops and her coat of burgundy brocade swept the floor as she walked, and caught the light and shimmered. Her hat was a sort of silver turban, which made her look a little like one of the three kings in a Nativity play, but Beth hadn't had the heart to tell her so. Chloë was in blue, and for once looked quite normal. Fiona wasn't going to risk having her as a bridesmaid and Beth could understand that. Her youngest cousin had a disconcerting habit of turning up with purple hair or wearing something outrageous, like a dog-collar studded with metal spikes as a bracelet.

The men, who didn't have the same opportunities for dressing-up, all looked good, Beth thought, except for poor old Alex. He hated ties of any sort and hadn't been seen in a suit since his schooldays. He seemed most uncomfortable, and Beth smiled at him. He grinned back at her, transformed. Funny how different he was, Beth thought, when he let himself go a little. Really quite nice-looking, when you took the time to notice him. For a fleeting second, Beth wondered whether he was ever jealous of his extraordinarily handsome brother. Did men think about such things? I'll ask him one day, she thought. Even though Alex wasn't much of a talker, when you did ask him anything, he always turned his full attention to the question and never dismissed your query as mere silliness.

'You may kiss the bride,' the vicar said, and Beth saw Efe lean over and raise the veil that covered Fiona's face. He kissed her full on the mouth, of course: no half-measures for Efe, even in church, and Beth closed her eyes. She had wanted very much *not* to see this kiss, but Efe was too quick and there it was, burning on the inside of her eyelids like a nightmare. Efe's mouth on Fiona's. For ever. Efe and Fiona in bed. *Don't think of that. Think of anything else, but not that.* She found herself going over the occasion when she first realized how serious Efe was about Fiona.

Efe had decided to give a dinner party.

'I want everything to be perfect,' he said. 'You didn't mind me asking you, did you, Beth?'

'Not at all,' Beth said, considering the available vases and wondering how the flowers Efe wanted arranged all round his flat could possibly be fitted into them. She'd met Fiona McVie a couple of times and didn't think that much of her. She was nice enough, and very pretty too, but somehow it was hard to imagine Efe madly in love with someone who was so . . . she couldn't think of the proper word to describe Fiona. She wasn't stupid, not at all, but she was, or seemed to be, completely unsophisticated, and so besotted with Efe that you felt her mouth was going to drop open with sheer adoration and awe at any moment – in fact, she naturally had a sort of open-mouthed air about her, even when she wasn't gazing at Efe.

Beth stabbed another tulip into a small forest of the greenery that you never saw in nature but only in a florist's shop, and wondered what Efe saw in Fiona. She was rich. She adored him. She would be biddable. All of this was true, but did his heart sing when he looked at her? Maybe it did. Efe was never one to show his feelings too much and he'd been going out with Fiona for a few months, which was something of a record for him. I'm being unfair, she thought. It's just that he's my cousin, practically my brother, and he deserves someone exceptional. Marvellous. Unusual.

'They're here, Beth. Are you ready?'

'Yes, Efe. Everything's looking great. Go and open the door.'

She stood in the living room and welcomed everyone into Efe's flat. Look at me, she thought. The perfect hostess. Fiona and the others, whose names Beth caught briefly only to forget them at once, sat down and Efe handed round the drinks. They went to the table at last, and the food came and went and everyone said it was delicious, but it could have been made of cardboard for all the pleasure Beth took from it. She sat across the table from Fiona, next to Efe, and the conversation drifted past her like smoke – Fiona's high, rather drawling voice; Efe sounding uncharacteristically gentle; all the others, making a kind of tapestry of noise all around her.

Something had happened to her. It felt like an earthquake of some kind; a profound shift in her feelings, in *her*, her body, her blood, every bit of her. She'd intercepted a look that passed between Efe and Fiona and something like a wave of pain washed over her. In that moment, during the seconds that it took for Efe to purse his lips in a silent kiss across the table in Fiona's direction, Beth knew that she wanted him. Cousins, blood brothers, that was all nonsense. She wanted him all to herself in every possible way there was to want a man. She wanted to lie down next to him at night and wake up beside him in the morning. She wanted him to kiss her. To touch her. The thought of him and Fiona together was so ghastly that she felt suddenly sick and began to push her chair away from the table, longing desperately to lock herself in the lavatory and weep.

'You okay, Beth?' Efe was looking at her now. She wasn't, but how could she say so?

'Fine, just a bit hot, that's all. Thought I'd just go . . .'

'No, wait a minute, please. I have an announcement to make, everyone. Fill your glasses. Go on. I'm going to propose a toast.'

Beth smiled and held her glass out for the champagne. Where did that come from? How typical of Efe! He wanted a toast this very minute, so any trips to the loo would have to be delayed. Never mind, she was feeling a little stronger now and wondered what it was he had to celebrate. Perhaps he'd been promoted at work. He stood up and beamed his smile all round the table.

'Right, everyone, here it is. Tonight's toast is to Fiona, who's just agreed to be my wife. We'll be married at Christmas. I'm the happiest man in the whole world. To Fiona!'

His words echoed in the room. Everyone crowded round the bride-to-be and Efe went to her side of the table to embrace her. Beth had just time to think that she'd never, ever be happy again when she fainted for the first time in her life and the darkness closed over her head.

Everyone was now in reception mode, laughing, drinking, letting their hair down. Weddings were all the same. Beth felt like an actor who'd gone through a gruelling performance and hadn't been praised nearly enough. She leaned against the wall and closed her eyes. The other guests were milling, dancing, standing around in small groups. She didn't feel like attaching herself to any of them.

'Have another drink, Beth,' said Alex, coming over to her. He was carrying two glasses. 'You look as though you could do with something.'

'I know. I look like hell, don't I? I can't help it. This bloody wedding has gone on long enough, don't you think?'

She could hear herself sounding pinched and crabby and more than a little drunk. She'd hoped to achieve some kind of dulling of the pain, but it hadn't worked. All the booze had done was make her feel weepy. Now Alex was going to be nice to her and that would really be the end. She'd definitely burst into tears unless she could manage to change the subject.

'Have you finished taking the photos?' she asked.

'No, not yet. I've done the album stuff. You know, bride, groom, relations, that kind of thing. Now I'm going to get some shots of the guests and so on. I'll just wander around for a while, see what I can find.'

'Don't take one of me. I look like a corpse.'

Alex shook his head.

'You don't, Beth, really. You always look great to me.'

She stood on tiptoe and kissed him on the nose.

'You're very nice to me, Alex. But you don't have to stay here, you know. You can go off and see if you can find someone who's more fun. Go and photograph my mum. She's always ready to pose for the camera.'

Rilla, Beth was pleased to see, was enjoying herself. She was flirting with the bride's father. The bride's mother was nowhere to be seen. No, there she was, chatting to Leonora in a darkened corner of the room. The McVies' house had been judged too small for the wedding party and they were in the ballroom of the kind of hotel that charged three figure sums for bed and breakfast. Small tables and gilded chairs were clustered at one end of the space, and a band played dance music at the other. Wedding guests sat about, danced around, walked from group to group and Beth, watching it all from her place by the window, half-hidden by a velvet curtain, hated the whole thing and just wished for it to be over.

The bride had gone upstairs to change into her travelling clothes. Efe and Fiona were flying off any minute now and spending their first night together in a snow-sprinkled chalet on some mountainside. Beth turned to look out at the London twilight. Someone touched her on the shoulder and she whirled round. It was Efe. She blushed and looked up at him. He leaned his arm on the wall above her head and she was conscious of the flash of Alex's camera going off somewhere near them.

'Lovely wedding, Efe. And if I haven't said so before, I do hope you'll both be very happy.'

'We will, but what about you?'

'What do you mean, what about me?' Beth tried to sound brave, but a lump was growing in her throat.

'Are you okay? Are you happy, Beth?'

She laughed. 'That's not the sort of question you ask, Efe. What's got into you?'

'I don't know. I just thought . . . well, I thought you looked a bit sad, that's all.'

'No, I'm fine, really. I'll be fine. I'll miss you.'

'I'll be back. In a couple of weeks. And then you must come round to dinner. Fiona's done amazing things to the dining-room in the flat. You'll love it, really.'

'I don't mean that, Efe. I don't mean I'll miss you now, while you're away. I'll miss our relationship. Blood brothers, remember?'

'Of course I do! That's not going to change, Beth. You know how much you mean to me, don't you? You must do. I don't say stuff like this very often and I'm not very good at it, but I couldn't love you better if you were my own sister. Don't you know that?'

Beth nodded without saying anything. What would he say if she told him the truth? His whole, neat, carefully arranged and newly decorated life would suddenly alter beyond recognition. She made a vow never to say one word about how she felt. She'd protect him; his life, his happiness.

'You still going out with, what was his name, Robert? Richard?' Efe asked.

'Robin.'

'Right. Silly sort of name for a bloke, I thought.'

'Robin's very nice. But I'm not seeing him, no. I'm not seeing anyone at the moment.'

'Then what're you doing hiding behind a curtain, when you could be out there finding a mate?'

'I'm not in a mate-finding mood at the moment, Efe, really.'

'Why? Is it that Robin? Has he messed you about? He'll have me to deal with if he has.'

'Don't be so pompous, Efe, honestly! You sound like my dad. I can look after myself. And no, he was nice. I dumped him.'

'Got to go, Bethie,' Efe said. 'Fiona's going to come down in a bit and I haven't said cheerio to Leonora or Mum and Dad. Give us a kiss goodbye.'

Beth closed her eyes and stood quite still as Efe leaned down to kiss her. For a long, blissful moment his body was so close to hers that she could feel its warmth through his clothes. His breath was on her face, and his lips on hers were for a second half-open; the kiss was so very nearly a proper kiss. If she were to open her mouth under the pressure, find his tongue with hers, twine her arms around his neck and press her entire body up against his . . . she should pull away now, before anything happened, before she lost control, but she was lost, lost in his smell and his taste and then, just like a dream, the kiss was over and he was walking away, looking over his shoulder at her and waving nonchalantly as though nothing had happened. That's it, she thought. That's all I'm going to get. Ever. She rested her head on the glass of the window and let the tears come, the ones she'd been holding back for hours, till the street outside blurred and smudged into a fog dotted with glittering points of light.

❧

Fiona managed to tuck Douggie up in his bed with Brarey, his favourite cuddly, who was a pink fleece rabbit. She'd not shed a single

337

tear while she sang him a song to soothe him. He stuck his thumb in his mouth and closed his eyes. Poor little thing, she thought. He's exhausted and I'll pay for this tonight. He'll never want to go to bed at his proper time if he has a sleep now. She found that she didn't care. She didn't care about anything but Efe and getting him back into a good mood.

What had got into him, down in the hall? Why had he been so horrible to her? More and more she was finding it hard to understand him and even harder to make up with him after quarrels. In the first months of their marriage, she had only to press her body against his and he would turn to her and make a moaning noise in his throat and they'd sink down on to the bed or the floor and once or twice they'd even done it standing up, in the kitchen against the sink.

They'd made love this morning, while Gwen was looking after Douggie. He'd laid her down on the bed and lifted her skirt above her waist and pulled her knickers off and pushed into her urgently and quickly, panting as he kissed the side of her neck. Fiona's body was still humming with pleasure, even though Efe hadn't said a word to her from beginning to end. Before that, though, the last time they'd made love (she couldn't even think of it in her own mind as anything else, much less say aloud the words that everyone seemed to utter at every available opportunity) was more than three weeks ago. She had no idea whether that was normal for people who'd been married for nearly four years.

She hadn't managed to work out in all that time what to do to bring Efe out of his black moods when lovemaking was out of the question. She didn't know whether he'd be annoyed with her if she stood up for herself, or if she apologized. The truth was she could never find the right words. Maybe I *am* just a pretty face, she thought, and a stupid one at that.

Efe came into the room, and Fiona didn't dare to ask him where he'd been. He went and stood at the window while she hovered rather tentatively before making up her mind to move across to the dressing-table. Once she was sitting safely in front of the mirror, she pretended to be doing her hair and kept an eye on Efe at the same time. She could see him reflected in the glass. She was about to say something neutral about Douggie being exhausted when Efe spoke to her. He didn't look in her direction, but went on staring out of the window.

'Alex is a fucking goody-goody,' he said. 'Bloody cheek he's got interfering in my marriage.'

Fiona had been full of gratitude for Alex's uncharacteristically macho behaviour, and she was still hurting from her husband's unkind words, but it didn't do to disagree with Efe when he was in this mood so she agreed with him instead.

'I know,' she said, and then rather guiltily, 'I don't expect he meant any harm.'

Efe didn't answer for a while. Then, still not looking at her, he said, 'I'm sorry, Fi. I don't know what got into me. I shouldn't have been so foul. It's all the uncertainty. About the pictures, you know. I'll be myself again when Leonora's made her decision.'

'That's okay,' said Fiona, amazed to get any apology at all. He found it almost impossible, she knew, to say the word 'sorry'. 'I knew you were joking.'

'Course I was,' said Efe, and Fiona knew he was lying but didn't care because his tone was lighter and the mood, she could see, was lifting. 'I'm going down now, Fiona. I could do with a drink, I can tell you, after all that. See you.'

He left the room, blowing her a casual kiss as he went. Tears welled up in Fiona's eyes. He never includes me, she thought, feeling increasingly sorry for herself. She could forgive his temper, his bad moods, being bruised when he took hold of her too roughly when he was angry, even being hit, if only he really, really loved her and wanted her with him all the time. He doesn't care, she thought, whether I'm around or not, most of the time. That's what hurts. I could be on another planet and he wouldn't even notice. Her tears spilled on to her cheeks and she brushed them away quickly. I'll have a nice cool bath, she thought, and then get ready for dinner. I'll put my hair up. I'll put a cool cloth over my eyes and lie in the water and rest.

She was on her way to the bathroom when she noticed that Efe had left his mobile phone on the table beside the bed. It wasn't like him to put it down and forget about it, especially not today when she knew he was expecting a call from Reuben Stronsky. She'd wondered whether it had been sensible to invite the poor man all the way over from America if the chances were that Leonora wouldn't give in over the matter of the pictures, but Efe assured her that Mr Stronsky was so charming he might even be able to sway Leonora. Fiona doubted it, but she certainly wasn't going to provoke a row by disagreeing with Efe.

She picked up the phone and saw at once that there was a text message for her husband. She hesitated, looking at the silver rectangle in her hand. She'd been brought up never to read other people's letters, and also believed that eavesdroppers never heard any good of themselves, but this was a little different. It might be an urgent message from Mr Stronsky that Efe needed to know about at once. She was ready for her bath and didn't fancy traipsing around Willow Court in nothing but her kimono looking for him, but if the call really *was* important, she could dress again and go and find him and have a bath later on.

Fiona sat on the bed, pressed the tiny silver button and saw that Efe was being asked whether he'd received some call or other. I'll listen to it, she thought, and only go and find him if it's urgent. It turned out to be a call from someone in Efe's office who actually said he'd be happy to wait till Tuesday. Before she'd had time to switch the message off, another recording of an old call began. She should have turned it off, there and then, but it was a woman's voice and once she'd heard the first few words, she had to go on listening.

For some moments after the voice stopped speaking, she didn't move. Not a muscle, not an eyelash. If I move, she thought, I'll fall into pieces. She was aware of her whole body trembling. Her mouth was dry and she was suddenly freezing cold in spite of the heat of the day. It was a mistake. It had to be. Something vile and malign had made its way into her head. Perhaps she was going mad and had imagined it. Or maybe there was such a thing as a phone virus, like an e-mail virus, that got into mobiles and soiled them. Made them revolting. It isn't true, Fiona said to herself. It can't be. This isn't happening. Not to me.

She forced herself to breathe. Breathe in, breathe out, and calm down. She knew that before she did anything else, she had to listen to that hideous message again. The hope flashed into her mind for a second that maybe the call was a wrong number. Did the person actually mention Efe's name? She had to know. She pressed the button again and the voice, distorted by distance and made thick by lust, spoke into her ear again.

*Efe darling.* There they were, the very words she was dreading. The worst words, those she'd have given anything not to hear. *Efe darling. It's me. Can you guess what I'm doing? I wish it was you doing it, sweetheart, just exactly as you did last time but maybe it won't be too long. I can't bear the waiting, I want you so much. Tomorrow. Will there be a chance for us to go somewhere for a bit in the afternoon? Otherwise I might disgrace myself . . . oh, God, Efe, I'm longing for you. I need you. Can you hear how much I need you?*

Fiona went on listening through several seconds of groaning and sighing. Oh, God, oh, God, how revolting and loathsome! She flung the phone away from her and it fell on the floor. I don't care. I don't care if it's broken. I can't breathe. Oh, Jesus, God. She closed her eyes and fell back on the bed, hurting too much even to cry. She stood up again. Her body burned as though someone had stripped her slowly of every bit of her skin. Her head was filled with disgusting images of Efe caressing that person – who was she? – touching her till she was panting and moaning like she had on the phone. Fiona put a hand over her mouth, certain that she was going to throw up, but she didn't, and the feeling passed. Her forehead was damp with the cold sweat that accompanied the nausea.

She walked over to the window in a daze. She had no idea when the call had come, but Efe hadn't deleted it. He'd kept it, and there was only one reason for him to do that; it turned him on to listen to it over and over again. For a moment she was so enraged that if Efe had been there, in the room with her, she would have stabbed him with a nail file or something and not have felt the slightest twinge of remorse.

Fiona looked down at her husband's car, parked near the top of the drive. The keys were still on the bedside table. I don't have to stay here, she thought suddenly. I don't want to see him and I don't have to. I don't have to be anywhere near him ever again if I don't want to. I can leave. I can pack up and leave. Her mind raced. They'll all be busy somewhere, talking and talking and making arrangements for the party. I don't want to go to the bloody party. Fuck the party.

She went to the wardrobe and took out the larger of the two

suitcases they'd brought with them and started to throw her clothes into it. She wouldn't write a note. What could she say? For a moment she wondered whether to leave a message on Efe's phone that he would hear straight after hers, whoever she was. No, fuck him. If he wanted to speak to her, *he* could leave a message on *her* phone, couldn't he? She didn't feel like saying another word to him ever again, though she probably would have to, one day. Just not now. It was a good thing Douggie was having a nap. She wouldn't wake him until she was ready to go. What would Efe say when he discovered she'd taken the car? He'd go ballistic. He would come home by train, and serve him right, only she wouldn't be there. She'd get to her parents' house before it was time for them to leave for Willow Court. Mummy would be cross to miss the party. She'd been looking forward to it. Leonora would be cross that two people who said they'd come wouldn't be there. It would spoil the table plans. Well, fuck the table plans. On Tuesday morning, her father would make her an appointment with his lawyer. Daddy would look after her.

Tears sprang into Fiona's eyes at the thought of how little Efe would probably miss her. He'd miss Douggie all right, and what would become of the new baby? The thought of her – Fiona was sure the baby would be a girl – was the final straw and she covered her face with her hands and sobbed uncontrollably.

Some minutes later, having wept more tears than she thought was humanly possible and with the breath ragged in her throat, Fiona sat up. She picked the mobile phone up from where she'd flung it, and deleted the message. Now Efe would know she'd heard it. He'd know, and, what's more, he wouldn't be able to listen to it however much he might want to.

'I'm not sure I get it,' said Alex. He was in Efe's room, sitting on Douggie's bed. Efe himself was staring out of the window and not saying much. Far too much was going on for Alex's liking. He was still light-headed from what had happened in the kitchen with Beth. Still couldn't believe it, and kept going over and over it in his mind, reduced to being like a teenager again, unable to concentrate on anything other than her, than Beth. Just saying her name in his head gave him pleasure. As soon as she'd gone into the garden, he'd started worrying. She was just being kind. She loved Efe, and was only making do with him because she was angry with his elder brother. She'd come to her senses and realize she didn't really mean it. That kiss. But he knew she did. He'd felt it in every part of her body, held close to his. He shook his head to dispel this memory, which was threatening to push every other thought he'd ever had straight out of his head.

No more daydreams, he said to himself. He could see that his brother was in a terrible state. Alex could have sworn he'd been crying, but that was unlikely. Maybe he'd been helping down in the marquee and got something in his eye. Alex had been on his way to shower before dinner when Efe came out of his room and nabbed him. The bedroom door opened so suddenly that it looked as though he'd been watching out for Alex to come upstairs.

Alex had taken his shoes off. His back was against the wall and he'd drawn his knees up under his chin. Efe came to sit on the edge of the bed and put his head in his hands. Alex knew he was supposed to be comforting Efe but he found it hard to understand exactly what had happened.

'It's perfectly simple,' Efe said. 'Fiona has buggered off. She's taken Douggie with her. She won't answer her mobile. On the way to her parents, I bet. What the fuck am I meant to do? She knows something like this could wreck Leonora's party. What she's done is a kind of sabotage. What's got into her, d'you think?'

'Are you quite sure you apologized?'

'Of course I bloody did. I told you I did.'

Alex said nothing. Efe often apologized in a rather inadequate way that left you uncertain of whether he really meant it.

'I know you told me.' Alex tried not to sound impatient. 'But did Fiona realize, that's the point.'

Efe nodded. 'She was absolutely fine when I left the room. I'd swear she was. We'd been getting on okay. We hadn't had a proper fight in ages.'

This wasn't the time, Alex thought, to go back over the day and the several separate things Efe had done that would have driven another woman away long ago. He said, 'I don't know what I can say, then, Efe.'

Efe flopped back on to the bed. It was something he used to do when they were children and, indeed, there was a part of Alex's mind, a part that stood outside a situation and looked at it dispassionately, which was thinking exactly that – they could have been their ten and eight-year-old selves, wondering how to get out of some trouble or other that Efe had landed them in. They used to sit in exactly this way, Alex against the wall and Efe on the edge of the bed. It was strange how your body was programmed into patterns that were difficult to change.

'I *do* know, actually,' Efe said. His arm was across his face now, hiding his eyes. A sure sign, again from their childhood, of guilt. 'She opened a text message of mine. She might have thought it was urgent. That led her to a missed call and then I suppose she just kept on listening and picked up a message I hadn't deleted from before. I know she heard it because I went to listen to it again and it's been deleted. I assume it was her. In any case, it's not there and neither is she, so I'm putting two and two together.'

Alex groaned. 'The message was from a woman, right?'

'Right. And it wasn't the sort of message I would have wanted her to hear.'

Alex was silent. He could guess why Efe hadn't deleted the offending words. He said, 'What are you going to do, then? D'you want her back? You could persuade her if you do.'

'Dunno what I want. That's the truth. But Fiona's leaving isn't exactly going to help the celebratory mood, is it?'

Alex thought of tonight's dinner.

'I reckon you shouldn't tell anyone. Not tonight anyway, and by the time tomorrow comes, everything will be in full swing and no one'll mind so much.' He looked at Efe.

'Did you say you went to listen to the message again?' A thought had suddenly struck Alex.

'Yes. Why?'

'No special reason,' Alex answered. How heartbroken could Efe have been if, in the midst of discovering his wife had left him, he'd wanted to listen again to what was probably an obscene message from his mistress? Not very heartbroken at all, but just annoyed because this was something he hadn't planned and over which he had no control.

'Right, then.' Efe sat up suddenly and got off the bed. He ran his hands through his hair and said, 'That's it. I'll tell them she's not feeling too good. Headache or something. Tired. Don't you breathe a word, okay?'

Alex nodded. Not breathing a word was second nature to him.

Rilla sat in front of the dressing-table mirror, but even though she was looking into it she saw nothing. The bath had helped a little but her mind was still crowded with images of the lake as it must have been that day, and her child calling out to a heedless Efe who could have turned, could have looked behind him, instead of plunging further and further into his game. She let out a breath she didn't even know she was holding and thought, poor Efe! How terrible for a child to have that always in his history. Knowing this about him made certain things about her nephew much clearer. He'd coped with guilt by becoming selfish, by going full-tilt for whatever he wanted without much thought for anyone else. Rilla realized now that his short temper and impatience with those who were weaker than he must have been made even worse by this suppression of guilt.

She wondered whether this confession that Leonora had dragged out of him would make him feel worse, and decided that it wouldn't. It might even make life easier for him. But Leonora hadn't done it for Efe but to make her, Rilla, feel better. She felt a lump forming in her throat. Oh, stop, stop, she told herself, don't start crying now. No need to feel that sorry for her. She would feel better too, no doubt about that. One always did after a confession. It was true, though, that over the last few days her mother had been far less acerbic than she normally was. Could it be that Leonora was mellowing in her old age? Rilla tried to recall any critical remarks, snipings, backbitings or exasperated looks, and only two or three came to mind. It's also me, she thought. I'm distracted by love.

Her mobile phone began to sing its ridiculous tune and Rilla groaned. I must change the tone, she thought. It drives me mad. As she picked it up, her heart literally sank in her breast. It could only possibly be Ivan. She'd never got round to phoning him after all. That was Sean's fault. As soon as she'd caught sight of him, poor Ivan had disappeared out of her head. Then she'd remembered about him and knew she had to tell him about Sean and hadn't phoned out of cowardice. She was going to have to dump him. That was what the young called it, and though inelegant as a phrase, there was a certain accuracy about it. She would try to stall him for now and arrange a meeting next week. She pressed the button and held the phone to her ear.

'Darling Ivan! How lovely to hear from you . . . yes, I'm so sorry. You cannot imagine what it's like round here. Military campaigns are sloppy in comparison with the arrangements that are going on. Tell me what you've been doing.'

She listened with half an ear while Ivan droned on about a party he'd attended, her mind wandering away from the words she was hearing to what she was going to wear for dinner tonight. When he got to the slushy stuff about how much he was missing her, and how he was longing to hold her, she took a deep breath.

'Ivan, I can't talk now, but we have to meet early next week. Could we? There are some things I really do have to talk over with you.'

'I think,' said the disembodied voice in her ear, 'that I hear a certain hesitation in your words, Rilla darling. Is there something you're keeping from me?'

'No, Ivan, of course not!' Rilla could hear the false jollity she was exuding and hoped very much it didn't sound so awful on the other end of the phone.

'You are sounding happy, but you are not really happy,' Ivan said. Shit, Rilla thought. So much for that. What now? She was considering whether she ought to tell him the truth and be done with it, when he interrupted her.

'You are making this arrangement so that you can . . . how do you say . . . finish with me. Am I right? You have perhaps met someone else. Am I right?'

A silence developed while Rilla thought franctically of what to say next.

'You cannot answer, because it is the truth,' Ivan sounded triumphant.

'Well, yes, there is someone, but I didn't want . . .'

'I know. I know. You wanted to do the proper thing. To see me.

To tell me to my face. This is very good of you, but I will release you from such obligations. You are as free as a bird, Rilla. I will not tie you down.'

His voice rang with emotion. Rilla couldn't help smiling. What an old drama queen he was! She said, 'It's very kind of you, Ivan. I don't deserve it, and I didn't – don't – mean to hurt you, but I've fallen in love. Does that sound ridiculous?'

'No,' said Ivan. 'I fell in love with you the very first time I ever saw you. Who is this man?'

Rilla couldn't help feeling that his so-called love wasn't what might be called the real thing. He didn't exactly sound as though he was suffering. She ignored the first part of what Ivan had said and concentrated on answering his question.

'He's the director of the TV programme that's being made about Ethan Walsh. His name is Sean Everard. In any case, I've got to go now, Ivan. You cannot imagine how busy it is around here. We'll talk properly when I get back to London, okay? We'll have lunch as soon as possible.'

There were a few more seconds of Ivan from the silver rectangle of the phone. It crossed Rilla's mind that he wasn't sounding exactly heartbroken, which was a good thing, even if not very complimentary to her. It made her life much easier.

'Goodbye, Ivan,' she said at last. 'I'll be in touch next week, I promise. Take care.'

One tiny click and he was gone. Rilla put the phone back on the bedside table and felt suddenly light-headed with happiness. It was going to be all right. The field was clear. Ivan had made it plain from his manner that he would recover, rather more quickly than she ever thought he would. He'd been much more understanding than she'd had any right to hope for. Some femme fatale you are, she told herself, and went to the wardrobe to consider her options for this evening. Black satin trousers again, and perhaps by the more forgiving light of the dining-room she could get away with the pink silk top. The weather was still sultry and a scarf around her neck might be unbearably hot, but it was so beautiful that Rilla thought she would wear it anyway. She could slip it over the back of her chair if it became too much.

A gentle knock at the bedroom door surprised her in the midst of these pleasant thoughts. Who can that be, she wondered, hoping that it wasn't anyone wanting her actually to *do* anything. She said, 'Come in,' and Leonora said, 'I'm sorry to disturb you, darling . . .' before her voice faded away.

'Mother!' Rilla didn't know whether this visitation was good news or not. She was almost sure that it was only Leonora checking up that she was okay after the revelations about Efe. She said, 'Sit down here, Mother. Are you all right? You look rather tired.'

It was true. In the conservatory, in the shadow of a large leafy plant, Leonora had seemed exactly as she always did, poised, upright, and young-looking for her age. Here, in the low sunlight of early evening, the thinness of the skin around her mother's eyes, the shadows that were, surely, darker than usual, the blue veins standing out on hands that suddenly looked spotted and almost gnarled . . . with a shock to the heart Rilla realized that her mother was an old woman. She'd never thought of her in those terms before. I'm a fool, she thought. She's my mother and she always will be and so I don't really look at her. She's supposed to stay the same so I haven't seen her changing. She has no right to be different from all the memories I've carried since childhood, but of course she is. How could it be otherwise?

'I'm fine, darling,' said Leonora, her voice exactly as it always was, strong, vibrant, ready to offer opinions and take no nonsense from anyone. Rilla smiled ruefully. So much for consigning Mother to the category of the aged and infirm.

'I came in because there was still something I wanted to say to you,' Leonora went on. 'First, though, I have to ask you a question. Do you mind?'

Was saying, 'Yes, I do mind' an option? Of course it wasn't. Rilla said, 'Not at all. Fire away.'

'Do you ever think of Hugh Kenworthy?' Leonora turned her head towards the window as she spoke, allowing Rilla to collect her thoughts. What kind of a question was that supposed to be? Imagine Mother remembering his name! Rilla would have bet good money that the whole episode had faded from Leonora's mind years ago. And how was she supposed to answer? In the end she said, 'Yes, of course. From time to time.'

I will not, Rilla thought, remind you how much I hated you for what you did, and how I still resented it bitterly, right up until a couple of days ago. I certainly shan't say a word about never forgiving you. And most of all, I won't utter a squeak about not giving a damn about the whole thing now that I've met Sean. I shan't say a word about that.

'I hesitated about coming to see you, Rilla, but I thought about it and decided that in the end, it was better that you should know everything.'

'About Hugh?'

'About why I sent him away.'

'I remember it all perfectly, Mother. He was married. He was unreliable in every way. He wasn't a bit suitable. I know all this. I was very young then – now I understand that you had to do what you did. I expect I'd have done the same thing if Beth had been in such a situation.'

Leonora said, 'There was something else, though, that I didn't tell you at the time. It would have hurt you too much, and I was deeply ashamed of myself as well.'

She's blushing, Rilla thought. How astonishing! What is all this?

'Hugh made a pass at me,' Leonora said. 'Up in the studio one afternoon while I was showing him round. I was sitting on the chaise-longue and we'd been chatting. He was such a good talker that I'd let myself get far friendlier than I should have, I suppose. He was terribly charming, and very handsome, wasn't he?'

Rilla nodded. There was nothing to say. Leonora was already going on with her confession as though she had to get to the end of it, otherwise she might lose her nerve.

'He came to sit beside me. I don't know when I noticed that his arm was around my shoulders, but there it was and then somehow I had turned to him and he was kissing me and touching me and it was minutes . . . whole minutes . . . before I came to my senses and pushed him away and told him to leave.' Leonora stared down at her hands and her voice was so small that Rilla had to lean towards her to hear what she was saying. 'The worst thing was, I wanted him, Rilla.

My love for your father was not like other kinds of love, you know. I've never, ever loved another man, and I would no sooner have married again than gone to the moon, and yet Hugh managed to get under my skin a little. I confess that.'

She shook her head. 'It's not something a child wants to hear about her mother, is it? I'm so sorry to have spoken of it, but I did think you should know. That all the anger you felt towards me was . . . how shall I put it? A little justified. Yes, that's it. A little justified. I was jealous of you, Rilla. Of what you and Hugh had together. That's a dreadful thing for a mother to feel. I'm so, so sorry, darling. Can you forgive me?'

The first thing that occurred to Rilla was that this was the first time in her whole life that she'd heard Leonora allude to her own sexual feelings. She was right. That side of her mother's life was not something Rilla ever thought about. Quite the reverse, in fact. The very idea of Leonora in bed with anyone at any time in her life made Rilla feel queasy. She remembered vividly how beautiful her mother had been when she herself was seventeen. Leonora was younger when I was going out with Hugh than I am now, she thought. This was a sobering notion, for what had Rilla been thinking about, to the exclusion of almost everything else since she'd met Sean, but sex? Oh, God, how complicated people were. How impossible it was ever to know anyone, especially your parents. She said, 'Mother, there's nothing at all to forgive. Hugh was very handsome and charming. Only a log would have been immune to that. You were a very beautiful woman, you know. And you were younger than I am now.'

Leonora smiled. 'Thank you, Rilla darling. I couldn't have done things differently but I *am* sorry that you were hurt. And I regret not talking to you about it before. I do regret that, very much.' She sighed. 'I haven't ever talked to you properly, I don't think. It had never occurred to me before and I'm ashamed to have to admit it, but I think the fact that your father died while I was expecting you coloured everything. It's a very shaming thing to confess and even after all these years I blush when I think of how terribly unfair it was. But I was, how do they put it, distracted with grief. Half mad, really. More than half. And I blamed you, my poor little baby. Blamed you for his death, although of course you had nothing to do with it.'

Tears stood in Leonora's eyes. 'I've never said anything like this to anyone before, but I was *too* much in love with Peter. And it's made me unfair to you, all your life, really. But you *do* know that I love you, Rilla, don't you?'

'Yes, Mother, of course I do.' She thought she could see the physical signs of relief in Leonora: her shoulders straighter, her head held higher, her eyes brighter.

'I'm glad. You're being very generous, darling. It's such a relief, because you've been on my conscience so much lately, and I find it hard to apologize for anything, as you know.'

She smiled to show that this last remark was not meant entirely seriously. Rilla smiled back. 'But,' she continued, 'I *am* sorry. Really sorry, darling. That's the main thing I wanted to say. I hope you can forgive me.'

Rilla bit her lip to stop herself from crying. Her mother had unexpectedly shown her a wound, and she wanted, illogically, both to comfort Leonora as though she were a child, and also to cry out and say stop, you're my mother. You're not supposed to be the one who's in pain. You're meant to look after me. She answered somewhat shakily.

'Of course, Mother darling. But there's nothing to forgive, honestly. It must have been so ghastly to lose a husband you loved so much. I can't even begin to imagine it. Please don't feel bad about it any more. Promise me?'

'You're being kind to me, darling, and I'm so grateful. I'm not very good at being looked after, am I? But I'm feeling better now. I'll go, and let you get dressed for dinner. But I did just want to warn you about something. You won't think I'm an interfering old busybody, will you?'

Rilla laughed. It was a relief to hear Leonora sounding like herself again; a relief to take on again the part she'd grown so used to, that of the less well-behaved of two daughters. 'Go on, Mother,' she said. 'What have I done wrong now?'

'Nothing. Nothing at all, Rilla. It's just that I couldn't help noticing that you and Sean were . . . how shall I put it . . . getting a little close. Don't you think you're rushing things a bit? You've only just met him after all.'

This is not the time, Rilla thought, to tell her roughly to butt out and mind her own business.

'Now, Mother,' she said as mildly as she could, 'what have you always told me about meeting Daddy and knowing within a few seconds that he was the one you would always love? Love at first sight, remember? And you were only a child. I'm nearly fifty. I do know my own mind, you know, and actually, I agree with you. It *is* quick, and at first I worried about that but now I've decided I don't care. I don't want to waste any more time. That's the truth, Mother, and I hope you don't mind me speaking so frankly.'

Leonora laughed. 'You're quite right. Of course you are, and none of this is my business at all. But I don't want you to be hurt, darling.'

'I'm sure I won't be,' Rilla said. 'But you couldn't prevent it, I'm afraid, whatever you do.'

'I know. I know that, Rilla, but I've learned some things about my own mother today which have made me reconsider everything.' She smiled. 'I'm being enigmatic, I know, and I will tell you everything at dinner, but I just wanted to say it. I worry about you, and I haven't always been the best of mothers.'

Leonora walked over to the dressing-table, and before Rilla could say anything, she felt her mother's hands on her shoulders and a kiss on the crown of her head. She hasn't kissed me like that, Rilla thought, since I was about five.

'I'm a silly old woman,' Leonora murmured. 'Bless you, darling.'

Rilla blinked back tears. 'You too, Mummy,' she managed to say, before Leonora turned and went to the door. As soon as she'd gone, Rilla thought, I called her 'Mummy'. I haven't done that for years and years. Had she noticed? Rilla looked in the mirror and considered the repairs she needed to make to her face. She smiled. All this emotion was hard on the complexion.

Sean let the cooling stream of the shower fall on his head and wondered how Leonora was managing. The visit to Nanny Mouse had been extraordinary. He'd caught all of what had been said on film, but it was doubtful that he'd use it in that form. He would have loved to discuss his thoughts with Rilla, but a promise was a promise and Leonora had been quite clear that she wanted no one to know what had been spoken about this afternoon. He turned his mind to what he'd seen from his window when he'd first come upstairs.

A car was going down the drive and he thought he saw a woman at the wheel; a flash of blonde hair. She was going much too fast, whoever she was. Not Rilla, or Gwen, who was dark, and neither Chloë nor Leonora, whom he'd seen walking up to the house from the gazebo. Who else was there, he asked himself, and then it came to him. Fiona was a blonde, and even though she'd barely registered on Sean's radar, he had noticed that she looked miserable for much of the time. In all probability, he thought, she's had a fight with Efe and driven off in a temper. He hoped very much that she would calm down a little before she got to the main road and then forgot about her completely as his thoughts turned to Rilla. Wherever she was, it would soon be time for dinner and she'd be there. Tonight he would see to it that they were seated next to one another. And perhaps whatever it was that was going on would be explained at last.

He stepped out of the shower, and hummed as he took a clean shirt out of his suitcase. The sight of his birthday present to Leonora made him smile. The family were all going to give her their gifts after dinner tonight and had kindly allowed him to add his parcel to theirs. His present was a small white television and video recorder, on which she would be able to watch his film when it was ready. He was longing to see her face when she opened the box which now stood in the corner, looking a little silly with a pink ribbon stuck on it as an afterthought. Sean didn't see the point of wrapping, but recognized the inappropriateness of brown cardboard for conveying a feeling of festivity.

Sean looked round the table. He'd missed dinner last night, but it struck him how different the atmosphere was now from what it had been for his first meal at Willow Court. All over the house, there was the sort of excitement in the air that he generally associated with Christmas; a sense of secret gift-wrapping, and getting clothes ready, and delicious smells coming from the kitchen. Various members of the family had been whispering to one another during drinks on the terrace, and every so often someone disappeared somewhere only to emerge later looking faintly embarrassed. Efe seemed distracted and his eyes were red-rimmed. If it had been anyone else, Sean would have sworn he'd been crying, but in his case it was probably some kind of allergy to the heat or the pollen.

The weather had been extraordinary for the last few days, as though Leonora had ordered up a perfect English summer to surround the house especially for her birthday. Sometimes Sean felt that Willow Court was separated from the real world; that the entire house and its inhabitants were part of a beautiful arrangement under some gigantic glass dome. He smiled to himself. Too much excellent Chardonnay, that was his problem. That, and being in love, which turned you into the sort of fanciful dork who might easily have a thought like that.

This time, too, the seating plan at the table was different. He was next to Rilla, who looked perfect and smelled of something so delicious that he had to restrain himself from burying his face in the crease of her neck. Fiona was indisposed. Efe had told them she was going to get an early night in order to be ready for tomorrow. She was, according to her husband, sorry to have to miss Leonora opening her presents. Gwen, even in a rather flattering ice-blue silk shirt, looked careworn, with that *have I covered all possible contingencies?* air that he recognized from every stage manager he'd ever met. Still, James, who had clearly been knocking back the wine, was talking to her in an animated way and she was gradually relaxing. Beth wasn't eating properly. Sean looked at her pushing Mary's salmon en croûte around her plate and wondered what was worrying her. She kept glancing across the table at Efe, but it wasn't the dazed, worshipping gaze he'd noticed when he first saw them together. She was sitting next to Alex and nodding as he spoke to her. There was another change. Alex was neatly dressed in a clean white shirt and dark linen trousers. Chloë and Philip were tucking into their food. He supposed that what she was wearing represented some kind of evening dress, but the effect of a deliberately trashy pearl and diamond tiara stuck into the gelled spikes of her blonde hair, crowning a beige lace blouse and a black taffeta skirt, was more comical than glamorous.

Leonora had chosen to wear black. She looked pale and rather fragile, and the pearls of her necklace were lustrous against the waterfall of chiffon that formed the lapels of her blouse. She had been quieter than usual, even though he'd tried to engage her in conversation several times. She'd eaten very little of the avocado cocktail and hardly any salmon at all. Sean had watched many, many after-dinner speakers and some of the more nervous ones behaved exactly as Leonora was behaving now. He wondered whether the excitement of the party tomorrow might have had this effect, and doubted it. There had to be something else. He was just on the point of asking her, tactfully, whether anything was wrong, when she tapped gently on the side of her wine glass with her fork. Everybody fell silent.

'Thank you, everyone,' she said. 'I have something to tell all of you now, which is somewhat difficult and also extremely important, and I thought it would be best to do it now, before dessert is served. This is going to be an ordeal for me, so I hope you'll all bear with me and let me finish what I have to say before you ask any questions.'

Sean looked round the table at the family, nodding and murmuring their agreement, turning their faces to Leonora. She opened her sequinned handbag and took out a sheet of paper, which she unfolded carefully and laid on the tablecloth. Then, very slowly, she opened her spectacle case and put on her reading-glasses. She did this quietly, but there was an element of theatricality in the way she then looked all around the table before she spoke.

'This,' she said, tapping the sheet of paper with one finger, 'is a suicide note written by my mother.'

For a moment, Leonora thought she would faint. The faces all round the table seemed to be blurring: white circles against the dark walls of the dining-room. Something caught the light and glittered. That ridiculous head-dress Chloë was wearing, which reminded Leonora of the kind of thing Rilla and Gwen used to like to take out of the dressing-up box in the nursery when they were little girls. She could feel the silence stretching out and knew that she had to speak again. It had taken every ounce of her strength to keep the contents of this letter to herself from the time that Chloë had brought it to her until now.

At first, she had been in a state of shock. While she and Chloë were still in the gazebo, she'd wept and sobbed in a completely undignified way, and the poor child hadn't known what to do to comfort her. Leonora had accepted the endearments and the soothing sounds she'd made, but couldn't begin to explain to her granddaughter that her tears were as much from blinding rage as sorrow. Ethan, her father. If he'd been in front of her at that moment, she would have attacked him with her bare hands. *How could he?* was the thought that exploded in every corner of her mind. How could he steal from his own wife the very thing that she most valued? How could he deceive his only daughter, and go on accepting the love of an innocent child when he'd behaved so badly? Leonora shook with fury at the sheer injustice of it. After a while, she had no more tears left to shed and told Chloë that she was fine, really, and would like to go back to the house now, please. She'd been led up over the lawn so gently that for a moment she really did feel like the old lady she was supposed to be.

She'd kissed Chloë and gone straight to her room, where she sat unmoving for a full fifteen minutes before all the separate pieces of what she had learned came together to make some kind of sense. She felt as though some giant had taken up her whole life and shaken it about and then set it down again, with everything about it differently arranged; all her memories, her entire past, everything. But in the end, she'd pulled herself together and had even managed to be her normal self when she'd spoken to Rilla. I'm used to it, she said to herself. I'm used to putting a brave face on things. It's what I've been brought up to do.

Now, she looked round at her family, who were all staring up at her in total silence. Ought she to explain the background before she started? Or later, when they'd listened to these words that had been hidden for so long? No, she would plunge straight in and let her mother's voice be heard at last. She coughed and began to read, concentrating on the marks on the paper; trying to think neither of her audience nor of the writer, but only of the words themselves.

Went up to the Studio where your voice didn't reach and painted every hour of the day. Solace. Comfort. Consolation, in those days. Didn't care if the pictures went out under another name. Didn't care at all. Unimportant, all that was. Paint mattered. What was coming to life under my fingers, that was the important thing. Light shone in from the window, brushing the side of a teapot and for hours and hours nothing mattered but getting that highlight exactly right. Not precisely as it was in life, but more than it was; object (or subject) had to *be* what it was and also be all the possibilities,

356

dreams, memories of what it was. Terribly hard to explain, all this, but when a painting was finished, wanted it to be like a source of light to whoever looked at it. Wanted everything to glow and shine and leap out of the frame. Wanted to make beautiful things, and knew how to do that and they didn't cry or break and didn't bruise under my hands.

Maude, me, I was the better artist, that was all it was. Ethan saw that. Even while we were still both at art school, my paintings were more praised than his. Also, he realized that there was a fortune and a reputation to be made. Clever. He is, clever and clever. Didn't know how to stop him. Didn't question his words for years. He said doesn't matter whose name it is on the canvas. He said the work abides. Paint never lies. You should be satisfied, he said, with being able to make such things, and not ask for fame and glory on top of that. He said you're delicate, Maude. He said you're fragile. You'll crack under all the attention. He swore he'd keep the world away from my door, and he succeeded and now I bitterly regret it all. Bitterly. Have tried to say this to him, but it is too late and he doesn't listen to me at all. Barely looks at me. Deception is too deep, and has gone on for too many years to change now, he says. If you say anything (he says this all the time, many times) I'll tell them you're mad mad mad, and point to my signature. I'll say you're deluded, he whispers in my ear. They would believe him. He is very believable. No one doubts him.

There is a way out. Will take it. Very soon. Am not braver than I used to be, only tired of everything, weary in my very bones of all the pain. Nothing pleases me any longer. Want to punish and hurt him, but not brave enough to speak of what he has made me do, because he would destroy me if I did. Know he would. He is a cruel man, however he may charm people with his smile and clever talk. Have lost count now of times he has hit me, but days and days have kept to my room so that world shouldn't see the bruises and red eyes from the crying. Eyes always red now, but shall stop it all soon. No more pictures, ever, from my hand, and that will hurt him more than anything else. That may make him cry. Not losing me, but losing the paintings he has almost persuaded himself are his own. He has swallowed me up so that everything of mine is part of him. My fault. My weakness and my cowardice. Am such a coward. Cannot forgive myself for that, for locking myself away from my darling baby when she was so tiny. For not speaking. For not packing a suitcase and walking down the drive. But how? How to leave my child and my garden and my house that I love? Am a coward, a dreadful weakling and hate myself beyond anything else. Cannot look at myself in the mirror without feeling disgust and horror. Will end it. But have made a surprise for Leonora's birthday . . . it's very soon and so will try to wait till after that is over before stopping my painting for ever. There is one thing he doesn't know. No one knows. Have signed my own paintings. There, said it now. My own paintings. Somewhere in each one have made an arrangement of lines or colours in the shape of a lion. Very tiny lion, for Leonora, who is fierce and unafraid like her father, and beautiful and for whom only wish is that she may face the light always and never turn away to cry into the darkness, like me, like me. Darling child, forgive me. Forgive me. Have loved you from the moment you were born and think of you every moment of every day. Your mother, Maude Walsh.

Leonora looked up from the page. The familiar faces around the table had been transformed into creatures from a nightmare. Beth gasped, her eyes wide. Gwen had her hand clamped over her mouth, and Rilla was openly weeping. Alex had both hands over his face, covering his eyes. Chloë and Philip were sitting very upright, and James was reaching for the wine bottle. Darkness had gathered in the corners of the dining-room while she'd been speaking. Leonora broke the silence.

'It's rather a long letter, I'm afraid, but I felt I should read all of it, so that you would understand. It was written on the back of the wallpaper used to cover the entire dolls' house roof, and I'm very grateful to Philip and Chloë for removing it so carefully that not a word has been lost, and for making me the typed copy I've just read. The original is very faint and hard to make out. Thank you, both of you.'

Still no one spoke. She continued. 'I hope that my mother's somewhat disjointed style wasn't too difficult to follow. What this letter does not make clear – how could it? – is that I found her. I found her dead, floating in the lake, just before my eighth birthday. The shock of it made me ill and when I got better, well, they'd decided – my father decided, I suppose, and Nanny Mouse went along with his plan – that I shouldn't be told the truth. I expect they thought it would upset me too much to be reminded of such a dreadful thing.'

Gwen and Rilla cried out almost in unison, 'Oh, Mother, Mother, oh how . . . how . . .' and both started to get up from their chairs. Leonora put out a hand to stop them, and they sank back. Gwen was as white as the tablecloth in front of her and Rilla's tears were running unchecked down her face. She saw Sean hesitate, then lean towards her, touching her arm to comfort her.

'I'm sorry,' she said, looking at him, and dabbing at her cheeks with a napkin. 'Only it's such a shock. It's so awful. I can hardly believe it.'

Sean whispered something to her and put an arm around her shoulders.

'I wish I could have kept this from all of you,' said Leonora. 'At least until after the party, but I know that I will feel easier in my mind if everyone is aware of the truth. When I say it baldly, out loud like this, I still find it hard to believe, but it's true. Maude Walsh, my mother, is the person who painted the pictures hanging all over the house. He, my father, took her work and passed it off as his. Oh, it's a monstrous thing to have done. Monstrous.'

'But I don't understand *how* he did it,' Efe said. 'He must have started out by doing some painting himself, surely? I mean, he was an artist, wasn't he? When did he decide on the deception? And how come he wasn't discovered during Maude's lifetime?'

Leonora said, 'I don't suppose we'll ever know the answers to those questions. The only person who might have been able to tell us is Nanny Mouse, and she's becoming more and more confused. But I think perhaps he realized almost as soon as they were married that Maude's paintings were much better than his own, and he couldn't bear it. Maybe a dealer offered a good sum for one of her canvases and that gave him the idea. I don't know. But he took the credit for her art while she was alive, and once she was dead, he made sure that her work was as near to being buried alive as possible. That, I think, and nothing else, accounted for the fact that he wouldn't hear of her paintings leaving Willow Court.'

'And don't forget, Leonora,' said James, 'that there *were* a few of his very early paintings out there, because he'd sold them before he was even married to your mother. If anyone had started comparing the early and late Walshes, his plan probably wouldn't have worked. Even as it is, he took a risk.'

'He could have said he'd changed his style,' Chloë suggested. 'Artists are always doing that. If anyone had asked him why the paintings were so different.'

'That's true,' said Efe. 'But what a scam!'

'You sound as though you admire him, Efe,' Beth said, angrily. 'It's one of the cruellest things I've ever heard. Worse than his physical cruelty.'

Leonora saw Efe blush as Beth glared at him. Had they been quarrelling? She had no time or energy to worry about it if they had. There was enough, quite enough, to take in without concerning herself with her grandchildren's squabbles. She took her reading glasses off and leaned forward. 'It *is* a dreadful thing, of course. No one would deny that, but finding it out like this, so many years later, is perhaps even worse, because now I have to look back at almost my whole life knowing that there was a lie at the heart of it. And my father acted in a way that I find quite unforgivable. Appalling. Terrible. He not only destroyed my mother with his physical cruelty and unkindness, but also stole from her the one thing, the *best* thing, she had and made it his own. And the very worst thing of all is . . .'

Leonora stopped speaking. She felt her lower lip tremble and tears come to her eyes. She blinked fiercely to stop them from falling and took two deep breaths before continuing. 'This is very hard for me. The worst thing of all is that I've helped him. I've spent most of my adult life making certain that his work, his art, should be shown to its best advantage. I've guarded the canvases from the world in exactly the way he wanted. And I've loved him. I've loved him and his memory all my life and now I can't any longer. The person I thought I loved didn't exist. Most of what he really was he covered up. He dressed himself in my mother's talent and helped himself to the honour that should have been hers. And to all my love. I didn't have any left over for her. I've overlooked her, not only since she died but also while she was alive. Ethan Walsh sucked up all the attention, everyone's attention, all the time.'

The sound that came out of her mouth resembled laughter, which surprised her a little, because it had felt like a scream as she voiced it. 'It was always a little eccentric, wasn't it? Not wanting your pictures to leave the walls of your home? All that talking and talking about how people wouldn't appreciate them properly, and how much they were an integral part of the house . . . it was lies, nothing but hideous lies and I believed them and helped him. I aided and abetted him in his deception and his unkindness to my poor mother so that he could go on hurting her even when he was dead. I'm sorry to be crying now, but I can't help it.'

Gwen and Rilla both stood up and went to comfort Leonora.

'Please, please don't say sorry,' Gwen murmured, her arms around her mother.

'You should cry if you want to,' Rilla added. 'As much as you like.'

'I'm all right, darlings, honestly. Do sit down again. Some of these tears are simply rage. I feel . . . I feel murderous when I think about him. The truth of it is this: he wanted the paintings kept at Willow Court not only because he didn't want to be found out, but because he wanted to make sure that my mother was never acknowledged as the artist. He wanted to see to it that she never, ever got her due. That much is clear to me. He wanted them here for ever, safe at Willow Court. He made me promise to carry out his instructions, just as he'd written them down in his will, and I told him I would. I promised. Now I see that that promise was unfairly extracted from me when I didn't know the truth. As you all know, there are instructions in my will, too, but on Tuesday morning I shall see to it that they're altered.'

She took a sip of wine. I must pull myself together, she thought and dabbed at her eyes with a lace-edged handkerchief.

'There's a prayer I used to recite when I was a girl, which said *If I should die before I wake*. I have no intention of dying before I wake and missing my birthday party, but just in case I do . . .' she smiled. 'I'd like to say in front of all of you, and you're my witnesses, that I have every intention of spreading the story of Maude Walsh's paintings throughout the art world, and Efe, dear . . .'

'Yes, Leonora?'

'Please get in touch with Mr Stronsky and tell him that nothing would give me greater pleasure than a purpose-built gallery to display my mother's work.'

Those words broke the spell and everyone began to applaud. Sean said, 'I'm going to have to add some things to my film, Leonora. Nothing I've got so far will need changing except for your two interviews. Of course I'm going to have to rewrite the commentary from beginning to end, but I'll enjoy doing that. It is such a dramatic story. Maybe we could get together next week?'

'You're welcome to come back whenever it suits you, Sean,' Leonora said. 'I hadn't given any thought to the programme, I'm sorry to say. And I should also warn everyone that I am going to tell all my guests about this at the party tomorrow. I want everyone to know the truth. I don't want any more deception.'

'She'll become famous, Leonora,' Chloë was exultant. 'Much more famous than Ethan Walsh ever was, because not only is she going to have a proper gallery built just for her, but this story will be part of it. How she was discovered so many years after her death. How her husband stole her art. She'll be a feminist icon. You'll get droves of women tramping all over Willow Court wanting to see where she lived.'

Leonora shuddered. 'I don't think I'd like that, darling.'

Efe said, 'I must get on to various people at once. D'you think we should tell the press? They could all be down here by tomorrow.'

'Efe, please behave yourself.' Leonora spoke sharply. 'It may have escaped your notice but tomorrow is my seventy-fifth birthday party and I would like to enjoy it with my family and friends. My mother's story has been unknown since 1935. I shall tell my guests but the world can wait, I think. Another couple of days will not make any appreciable difference to her future reputation, I'm sure you'll agree.'

Efe had the grace to blush. 'I'm sorry, Leonora. Of course I don't want to spoil your day, but I just thought . . . I don't know. You and your birthday are a part of the story. You found her, after all. It's very dramatic. A human interest angle, the suicide and everything.'

'It will be just as humanly interesting next week,' Leonora said in a tone that managed to bring the discussion of the press possibilities to a full stop. She noticed that Rilla was looking towards the door and asked, 'What's the matter, Rilla? What are you waiting for?'

'It's a surprise,' Rilla said. 'Are you ready to ring for dessert?'

'Rilla darling, you can always be depended upon to bring the conversation back to earth, can't you? But you're quite right. We must get on with the meal otherwise we'll be here for ages and we should all get an early night.'

Sean leaned a little closer to Rilla as everyone round the table began to talk about the party. He whispered in her ear, 'Not us, please, Rilla. We're going for a walk, aren't we? In the dark. By ourselves. Aren't we?'

Rilla nodded, and put her hand on Sean's knee under cover of the tablecloth. He took her hand and stroked her palm gently. 'We certainly are,' she said.

Mary came into the room then and put the strawberry shortcake in front of Leonora.

'What's this, Mary? I thought we were having fruit salad tonight.'

'Rilla had other ideas,' Mary said, with a smile.

'I made it, Mother,' Rilla said. 'Last night when everyone was asleep. It's a surprise for you.'

'It looks wonderful,' Leonora said. 'Thank you, darling. I hope I can manage to cut it neatly. It looks too beautiful to spoil, doesn't it?'

'No, it doesn't,' said James. 'It looks far too good to leave on the plate, that's what I say.' He held out his plate and grinned. 'Get cracking with the knife, Leonora! I can't wait.'

Alex wished he'd taken his camera into dinner. The faces round the table when Leonora was reading her mother's words should have been caught on film. Gwen and Rilla with tears in their eyes; Efe looking at first as though someone had dealt him a knockout blow and then slowly realizing how he could turn the situation to his great advantage, and especially his financial advantage. He could scarcely manage to sit still through the strawberry shortcake that Leonora had somehow managed to distribute. It was sort of typical of Rilla to make something completely delicious which broke up into a mess of biscuit and cream and fruit as soon as you cut into it. Alex wished he could have got a shot of her getting ready for the first mouthful, her lips shining and Sean looking on as though he wished she'd take a bite out of him instead. And in the background, Leonora, with a frown that expressed disapproval of such greed.

Alex was alone on the terrace in the soft darkness waiting for Beth to appear. She was helping Leonora carry all the presents she'd opened up to her bedroom but she'd said she wouldn't be long. She'd been quiet all through dinner. He'd managed to sit next to her, and at one point he'd even asked her what the matter was, but she only shook her head and whispered, 'I'll tell you later.'

'Alex?' Her voice broke into his thoughts. He stood up and said, 'I'm over here, Beth. In the alcove.'

She sat down next to him, and leaned back against the wall. 'I'm totally exhausted,' she said. 'Too much has happened today. I can't take it all in properly.'

'More than you know, actually,' said Alex. 'Have you spoken to Efe?'

Beth snorted. 'Don't talk to me about Efe, honestly. You could practically see the dollar signs flashing in his eyes when he heard Maude's letter. When Chloë said that about her becoming a feminist icon, he was almost jumping up and down. I'm glad Leonora's put a stop to him filling the place with the press tomorrow. He's so greedy and selfish.'

'Haven't you always known that?'

Beth thought for a moment. 'Yes, I suppose I have. Only I've never minded before because I never saw the effect his behaviour had on people. But look at poor Fiona! She's not my favourite person, but she doesn't deserve to be hit. Or bullied. No one does.'

'She's left him,' Alex said.

'What? Fiona's left Efe? I don't believe it! She wouldn't dare. She'd be afraid of what he'd do to her when he found her again.'

'He may not go looking for her. That's the impression I got, anyway. Don't say a word, Beth. I'm not supposed to have told anyone. Efe doesn't want the party to be wrecked.'

'Something drastic must have happened. Tell me, Alex, go on. I shan't say a word. She's put up with so much. And what could he have done that would persuade her to miss a party?'

'She listened to a message on his mobile. By accident.'

Beth was quiet for a moment. She said, 'From a woman, I suppose. Melanie, maybe.'

'Worse than that. Telephone sex, from what I can gather.'

Beth sat without speaking for a few moments. 'Efe has had quite a lot happening to him today. I feel rather sorry for him.'

'He seems okay to me,' Alex said, feeling a stab of jealous anger.

'Leonora spoke to Efe and Rilla in the conservatory this afternoon – don't tell anyone about this, Alex, promise? – she made Efe tell Rilla about the day Mark died. Was that what you were trying to tell me earlier? About Efe not saving him? Being too involved in the game to bother?'

Alex nodded. 'I should have said something, I suppose, only Efe told me it was an accident. That Leonora said it was and we shouldn't say a word about it. And I haven't. I've felt bad too, Beth, sometimes, wondering whether I could have done something. Told Efe to look behind him. Something.'

'You weren't that much older than Markie, Alex. And no one can tell Efe to do anything, can they? You mustn't blame yourself. It *was* an accident. Maybe it could have been prevented, but that's what it was. I think we should try to put that day behind us.'

Alex listened to the night sounds all around them. The delicious scent of evening filled the air and he closed his eyes. This was a chance. He sensed that if he didn't speak, Beth would stand up soon and go to bed. It was late, she was tired, she had a great deal to think about. He knew all that. He said, 'Beth?'

'Mmm?'

Alex looked at her. She had her eyes closed. She hadn't mentioned what had happened earlier, in the kitchen. Did that mean she regretted it? Could he perhaps have imagined her reaction to his kiss? Should he say something? Her satin shirt glowed pearly white. What should he say, if he did decide to speak? *I love you* was out of the question. Not those words, not just like that, out of the blue. Nor could he ask what he really needed to know: *what about Efe? Do you still love him? Am I a sort of second-best?* Maybe he shouldn't speak at all, but just kiss her. He bent over her and touched his lips to hers as lightly as he could, a butterfly kiss, just in case.

'Nothing,' he said. 'I don't know what to say.'

Beth opened her eyes. 'You're wondering, aren't you, about this afternoon? If I really meant it. Well, I did. I don't know why it's taken me so long to realize.'

Before he knew what was happening, she'd wound her arms around him and her mouth was on his, open, eager, sweet. Alex closed his eyes and returned her kiss. They clung together for a long moment and then came out of the embrace, surprised and breathless.

'Never mind.' Alex spoke breathlessly. 'As long as you realize now . . .'

'You're talking too much,' Beth said. 'Shut up and kiss me again.'

'This is all beginning to remind me,' said Rilla, 'of a rather lavish production of *A Midsummer Night's Dream*. Couples wandering about in the dark in a mysterious wood.'

They were walking together through the wild garden and heading for the lake. They both knew this, but neither Sean nor Rilla mentioned the fact.

'Can't think what you mean,' said Sean. 'Gwen and James and Fiona and Efe and Chloë and Philip are probably all safely tucked up in their beds, the lucky things. Also I can't see any woods. Apart from that . . .'

'You're behind the times, Sean. I know something you don't know, and I'm not meant to tell you.'

'Go on. I won't breathe a word, I promise.'

'Efe and Fiona's bedroom door was open when I went upstairs to get my shawl. I looked in, thinking I'd see if she was feeling better and guess what?'

'I'm useless at guessing. Tell me.'

'She's gone. Fiona's gone. She's left him, apparently.'

'I'm amazed. I didn't think she'd have the nerve to do something like that. She'll go back to him, no doubt.'

Rilla sighed. 'She would, I think, but I'm not at all sure that he's that keen. He's a strange boy, Efe. Not a boy at all, of course, but that's how I think of him. I told you about what happened this afternoon. When I saw him crying like that, well, I felt desperately sorry for him. He's had to live with the memory for all these years. It must have been a terrible thing to bear.'

Sean was silent. He didn't have the heart to disillusion Rilla about her nephew's sensitivity, but he would have sworn that the sleepless nights Efe had experienced over the years on account of his grief wouldn't even get into double figures.

They went on walking towards the lake. Rilla stopped as they left the wild garden.

'That's where we're going, isn't it? To the lake.'

'If you can,' Sean said. 'I don't want to force you but I thought we might exorcise some of the bad memories if we went together.'

Rilla nodded. Sean was holding her hand and he could feel her stiffen slightly. She said, 'It'll be all right. If I'm there with you. I shan't feel so scared.'

There was hope in her voice, a rising inflection.

'Here we are,' Sean said gently. 'This is it.'

The lake glittered where the moonlight touched it. The willow branches were black against the sky, and only the small noises of water lapping at the shore broke the silence.

'It must have been here,' Rilla whispered. 'I'm sorry, I shouldn't cry. I'm so sorry.'

Sean took a handkerchief from his pocket and wiped away Rilla's tears. 'Take it,' he said. 'Cry as much as you like.'

'No, no, I'm fine. Really. It's better here, in the place where it really happened. Perhaps I should have come a long time ago, only I didn't dare. But I can be here if you're with me.'

Shadows moved on the surface of the water. Rilla said, 'Isn't it strange that however black something is, there's always something a little darker ready to make shadows on it? I can see, or I think I can see, movements in the water if I look hard enough, and I can't get the thought out of my mind of my mother as a little girl, finding this floating horror and knowing what it was and not wanting to know and screaming as she runs back to the house. It's because of that portrait of her, at about that age. We know not only what she looked like, but what sort of a child she was. From the portrait. I can imagine every single moment of it. Leonora running out into the garden and down here to the lake to get away from the house, and then finding the body. And it's sort of mixed up with Mark and what happened to him. Let's walk to the other side. I might feel more comfortable there.'

'And you get a really fine view of the house from over there.'

They walked without speaking until they were opposite Willow Court. The building was a black shape at the top of a slope. Light showed at some of the windows; Chloë and Philip's and, more surprisingly, Leonora's.

'You can't see much at night,' Sean said. 'It's better during the day, when the garden looks terrific.'

'You're a fraud,' Rilla laughed. 'Promise me a decent view and all I get is a few lights against a black background.'

'I didn't bring you here to show you the view.'

'I know you didn't,' Rilla said. 'And I don't care about the view, if you must know.'

'Good,' said Sean. He drew her to him and she closed her eyes as she stepped into the circle of his arms.

Leonora sat on the armchair in her bedroom with her eyes closed. It was not even eleven o'clock and she was determined to have an early night. There was a good chance she would be asleep before midnight, and this was important to her. She wanted to wake up fresh tomorrow on her birthday, and not slide into it at the end of the most exhausting few hours she had experienced for many years.

The presents her family had given her were all over the room. The smaller ones were laid out on the bed, in exactly the same way that she used to arrange her presents when she was a small child, so that Maude and Ethan could come and look at everything and create a scene that said, we are a happy family that does everything together. Chloë's favourite childhood expletive came into her mind and she said it aloud: 'Bobbins!'

Saying it made her feel stronger. She had been in danger, at dinner tonight, of breaking down and weeping all over again, after all the tears she had shed earlier in the afternoon. Leonora prided herself on not being sentimental. She had never been one to weep in the cinema, and believed that a certain amount of restraining your natural feelings never did anyone any harm, but it had been difficult to keep herself under control while reading Maude's words.

I'm not the same person I was when I woke up, she thought. I feel as though there's been an earthquake somewhere deep inside me. A huge upheaval that's hurt and shaken every part of me. There had been a few other days in her life when she'd also felt altered. Her wedding day. The days when she'd given birth to Gwen and Rilla. The day Mark died. Every death was sad but some were out of the natural order of things, and you were never the same after that.

She thought about her mother's death, and tried to imagine the weight of misery and desperation that had led her to do such a thing. Leonora had always firmly believed that suicide was a supremely selfish act for the mother of a young child. Because, she thought, I could never do it, that's why. And Maude must not have felt like my mother at all. It must have seemed to her that Nanny Mouse was more of a mother to me. Did she think I loved Nanny Mouse best? This fear brought new tears to Leonora's eyes. Maybe I added to her misery by not loving her enough. By not preventing her suicide with my love. Oh, I'm sorry, Mummy. So sorry.

Leonora took a deep breath and resolved to spend all her energy and time in promoting Maude's genius, and in telling her story. It was the least she could do. She looked up at the painting above her bed. White swans on the lake, always on the point of moving. Feathers that seemed about to ruffle in the breeze.

Her eyes were not up to searching for the hidden signature, the little lion, among the green and the white and the dark blue brushstrokes. It struck her as astonishing that no one had noticed it all through the years, but Maude had gone to great lengths to hide it, and no one was looking for it. Tomorrow . . . no, not tomorrow, that was going to be busy enough . . . on Monday she would ask Alex to find it for her. A thought came to her suddenly, and she wondered whether little Douggie might have found one of Maude's hidden lions on the dolls' house wallpaper and that was why he'd pulled at it, and stripped it from the roof. That would explain, perhaps, why such a quiet and undestructive child might have been tempted. She would look at everything after the party.

She turned to the presents. How lucky she was! Chloë's little cupboard with its tiny drawers full of items which brought back her past was quite lovely. There was a miniature locket holding a portrait of Mr Nibs, her very first cat. Chloë must have remembered him from the times she'd sat on Leonora's lap and looked at the old albums. There was a wedding-ring and one dried pink rose to represent her wedding, and baby boots for Gwen and Rilla. There was a corner of Efe's first school report; a copy of a bookmark Chloë had made when she was about twelve, one of Alex's earliest photos. All sorts of things that brought back good memories. Clever, talented Chloë!

Efe and Fiona had given her a most beautiful cameo brooch, set in gold, and matching earrings. They would look perfect with her dress tomorrow, which was fortunate. Leonora hoped very much that Fiona would be feeling better by then. She wouldn't want to miss the chance of dressing-up. Douggie had slept particularly well tonight. She couldn't remember when she'd last seen him, which puzzled her a little. Efe generally brought him in to say goodnight to her before he went to bed, but today was such an unsettled kind of day that all the routines of Willow Court had been thrown into confusion.

Gwen and James's gift was in an envelope, two tickets for a long weekend in a very good hotel in Venice, in October. All expenses paid. Who should she take with her? There would be time enough to decide that when the party was over, but what a glorious thing it would be to look forward to.

Sean's white television set stood on the small table at the end of her bed. She smiled. She'd held out for so long against television in the bedroom that it would be an admission of defeat to confess how much she was longing for the winter evenings when she'd be able to lie on her bed under a soft blanket and watch her own set all by herself, without having to consider what other people felt like looking at. Never mind, she'd admit to being wrong. It would be bliss. Sean had also promised her a tape of the Ethan Walsh – no, the Maude Walsh – programme, and she could put that in her video machine and play it back whenever she felt like it. It was, she considered, a very thoughtful present.

Beth had bought her an antique cheval glass, which she'd put near the window. I can take down the old full-length mirror on the inside of the wardrobe door now. She smiled. Beth never did like it, and always wrinkled her nose when she saw it, saying that it was no better than the average changing-room mirror and dreadfully unflattering.

'Good enough for me,' had been Leonora's answer. 'I'm not as interested in what I look like as I used to be.'

She smiled to read what Beth had written on the card attached to the mirror. *For someone beautiful who deserves a proper reflection.* She was surprised at how moved she was by Beth's kindness and devotion.

She leaned forward to touch Rilla's present. When the packet fell open, she wasn't a bit sure that what she could see would be her sort of thing. She'd thought (and now she felt ashamed for thinking it) how typical it is of Rilla to buy me something she'd like to wear. She didn't even know what to call it. 'Dressing-gown' wouldn't describe it. Of all the words in the language, those signalled cosy, comfortable, woolly, fleecy. *Peignoir* was wrong. That brought into her mind something flimsy and probably transparent. This garment was most probably a *robe*, with all its associations of grandeur and splendour. Leonora picked it up from the bed and put it on over her clothes, and it fell to the ground in a glitter of brocade, gold thread in a rose pattern on a darker gold background.

She looked in the cheval mirror and smiled. I look resplendent, she thought. I look like an empress. She was surprised at how satisfying the fabric felt on her body. The robe fell open to reveal its secret beauty: from shoulder to hem the whole thing was lined with pink velvet, silky, opulent, and exactly the sort of pink she adored, which was neither too bright nor too washed-out, but what she always thought of as 'dusty'. It was a shade which had something in it of grey, like a rose that had started to fade. She stared at her reflection in the glass and thought, I love it. I love how I look in it. I don't ever want to take it off. Clever Rilla! I must make a point of telling her tomorrow how very beautiful her present is, and how much I appreciate it.

Still in the robe, she sat down at the dressing-table to look at Alex's gift. The album which he had promised to fill with images of Willow Court and of her birthday was almost empty, but there were a couple of photographs already in place. One was an exact copy of the painting which depicted the vista up the drive, with the oak trees showing scarlet and the house grey and small at the top of the avenue. Alex must have taken this last October and kept it to start the album off. On the next page, there was a portrait of her, and however long she looked at it, she couldn't recall when she'd been in exactly this pose. She was in the nursery, sitting next to the dolls' house with one hand on the roof and the other on her lap.

I look as though I'm talking to someone, she thought. Talking to Alex, it must be, because he took the photograph. She examined the picture more closely. Why had she never had the dolls' house photographed before? It looked magnificent, perfect in every detail, with all the dolls visible and seeming to be almost on the point of moving. The green of her blouse exactly matched the willow branches on the wallpaper. She blinked tears from her eyes. Mummy chose that paper, she thought, and closed the album. There was still one more thing she had to do.

She opened the drawer where she kept her scarves and took out Rilla's home-stitched purse. The dolls that had lain in it for most of the last half-century were exactly as they were when Leonora had stopped playing with them. She placed them one next to the other on her dressing-table. There we are, she thought. That's what we looked like then. The lilac dress of the little-girl doll was unfaded; her face was pink and the embroidered smile was quite unchanged. The mother and father dolls reminded her of Ethan and Maude, and yet of course they were nothing like the real people. Dolls did what you wanted them to. Dolls were actors in the dramas that children created. It occurred to her that she ought to have let these three be played with. She ought to have allowed them some kind of life instead of burying them deep. It wasn't too late.

Leonora went to the bedroom door and opened it. There was no one in the corridor and she walked along to the nursery. The bulbs in here, she thought as she switched on the lights, could do with being brighter. The strips of wallpaper from the roof had been put away safely in her desk until she could think about what should be done with them.

She took off the dustsheet that covered the dolls' house and folded it up. It oughtn't to be hidden, she thought. I will keep it open for everyone to look at from now on. It should be visible. Maybe there's even time for Sean to put it in the film. She stroked the roof. What would she be doing now, thinking now, if Douggie hadn't started tearing at the paper? If the nursery door had been locked, or if he'd found something else in Willow Court to interest him? Maude's sorrow, Ethan's secret, would still be lying there, undiscovered. She would have told Efe that the paintings were on no account ever to leave this house. The memory of that black shape in the water, the strands of her own mother's hair floating on the surface of the lake, everything she'd remembered about that day, would still be buried somewhere in her heart. All our lives, she thought, hinge on the tiniest of events. If this girl doll, she thought, comes in too early from the garden, she might see Daddy Doll hitting Mummy Doll about the head.

No, she thought. I'll give them some comfort. She took all the Delacourts . . . wasn't that what Gwen and Rilla used to call them? . . . out of the house and put them on the window sill. I'll tell Gwen that's what I've done, she said to herself, and after the party she and Rilla can decide what's to become of them.

She knelt down carefully and placed her own precious dolls around the table in the miniature dining-room and put a tiny roast chicken in front of them. Then, for good measure, she added a red jelly made of *papier mâché*. It's going to be a lovely meal, she decided. Everyone will have the most wonderful time. There will be no quarrels. Never again. They are going to live happily ever after. Leonora gathered the folds of her rose-and-gold robe around her and left the nursery, closing the door quietly behind her.

Sunday,
August 25th,
2002

Leonora's Birthday

Even in the midst of her nightmare, Leonora was aware that she was dreaming. A man was standing next to her bed and singing. It wasn't a proper song and his voice was not a human voice but something between a bird's cry and the grinding of gears. His face was turned away, and Leonora knew that this was precisely the right time to wake up because, if she didn't, the man would turn round and his face would be unspeakable. She opened her eyes and settled into the comfort of finding her own bedroom all around her. Who was he? Ethan? Efe? Peter, even? She still felt, as she had felt every single morning since Peter's death, a tightening around her heart; a little fluttering of sorrow that he was not sleeping *there*, just there beside her. What would he look like, she wondered, if he were still alive? Eighty-two years old, he would have been. White-haired. Wrinkled. Perhaps, like Nanny Mouse, wandering in his thoughts. She shuddered. It was too dreadful to think about.

She pushed back the covers and sat on the edge of the bed, with her heart beating a little too fast. Her bedside clock told her that it was just after half past four. It was far, far too early to get up, but Leonora knew that she wouldn't fall asleep again. She walked very carefully across the room and drew the curtains. When I was a girl, she thought, I used to bound out of bed and be at the window in two strides. Never mind. I'm here. I'm seventy-five. It struck her suddenly as a very long time to have been alive. Streaks of gold and pink and palest blue lay across the sky, and soon the sun would appear and the day would begin. She made her way to the bathroom and thought, I'll just go back to bed and lie quietly until I hear someone else getting up.

Once she was settled against her pillows, she closed her eyes and thought of her birthday guests, all over the county and even further afield, getting up and choosing their best clothes and making their way towards Willow Court. She'd always thought of herself as having led a quiet life, with very little of what she called 'gadding about', but it seemed as though all those afternoons spent sitting at one or another polished table, contributing to the deliberations of this or that committee was a more sociable activity than she had realized. There were the Heads of several schools of which she had been a governor until very recently, with whom she'd formed rather formal friend-ships, but they were friendships nontheless. I've got quite enough going on in the family, she thought, and came to the conclusion that she valued her friends precisely because they *weren't* caught up in any emotional turmoil. They were restful for the most part. Talking to them allowed her to participate in a world outside Willow Court and she was looking forward to seeing them again.

She felt rather like the conductor of a large orchestra, waiting to raise her baton and start the whole thing off: conversation, laughter, food, the meetings with old friends. Everything. Whatever could have been done to make sure that the day went well had been done. She'd even remembered to ask Sean to go down to Lodge Cottage in good time and fetch Nanny Mouse and Miss Lardner up to the house in his car. He didn't mind. In fact, he appeared delighted. Rilla probably thought that her new *amour* was something between herself and Sean and that no one else was aware of it. Leonora smiled. It was perhaps rather impulsive of Rilla to attach herself to him so quickly, but he was, as far as Leonora could see, a good man, a kind man, and he appeared to be fond of Rilla. Perhaps her daughter was right and the only thing that really mattered was to be as happy as possible whenever you could. Peter . . . Rilla had been right to remind her of that moment, all those years ago, when a young soldier had walked into the kitchen and she'd known she loved him before he'd even opened his mouth to speak. She's not a child, Leonora thought. She can look after herself.

Gwen had set her alarm for half-past five but found herself wide awake at five o'clock. She was excited. She couldn't help it. She sat up and started to get out of bed as quietly as she could. There was no need for James to be woken this early, but he stirred as he felt her push back the covers and said, 'Surely it's not morning already?'

'Not for you,' she whispered. 'Go back to sleep. I'm just going to do a few things before Bridget arrives.'

'Mmm,' James said, and buried his face in the pillow.

Gwen pulled on a tracksuit and went to brush her teeth. Ever since childhood, she'd loved the feeling of being up and about when everyone else was asleep. She looked out of her bathroom window and thought, as she always did when she woke up early during the summer, that this was easily the best part of the day. The sky was pearly with new light and still faintly pink where the sun had just risen. A few fluffy clouds were dotted about the blue, like those a child might have painted. The dew was still on the grass, sparkling where the light caught it just as dew was meant to do. Gwen smiled. She would go down and have a cup of coffee and a slice of toast before everything got too hectic. In her experience, on occasions like this birthday party alcohol began flowing as soon as two or three people were assembled anywhere and it was just as well to get some nourishment inside you. She felt a knot in her stomach somewhere, and thought, it's like going into battle, or something.

She tiptoed downstairs and into the kitchen. It struck her as strange that Douggie was still asleep, but maybe he'd had a disturbed night. As she put the coffee on, it occurred to her that she hadn't heard him in the night. She frowned. I'm sure I'd have woken up, she thought. That must mean he slept right through. What a good boy he is. She put the bread into the toaster and fetched the butter from the fridge.

As she ate, she made a mental note of everything that needed looking at before she went out to meet Bridget. The vases of flowers all over the house, the present tree (just to make sure that all the latest gifts had been added to the pile), the downstairs lavatory to check that clean towels had been put out and new pot-pourri arranged in the blue and white bowl on the shelf. After I've done all that, she thought, I'll go and wake Mother with a cup of tea and bang on Rilla's door. She won't want to have to hurry with her titivating.

'Made any extra for me, darling?' James came into the kitchen, smiling. 'Lovely day again, I'm glad to say.'

He sat down opposite her and Gwen marvelled, as she always did, at the way her husband was instantly awake and completely himself first thing in the morning, however much he'd been drinking. There used to be days, after particularly bad nights when the children were little, when she felt she could scarcely keep her eyes open at the breakfast table and was rather irritated by James being quite so (in his own words) 'bright-eyed and bushy-tailed'. Now she was grateful for his cheerfulness and energy.

'Get that toast down you,' he said, 'and we'll go out and see if Bridget's here yet. I want to give the marquee a last look round.'

'It was fine last night,' Gwen said. 'Just needed the flower arrangements on the tables and the place settings.' She sighed. 'Everything's gone rather too smoothly, as far as the catering's concerned. I'm nervous. Holding my breath in case something goes wrong.'

'Nonsense, darling, nothing will go wrong. Everyone will have the time of their lives. I just hope your mother is herself. That suicide note must have been a shock for her, don't you think? Still, she's a tough old bird, isn't she?'

'James!' said Gwen, trying to sound offended and not quite succeeding, because after all he was speaking no more than the truth. Leonora *was* tough, but probably not as strong as she and everyone else liked to believe. 'Come on, then. Finish up your coffee and let's go.'

Reuben Stronsky spent the first part of his drive to Willow Court thinking about the call he'd taken on his cell phone just before he set out. It was from Efe, sounding hurried and anxious, as though there were some kind of emergency happening where he was. Maybe that was just the bad reception in this part of the world. 'A turn-up for the book' he called it, and that quaint British expression meant that Leonora Simmonds had changed her mind and was going to allow the Walsh pictures to be housed wherever he, Reuben, thought best. He couldn't help smiling and wondered what had swung it for him. When Efe told him about the real creator of the pictures, he was overwhelmed and wanted to discuss it further, but it was clear that Efe was eager to get off the phone and said only that he'd asked the parking staff to watch out for Reuben's car. Details of the revelations would have to wait.

'I might get there early,' Reuben said. 'I'm making good time.'

'Come in and meet Leonora then, and have a cup of coffee before the shindig gets going.'

*Shindig.* Another good British word. Reuben said, 'I'll take a raincheck on that, Efe, if you don't mind. I want to walk in those lovely gardens for a while. Would that be okay?'

Reuben was assured that the gardens were at his disposal. He glanced out of the window. This was the sort of day, he reflected, that earned England its reputation as a beautiful country. In this weather, the Wiltshire villages he was driving through had 'traditional idyllic landscape' written all over them, and there were stretches of the route when he felt that he was driving through a film set. Rain, grey streets, sidewalks covered in litter, boring suburbs and featureless estates on the outskirts of cities might have belonged on another planet, and it amazed him that in a country this size there could be so many different views out of a car window.

He'd left London early to beat the traffic and was just beginning to get the hang of the white BMW he'd hired. Beside him on the passenger seat was the perfect birthday present. Leonora would never expect such a thing, and Reuben was sure that the serendipity of how he found it would be part of its appeal for her. It was, he knew, unique, and would stand out from every single thing anyone else could possibly have thought to give her.

Reuben had not been looking forward to his meeting with Leonora. Persuasion, charm assaults, bringing pressure to bear; he hated anything that forced him to be something other than what he naturally was, and he had a pretty good idea what that was. He was a quiet man who hated the limelight. 'Strong and silent' his ex-wife called him once, but that was a long time ago and now, at the biblical age of three score years and ten, he could no longer claim strength as a distinguishing characteristic. Tall. He was tall and quiet. Some people said he was stubborn, but he preferred to think of himself as determined. He'd been ready to put his case to Leonora as forcefully as he could, but he wasn't sorry that none of that would now be necessary. Now, his gift was a way of thanking her, rather than a kind of bribe. Reuben began to hum 'Oh, What a Beautiful Morning', as the green and gold countryside slid past at high speed; white clouds in the blue sky looked as though they were racing to keep up with him. I'm on my way to Willow Court, Reuben said to himself. He couldn't help feeling optimistic and younger than he had for years.

Alex had set his alarm for seven o'clock, thinking that he'd be the first up and could wait quietly outside the marquee for the caterers to start setting the tables with glasses and flower arrangements and so forth. He wanted some shots of everything in preparation.

Before he got out of bed, he did a mental check to make sure that what he thought had happened last night wasn't a figment of his imagination. Beth. She'd made it quite clear how she felt about him. He wasn't second-best to Efe. He hadn't dared to bring the subject up, but characteristically, she had. She'd talked and talked about it and he just sat there listening to her. She went over the whole history of her relationship with his brother. He smiled. Had she realized that half the time he wasn't even taking in what she was saying? That he was too busy wallowing in the nearness of her body to his?

The love he felt for her! It was as though someone had blown up a balloon somewhere inside him. It was weird. He felt full to bursting with unaccustomed emotion, which made him feel like laughing and crying and leaping about like a fool. Was it any wonder people behaved so stupidly half the time when they were in love? He got out of bed, and washed and dressed, and had a cup of coffee standing up in the kitchen. Then he stumbled outside at about half past seven only to find that both his parents were in full organizational mode. James was wasting Bridget's time by chatting to her while she was trying to oversee the table settings and get started on the food. Gwen was hovering around, watching the comings and goings of the staff, still in their jeans and T-shirts. She was looking as though she were not quite sure whether there was something she ought to be doing.

'Stand still, Mum,' Alex said. 'I'm going to take a photo of you.'

'Oh, not looking like this, Alex, please!' Gwen said, and added, 'How come you're up so early? I was going to wake you all at nine o'clock.'

Alex took one photograph after another, taking no notice of his mother's protestations about not being presentable. He said, 'I wanted to get some shots of what it all looks like before the crowds get turned loose on it. When's everyone coming?'

'Drinks on the terrace from noon or so. Lunch from one onwards. Oh, goodness, I really do hope everything goes without a hitch.'

'Course it will.' Alex spoke soothingly, wondering at what exact point in the morning's activities his mother and Leonora would need to be told about Fiona. He raised the camera to his eye and focused on a young woman carrying a tray into the marquee. The sunlight caught the glasses and made them sparkle. Even at this distance, Alex thought, that'll look good.

This is the very best bit of any social occasion, Rilla said to herself, as she lay in the bath and let the scented water cover her. Not vanilla at Willow Court, but Gwen's favourite, Crabtree and Evelyn's 'Nantucket Briar'. The wonderful part is always before something begins. Deferred gratification. Expectation. Anticipation. For a moment, she closed her eyes and thought about last night. Sean had been so kind. Being near the lake was hard for her, but she'd done it, after years and years, and it would get easier. The taste of his kisses couldn't possibly still be on her lips but if she concentrated hard she could call it to mind exactly, and she felt her whole body become as warm and liquid as the water that surrounded her. She smiled. Talk about deferred gratification! This delaying of pleasure meant that she was in an almost permanent state of sexual excitement. Stop thinking about Sean, she told herself. This is Leonora's day.

Getting ready for the party was like 'the half' in the theatre, the thirty minutes before a performance when you sat in front of the mirror and saw your face framed by lights, waiting to be worked on and full of possibilities. Behind you in the dressing-room, your costume would be hanging on a rail and soon, you'd step into it and become someone else. Here, the dress was in the cupboard, and Rilla imagined the folds of chiffon floating in the darkness, waiting for her. She'd hesitated before buying it. There was a superstition in the theatre about wearing green but Rilla prided herself on being rational and, in any case, this wasn't the theatre and the colour wasn't properly green. It had so much blue in it and was so pale that the first

383

thing you thought when you saw it was, that dress looks like the ocean. Perhaps it was nearer turquoise. Or pale peacock. Whatever the shade, it was the way the skirt drifted round her legs, the way the neckline flattered her bosom and shoulders, that made her fall in love with it. She could hardly wait to put it on.

But it wasn't a costume or a disguise. I don't want to be anyone except myself, she thought, getting out of the water and silently congratulating Leonora on the luxury of the Willow Court towels as she wrapped herself in one the size of a small blanket. I'm going to concentrate on making myself as beautiful as I possibly can.

On the way back to her bedroom, she noticed that the door of the nursery was open. Oh, God, she thought. Had Douggie got in there before Fiona drove off with him? Rilla went to see what he might have got up to, not even daring to think of Leonora's reaction to any new damage.

'Beth! What are you doing here? I thought it was Douggie. Why aren't you getting ready?'

'Sorry, Rilla. I just wanted a place to think quietly for a bit.'

She was kneeling on the floor, looking at the dolls. Looking as though she were just about to pick them up and play with them.

'Something wrong?' Rilla sounded tentative. Beth seemed to her quiet rather than miserable, but it was important to make sure.

'Well, not wrong exactly.' Beth sighed. 'I suppose I can tell you, though Efe doesn't want anyone to know yet. Fiona's done a runner.'

'Yes, I knew about that. I looked into their room and saw that her things were missing. What I don't really know is why she chose this exact moment.'

'She found a message on Efe's phone. An obscene message from what I've heard. Did you know that Efe was cheating on her?'

'I hadn't thought about it,' Rilla frowned. 'But now you mention it, it seems in character. And look at this, Beth. Mother must have been in here during the night. These are the real dolls. The ones Maude made for her. The ones we were never allowed to play with. How astonishing! I wonder why she did that. She never does anything without a reason. I wonder if I dare to ask her.' She picked up the little girl doll, and looked at her and then put her back carefully, knowing Leonora would notice if she'd been moved.

Beth sat back on her heels. She took the father doll and put him to stand at the dining-room window, looking out. Rilla wondered whether she ought to say something, tell her not to touch the Ethan figure. She was just about to speak when Beth said, 'I've had my mind changed, Rilla. These few days. I don't think we've been together for so long and at such close quarters since we were kids. I think I had a distorted opinion of him.'

Rilla looked at Beth. She could hear a slight trembling in her daughter's voice and chided herself for being a bloody fool.

'Oh, Bethy, no. You love him, don't you? Efe. You really, really love him. I never knew. I'm so sorry. I'm always too caught up in my own things to notice. Poor darling . . .'

'I *did* love him but I don't any more. Not at all, really, in the way I used to. I've been a bloody fool, honestly. I mean, even after he married Fiona, I sort of hoped. I had these fantasies, you know? That one day he'd just say *no, it's you I really love, Beth. Not Fiona at all. I've made a terrible mistake.* But he didn't, of course. And I've been so horrible to Fiona. I hated her, for no real reason except that Efe loved her. Poor thing. He might have loved her once, but he doesn't exactly seem broken-hearted, does he? More concerned with the Maude Walsh revelations than the fact that his wife has left him.'

'Oh, Beth, it's not fair! I really wanted you to have a lovely time at this party. You deserve it.'

Beth got to her feet and smiled. 'I intend to. Efe will never spoil anything for me ever again. I don't know why I came in here. I think I just wanted to look at the dolls to remind myself of . . . I'm not quite sure what I wanted to remember. Maybe that real life isn't as easily arrangeable as dolls' house life. I'm going to get ready now, I promise. But I can come in later and put your hair up. Would you like me to?'

'Oh, darling, would you?'

'Sure. I'll come and do it when I'm dressed.'

Beth left the room with such a light step that Rilla wondered briefly whether there was something else Beth should have told her but hadn't. She made her way to her own room and sat down at the dressing-table, thinking about Fiona. Well, she said to herself as she massaged moisturiser into her face and neck, I'll ask her when she comes to do my hair. I'd never have credited Fiona with the nerve to walk out like that. She wondered what Leonora would say. And Gwen, too, when she heard that there would be a space at the family table. Fiona's parents probably wouldn't be here either, which meant the disruption of all her careful arrangements.

Gwen, she was quite sure, had been up since dawn, but soon the corridor would be full of the excitement of everyone else getting ready for the party. There would be many different perfumes in the air. Rilla sprayed Vivienne Westwood's *Boudoir* all over her body, and was just thinking how divine it was, when someone knocked on her door.

'Come in,' she called, and there was Gwen, dressed in a tracksuit and looking harassed. 'What's the matter?'

'I've just spoken to Efe, Rilla. Do you know what's happened?' Something, some instinct told Rilla to lie. Gwen might be put out to realize that Rilla knew something about her son before she did and there was no point in asking for an argument.

'No, Gwen . . . it isn't Mother, is it?'

Gwen shook her head. 'It's Fiona. She's left him. Left Efe, I mean. I can't imagine why. He wouldn't tell me. I don't know what I'll do.'

She sat down on the edge of the bed, and took out a hankie.

'Gwen, you're crying. Oh, please don't cry. I'm sure they'll work something out. They'll be all right. Really.'

'What if they aren't? What if she never goes back to him?'

Rilla bit back her first thought, which was that she never realized Gwen was so devoted to Fiona, and murmured something soothing.

'Oh God, Rilla, it's so difficult to explain!' said Gwen. 'It's not Fiona. It's not even Efe. If he wants to risk his marriage with a whole string of sordid affairs, that's his business, but it's Douggie. I may never see him again, Rilla. I couldn't bear that. Couldn't bear it.'

She started crying again. 'I'm so sorry, Rilla, I didn't mean to burden you like this, wailing like a banshee.'

'Don't be silly, Gwen, you can burden me, as you put it, all you like, but I think you should stop crying. Your eyes will be red for the party and Mother'll want to know why, and you'll never hear the end of it. Besides, you *will* see Douggie. I'm sure Fiona won't keep him away from you.'

'She's quite capable of it. I'll become one of those absent grannies. Oh, God, Rilla, that awful McVie woman will have him for Christmases and birthdays and I'll never see him.'

'You don't know that. Even if they *were* to divorce, Efe will get good visitation rights and you can make sure he brings Douggie here whenever he has him. Efe won't want to look after Douggie on his own. He'll need you. Really he will.'

Gwen looked happier. 'Yes, I suppose he might. Thank you for saying that. It makes me feel a bit better.'

'And in any case,' Rilla added, 'you don't know she's gone for ever. She might just want to give Efe a bit of a shock. She might well be back.'

'That's true. I hadn't thought of that.' Gwen stood up. 'I'm so glad I told you all this. Thanks so much for letting me witter on. I must go and do a repair job on my eyes.'

'Take this,' Rilla said, and pressed a tiny tub of concealer into her sister's hand. 'Dab a bit of this round your eyes just before you put your powder on. Magic stuff.'

Gwen looked down at the make-up uncertainly. 'I've never used this sort of thing before.'

'You've not had anything to conceal up to now, I expect, but needs must,' Rilla said. 'Go on. Spoil yourself.'

After Gwen left the room, Rilla thought how surprising everyone was. She'd never have guessed that her sister was so besotted with Douggie. Poor Gwen. For a while, she considered the chances of Fiona going back to Efe but then she thought, what the hell! Why should I worry with such things today? Time enough for discussing family troubles tomorrow. I'm going to a party, dammit. She turned her mind to the question of earrings. Dangly crystal drops or gobstopping Baroque pearls? That was the kind of problem she was willing to wrestle with.

Reuben Stronsky stopped the car just outside the gates of Willow Court and looked down the avenue of oaks to the house at the top of the drive. What a sensational view this is, he thought. If only the whole place was in the middle of London instead of here in the boondocks, then the possibility of turning the house into a decent museum would be a distinct possibility.

He drove up and parked the BMW in the area to one side of the house that had been set aside for cars. A discreet board with an arrow painted on it showed him the way. He remembered the very first time he'd ever come to this house, as a visitor among others, years ago now. The pictures had hit him right between the eyes and he'd been haunted by them ever since.

A young man was approaching the car.

'Good morning, sir. We've been expecting you.'

'Thank you. I'm rather on the early side, I'm afraid. I'm going to walk about for a while and then it's drinks on the terrace, am I right?'

'Yes, that's right, sir. At about eleven, I believe.'

'I'll be there,' Reuben said. The young man disappeared in the direction of the house. Reuben got out of the car and unlocked the trunk. It was called a boot over here, which made no sense to him at all. He put the parcel under a blanket and locked the car up. He wasn't going to go up to the house clutching the present. It was important that Leonora received it without any distractions. He'd go and get it later on, when the party was over.

Reuben began to walk towards the gardens, then paused. He took out his mobile phone from a pocket in his jacket and punched in Efe's number.

'Efe, is that you?' he said after a few moments. 'This is Reuben. I'm in your carpark right now.'

'Can you remember whose birthday it is today, Miss Mussington?'

'It isn't my birthday, is it?' Nanny Mouse frowned and tried to concentrate. She had eaten her breakfast and she was ready for the party. She knew that there would be a party but was it for one of the children? Efe, perhaps. No, that wasn't it. The effort of thinking tired her and she said, 'It's slipped my mind for the moment, Miss Lardner. Please remind me.'

'It's Leonora's birthday. She's seventy-five today.'

'What nonsense! Seventy-five! Why, she can't be a day over forty.'

Nanny Mouse stroked the fabric of her dress and smiled. 'This dress is very pretty, isn't it? I shall be the belle of the ball. That's what

I used to say to Leonora whenever she went out. I used to say, you'll be the belle of the ball.'

She closed her eyes. Miss Lardner looked at her, sitting in her wheelchair. They'd had to get up specially early to make sure to be ready in time, dressed in their best clothes. She herself was wearing her dark green summer costume, with a straw hat that she'd cheered up by the addition of some artificial cherries of quite astonishing glossiness. Miss Mussington was in her navy blue silk. A pearl and amethyst brooch was pinned in the exact centre of the lace collar. Her hair was neat and tidy, pulled back into a bun at the nape of her neck.

'Mr Everard is coming to pick us up in his car and take us to the house. Aren't we lucky?' She was looking forward to going up to Willow Court, which was not something they did very often. She was also more excited than she would have admitted at the thought of seeing herself on television. Mr Everard had asked her to make sure the video recorder was all ready because he had a tape of the recording he'd made of his conversation with Miss Mussington and he was going to show it to them.

'You are in several shots, Miss Lardner,' he'd told her. 'And looking very handsome too.'

'Miss Mussington will be very pleased,' she'd answered. 'We look forward to seeing you.'

Efe fully expected to be alone at breakfast, but to his surprise Leonora was sitting at the table in the kitchen, drinking Earl Grey tea and looking rather frail in her dark blue dressing-gown. He was used to seeing his grandmother dressed, made-up, with her pearl earrings in place and black court shoes on her feet. She's old, Efe thought. Really old. He noticed, perhaps for the first time, the wrinkles around her eyes, the blue veins standing out on the backs of her hands.

'Happy Birthday, Leonora!' he said, and came over to give her a kiss.

'You're the first person to say that, Efe. Thank you, darling. I've just come down for a cup of tea before getting ready for the party. I'm rather excited.'

She smiled at Efe, and oddly, she suddenly looked not like an old woman but more like a kid. Efe hesitated. He knew he ought to tell her about Fiona, but part of him was seriously considering lying. Saying something about her still not feeling well, not in a state to go to the party. He was just about to speak when Leonora interrupted him.

'Something's the matter, Efe, isn't it? I know it is, so there's no point looking away. And don't lie to me, please. I don't need to be protected. I've always known when you're lying.'

'Wouldn't dream of it, Leonora. There *is* something, actually. I was going to tell you later. I didn't want to spoil the party.'

'Tell me.'

'It's Fiona. She's left me. That's it. She's taken Douggie and gone.'

Leonora was silent for a moment. Then she said, 'Are you very upset, Efe? Do you want to go after her? I won't mind if that's what you feel you have to do.'

'Certainly not! I wouldn't miss your party for the world. Besides, it's up to her to come back, not up to me to go chasing her all over the country.'

'I'm touched, darling. But Efe,' Leonora's voice became sharper, 'perhaps that attitude has something to do with why Fiona left in the first place? What about Douggie? Surely you want him back?'

'I'll get him back, don't you worry,' Efe said, privately wondering how on earth he would look after Douggie on his own.

'Anyway, thank you for telling me, Efe. I'm sorry Fiona will miss the party. She was looking forward to it, I think.'

'More fool her, then, for going. I refuse to worry about her today. Today is your day, Leonora. It's got to be fun from start to finish.'

'Well. I'd better go and get my glad rags on then. As you said when you were about sixteen, I think dressing-gowns after eight o'clock in the morning are a sign of loose living. I shall see you on the terrace for drinks, then.'

'Right,' said Efe, and when Leonora left the room, he turned his attention to his mobile phone. Getting-up noises were coming from upstairs now. That was Chloë, shouting something out as she ran along the corridor. It was a sound he recognized from their childhood – excitement, the thrill of getting ready, the sort of holding of your breath till the event that you were waiting for happened.

He helped himself to another slice of toast. It would be ages before they all sat down to lunch and he intended to start drinking very soon. He had, he felt, every justification. It wasn't every day that your wife left you. Saying it over to himself like that was a kind of test. He was missing Fiona, wasn't he? Of course I am, he thought. And Douggie. I really am missing him. It's just because there's so much else going on here that I'm not completely miserable. Reuben is here. He's walking around the grounds. He'll be coming to the terrace at eleven and I'll introduce him to Leonora. Efe intended to be good, and circulate for most of the afternoon, but he was longing to see Melanie again. There would, surely, be some time for them to sneak off somewhere, away from everyone.

His mind turned to their last meeting, which was three weeks ago. Far too long. He remembered that they'd barely managed to shut the door of the back room of Melanie's shop behind them before she'd started to tear his clothes off. She'd been waiting for him to arrive, so she was naked under her thin frock. Efe put the remains of his toast down, suddenly overcome with desire. He had intended to try Fiona's number again, to talk some sense into her, but this wasn't the right time. He was going to be in the money now, thanks to the revelations about Maude Walsh. He wondered whether that fact would influence Fiona in any way and decided that it wouldn't make any difference. She'd always had exactly what she wanted from her parents, who were certainly not short of a bob or two. No, if Fiona came back it would be because she couldn't bear to live without him. She needed him, he knew that, and he was reasonably sure of being able to win her round if he wanted to. The only thing he had to work out was whether he did or not, and there was time enough to worry about that after the party.

Gwen went over everything in her mind. All nine tables in the marquee were ready. Jane the florist had two helpers and together they were seeing to the flowers. The theme flower at the family table, set for twelve people, was pink roses. There were eight other tables, each seating eight, and the theme flowers for those were white roses, gerbera, freesias, iris, carnations, lilies, scabious and marigolds. Flowers to give out to the guests were ready in their baskets. The food was being prepared and delicious smells hung in the air. The champagne had been set up on the terrace. Everything was ready.

'You look great,' said Chloë, peering over her mother's shoulder into the dressing-table mirror. Gwen was wearing a bronze linen dress and sapphire earrings. Gwen smiled gratefully up at her daughter, who seemed to be in a good mood.

'So do you,' she said gallantly, though she thought Chloë's dress looked exactly like a nightie.

'This dress is a nightie,' Chloë said. 'I found it in a brilliant second-hand shop. It's the most beautiful fabric, isn't it? I can't believe anyone would wear it to bed.'

The fabric was apricot satin. There was a panel of lace set into the bodice and it occurred to Gwen that Leonora used to possess a garment very like this long ago. She hoped that today her mother's mind would be on other matters or she might very well be reminded of it, and make some remark.

Chloë sat down on the chair near the window. She said, 'Do you think I'm a horrible brat, Mum? Do you wish you had a good daughter like Beth? Someone who wasn't so . . . I don't know. Rude, or something.'

Gwen hesitated. She realized that what she said now was important; would set the tone for the future, perhaps. This wasn't the moment, she knew, to say anything at all critical or carping. She said, 'You're exactly the daughter I want, thank you very much. I wouldn't swap you for anyone. And there's something else I wanted to say.' Gwen paused. 'I'm so grateful for the way you told Leonora about Maude's message. You were very discreet and thoughtful and I know you must have helped her greatly. It can't have been an easy conversation.'

'No, it wasn't.' Chloë stood up and came over to the bed, and lay across it, Gwen noticed, in exactly the same way she used to do as a little girl. 'Leonora went so pale, and then she cried. She just sobbed and sobbed and I didn't know what to do really, but it was awful. I always think of her as so strong and, you know, competent and then all of a sudden, she was like this little old lady.'

'What did you do?'

'I just hugged her. She's dead thin, and I could feel how . . . how fragile she was.'

'That's splendid of you, Chloë. No one else could have done that as well as you. Really, Leonora's always adored you, hasn't she?'

'Well, whatever she thinks about some things I do and everything I wear, she never gets on my case in the same way that you do, Mum.'

'I do not get on your case, as you put it,' Gwen smiled. 'It's just that sometimes I think certain things you do are a bit . . . well, off.'

'I can't help it, Mum. That's me. I'm not like Beth. I do love her to bits but she *is* little Miss Perfect, isn't she?'

'I wouldn't have you be anything like anyone else at all, Chloë darling. I love you. You know that, don't you, even though I probably don't say it nearly enough. And I'm not exactly a tolerant mother, am I? I expect you wish you had a mother like Rilla.'

'No, I don't,' said Chloë. 'Of course I don't. Though Rilla's a smashing aunt.'

'And I'm very proud of you too,' Gwen added. 'Your tree in the hall is lovely. I don't remember, what with everything that's gone on, whether I've told you how much I love it.'

'Okay, Mum,' she said. 'Ta very much. But we're beginning to sound like people in a soap, don't you think? Better change the subject, right?'

Gwen was about to answer when there was a knock at the door. She said, 'Come in.'

'Hello, darlings!' Rilla said. 'It's only me and Beth. Are you ready? Oh, you both look gorgeous. Let's all go down together and find Mother.'

'God, Rilla, you've rather overdone it with the perfume, haven't you?' Gwen wrinkled her nose.

'Don't be a bore, Gwen,' said Rilla lightly. 'I'm not going to get into any spats this morning, so you can say what you like. I shan't take any notice. Just spray yourself with something or other and join in the fun.'

'Wow, Beth!' said Chloë. 'That dress is fantastic. You look amazing.'

'So do you,' said Beth.

Gwen added, 'It's lovely. A wonderful colour for you.'

Beth was in a plain sheath of heavy red silk. Her only jewellery was a pair of long earrings in some pale, translucent stone.

'Are they marble? Can you have marble earrings?' Rilla asked. 'They *are* super.'

'They're agate,' said Beth.

'I think,' Rilla said, 'that we should go and find Leonora and wish her happy birthday and prepare for the fray.'

They went downstairs two by two, Beth and Chloë first, followed by Gwen and Rilla. Gwen said, 'It's going to be all right, isn't it? The party?'

'It's going to be sensational,' Rilla answered. 'Don't worry about a thing.'

'Is that me?' Nanny Mouse leaned closer to the television set and put out her hand as though to stroke the picture. Her mouth was slightly open, and her eyes were wide. Sean thought that it was like watching a child, or someone who'd never seen a television film before. She was muttering as she listened to herself talking, as though she were saying the words all over again, joining in with the Nanny Mouse on the screen.

'It's you,' Sean said. 'Star of the show. You're a very natural performer. You come across very well. And you look good, too. Not as smart as you do now, of course, but then we're going to a party today. Your brooch is very pretty.'

'Thank you,' said Nanny Mouse with a flirtatious dip of the head. For a moment, Sean could see a shadow of the young woman she used to be in her movement and her smile and then it was gone and she was an old woman again, her small, mouse-like hands trembling slightly as they rested in her lap.

She watched the interview to the end, without saying a word and then turned to Sean.

'Have you spoken to Maude? You ought to speak to her. She's the one who really knows about the paintings. She'd look lovely on the television. She's not a striking woman, but very pretty if you get to know her. You need to talk to her for a while though, before you turn on the camera. She's rather shy. She might be hiding you know. She's always hiding. Well, you can't blame her for that, but still, on Leonora's birthday, she should be there to greet the other children, don't you think? I usually do it, of course, but I think you should see if she wants to do it, just this once.'

'I think we should be off, Nanny,' Sean said. 'I'll help Miss Lardner get the wheelchair into the car. The guests will be arriving soon.'

Nanny Mouse's eyes shone. 'There will be cake, won't there? And balloons?'

'No balloons, I don't think, but certainly cake. I think I can promise you that.'


That must be her, Reuben thought. Leonora Simmonds. Looking at her from this distance, across the lawn that stretched like green velvet for about a hundred yards from where he was standing to the terrace, reminded him of Shakespeare's Cleopatra, 'The barge she sat in, like a burnished throne, burned on the water.' There was no water anywhere near Leonora, and the burnished throne was simply the sunshine bouncing off the metal back of her chair, but still, there was something regal in her carriage. She was sitting up very straight. He couldn't see the detail of what she was wearing but there was a general impression of a colour between grey and blue.

All around her, guests were already doing that party-guest thing that he'd noticed so many times: standing and talking and then moving on to the next person and then standing and talking again, in a pattern that was something like a dance.

Willow Court was the perfect setting for her. The walls, golden-grey against the blue sky, seemed almost to reflect the sunshine. Begonias spilled out of their stone urns in a flood of pink and apricot and scarlet. Reuben saw that Efe was talking to Leonora. He was sitting on a chair pulled up very close to hers. She listened for a moment and seemed surprised and then looked around. This was the signal Reuben had been waiting for. He and Efe had arranged for Leonora to be forewarned. It would have been unkind to catch her quite unprepared. He made his way over the grass and up the steps to the terrace. Then he found himself in front of her, and her clear blue-green eyes were looking straight into his. Before he could say anything, she smiled at him and said, 'Mr Stronsky? Welcome to Willow Court.'

Reuben took off his Panama hat and bowed from the waist. 'It's a great honour and a pleasure to meet you, ma'am,' he said.

'Efe, bring Mr Stronsky a glass of champagne.' Leonora patted the chair beside her as Efe stood up. 'Come and sit down and tell me all your plans.'

'It looks choreographed, doesn't it?' Beth was talking to Chloë and Philip and Alex and watching the guests on the lawn below the terrace. She had a champagne glass in one hand and her gaze was fixed on a stick-thin woman with surprisingly large breasts and a wide, red mouth who had squeezed herself into the tightest of white dresses.

'That's Melanie,' said Alex, noticing where she was staring. 'Eye-catching or what? Look at Efe.'

'I've heard of body language,' said Philip, 'but that's taking it a bit far, I reckon. He looks pissed to me.'

Efe had one arm draped round Melanie's shoulder and showed no sign of leaving her in order to circulate among the other guests. Beth saw James approaching the couple. He said a few words in Efe's ear and the result was that Efe moved away at once, but not before he'd given Melanie's bottom an affectionate pinch. Her laughter was audible to them all.

'Efe is clearly,' said Alex, 'devastated by Fiona not being here.'

'Clearly,' said Beth and burst out laughing herself. The champagne was getting to her as well.

'It is,' Rilla said in a whisper to Gwen. 'It's that poisonous old busybody, Mrs Pritchard. How old must she be?'

'You knew she'd be here, didn't you? Mother's known her for years. She couldn't have a party without inviting her.'

'I suppose not,' Rilla said. 'I'm going to go over and say hello.'

She approached the old lady, who had taken a seat on one of the chairs on the terrace. She looked, Rilla thought, like a very large walnut, dressed rather inappropriately in a tweedy affair with no discernible shape to it.

'Hello, Mrs Pritchard!' Rilla said cheerfully. 'How lovely to see you looking so well.'

Mrs Pritchard poked her head towards Rilla. Perhaps she's more like an old tortoise than a walnut, Rilla thought.

'How do you do,' said the tortoise. 'Do I know you?'

'I'm Rilla. Cyrilla. Leonora's younger daughter.'

'Ah. Well, you've aged somewhat since I last saw you. I remember you very well. You became an actress, I believe.'

'Yes, I did,' Rilla agreed, and searched around for something witty to say along the lines of *and you're in the pink of condition yourself* and decided it wasn't worth the effort. This exchange had probably exhausted everything she and Mrs Pritchard had to say to one another. Mercifully, someone else came up to speak to her and Rilla slipped away. There would have been no point in reminding the old bat how she used to spy on them, her and Hugh. She's probably forgotten all about those days, Rilla thought, and so should I. I'll go and talk to Sean. The crew was filming the guests on the lawn with a hand-held camera but Sean had been detailed by Leonora to look after Nanny Mouse and was valiantly pushing her wheelchair from one group of people to another.

Leonora took a deep breath. The mozzarella and basil fritters, the salmon crêpes, had come and gone and the chocolate mousse cake was on its way. She could tell from the happy murmurings coming from the other tables that the food had been a complete success. She had watched the black and white figures of Bridget's staff winding in and out between the tables like dancers, managing to fetch and remove and distribute the different parts of the feast. She'd even eaten every mouthful set before her, but she hadn't tasted anything properly. There was too much going on; too much to look at. There was also the matter of her speech.

She hadn't wanted to give one, but Efe and Gwen and James said that everyone would be expecting her to.

'I detest speaking in public,' Leonora had murmured while they were still having drinks on the terrace.

'These people are your friends,' Reuben Stronsky said. 'You don't have to say anything fancy.'

'Well, I'd always intended to say thank you to everyone for coming of course, but a proper speech, that's a different matter.'

'I thought you wanted to tell everyone about Maude Walsh,' Efe said.

And so now here she was, having undertaken to speak. For the moment, though, she let herself enjoy the chocolate mousse cake. How clever of Bridget to serve it with these heavenly strawberries and raspberries! A perfect dessert, Leonora thought, and let it melt in her mouth. Then she looked around the table at her family.

As it turned out, Fiona's absence was fortuitous. It meant that Reuben could sit with them. He had been quite a surprise to Leonora, though she'd tried to hide it when she met him. *American Millionaire* made her think of someone fat and red-faced in a big hat and he was the exact opposite, thin and tall and quiet, with a shock of white hair. His eyes were very dark and his manners were impeccable. He'd even brought her a gift, which was more than kind of him.

'I'll wait till later to give it to you, if you don't mind,' he'd told her, and she was immediately curious and intrigued. Why could it not join the other presents under the tree and be opened along with them?

Nanny Mouse was enjoying herself. Miss Lardner sat next to her, making sure that she ate a little, but for the most part, the old lady just looked about her with the air of a child at the circus, her eyes wide with wonder. Sean was on her other side and talked to her all the time, which was angelic of him. He may have been trying to impress Rilla but Leonora knew that he genuinely liked Nanny.

Miss Lardner had handed over Nanny Mouse's present with a somewhat apologetic air, but Leonora was touched by the hand-embroidered cross-stitch book mark.

'Miss Mussington's eyesight isn't what it used to be,' Miss Lardner explained, 'but she insisting on making it for you, Mrs Simmonds.'

'I love it,' Leonora had said quite truthfully. 'I'll make sure to thank her later.'

'Mother!' said Gwen, breaking into her thoughts. 'They're bringing the birthday cake in. Look!'

All the guests were craning to see the cake, which was being taken round the marquee on a sort of lap of honour. Leonora had vetoed candles absolutely. She had no intention of being seen puffing out air in public. The huge tray progressed round the marquee, and spontaneous applause broke out as everyone realized that the icing was a perfect reproduction of one of the paintings from the Walsh Collection: the portrait of Leonora as a young girl, sitting on the edge of a bed, wearing a lilac dress.

'How marvellous!'

'Too clever for words!'

'What a wonderful idea!'

Everyone started talking at once, so that James had to stand up and call for silence.

'Thank you, everyone. I'm sorry to have to stop the talk but it's time for the cutting of the cake. Beautiful as it is. And I am going to call on Leonora to say a few words but before we do all that, let's sing to a great lady. Happy Birthday, Leonora.'

'Happy Birthday' had always been one of Leonora's least favourite songs, but she smiled graciously while the assembled company tried, without much success, to fit 'dear' plus her name into the notes provided by the music. As soon as it was over, she stood up and raised her hand to bring the renewed applause to an end.

'You're very kind,' she said. 'I'm so pleased that you've all come to help me celebrate. And I thank you for your wonderful gifts. So generous and thoughtful. I will have a splendid time opening them this evening.'

Leonora looked out over the tables. These are friends of yours, she said to herself. Nothing to be afraid of. She took a deep breath and began. 'I'm not going to make a long speech. I know how much you're all longing to eat this most beautiful cake. It's such a wonderful surprise, and I really wasn't expecting it, so thank you to my family for arranging it. I hope someone has thought to photograph it before it vanishes – thank you, darling Alex, I knew I could rely on you – and the first thing I must do is thank Bridget for a perfect meal and Jane for the glorous flowers.'

Cries of 'hear hear' rose from every corner of the marquee and Bridget bent her head in acknowledgement.

'I have also to thank my daughter Gwendolen and James, her husband, as well as the rest of my family, but there is something in particular I wanted to tell you.' She hesitated for a moment and then went on, 'You all know the paintings of Ethan Walsh, my father. You've all been tremendously helpful and kind to me while I've been

399

in charge of Willow Court and so I feel I must tell you the truth. It'll be public knowledge soon enough because there's going to be a television programme about the pictures, directed by Sean Everard who's here today. Some of you will have met him before lunch, I'm sure.'

Leonora took a deep breath and went on. 'The truth is this. It wasn't my father, Ethan Walsh, who painted the pictures hanging in the house, but my mother, Maude. I can't go into detail now, because it would take too long, but briefly, my father deceived the whole world and drove my mother to take her own life. I found this out by accident. A very happy accident. I'm now just beginning to get over the shock but I can tell you that Maude Walsh will have her fame restored to her, thanks to Reuben Stronsky, who's here today.'

Reuben half rose to his feet and smiled at everyone and sat down again.

'Mr Stronsky will make sure that the pictures are properly displayed for future generations in a purpose-built gallery, and I'm very grateful to him for helping me in the work that will occupy me for the rest of my life, that of ensuring that my mother's work is seen and her story told. Thank you very much for listening to me, and for making this party so special. Thank you.'

Leonora became aware of the applause, and of Gwen putting a knife into her hand.

'You must cut the cake, Mother,' she whispered, and Leonora bent forward to make the first stroke. She also made a wish, just as she used to do when she was a girl. Please, let everyone be happy, she thought, and then instantly chided herself for being stupid. Everyone couldn't possibly be happy. She amended it slightly in her head: please let everyone be as happy as they can be, whenever they can. That was better.

The singing broke out again as Bridget and two helpers came to remove the cake so that it could be cut into more than seventy pieces. The tune this time was 'For She's a Jolly Good Fellow', which was better than 'Happy Birthday', but not much.

'What a very inadequate song,' said Reuben, leaning in to whisper in her ear. 'You deserve something more dignified, Mrs Simmonds. Something grander.'

'Please call me Leonora,' said Leonora. Reuben Stronsky, she decided, was a real gentleman.

Beth walked round to the Peter Rabbit garden to get away from the party. Alex was photographing the revellers down by the lake, and in the gazebo. Many people had left already but there were still enough to make it worth his while. The lunch had been perfect in every detail, and she could see Gwen relaxing as one delicious course after another had come and gone. The Persian omelette provided for the vegetarians was heavenly, and as for the mozzarella and basil fritters, they were quite the tastiest thing she'd ever eaten.

Everyone, at every table, seemed to be having a marvellous time. Melanie, she noticed, was drinking rather heavily and flashing her cleavage at anyone who would look, and that seemed to be most of the men she went near. At one point before lunch, Beth had seen Efe with his hand on Melanie's – could you call it her lower back? Or her bum? – again. He couldn't keep his hands under control even in public.

She walked up the path towards the shed. All at once, it seemed to her exactly the right place to go to get away from the party for a while. She went up to the door and was just about to open it when she heard a noise from inside. Not voices, but something. She didn't need to listen for more than a moment or two to realize what was going on. Some couple or another was having a quickie. It could have been anyone but a sick feeling in the pit of her stomach warned her that it might be Efe and Melanie. I have to check, she thought. No, I don't. I could easily walk away and leave them to it. What do I care? It's none of my business. She hesitated and then glanced in at the small, rather dusty window.

She couldn't see very well, but there was a pale flash of legs moving and Melanie's black hair was spread out over the work table in the corner. There were grunts and moans and Melanie's ringing voice giving the game away.

'Oh, Efe, Efe, yes . . . yess.'

Beth ran away down the path between the lettuces and carrots towards the house, trying to put what she'd just seen out of her mind. Poor Fiona, she thought. He really doesn't give a shit about her. Efe looks after his own desires, she said to herself, and that's that. She was happy to notice that thinking about Efe didn't cause her any pain at all. She loved him, of course she did, but every element of desire had gone. What remained was concern and affection and family loyalty. What astonished her now was the strength of her feelings towards Alex. How could she have been so blind for so long?

'You were a star,' Rilla said to Sean. 'Looking after Nanny Mouse all day long. A real treasure.'

They were sitting in the alcove, smoking. Even after such a short time, Rilla felt sentimental about this part of the house. This, she thought, is where we first spoke properly to one another. This was where it started.

'You can drop fag ends among the roses today,' Sean said. 'Leonora's talking to Reuben Stronsky and she's had such a busy day she'll never notice.'

'Oh, yes she will. You don't know my mother. But it was a lovely party, wasn't it? I thought that chocolate mousse cake was the best thing of all. I wonder if Bridget would give me the recipe. And Gwen looks much more relaxed now that the party's over.'

'There's still lots to be done on the film,' Sean said. 'I'm going to have to come down here next week, maybe on Wednesday, and interview Leonora all over again.'

'What about Monday and Tuesday?' Rilla said. 'What are you doing then?'

'Well, Monday's a Bank Holiday but I have to go into the office on Tuesday, of course.'

'Of course. But what about after work? Will you come and have dinner with me, on Tuesday night?'

'I was hoping you'd ask.'

'I'm asking.' She turned to kiss him.

'Someone might see us,' he murmured rather half-heartedly.

'I don't care if they do,' said Rilla. 'Kiss me.'

After some moments, she murmured: 'On Tuesday night, I forgot to say, remember to bring your toothbrush.'

Gwen looked towards the marquee. All the tables would be folded away soon, and she was happy to think that the washing-up and clearing away were going to be seen to by someone else. Soon, it would be just the family left at Willow Court, and Leonora would open her remaining birthday presents. They could get an early night. She began to walk through the wild garden towards the lake, feeling as though she were letting out a breath she'd been holding for much too long.

She bent down and took off her sandals and left them lying on the grass. No one would be coming this way, she was almost sure, and anyone who did would know to leave them there for her to pick up. The wild garden was not the place for high heels and party dresses. Gwen wished she were wearing trousers. I'm alone, she thought, for the first time in days. No one is asking my opinion, or telling me things. It's bliss.

As she approached the lake, she saw someone – a woman – sitting on the old tree stump. The swans had gathered there, too. Gwen was surprised at how disappointed she felt to find that she wouldn't after all be on her own. Should she go back to the house? No, damn it, why should I, she thought, and then she noticed that the woman was Rilla.

'Rilla?' she said tentatively. 'Are you all right?'

'Hello, Gwennie. Of course I'm all right. Why shouldn't I be?'

Gwen began to speak but Rilla interrupted her. 'You mean being here by the lake, don't you?'

Gwen nodded. 'I'm just surprised that you chose to come here all by yourself.'

'It's a test,' said Rilla. 'I was here with Sean and it wasn't so bad. I could look at the water quite steadily, really. And so I thought I'd give it a go on my own.'

'But . . .' Gwen wondered what Sean could have said to persuade her sister to come down to the water's edge and as if she'd read her mind, Rilla said, 'It was Mother's doing really. She . . . she explained to me properly what happened when Mark died. She made me feel . . . well, a little less guilty that I wasn't here.'

'We've never spoken about it either, have we?' said Gwen. 'I should have looked after you more, I know, but there were the children . . .' She bit her lip, suddenly remembering that hideous time, when Efe kept waking in the night with bad dreams, and no wonder, and Alex had stopped talking altogether for a few weeks. If she hadn't had Chloë to look after, she would have gone mad. At the time she'd been grateful to Leonora for keeping everything under control.

'You didn't do anything wrong, Gwen,' Rilla said quietly. 'I've never blamed you in the least, and now, well, let's just say that everything's clearer now and I'm here, aren't I? Standing by the lake. Dealing with it, as Beth would say.'

Rilla stood up and started walking. Gwen fell into step beside her.

'It was a super party,' Rilla said, in a tone that marked a change of subject; a lightening of the atmosphere.

'No disasters, thank heavens.'

'And I don't know if you've noticed,' Rilla went on, 'but Beth and Alex are always together, aren't they?'

Gwen smiled. 'They've always been friends, from childhood.'

'Not that sort of close, Gwen. I mean . . . well, I came across them in the kitchen yesterday and they'd been kissing.'

Gwen stopped and stared at Rilla.

'Are you sure?'

'Positive. What do you think about that?'

'I don't know.' Gwen thought abut it for a moment. 'God, Rilla, might we become in-laws as well as sisters? It's quite odd, isn't it?'

'I think,' said Rilla, 'that our children are lucky to be spared any surprises in the mother-in-law department.'

Their laughter broke the silence of the late afternoon.

Almost everyone had gone home. It was six o'clock and the last visitors were drifting towards the car parking area.

'Lovely party!'

'Thank you, darling Leonora!'

'Goodbye, goodbye . . .'

Gwen and James made their way to the kitchen.

'Where have you been, darling?' James asked. 'I was searching all over the place for you before.'

'I went down to the lake. Just to be alone for a bit, but Rilla was down there.'

'Really? By the lake? That's a bit unexpected, isn't it?'

'I'll tell you all about it later, but now I'm longing for a cup of tea.' She sank into a chair. 'I'm completely exhausted.'

'It's been a triumph, my darling,' said James. 'You deserve a medal. Whole thing went off without a hitch, I think it's fair to say.'

'Yes, I suppose so,' Gwen agreed. 'And did you notice how many people told Chloë that her tree was the most beautiful thing they'd seen in years?'

'*You* were the most beautiful thing I'd seen in years. Radiant.'

'Nonsense, James. Don't be silly.'

'No, I mean it. The belle of the ball. And I'm a lucky man to have you. I don't tell you that nearly enough, do I? But I do love you, darling. You know that, don't you?'

Gwen tried to stop the tears from gathering in her eyes. She blinked rapidly. How long had it been since James had said it in so many words?

'Course I do,' she said, as lightly as she could.

'Good!' said James. 'Now could you manage a biscuit after all that lot at lunch?'

'I'll never manage a biscuit again,' Gwen answered. Just at that moment, Rilla came into the kitchen.

'Oh, hello, you two,' she said. 'What a good idea . . . a cup of tea. And I could do with a biscuit as well. Or even two. It's ages since lunch, isn't it?'

Gwen and James both started laughing.

'What's so funny?'

'Nothing, really,' Gwen said. 'I expect the champagne has gone to our heads.'

Beth was upstairs fetching her jacket. She and Chloë and Philip and Alex were going to the pub. They'd decided unanimously that they needed a change from Willow Court. On her way downstairs, she saw Efe standing at the door of his room.

'Hi, Efe,' she said, trying hard to eradicate from her mind the image of him and Melanie in the shed. 'All alone?'

'Come in for a bit, Beth,' he said. 'Chat to me. I'm feeling miserable.' She could hear from his slightly slurred speech that he'd drunk far too much. She looked at her watch.

'Not got the time?' he said. 'No time for poor old Efe, eh?'

'Oh, God, Efe!' she said. 'If you're going to be pathetic, I'm off.'

'No, I won't. Won't be pathetic. Promise. Just come in and have a chat. I'm all alone.'

She went into the room and sat down on the chair by the window. 'You could,' Efe said, 'come and sit here on the bed with me.'

'Why would I want to do that, Efe?'

'We're blood brothers, remember? Or sisters. Blood sisters doesn't sound quite so good, does it? No. She's gone, Beth. Fiona. And now you're going. But you've always been my best, you know. The one I admired. The one all my other women had to measure up to.'

How ironical, Beth thought. She looked at Efe, and knew, as definitely as she had ever known anything, that it was Alex she loved. And Alex she wanted. Any doubts that might have been there, lurking at the back of her mind, even as she kissed him, had gone, blown away for ever.

'I've got to go, Efe,' Beth said, a little more gently. I loved him so much, she thought. How come it's all evaporated so quickly? It had, though. Now all she felt for Efe was a kind of affectionate pity, mixed with something like contempt.

'You all fucking leave, don't you? Fiona left.'

'You're not exactly missing her though, are you?' Beth said. 'That Melanie looked as though she was doing a grand job of cheering you up.'

'Just a good shag, that's all she is, Beth. I can talk to you. I can't talk to anyone else. Not Fiona and not Melanie. You. I think I love you best, Beth. Yes, I definitely do. Come over here.'

'No, Efe,' she said, as firmly as she could. A few days ago she'd have given anything to hear Efe say that. *I love you best, Beth.* Not only did she not believe a word he said, but even worse, she wouldn't have been able to face him even if it were true. She'd seen too much of how he treated the women he was involved with. She went on, 'You don't love me best. I don't know what you think I can do for you, but I'm off now. I'm going to the pub with Alex. So I'll see you tomorrow, I suppose.'

'Fucking Alex! Stolen you from under my nose. Bastard. I'll have a word with him. Tomorrow.'

He sank back on to the bed and covered his face with one arm. 'Piss off, Beth. Piss off back to Alex if that's what you want.'

''Bye, Efe,' she said and left the room. He'd sleep it off and might even forget all about what he'd said to her. Too late, she thought. He's said it far too late. And I don't care. I don't love him like that any more. She ran downstairs to find Alex.

Nanny Mouse was tucked up in bed, with her hands folded on top of the duvet.

'It was a lovely party, wasn't it? I did enjoy it,' said Miss Lardner. Her straw hat with the shiny cherries on it had been put away.

'Yes,' said Nanny Mouse. 'It was a very good party. Did we take a present?'

'We did. Didn't Leonora thank you for it? She told me how much she liked it.'

'Someone thanked me. An old lady. Not Leonora. I wonder why she wasn't there. I expect she's at school, don't you think?'

'I expect so, dear,' said Miss Lardner. 'Goodnight, Miss Mussington.'

'Don't let the bugs bite,' said Nanny Mouse. 'That's what I always used to say to Leonora. Don't let the bugs bite.'

'You must be very tired,' Reuben said. 'I won't keep you long, Leonora. It's been a most memorable day.'

'I'm a little weary, but I don't think I'll be able to sleep tonight. This is the first moment of peace I've had all day. I am also very curious about my present. I admit it. It's childish, I know.'

They were sitting on the bench under the magnolia tree in the Quiet Garden. The shadows were creeping over the grass. Soon, it would be dusk.

'I guess,' said Reuben, 'I could have saved myself a deal of trouble if I'd come to see you two years ago, when I first started thinking about the Walsh Collection.'

He smiled. 'You were away from home when I saw the pictures and fell in love with them. It was the dead of winter and I never even glanced at the gardens. In a hurry, as usual. I'm always in a hurry.'

Leonora said, 'My father had such dreadful reasons for keeping the paintings here that now I want them to be out in the world as soon as possible.'

Reuben sat up straighter on the bench. 'We won't discuss business now, Leonora. It's your birthday. But I'm seriously thinking of some kind of twinning arrangement. A small gallery here, just down by the gazebo and maybe even built in the same style . . . you know, a lot of glass and white wrought iron . . . and another one over in the States. We'll talk about it tomorrow.'

'I'm so grateful to you, Reuben, for everything.'

'For what?' Reuben said. 'I feel privileged to be part of your celebration. This is a most beautiful place.'

'I love these evenings at the end of summer,' Leonora said. 'Autumn's coming and you can feel it, can't you?'

'Yes, I guess you can, but it's still a long way off. Hard to imagine such a thing as winter on a day like today.'

He put a small parcel in Leonora's hand.

'Let me tell you the story of this gift,' he said. 'I was in Paris last month and hunting about as I always do among the stalls on the Left Bank, the *bouquinistes*, where they sell second-hand books and maps and such.'

Leonora nodded. 'Yes, I love them too.'

'I found what's in this parcel at the bottom of a large pile of rubbish.'

Slowly Leonora unwrapped the package. Inside was a small, framed picture. Pastels, she could see at once. The pastel portrait of a young woman, leaning on the parapet of a bridge in Paris. There was Nôtre Dame sketched in behind her.

'Is it Maude? How astonishing! She's beautiful,' Leonora said. She's happy! Maybe in love. That's what she looks like to me. Like a happy woman in love.'

'That's right. But you haven't noticed the signature.'

'I can't quite make it out, without my glasses. Who's the artist?'

'Ethan Walsh. This is a genuine Ethan Walsh. One of the very few. I figure he did it while they were living in Paris. I asked the bookstall guy where he'd come across it, not really hoping for much, but he told me exactly. Someone called Jacques Noiret had sold it to him. It was part of a whole lot of stuff that used to belong to this Noiret's mother, who'd owned a small pension, it seems. Can you believe the serendipity? That I should come across it like that? A few weeks before I meet you? I think it's amazing. Astonishing.'

Leonora was silent for a long time, staring at her mother's face, young, carefree, full of love for the man who was putting her likeness down on paper. Ethan. Not cruel then. Not bitter at Maude's superior talent. Not deceiving anyone but telling the world how much he loved this woman in front of him. This was her mother before Willow Court became her prison. Leonora could imagine Maude in Madame Noiret's pension, leaning against lace-edged pillows in a high bed with a brass bedstead, looking at the husband who loved her sketching by the open window, watching him turn his gaze from the roofscape outside to smile at her. There was nothing in the face in this picture that foreshadowed hair floating on dark water behind a screen of willow branches; nothing of pain, or anger or despair.

'Thank you, Reuben. I can't think of anything in the whole world I'd have liked better. I only have sad memories of my mother but you've given me another Maude. And also, something good about my father to hold on to while I take in what he did. He must have loved her very much, don't you think, when he did this? Even though it changed later.'

'Sure he did,' said Reuben. 'He loved her a whole lot. I think we should go in now, Leonora, don't you? It's getting late.'

'You go, Reuben. I'll come in a minute. And thank you, more than I can say.'

Leonora watched him leave the garden. She half-closed her eyes, and found that she was looking at the border where the late summer flowers were nearly over. The memory came to her out of nowhere. Maude, sitting on a small stool, with a sketch book in her hand. The flowers, the folds of her mother's skirt. I'm so close to her. It must have been one summer when I was very small, Leonora thought. I can recall how she smelled, of sun and lily of the valley, and she had a hat with a wide brim and a pale mauve ribbon. I can remember everything about that moment. She smiled. She had retrieved a picture of her mother to set against the bad images that filled her head. Maybe later, she said to herself, I will recall other things, different glimpses of Maude's life.

Leonora went on sitting under the magnolia tree holding the portrait in her lap until the sun dipped below the top of the garden wall. Then she stood up and made her way back to the house.